Sun, Sea, & Steve!

A Novel

By

Paul Cook

First published via Amazon/Kindle Publishing 2019
© 2019 Paul Cook
2019 BrainFatBoy Press

Foreword.

Dear Reader

What follows is a simple tale of loss, love, and redemption, with a few surprises and lots of hilarity. Whether you're reading this in an old school paper copy or a new school electronic version, this is the realisation of a dream, and I offer you my sincere thanks for choosing to read it.

Before you do start the story, I should point out that, whilst this is a work of fiction, some of the characters are based on real people, Steve especially. You should also be aware that some of the events that occur in the book are based on real situations and experiences. Which ones? That would be telling.

Enjoy

Paul Cook
July 18, 2019

P.S. This really has been a labour of love and I truly hope you enjoy it, and if you do enjoy it, I'd be incredibly grateful if you'd be kind enough leave me a review somewhere and recommend it to your friends and family.

For Nicky, Hannah, Charlotte, and Ollie.

For my Dad for being my sounding board through the whole process, and for pestering me for the next chapter when I slacked off. I might not have got it done otherwise.

But most importantly, for Lisa: There's never a day goes by without me being thankful for the joy and the privilege of having you in my life. x

Chapter One: Old Tragedies and New Beginnings!

Newcastle Airport.

13.45pm.

On a Tuesday.

As Pete Kelly sidled up to the Easyjet desk in Newcastle International Airport, he was confident of two things; he was nursing what was quite possibly the worst hangover of his life, and he was quite sure that his life was most definitely in the toilet and fate just kept on flushing. Two weeks prior, he'd had it all: a good job, a nice house, a lovely wife, and a relatively great life. Pete thought, though, that the speed at which utter devastation had spread through that great life was enough to make the Pope swear. The queue moved forward, slowly, and Pete moved with it. As he nudged his bag along the floor with his foot, his mind wandered, and his thoughts turned to recent events again. Ruminating was the technical term for it. He'd been ruminating a lot lately, at every opportunity, actually. The fact that he was now unemployed and had all the time in the world meant that he was spending nearly every waking moment contemplating where his life went wrong.

Flashback to two weeks earlier:

No, wait! Let's go a little bit further back.

Meet Pete Kelly — Pete to his friends — born twenty-eight years ago in the little Irish town of Edenderry. Edenderry thrived briefly in the latter half of the last century, but it had long since ceased to be self-sufficient, and most of its residents now commuted out of town to work, relegating it to a 'Dormitory Town'. About eighteen years ago, Pete's dad had died and his mum, in some grief-stricken whirlwind romance, had fallen in love with a British travelling salesman and moved to Northallerton, up in the wild North of England. Pete was a nondescript kid. He had a few friends; he didn't get into any trouble; he did okay at school and was actually really bright and could have done better, but he just couldn't be arsed!

Throughout all his formative years, he never lost his Irish brogue, and he found it a blessing and a curse, especially after school ended. A lot of his friends used college as a way to escape the unremarkable existence that Northallerton had to offer, but not Pete. Pete wanted to start earning money; besides, his exam results didn't really lend themselves to going to college. He started applying for jobs and got plenty of interviews, but he kept getting knocked back, partly because of his age, he was only sixteen after all, and partly because of his accent. Even though he was born far away from the 'troubles', Pete found that most English folk at that time still held distrust for anyone with an Irish accent, despite the Good Friday Agreement. Eventually, he landed an interview at one of the only two supermarkets in the town. The manager, a Mr Percival, had seen potential in him and taken him on and, to be fair, Pete did incredibly well and made it to Supervisor within three years.

He may have stuck to life in retail, but fate had other plans for him. After a brief yet incendiary flirtation with a girl called Gemma, Pete finally headed off to college. He initially enrolled on a Business Studies Diploma at the York College of Art and Technology intending to be the next Donald Trump, but within a month he realised that he hated everything about it, not least his fellow business students! A brief encounter with a fellow student, a girl called Wendy who enrolled on a design course, led to him jumping ship and switching to study Art and Design. He did very well, passing his diploma with distinction, and he might have made quite a career out of being an artist save for a chance encounter with Gemma (again) while out socialising one night.

Pete and Gemma weren't strangers; they'd had a couple of tempestuous liaisons in the past that always ended in some level of disaster, yet somehow they always gravitated back to each other. It was some sort of real-life fatal attraction, but without the boiled bunny and sexual encounters in random places. Pete's judgement was always clouded when it came to Gemma, and he often joked that she had put some kind of magic spell on him. The night he proposed he was actually living with another girl. He'd gone out for a few beers with a mate - his best mate, Jack - and bumped into her in a pub. At first, he avoided her but after a few more pints - and possibly vodka, there was usually vodka - they were sat at the same table chatting away. A lot of what followed is very fuzzy in Pete's memory, but by the end of the night, they were locking lips on the town hall steps, and Pete had actually proposed marriage to which Gemma had gleefully, and drunkenly, said yes. The next morning, Pete woke up in a strange bed with another one of those hangovers that take away the memory of the last twelve hours and, worse still, another human being that Pete was sure wasn't his current girlfriend. He looked around the room to try and get his bearings, but nothing rang a bell. No photos, no familiar looking items, not one single clue that gave him the slightest inkling as to who his mystery host was. Then he thought of Anna.

"Shit!" he exclaimed softly. He had been seeing Anna since college, and they had since moved in together in a rented cottage just outside Northallerton. They'd been together almost two years now and, although Pete wasn't convinced she was 'the one,' he was not the sort of guy who usually went in for cheating on his girlfriends. In fact, he'd never done anything like this before, ever. "This is bad." He thought. "This is REALLY bad." He slowly rolled over to try and get and a better idea of whom his bed buddy was without disturbing them. He managed not to disturb the still anonymous companion, but he did, however, agitate the seemingly enormous and luxurious duvet which in turn caused a sudden gust from 'under the canopy'. Pete's nostrils suddenly took a punch of the strong odour of farts, sex, and was that...was that Trésor? The perfume, coupled with the brown hair and lightly tanned skin that was now visible, caused his memory to activate several lightning assaults on his fragile psyche. His already critical headache went into overdrive, his heartbeat increased exponentially as each fragment of last night began to reassemble into one grim and vivid picture.

"Oh, no!" Breathe. "Oh, hell, no!" Breathe, dammit! "Shit! Shit! Shit! No!" It was like a recap from a Netflix show - "Previously on 'Life with Pete'" as all his memories came flooding back: Meeting Jack at his parent's house followed by the walk into town. Then the pair of them were drinking beers in all of their favourite hotspots, before settling in at their super favourite hotspot; The Fleece. Then they were mingling with a few familiar faces. He vividly remembered seeing Jimmy talking to Gemma and being pissed off at first but then, being incredibly drunk, going over to speak to her too.

His memory seemed to jump from that to being stood on the steps of the town hall with Gemma. As he tried to remember, icy fingers gripped his heart and squeezed as he remembered the four little words he said to her: "Will you marry me?"
And her answer: "Yes!"

Despite his initial shock at the memory, Pete realised that he was quite sincere and that, right there and then, he did indeed want to spend the rest of his life with this woman. The rest of that day was pretty horrendous, and having to deal with Anna was definitely the highlight of the lowlights. She was an incredibly sweet girl, and she really didn't deserve to be betrayed this way. When he'd eventually found the courage to look at his mobile phone, he had around 30 missed calls from Anna. Every time she'd called, he just let it vibrate, too afraid and ashamed to answer. Finally mustering up the courage, he called her from Jack's parent's house just after they got back - Jack, incidentally, had happily passed out on the sofa at Gemma's while Pete and Gemma had gotten reacquainted. She picked up the phone, and her anger was tangible. In his defence, he was honest right from the start, telling her where he had been and what had happened and apologising profusely. Jack was in the room, and he could hear Anna punctuating the call with "you bastard," and "you absolute bastard," and — a particular favourite — "you absolute bastarding shit!" The call finally ended with what Pete presumed was the phone flying across the room, or possibly through a window, it was hard to tell.

Later that day, when Pete arrived back at the cottage, they shared, as he got out of the taxi. The first thing he noticed was the hole in the lounge window. "Oooooh, right," he said out loud, to no one in particular. He took a deep breath and headed inside. When he got in the house, he was amazed to find almost no trace of Anna. She had surgically and ruthlessly removed herself from their home, and Pete's life, in the space of a few hours. She had left a testament to her disgust, though. Over the last few years, Pete had built up quite a collection of Compact Discs. Mainly rock and heavy metal, some obscure, some imported, many rare. They all sat in a massive heap in one corner of the lounge. As Pete approached, it appeared it was mainly the cases that were trashed as the discs looked entirely intact. As he got in for a closer look, though, he became aware of the smell of acetone - nail polish remover. "Yep," he thought, "they are knackered!" This was followed quickly by a loud and angry exclamation of "Shit!"

She had also placed all his t-shirts in the washing machine. No big deal except it appeared she'd substituted conditioner with bleach. "Shit!" Still, it was a proportionate response, he reckoned. He had really done the big dirty on her. He was getting off lightly, really.

Pete didn't find the final piece of vengeance until he got into bed early in the evening. He was surprised he didn't notice sooner. I mean the smell alone should have been a massive giveaway. That is to say, the smell would have been a giveaway had Anna not cleverly emptied a bottle of Zoflora all over the upstairs to mask the smell - Pete knew she loved that horrible smelly stuff and she counted on that fact. As soon as he slipped under the covers, it hit him, hard: the unmistakable stench of shit. Panicking, Pete scrambled to sit upright, pulling his hand from under the duvet, revealing what looked like 'Kevin's Famous Chilli' dripping from his fingers. More panic ensued as he tried to shuffle up against the headboard. Steeling himself, he threw the duvet back, to uncover the real horror of what lay beneath. Anna had literally taken a huge, and I mean massive, shit in their old bed. Picture the scene. It was like Jack Woltz discovering his prized Stallion's head in his bed, only it was Pete, and the horse's head was actually an almost inconceivable amount of shit! Pete marvelled at how much shit there was and at the fact that Anna had managed to do so much damage in such a short space of time. Anyway, life went on, and within six months, Pete had moved in with Gemma. Within another six they were married and had moved into their own house, further up the road in Darlington. Despite the shitty start - no pun intended - life was good. Life was perfect.

Ultimately, instead of being a world-renowned artist (okay, maybe that's an enormous stretch) Pete ended up as the Production Manager at a local, independent engineering company in Darlington. He'd started there as a labourer six years ago, just after he and Gemma were married, and he'd quickly proved his worth in the business and made his way up the ladder to be the right-hand man of Terry Drake, the Managing Director. They got on well. You might even call them friends, as much as Terry had friends. He was an odd sort, very full of himself and quite aloof emotionally, so Pete thought, at least. Terry seemed to not so much have friends as people with whom he could enjoy a mutual exchange of services. At any one time, Terry only seemed to have three or four people in his life that matched that criteria and they seemed to rotate in and out with alarming frequency. Pete marvelled at how long he'd managed to stay in that inner circle, and he suspected his willingness to overlook Terry's bullshit had no small part in that.

Terry Drake, aside from loving himself, was quite narcissistic. Whereas it's true, he always seemed to come out on top, and Terry was forever over exaggerating his qualities and abilities He was constantly bullshitting to anyone who was in earshot and always bullshitted the customers, which in turn led to some pretty tense situations from time to time when impossible deadlines were promised. It was the shit that came out of Terry's mouth that always amazed Pete, though. He remembers one of the first things he'd said to him, during his interview for the labourer's job: "I'll tell you what it is, big lad." It seems he called every one, everyone with a penis, 'big lad'. "I am brilliant. I mean, if I want to do something, I'll do it. I said I wanted to own my own company one day and look at all this. If I wanted to go to the moon, I'd get to the moon." He was nodding with an intense look in his eyes as he said this last part.

Pete knew he shouldn't, but he couldn't help but ask: "Are you?"

Terry paused a moment. "Am I what?"

"Are you going to the moon, then?"

Terry seemed thrown by this as if he'd never actually been challenged on this claim before. With slight frustration in his voice, he responded: "You don't understand, big lad, I don't want to, but I could if I DID want to!" Terry always likened himself to some sort of Jerry Maguire figure, regularly proclaiming: "you want it, big lad, you want it, you want it, you KNOW you want it!" The staff out on the factory floor were always saying that when he wasn't around, affecting his accent and mannerisms perfectly. Pete too, on occasion, would manage a reasonable impression of Terry when he'd had a bad day with him. But for all his faults though, Terry had looked after Pete. He'd recognised his potential and promoted him up the ranks until he was his right-hand man. In the process, they seemed to become firm friends. When Terry had his first child, he asked Pete to be godfather. Pete and Gemma would often double date with Terry and his wife, Claire, like one big happy family.

As things moved along, Pete fell into a routine that pushed him hard but allowed him to live a great life outside of work. Fast forward six years, Pete and Gemma are still married and, on the face of it, still happy and, to all appearances, crazy in love. Two weeks before Pete ended up at the airport, it all went horribly and spectacularly wrong!

Pete and Gemma always had breakfast together before both set off for their respective jobs. Pete usually left first as he always parked in front of the garage doors. Gemma would then set off for her role as a pharmaceuticals sales manager. After his usual, short commute, Pete arrived at work to find a message from Terry. Apparently, he'd had to make an impromptu trip down to Leeds to meet with a potential new client. Terry had also forgotten to mention that Mr Hashimoto — the Managing Director of their biggest client company — was coming over for afternoon tea and to discuss some potential new contracts. Terry had a lot of faith in Pete's abilities, and it was not uncommon for him to leave Pete to deal with high-value customers, he was the factory manager after all and who better to discuss new work requirements? At about eleven thirty that morning, it occurred to Pete that he wasn't correctly dressed to receive guests and, since respect was a big part of Japanese culture, he pondered popping home for a quick costume change.

It was a Tuesday, the weather was beautiful, and nothing was going on locally that would hinder his journey. Mr Hashimoto was due at one thirty, which gave him enough time to get home, get changed and get back. He spoke to Karen, the company secretary, to make sure that there were adequate refreshments in place for the visit. He then quickly pulled the team leaders in to make sure they knew of the visit and that they had briefed the workshop staff so in case a tour was requested, and then he set off.

He arrived home just after midday and expected to be able to pull into an empty driveway but was perplexed and annoyed to find the space occupied. This situation was not uncommon as he and Gemma didn't live far from the local train station, and people often looked to park their cars in the streets and sometimes even driveways to avoid the extortionate parking fees. This wasn't the first time the driveway had been used, and in all honesty, Pete wasn't that bothered. He figured he'd do the same thing if the shoe were on the other foot, although he might ask permission first. So long as the cars were gone by the time Pete and Gemma got home, no harm was done.

He pulled up just past the house, got out and locked up, then headed for the front door. Pete was just about to put his key in the front door when it hit him. 'T3RRY 1'. That was Terry's number plate. The car belonged to Terry! How could he have missed that? "That's not any car, that's Terry's car!" He softly exclaimed. "Surely there's some simple explanation," he thought, though for the life of him he couldn't fathom it out. He knew Terry's wedding anniversary was coming up and he recalled him asking Gem for some help in organising some surprise event, maybe that was it? Pete knew, deep down, he was clutching at straws. There was no logical reason for Terry to say he was headed to Leeds then turn up here with Pete theoretically tied up at work. Stopping a moment, Pete took a few deep breaths. He didn't like to think about what possible reason Terry might have for being there. The thing that really bothered him was that over the past six years, there had been more than one occasion when Pete felt uneasy about things Gemma did. Late nights at the office, sudden overnight stays in Harrogate (where the company's regional headquarters were located), to name but a few. She'd always managed to explain away these occurrences and Pete had never had any reason to doubt her overall. He'd certainly never had any reason to suspect anything untoward between her and Terry. Terry! For shit's sake! He needed to keep calm because if they were doing what he thought they were doing, he wanted to catch them in the act, and that meant not alerting them to his presence. Strolling over to the car, he placed his hand on the car bonnet. Cold! That suggested it had been there a while, long enough to cool down at least. Next, he went over to the front window and cautiously peered into it from the bottom corner nearest him. Although the TV was on there was no sign of life. He wasn't sure if this was a good sign or a bad sign.

"Hot tub!" He thought.

The hot tub was a relatively recent addition to his garden furniture. Gemma had bought it for him for Christmas after he'd seen one round at Terry's. It sat under a canopy on the rear patio, and Pete loved it, happily sitting out in it in all weather, with beer, snacks, music, and his iPad. It was his own little slice of heaven. Of course, there were many times when they both shared it, and not just to relax. The thought Gemma and Terry 'using' it made his chest feel tight. Pete decided to have a look, to rule it out, silently reassuring himself that Gemma and Terry surely wouldn't be stupid enough to conduct an illicit rendezvous in such an open place. It was one thing to get frisky at night with the patio lights off but in broad daylight? Surely not? Carefully unlocking the side gate with his keys, he headed along the side of the house, Relief swept over him when he saw the hot tub was all covered up, just like he'd left it two days earlier. A quick and quiet peek into the kitchen and conservatory also came up empty.

That left only two options.

The first and least likely reason was that they had driven off somewhere in Gemma's car. If they indeed were heading somewhere else, then they surely would have met there rather than risk any discovery.

The second, logical and much more likely scenario was that they were upstairs, maybe bumping uglies, maybe doing something innocent. If that was the case, as much as Pete wanted to give them the benefit of the doubt, he didn't think they were having a two player round of 'Goldeneye' on his prized vintage Nintendo N64.

Pausing for breath again, he considered his next move. The need to know what was happening was overwhelming, and so he thought about how he was going to proceed, deciding that stealth was still in order so as not to alert them. It occurred to him that if Gemma hadn't left the house, then it was more than likely that the alarm was still active at the rear of the house because she was always too damn lazy to fully disarm it if it wasn't necessary. The downside of this was that the control panel would beep if he entered through the back door or the conservatory door. The front door was the only way forward then, Pete reasoned, heading back to the front of the house. Quietly and slowly, he pushed his key into the lock. Movement caught his eye to his left. His elderly neighbour, Mrs Hennessy, was stood watching him with her pen and notepad in hand.

Mrs Hennessy was, in some respects, the perfect neighbour. She lived alone and never had big parties or played loud music. Kept her garden lovely and her house spotless, and she always sent a card at Christmas. She did, however, have one huge flaw. She was, as Gemma often commented, "A proper nosey cow!" She was, in fact, a one-woman Neighbourhood Watch Scheme. No one else bothered because they knew 'The Hawk' - as they fondly dubbed her - was always on the case and she was rarely seen without a pen and her notebook in hand. The notebook was her record, her ongoing log of all the comings and goings in the cul-de-sac where Pete and Gemma lived. She took it all very seriously.

Leaving his key in the door, and almost tiptoeing, Pete went over to speak to her, looking up at the front bedroom window as he moved. "Morning Mrs H! How the devil are ya?" He greeted her as quietly as he could without wanting to seem odd. The house was double glazed, but he didn't want to take any chances. Mrs Hennessy looked at Pete and then she looked at the car.

"That car is back again." She observed.

"What?" Pete spluttered. "The car? Oh, yeah! Wait a minute. Again?" Mrs Hennessy looked at him, expressionless. "Mrs H, did you say that it's here again?" Pete asked, pointing back to the car.

Mrs Hennessy stared at him a few moments before answering. "Yes. Again!"

"That car?" Pete asked, still pointing. The Hawk nodded her confirmation. "You're sure, Mrs H? That car has been here before when I haven't been here?"

The Hawk gave him an exasperated look. "Mr Kelly, surely you know by now how accurate my records are!"

Pete nodded "yeah, to be fair. You're never wrong, and you don't seem to miss a trick. So, if you don't mind my asking, how many times before has this car been here, Mrs H?"

Mrs Hennessy licked her thumb and began flicking through the pages of her notebook. "This month, three times." Came the response.

This revelation took Pete by surprise. He wasn't expecting this to be a repeat performance, let alone a regular one. "This month? Three times this month!" Struggling to keep his voice down. "What about last month? Was it here the previous month Mrs H?" Pete was getting a bit agitated now.

She calmly licked her thumb again and flicked further back in her book. "Five times last month. This notebook is new, so if you want any more information I'd have to go and check my archives!" she exclaimed.

"Shit me!" Pete retorted, quickly apologising when The Hawk shot him a very disapproving glance. "Right, well, er, thanks for that Mrs H. I, er, I'll certainly be making sure it doesn't happen again. Okay?"

The Hawk looked at him. "Not my driveway, none of my business! You take care now." She replied, before turning around and heading off to her own front door.

Pete stood and watched her depart with a confused look on his face. "You too, Mrs H! You too, thanks!" he gingerly called after her.

Shaking his head and cursing under his breath, he turned and quickly headed back to his front door to resume breaching into his own house. Gently turning the key, he slowly eased the door open, pausing for what seemed like the most extended second ever while he waited to hear if the alarm control panel was going to announce his entrance. Silence. "Thank Christ!" After carefully closing the door, Pete stopped to take stock. With his heart racing, he had another quick check of the downstairs rooms but found nothing untoward.

Cocking his ear, he could hear music upstairs through a closed door. The muffled tones of Kenny Loggins belting out 'Danger Zone' drifted down. Pete took a few moments to process that information before heading up the stairs towards the source. As he apprehensively ascended the stairs, he became suddenly aware of his situation: He was heading up his stairs to possibly catch his boss and relatively good friend in the process of possibly banging his wife. Possibly banging his wife to Kenny bloody Loggins! In his bed, the marital bed, the bed he shared with the love of his life. "Jesus bloody Christ," He thought. "How bloody disrespectful can you get?" All too soon, he was on the landing and faced with the choices that represented:

Option one: Go through all the doors one by one, leaving the main bedroom until last.

Option two: Go for broke and double down on the main bedroom being the winner.

While he wrestled with the decision, he heard the distinctive 'ba-da-ba-bow-bown' synth intro to Danger Zone as it fired up again. This whole situation was becoming very surreal to Pete. "Maybe 'Footloose' or 'Heart To Heart,' but 'Danger Zone' again? What the actual hell, man!" Don't misunderstand, Pete fully appreciated Danger Zone and its place in pop culture history. It was a genuine 80's classic song off of the soundtrack of an actual 80's classic film and, aside from those accolades, it always made him think of Sterling Archer - it was always a win/win as far as he was concerned. Right now, though, he was about to open a door that, unless it had Tom Cruise behind it, doing a very personal one-man show based on the life of Maverick, was about to turn his life upside down.

Option number two, then.

Deep breath!

He gripped the doorknob, then let go as anxiety began to tear his chest apart. Bending over, he placed his hands on his knees and put his head down, taking some deep breaths. Standing upright again, he focussed on the doorknob and took another deep breath, then he gripped it and just 'ripped the plaster off,' bursting straight in. Sadly, Tom Cruise was definitely not in the room. Instead of Tom, Pete was greeted by the sight of Terry on the bed, kneeling behind Gemma with his arse banging away, the slap of his flesh hitting hers barely audible above the not so dulcet tones of Kenny Loggins.   Pete was like a deer in the headlights. He found himself both utterly repulsed at what he was witnessing yet utterly transfixed at the absolute car crash of it all. Pete stood, motionless, rooted to the spot, for what seemed like an age before his mind rebooted and threw him an idea.

Fumbling in his pocket, he managed to retrieve his iPhone and open the camera. Quickly, he swiped it along to the video function and started recording the utterly depraved scene in front of him. Meanwhile, Terry was as oblivious to Pete's presence as Gemma was while he hammered away at her. Things began to pick up the pace, and they both began grunting with each thrust. Sensing things were about to 'come to a climax,' so to speak, Pete grabbed the remote for the stereo from where it lay on the nearby vanity desk and hit standby. The music stopped just as proceedings wrapped up on the bed.

Had it not been for the seriousness of the situation, Pete was sure he wouldn't have laughed when Terry, at the height of his climax, shouted: "I feel the need."

In fact, he might have even managed to keep an entirely straight face if Gemma Hadn't retorted "THE NEED FOR SPEEEED" at the top of her voice.

It was at this point that Pete broke his cover, albeit unintentionally, as he began to laugh. "You've got to be kidding me!" He blurted this out as he stopped filming and returned his phone to his pocket. He was trying to keep his composure, but he couldn't help but laugh as he said it. The scramble on the bed was British Slapstick in its purest form. Arms flailing, legs akimbo, bodies falling. Terry couldn't move fast enough, but he made little progress as his foot was tangled in the bed sheets, swearing profusely as he tried to free himself and cover his nakedness simultaneously. Gemma wasn't quite as constrained and was doing a reasonable job of covering herself.

She managed to squeak out "Pete. SHIT!" right before Terry, still flailing like Crazy Legs Crane, accidentally elbowed her right in the nose. "Ow, Shit!" she exclaimed. "Shit, shit, FUCK!"

"Shit, I'm sorry, Gem, I.." Poor Terry, he was like a little boy.

"It's actually bloody bleeding, you absolute, clumsy bloody goon! FUCK!" She pulled the sheet up to her nose to wipe the blood.

Terry, now finally footloose and covering his modesty, was clearly out of his depth right now. He just looked from Gemma to Pete and back to Gemma again, like he was watching some invisible tennis match. He fixed his gaze on Pete with one of those stares where you look at someone's face but avoid eye contact, "Pete. Big lad" There it was, his 'go to' greeting. Pete raised his eyebrows but stayed silent. Terry could be a dick sometimes, but Pete always thought they were friends, and they had both worked hard to build the business, but this? "Pete, mate look…"

Pete held up his hand to silence Terry, "Shut it, Goose" Gemma drew a breath as if she was about to speak, "You too, Maverick. Shut it! Just…" Pete grimaced and shook his head as Gemma dabbed at her nose with a tissue and looked down at the bed. Terry gave an exasperated huff, puffing his cheeks out, then he fell silent. "Seriously guys, what in the hell is going on?" Pete looked from one to another and waited for a response. The silence was starting to get awkward when Terry piped up.

"Look, big lad, Pete mate, It's not what it looks like…well okay, it *is* what it looks like, but it was an accident. Mate, we didn't …"

Pete held his hand up again to silence Terry. Terry obliged. "Terry! Firstly, I think that at this point it's pretty safe to assume that we are definitely not mates. To be honest, *mate*, I'd go as far as to say we are pretty bloody far from being mates. You've got more chance of getting a hand job from the Pope than you have of actually getting to call me 'mate' at this point, *mate*. In fact, the only scenario in which any of this is okay is if terrorists have kidnapped Claire and, in place of a cash ransom, they are demanding that you bang my wife in a tragically comic fashion to get her released." Pete motioned to the stereo at this last part as if to suggest that most normal people don't have sex to Danger Zone on repeat. "Except, maybe, Sterling Mallory Archer," his inner voice conjectured. Terry looked up at Pete and started to say something; he changed his mind and returned his gaze downwards again. Pete continued, calmly. "Secondly, mate, reversing your car into my garage door is an accident. Dropping one of my limited edition 'Sideshow Collectible' Star Wars busts is an accident."

He suddenly turned the volume up," but sticking your dick!"

A bit louder now, "In my wife!"

Louder still, "In my OWN fucking bed!"

Pete got really loud and quite visibly angry, " That's not an accident. '*Mate*!' That's an ABSOLUTE BLOODY LIBERTY!" He threw the HiFi remote at the wall behind them, causing them both to jump as it shattered into a cascade of plastic and triple-A batteries. He paused a moment and took a few deep breaths. "Guys, seriously! What the hell is going on? Gemma?"

Gemma looked up at Terry then returned to looking at her knees and dabbing her nose. Pete continued. "Gem? Come on." He then pointed at Terry. "Terry? You had to be banging Terry? It's bad enough that you're screwing someone else in our bed, which by the way, has pretty much broken my heart, but did it have to be Terry?" Shaking his head in disgust, he looked at Terry. "Offence well and truly intended, Terry."

"None was taken." Mumbled Terry without looking up. Pete turned his attention to him.

"Terry! What the hell, man? We were mates. We were mates, and we were making tons of cash together. I'm godfather to little Annabel, for shit's sake! How could you do this to me? To her? To Claire? To top it all off, you're having some adulterous, midday sex-fest to Danger Zone? So, you've not only ruined my life, but you've totally robbed me of one of my all-time favourite films. I'll never be able to watch it again without…" He shuddered. "I mean, the whole thing is just bloody disrespectful, man."

Neither Terry nor Gemma looked up as a deafening silence washed over the room. Pete rubbed his face and walked over to the window and looked out to see The Hawk loitering in her drive, throwing furtive glances up at the house now and then. He thought back to his earlier conversation with her, about the car, and then turned back to the dastardly duo. "How long?"

Gemma cocked her head, like a curious puppy. " Excuse me?" Both she and Terry looked at each other before they looked over at him.

"How long has it been going on? I mean, was this the first time?"

Gemma and Terry looked at each other before Gemma replied. "Sweetheart, this was the first time. It just…it just sort of, happened." She offered.

"First time? For real?" Pete looked at her and opened his eyes wide as in relief.

"Oh yes, yes, the first time. Honestly!" Gemma, sensing a chance to pull this back maybe, really laid it on. "Almost Oscar-worthy," thought Pete.

"Is that right, Terry?" Pete looked at Terry, his eyes almost pleading, leading Terry to think he was desperate for some semblance of reassurance that this was, indeed, an anomaly and a one-off.

Like a trained dog, Terry bought right into Pete's ruse and, picking up on Gemma's cue, he concurred. "Oh absolutely, big lad, absolutely, I mean. It just sort of happened. It certainly wasn't planned. It was just, ya know, a bit of fun." His voice went up nearly a whole octave on that last word. Gemma shot him a look that suggested he shut up. He duly obliged.

It was Pete's turn to appeal to the Oscar Panel: "A bit of fun? Wow. This time was the first time, though." Pete looked at them both. "First!" They were both nodding. "Time!"

Terry and Gemma both looked at Pete as he darted his eyes back and forth between the pair of them. After what seemed like a very long period of glances passing back and forth, Pete started laughing. "Thank Christ!" He exclaimed. Gemma and Terry began to laugh too. Not the kind of laughing that accompanies a shared joke or a funny mishap. More the sort of nervous laughing that East Germans might have cracked upon finding themselves sat in a bare room with a wisecracking Stasi Officer. Still chuckling, Pete looked out of the window and down at The Hawk, then back at the pair of them. "Man, that's such a relief. Such a bleeding relief! Just once! Only the once, eh?" Terry and Gem both mumbled and nodded in agreement, their faces pinched in nervous confusion. "Only once?" Pete chuckled again then continued as the other two nodded solemnly. "Only once, that really is, you know, it's a massive bloody relief. Because according to our lovely, and ever vigilant neighbour, The Hawk, your car is on my drive more times than next door's kid's football! You know? It's such a relief because I thought you'd maybe been BANGING HER FOR MONTHS!" He grabbed the nearest thing which happened to be a delightfully horrid Caithness Glass paperweight Gemma's aunt and uncle had given them as a wedding present, and he launched it after the remote. Gemma and Terry both ducked again as it hit the wall behind them. Everyone was surprised when, instead of shattering, it made a sizeable dent in the drywall before dropping to the bed and resting between the gruesome twosome. "Bastard!" exclaimed Pete, not hiding his disappointment. Regaining their posture, the two transgressors just stared ahead, neither of them making eye contact with him.

Gemma then closed her eyes and started gently sobbing. "Shit!" she whispered, between gasps of breath "Pete, sweetheart, I'm so sorry."

Pete was quite angry now. "You pair of absolute gobshites! You must think I'm totally stupid." He moved back to the window. Although raging on the outside, inside, he was perfectly calm. It was like there was another, clear-headed Pete inside him, directing him. He regarded his neighbour, The Hawk, as she tried to pretend she was sweeping her already pristine drive while every fibre of her being was visibly straining to see or hear what was happening in the Kelly household. "Right." He said, with a suddenness that caused Gemma and Terry to jump. "First things first, let's give The Hawk a bit of a bonus for helping me break up the…" he paused as he searched for the right words, smiling as he added: "Midday, Danger Zone, Sex Ring!" He threw the window open and then started gathering Terry's clothes up.

"Whoa, Pete, big lad, big lad! No, no! Big lad! No, no! Come on, mate!" Terry leapt up off the bed but quickly realised he was naked and tried to pull a cover off the bed. Gemma was having none of it. She grabbed the sheets, pulling them to her body, and kicked out at a rather frantic Terry. "Fuck off, Terry." Pete threw Terry's clothes out of the window.

Although Pete had balled them up, they seemed to billow out and cascade towards the ground in a slow-motion rain of shame. The Hawk, notebook in hand, nearly fell over her sweeping brush as she rushed closer to get a better view of the action.

Pete leaned out of the window and waved at her. "All right there, Mrs H?" She shot him a strange look, her face halfway between unbridled glee and solemn disgust. "Oh, Hang on a mo!" he called down to her. Pete turned back into the room and scanned around, then back to the window. "Shoes!" He exclaimed. He turned away from the window again and looked at Terry. "Where are your shoes, big lad?" The look of horror on Terry's face intensified as he gave up his tug of modesty with Gemma and began scanning the room for his shoes. They both set their eyes on them at the same time and made a move. As the two of them raced towards them, Pete had the upper hand. He was closest, and he was fully clothed. Terry went to grab Pete, and Pete stopped dead and turned to face him, "I wouldn't, mate. I really wouldn't!"

The look he shot Terry was enough for him to step back a few paces. Pete scooped the shoes up. For a moment, he held them up and inspected them. "Ooh, Bally Swiss, nice!" He launched them through the open window. Terry raced to the window as if by doing so, he might save them. Outside, The Hawk was now positively giddy with excitement. This was the most fun she'd seen since the infamous 'mischief night' of 2013. She looked up at Terry and gave him a cheery wave and a smile before scribbling something into her notebook. Pete laughed, "Of course she's making notes."

"Bloody hell, big lad!" Terry was more than a bit annoyed now. "Was that really necessary?" He could hardly contain himself. All attempts to cover his modesty had ceased. This sight gave Pete some comfort, as he couldn't help but notice that the 'tiny cannon, big cannon balls' rumour was true.

"I don't know Terry, was it really necessary to stick your dick in my wife on, apparently, numerous occasions?" He didn't wait for a response. "Also, I have to ask; what the hell is up with Danger Zone? That song was on repeat!" Terry began to blush, "And while we are about, what the bloody hell is up with all that, '*I feel the need*' malarkey? Double you, tee, eff, Terry?" Pete was laughing now.

Terry had had enough. "Right big lad, that's it! You've had your fun." He started jabbing his finger at Pete, punctuating his words. "You caught us out. You've punished us. This whole thing has gone far enough!"

Pete let out one last little chuckle. "Okay, Okay. Sorry, Terry, you're right. Time to wrap this up and move forward." Terry looked both amused and slightly proud that he had disarmed the situation. He straightened up his posture, despite his nakedness, and puffed his chest out masterly. He wasn't quite sure what happened next. He was suddenly doubled over, clutching his stomach and retching hard. He dropped to his knees.

"Sorry, man." Said Pete. "I meant to say; 'head or gut?'"

"Wha…what?" rasped Terry as he started to vomit.

"Y'know! Like in Last Boy Scout, when Bruce Willis catches that fella banging his wife. I mean, I think his marriage was over, and he was doing it on principle because that man was his friend. Talk about art imitating life, or is it the other way around? Anyway, he gives him a choice; 'head or gut'. Haven't you seen it? Come on; you must have seen it, Goose." Pete started laughing. Terry vomited on the carpet again, and his feet. Pete quickly retrieved his phone and took a quick photo. "Right 'mate!'" He exclaimed. "I'm giving you three minutes to get out of this house." Terry looked at him, spitting the last of his vomit out.

"You're goosed, big lad. This is the end of the line for you. You're fired for, for, gross misconduct. You can't just treat me like this, regardless of what I've done. I'm your bloody boss for shit's sake! As far as I'm concerned this is instant dismissal and you can forget any kind of severance, too."

Pete laughed. "Do you honestly think I'd still be coming in and working for a backstabbing, wife shagging, dick hole like you?" He laughed hard. "You are insane! Now you have two minutes to get out." He looked around the room and his face lit up when he spotted what he needed. The hatch to the attic was in the bedroom and access was via a set of folding stairs that one pulled down with a hook at the end of a thick, four foot long, wooden pole. Pete went over and picked it up. "ninety-seconds left, dickhead. The clock is ticking. Better get a crack on!"

Terry's anger quickly turned back to fear as he started towards the door, stopping briefly to pick up Gemma's discarded dressing gown. BAM! Pete brought the pole down hard just in front of Terry's hand. "Ah, ah, ah! No, you don't. Now, sod off before you end up as an episode of Forensic Files!" Terry took off running. Somehow he managed to trip on nothing and roll down the stairs. Pete, having followed him out onto the landing, grimaced at the sight of it. Terry came to rest in a heap at the bottom of the stairs, a bruised, dazed and confused pile of legs, arms, and balls. "Clock is ticking, number one! Go on. Get the hell up, and get the hell out!"

Terry managed to stand, and he limped over to the door. After a brief struggle with the lock, he was outside, naked. The Hawk had already anticipated a nude retreat and, taking advantage of the slight lull in proceedings; she had popped inside to get her camera. This was a glorious day for her. This was a tale to be told through the ages! As The Hawk began snapping away, Terry fumbled with his trousers. After he managed to get them on, he began scrabbling for his keys. Not in his trouser pocket. Not in his jacket pocket. "Shit!" He looked up to the bedroom window just in time to see Pete, right before his keys smacked him right on the forehead. "Ow! Ah, shit, shit, shit! Ow, shit!" Spit flew out of his mouth as he screamed so hard that the veins stood out on his neck. Terry stood there, panting with drool on his lip, staring up defiantly at Pete. Pete cocked his head and raised his eyebrows then he nodded and left the window. "Oh, shit!" Terry turned and ran to the car. He jumped in and started to reverse but then stopped and jumped back out of the car when he realised that the rest of his clothes and his shoes, his beautiful £400 shoes, were still strewn across Pete's lawn and drive. He started to pull back into the drive just as Pete emerged from the front door. "Nope! Bugger the shoes!" He said, to no one in particular as he pulled back out and sped off out of the cul-de-sac. Pete, in the driveway now, was picking rocks up from his garden and pelting them at the fast retreating car. Most missed, but one connected with the rear window, surprisingly sending glass everywhere inside the car. Terry nearly swerved off the road, but he kept driving as if his life depended on it, which it quite possibly did by this point.

Back at the house, Pete was sitting on the front step with his head in his hands. The warm August sun had passed its zenith, but its caress was still bright and comforting. The Hawk approached Pete silently and took a seat next to him on the doorstep. Pete slid along a little, to give her some room, then he looked at her for a few seconds before returning his gaze frontwards. They both just sat and stared out at the world, Gemma's faint sobs drifting out from inside the house.

The Hawk was usually quite stoic. She rarely talked to anyone in the cul-de-sac, keeping herself to herself and keeping watch like Uatu, always observing, never interfering, well, rarely interfering. Because of this, Pete was quite taken aback when she put her arm around his shoulders and asked him, in a quite motherly way: "Are you okay, Pete?"

Right at that moment, amid this unexpected kindness, Pete just let go. He started sobbing. "No, Mrs H. No, I'm not okay." He sniffed and wiped his nose on his bare arm, regretting it instantly and wiping his arm on his jeans. "I'm not even sure what 'okay' is right now! I love her, I love her, and she has torn my heart out and taken a massive shit in the hole it left. What did I do to deserve this?"

The Hawk squeezed his right shoulder and brought her left hand up to grasp his other shoulder. "I don't know you that well, Pete Kelly, But I know a decent person when I see one. You are a decent person. You always have a smile for me, and you always wave and say hello, not like some of the other miseries in this little hotbed of gossip and sin. You're a decent person, and you don't deserve this. I can't see as you have done anything wrong. Some people are just never satisfied." Pete shot her an odd look. "No, sorry, poor choice of words. Some people are just never happy. I think she's one of those people." The Hawk jerked her thumb over her shoulder to reinforce her point. She continued: "Look, I know the world seems like a dark place right now, but it will get better. You'll get past this. If I can offer you a bit of advice?" Pete looked at her and nodded. "Ditch her. She's a whore. You mark my words; you'll never be able to look at her the same way again. Every time she's late home from work, you'll wonder where she is and what she's doing. Every time you're away from home, you'll be wondering what's going on. It will never, ever be the same again. Also, I think there's more chance of Madonna and Guy Ritchie staying together than that girl's knees." Pete mentioned that the celebrity couple had gotten divorced in 2008. "Exactly, my dear! What I'm trying to say is, you're too good to put yourself through that."

Pete looked at her face, and he saw a softness and sorrow he'd never noticed before. "You sound like you're talking from experience there, Mrs H?"

The Hawk smiled. "I've been around a bit, you know." She winked at him. "I'm just over here if you need me." She motioned to her house.

As she got up to leave, Pete looked up at her. "A hotbed of sin and gossip?"

The Hawk looked down at him and smiled again. "Dear boy, you would not believe what goes on around here. You must pop over for a coffee sometime, and I'll fill you in."

Pete smiled. "I might just do that." He said. "Mrs H!"

"Yes, dear?"

"Thank you."

The Hawk gave him another wink and a smile and headed off back next door. Pete sat and enjoyed the warmth of the sun for a few more minutes and then jumped up as if startled. "Shit!" He said out loud. "The meeting with Hashimoto!" He checked his watch; it was coming up to One O'clock and this meant he could make it back in time if he wanted to. He stood up intending to go to his car, but then he paused and sat down again. His recent 'dismissal' had come flooding back to him. He had no obligation to sort that rat bastard's shit out anymore. Besides, he knew he couldn't just leave things like this with Gemma. He sat and thought about this for a little while. It was a sure bet that an almost naked Terry, wouldn't have gone back to the factory. Terry has probably forgotten all about the meeting, too, to be fair. Wheels began to turn in Pete's head. Hashimoto Automotive Engineering was TELCO's biggest customer. They supplied HAE with numerous small components. These components were assembled with other elements, from various suppliers, to create more significant items that, in turn, were shipped to major car manufacturers across the country. It was high volume precision engineering, and it was quite lucrative.

Mr Hashimoto was a middle-aged Japanese businessman and, if nothing else, one thing that Pete knew was that Mr Hashimoto was old school. He was big on tradition and culture, and he placed great emphasis on honour and respect, and Pete had spent a lot of time with him both at his workplace and his home. He was lucky enough to be invited to dinner on more than one occasion and was also privileged to attend a couple of weekend barbecues. Each time, it was a straightforward affair in very austere surroundings. Everything was simple yet refined. Pete thought about this and considered how Mr Hashimoto might react to his current predicament and concluded there was only one way to find out. He once again pulled his phone out of his pocket, opened his contacts and located Mr Hashimoto's direct number. He hesitated for a moment, weighing his actions in his head. "Here we go!" He pressed the call button.

The phone rang twice and then. "Hello, Kelly san! I am just on my way to see you for our meeting!"

"Mr Hashimoto! Thank you for answering. I am so very sorry to call you directly, but I have a dilemma." Pete began.

Without hesitation, Mr Hashimoto responded in his thick Japanese accent and impeccable English. "Oh, dear, Kelly san! What could be the matter?"

Pete took a deep breath. "Mr Hashimoto, I am afraid I will not be able to meet with you this afternoon. I offer my sincerest apologies for this short notice. Unfortunately, I have, er, I have been fired."

There was a long pause. "Fired? I don't understand, Kelly San. What could you have possibly done to be fired? You have been instrumental in the synergy between our two companies. What on earth have you done that has led Drake San to this?"

Pete let out a sigh. "Mr Hashimoto, In truth, I punched Mr Drake."

Another short pause as Mr Hashimoto processed this information. "I see. Forgive me, Kelly San. I have worked with you both for five years or so, now. I do not wish to pry, but can I ask why you punched Masters San?"

Pete hesitated, he might have said nothing else on the matter, but then his mind forced the image of Terry's arse going like a slightly worn out jackhammer behind his wife. "Well, sir, would you believe I came home to get changed for our meeting and caught him balls deep in my wife?"

"Balls deep?"

"Sorry, he was, how do you say…making sekusu with my wife!" Pete had once started to try to learn Japanese. He only really got as far as a few greetings and some insults and words for rude things.

Mr Hashimoto fell silent again. Sensing the mood on the other end of the line, Pete just waited for him to respond. After what seemed an eternity: "I see." Another pause, "and you punched him?"

"Yes, yes, I'm afraid I did."

"And, he fired you?"

"Yes, yes he did, Mr Hashimoto, sir."

"Hmm. Okay. I am sorry, Kelly San. I am grateful to you for being so candid with me." He said something in Japanese, to his driver, Pete presumed. "I will go back to my office. You must deal with your personal business." Pete couldn't gauge his mood, although he did sound sincerely concerned for Pete.

"Thank you, Hashimoto San."

"Pete?" This was a first; it was always formal with Mr Hashimoto.

"Yes, sir?"

"Take some time, sort your personal business out. When you are done, call me. I am always looking for men of your calibre in my organisation."

Pete was taken aback by this. "I, I don't know what to say. Domo Arigato, Mr Hashimoto."

"Take care, Kelly San." With that, the call ended.

Pete stared at his phone. For the second time in less than ten minutes, he'd been caught off-guard by the kindness of others. Tears started to fill his eyes again, and he wasn't sure how much longer he could keep it all together. The sound of Gemma sobbing upstairs snapped him out of it though. "Right!" he thought, "let's get this shit done." As he headed for the stairs, he remembered the video he'd taken earlier. "Well, if we're going for broke here!" Pulling out his phone again, he went to messages and selected 'New Message.' He set the recipient as Claire Drake, and he began to type:

"Claire, I am so sorry to be the one to do this, but I wouldn't be any friend if I didn't. Also, you deserve to know the truth. Just in case it's not clear in the attached clip, that is Terry and Gemma doing the worst Top Gun reenactment I've ever seen. Pete. x"

He attached the video clip and hit send.

"Right! Let's go and sort this shit out," he said before heading back inside. Gemma was still sobbing on the bed when Pete got back upstairs. He walked over to the window and closed it before sitting on the end of the bed. "What the Hell Gem?" He looked at her then laid back on the bed, staring up at the ceiling. Gemma sobbed a bit then blew her nose on the bed sheet. "Rude!" thought Pete. Then he considered what else might be on the sheets and he sat up sharply. "It's bad enough you've cheated on me, you know? But Terry of all people. You've really gone for broke here." He got up and walked over to the chair near the dressing table, turning it round so he could see Gemma before he sat.

Gemma kept her head down. She just stayed silent and fiddled with her fingers. Finally, she sighed and looked up. "Pete, I'm so sorry. If it helps, I really couldn't feel any shittier than I do right now." Tears filled her eyes again.

Pete studied her. He was always amazed that he'd managed to get married to a girl that was so amazing. She had the body of a model, albeit a relatively short model. She was funny, intelligent, kind. She wasn't a massive animal lover, but that was a small trade-off in Pete's eyes. He looked at her face, framed by her dirty blonde hair. Those eyes that had mesmerised him the first time he met her all those years ago. Those lips, shit! He was going to miss that smile. "Gem, I don't want to be 'that guy,' but please, it's little crass to try and be a victim right now." He rubbed his face with his hand, before running the hand through his wild (smart casual, he liked to call it) shock of curly black hair. "You know there's no coming back from this, right?" Gemma sat bolt upright and looked at him like he'd just shot her mother. "Oh... oh," Pete laughed. "Did you honestly think we'd go back to happy families after this? Holy shit! You did, didn't you?"

"Come on, sweetheart, it's just a little hiccup." There was a desperate edge to her voice. "Call it an early 'seven-year itch' or something. After all this time, surely I deserve a second chance? We're together forever, remember?" Gemma referred to something they always said to each other during peak romantic times. After a nice meal out, during a romantic riverside walk, always after sex. "Together forever?" She'd say. "Forever and a day!" He'd reply. The memory of it made Pete cringe suddenly. "We can get past this babe." She continued.

Pete shook his head. He thought about what The Hawk had said to him out on the doorstep earlier. "You know, Gem. Sitting here, after all this, I can't help but wonder how many other guys you've banged since we got married."

"Don't be stupid." Gemma spluttered. "That's not just daft; it's bloody insulting!"

"Nah, it's not. Not really," said Pete, shaking his head. "It's only an insult if it's not true. The more I sit here and think, the more I wonder just what the body count is. All those office Christmas parties where you insisted on booking a hotel room instead of having me

36

come to get you. All those times you were three hours late home because you had a client meeting. Oh god! I am such an idiot!"

"No, no, no! You're not an idiot love. I've never done this before, honestly. Terry was the only one, I swear." Gemma looked him right in the eyes and clutched at her breast in some weird mea culpa gesture. Pete was having none of it, though.

"Gem, come on love, the game is up." He gestured around the room, "This is over, whatever you tell me, so why not just come clean, eh?" Their eyes locked, and for a split second Pete almost felt pity for her. Then he remembered he was in the Danger Zone, and he switched his gaze to the window.

"It can't be over, Pete. It just can't be. I love you." Pete looked back her, a look of bemused disbelief on his face. "Come on; we can get through this. I know we can." Gemma's voice began to rise as she tried to convince him. "We can get some display cases for all your toys and stuff." She was referring to his extensive collection of action figures and other cool pop culture memorabilia. He'd been collecting for years, and when he had his own place, it was all out on display. When they moved in together, though, she'd insisted it wasn't going to be part of the decor. He hadn't even unpacked any of it, just placed it all up in the attic, where it still remained. "Let's get a dog; you've always wanted a dog. We'll get a dog and you and me, we can."

"Stop it, Gem!" Pete interrupted. "Just... stop it! There is no you and me anymore." He sighed. "I'm not even bothered that there were others or not; one was enough. Terry was enough to bring all this burning down to the ground. You've broken my heart, Gemma. I can't stay married to you. Hell, I don't even want to know you." Gemma burst out crying, not the soft sobs of before; this was a three-alarm crisis. She leapt off the bed and ran to the bathroom, slamming and locking the door behind her. 'Calm Pete' took over again. He knew he couldn't stay here with her, but this was his home. Where else could Pete go? For now, he figured the best thing to do was pack a bag, jump in the car and consider his options from the safety and comfort of a Premier Inn.

Up in the bedroom, as he began to stuff a few clothes into a bag, he became aware of Gemma staring at him. He wasn't sure how long she'd been there. "I'm going to spend a few days in a hotel, Gem." Pete didn't even look up from the task at hand. "I think it's for the best, don't you?"

Gemma sighed a sigh of exasperation or frustration. This display of frustration made Pete stop; he turned to look at her. "Come on, Pete, let's stop this." She was visibly annoyed, much to Pete's amazement.

"She's going 'Full Terry' now," he mused.

"I've screwed up; I admit that, and you caught me out. Fair play to you! You've made me sweat, and now it's time just to draw a line and carry on with our lives. We can't split up. I mean…what'll I tell my mum?"

'Calm Pete' took over again. "Wow!" he said while opening his phone again. "You really are a piece of work, Gem. You do know that, right?" He selected the video clip. "You are just this spoilt little girl who always has to get her own way." Added the clip to a text message. "You think it's perfectly acceptable to bang my boss and ex-friend and then, what? Order a Chinese and catch up on 'It's Always Sunny?'"

As he spoke, he started to go through his contact list, adding all of their mutual friends, Gemma's friends, and finally, her mother - Andrea. Andrea was like an older and slightly fatter version of Gemma. She was incredibly overbearing, and Gemma seemed to always strive for her approval. Andrea had lived on her own for the past two years since her husband died in a bizarre 'DIY' accident, the details of which were unclear. Suffice to say he was found hanging from a joist in his attic den, naked from the waist down with video footage of Olga Corbett's 1972 and 1976 Olympiad routines playing on a loop on his computer. Pete was unclear as to why it was considered a 'DIY' accident, but that was not the issue here and now.

Gemma started to protest, but Pete just powered on, speaking louder to be heard over her. "What cracks me up though, is the fact that you really couldn't give a shit about me!"

"That's not true! I love you, babe. You know I love you." She pouted.

"Oh Gemma, come on love. You can do better than that. Let's face it, the only reason you don't want me to leave you is that you'll have to explain it to your mum. That said, I'm sure you'd find a way to spin it to her, so I come off as the villain. After all, we can't have mummy's little angel painted as a scarlet woman now, could we?" He hit send. "Mind you; I do think you might have your work cut out this time."

A curious look crossed Gemma's face. "What do you mean?" She asked. Pete smiled and picked his bag up. "What do you mean, Pete?" He started heading for the door just as Gemma's mobile began to ring, and the house phone. "Pete? Pete! What do you mean?"

Pete stopped in the bedroom doorway and turned to look at her and motioned in the direction of her ringing mobile. "I would get that if I were you. See you soon." He winked, turned on his heels and headed out. As he descended the stairs, he could hear Gemma on the phone, pleading with her mother to let her explain. He laughed and was gripped by a sudden compulsion. "I FEEL THE NEED," he bellowed as he headed down the stairs, "THE NEED FOR SPEEEEEEEEEED!"

Over the next few weeks, Pete found out just how little he meant to Gemma and just how easy it was for her to cut him out of her life. Within two days of him leaving, he had received divorce papers care of his parent's house. Pete had been back to the marital home with a trailer to pick up his other belongings. He'd filled the car and trailer with as much as he could. Pete was careful to get the things he valued the most, including his prized vintage video game collection, the TV from the lounge, and his stereo and music collection and, of course, his beloved pop culture memorabilia collection, all that was left were some clothes and some household odds and ends. He'd gone back the next day to collect them, only to find Gemma had changed the locks. He couldn't break in though as, technically, the house wasn't his.

When they were first married, Gemma's father had put up the deposit for the house. He'd also taken the mortgage out for them as Pete had credit issues. They'd paid him every month, and he'd put the money into the bank. Pete was quite convinced, however, that he was the only one paying as he was sure his father-in-law was paying Gemma's share while he was alive. When her father had died, Gemma had taken over the mortgage, so the house was legally in her name. Pete was happy enough with this arrangement as he never expected to be in this position. With a divorce on the way, Pete worked out that he must have paid in around £16,000 over the last six years. The house was now valued at about £180,000, and Pete was pretty sure he could push for half of this, despite not being named on the mortgage or deeds. He did see an alternative, though. They'd both had jobs that paid well, and so they had both been paying half their disposable income into a joint bank account. The idea was that they would save their money and that way they'd always have something for holidays or other little extras. Pete had rarely dipped into it, but Gemma always seemed to find a reason. At the end of the day, the final balance stood at just shy of £15,500. He weighed up fighting for half the house in the pending divorce, or just taking the cash. Luckily, Pete had been one step ahead of Gemma regarding the joint account, and he'd transferred the balance out into his own current account before he'd even put his key in the ignition to leave on that fateful day. When Gemma found out about the money, she went ballistic. He told her that this was fair and if she wanted to pursue it, he was going to launch a counter divorce claim stating she was a "lying cheating whore." She protested more, but when Pete reminded her he had some pretty compelling evidence on his phone, she quickly warmed to the deal that Pete had offered. She could keep the house. He would keep the money. She would let him in to get the last of his stuff, and he would then let the divorce go through without contest, providing there were no stupid or unreasonable settlement requests. She had no choice but to agree to this. Pete had her over the proverbial barrel.

The day he collected his stuff, she'd left the key with a neighbour — not The Hawk though. Things had been considerably frosty on that front since 'the event.' Pete had gotten up early as he wanted to get it done and dusted. He saw this as the symbolic end to everything. A sort of 'ceremonial emptying of the marital home'. The first thing he did when he arrived was pop next door to see The Hawk. He'd stopped on the way to buy her a small bouquet which caused a few tears to roll down her cheeks. She invited him in for a coffee, and they sat and chatted a while. He filled in the blanks for her as to what happened on that day and what he'd been up to since. The Hawk had roared with laughter when he told her about how he'd sent the video clip to just about everyone Gemma knew. In return for Pete's candid storytelling, Mrs Hennessy regaled him with tales of sin and scandal from within the cul-de-sac, just as she had promised. Some of the tales made Pete's jaw drop. Finally, Pete was forced to make his excuses and get on with the task at hand. He stood up and searched for his keys in his pockets. "Mrs H, it's been a pleasure, but I really must get on." The Hawk placed her cup onto the tea tray and stood up to walk Pete to the door.

"Of course, Pete. I understand. It has been so nice to see you. I do hope you won't be a stranger." She looked at him and smiled.

"Oh no, I promise I'll keep popping back, if for no other reason than to piss Gemma off." They both laughed. Standing at the front door, Pete looked across the Cul De Sac, "I'd better pop and go and get the key from number twenty-eight." He said, motioning across at the house opposite. "I hope she doesn't offer me any cucumber sandwiches," he added, a reference to their earlier conversation about all the scandals from behind the closed doors of their idyllic little close. They both burst out laughing. The Hawk moved closer and gave him a warm hug, pecking his cheek.

"Take care of yourself, Pete." Pete smiled and winked then headed off to collect the last of his gear.

It didn't take long to gather up the last of his belongings. As he moved about the house, he was amazed at how untidy it was. Food ridden plates languished in the kitchen. Half drunk cups of tea sat about on most surfaces throughout the house. As soon as he entered, he noticed the big pile of clothes on the floor, as if Gemma just came in and stripped off. He assumed the dressing gown over the bannister was a part of that ritual. On the verge of locking up, Pete was suddenly transported back to the beginning of this turbulent chapter of his life. In particular, he was reminded of the ingenious way that Anna had taken revenge. It wasn't so much the super clean washing machine prank that sprang to mind, more the 'Godfatheresque' bed incident. Ten minutes later, he was heading down the drive. "Thank you for the dinner and an enjoyable evening." He said out loud in a rather convincing American accent. "If your car could take me to the airport. Mr Corleone is a man who insists on hearing bad news immediately."

Pete spent the next few days in a bit of an alcoholic stupor. He'd dropped his stuff off at his folks and headed back to the comfort of his Premier Inn room. His parents knew what had happened and had sympathised and offered all the help they could. Pete's mum was secretly over the moon as she had never really cared much for "that flighty girl." Although she'd never really discussed her feelings with Pete, he knew his mum well, and he could always tell what was going through her mind when Gemma was in the same room. His dad wasn't bothered what he did so long as he was happy and so long as he didn't get any grief from it. They'd offered to put him up, but there was just no space and, at thirty-one years old, moving back in with his parents was not high on Pete's 'must try that again' list and so he continued to stay at the Premier Inn. It was cheap and cheerful, but it was comfy enough for him with the added bonus of having the usual pub and restaurant attached, which meant Pete didn't have to go far for a pint or four. One thing that struck Pete, particularly in the middle of the night, when the brain tends to torture you by replaying everything in minute detail, complete with director's commentary and deleted scenes, was that he was less bothered about Gemma cheating on him than he was about Gemma cheating on him.

Now, I know that doesn't make sense, so allow me to elucidate: He was pissed off that Gemma had been dishonest, that she had done something underhanded and inconsiderate and selfish and all the other adjectives that sprang to mind. However, he wasn't bothered about the fact that his wife, the 'love of his life,' his soul mate, his life partner, had cheated on him. He was more bothered about the deception than the emotional impact. He found himself spending more time wondering about who else, and when, and how. That is, how she managed to cheat and hide it, not how she... you know... did it. The real sense of loss he was feeling was more to do with how his life had completely turned on its head rather than the actual loss of his job, his home, and Gemma. It occurred to him that losing Gemma was more like losing a recurring character in a favourite TV show, than losing the love of his life. The more he laid awake at night - every night - the more he realised that his life hadn't been as idyllic as he used to think. He was in love with the idea of Gemma, but not actually in love with her. This realisation offered little comfort, though, and he found himself in a vicious circle of rumination and self-medication as he kept drinking his sorrows away.

Eventually, the isolation, the poor sleep pattern, the alcohol and poor diet, all took its toll. Pete felt like he was trapped in some shit groundhog day where there was no lesson to be learnt, just the constant repetition of shit and misery. Sitting in his hotel room that Tuesday morning he had an epiphany, of sorts. "Screw it!" He didn't have much stuff with him; his Macbook, some clothes, toiletries, his iPod. He quickly went through his clothes and picked out a few bits that would pass for relatively clean, and that might do for warmer climes, separating them into a bag. He grabbed all his dirty clothes underwear and, after a little deliberation, tossed it into the bin, stuffing them down into the little wastebasket with enough force to rupture the fragile mesh. Everything that was left was forced to fit into his small backpack. With that in hand, he did a quick, final sweep of the room and then went down to reception and checked out, also asking for a taxi. When the perpetually cheery receptionist asked for a destination, Pete thought for a moment then replied, "Ask them how much to get me to the nearest airport." It was time for an adventure!

Chapter Two: Calella? I Hardly Know Her!

"Well, Mr Kelly. The next available flight we have with any space on is to Barcelona International Airport. It leaves in two hours and will cost you…£130." The girl behind the desk didn't even look up.

"Would that be a return ticket?" Pete asked.

"No, but I can secure you a return flight for an extra £60."

"Ooof!" A look of dismay crossed Pete's face. "A hundred and eighty quid? I thought you guys were meant to be cheap!" He pointed up to the big advert behind the desk clerk. "'Affordable seats to premium destinations!' Can I have one of those 'affordable seats' please, love?"

The attendant gave Pete a look of feigned frustration. "Mr Kelly," she began, in an exasperated tone, "If you book well in advance, you'll find we are cheaper than almost all of our competitors. However, you have arrived here looking for a cheap flight on the same day and, I'm afraid, that's just not possible." The boredom and irritation in her voice were very noticeable at this point; this obviously wasn't her first rodeo with a troublesome customer. "Now, would you like me to book this seat for you, or would you like to have a look at some other prices elsewhere?"

Pete knew it was pointless, looking elsewhere. The girl did have a point, though, it was all rather last minute. "No, no, I'm sorry, I've had a rough few weeks. That's fine, I'll take it please."

"The return for £180?"

"Yes, please!" And that was that. Ten minutes later, all checked in, Pete's getting settled in the departure lounge to wait for his flight to board. He took a seat in one of the many restaurants there and looked about. Pete had a nagging feeling that something was missing. He had his bag, his passport. Money! He needed to grab some cash for the trip. He knew he could probably get it when the plane landed, but he was going to get shafted for commission whichever airport he did the exchange in, may as well get it done now. It then occurred to him that, as he was currently flying to Spain with absolutely no idea of where he was going to stay, it would be a great idea to go online and see about finding some accommodation once he got there. Getting money changed from sterling to Euros was a painless affair, and he was pretty happy with the rate they gave him, having been prepared to have his pants pulled down at the Exchange Kiosk. With his Euros sorted, he headed to Burger King, got a large Whopper meal with no pickles and diet coke before he got settled at a table and started his search for somewhere to stay. As much as Pete had always wanted to visit Barcelona, he decided he also wanted to have a bit of sand and sea. He also wanted something relatively cheap too, mainly because he had already blown through a grand in two weeks. With this in mind, he did a quick hotel search on his phone and came up with a reasonably priced (i.e., dirt cheap) hotel in the sunny, seaside resort of Calella. It's worth mentioning at this point that Pete was not one for doing research. You or I, for example, when booking a holiday, we might look at things like reviews to see what other people thought of it. We might check to see how far from the airport the hotel is too. Little things, I'm sure you know what I mean.

Pete was happy enough that the hotel he picked - the rather grand sounding 'Olympiad' - was listed as a three-star hotel. He knew that it would be cheap but cheerful, and that was okay. Pete had searched for 'hotels near but not in Barcelona with a beach,' and Hotel Olympiad had come at the top of the page of results which, to Pete, meant it was the closest one. He checked availability and booked a room with a balcony for the week ahead. "Sorted!" Fed, watered, and now with shelter all planned, Pete headed for his gate to wait to board. There was still around forty minutes before boarding, and the gate was pretty quiet. Sitting in a seat near a power outlet, he plugged his phone in to charge. As he sat and waited to board, he began scanning the waiting area, and he could see there were only about five or six people sat about, almost all of them were busy scrutinising their phones or tablets, all except one person. He saw one, slightly portly lad, sat facing away from him. The young man had a blue sun hat on with a small amount of what appeared to be almost ginger hair poking out. As far as Pete could see, on his upper half, he was wearing a red and white striped rugby shirt. He appeared to be just looking around, and from the way his shoulders and head were moving, Pete was pretty sure the lad was chatting away to himself. Pete was too far away to hear what he was saying, but he could see the side of his jaw moving and, if he turned his head slightly and strained his ear, he thought he could hear faint mumbling. Pete was sat transfixed as the young man looked left then right, straight ahead for a little while, then left then right again. It wasn't so much the act that had Pete mesmerised, as the hypnotic rhythm with which it was executed. A middle-aged couple approached the young man and appeared to give him something, his boarding pass maybe, and they were saying something to him. The man was almost six foot tall and skinnier than a scrapyard rat, Pete thought. The woman was a little shorter than Pete, with a tan as fake as her blonde hair and massive duck lips. He winced as he saw her try to open her mouth to pop in a piece of chewing gum. With his curiosity getting the better of him, he casually stood up and sauntered over to the window nearer the group to try and get a better idea of what was going on.

"Okay, Son, this one is for your coach connection, okay?" The young man nodded. "Coach 52. You're at the Olympiad, so that's where you need to get off. Now, I did some research, and it should be the last stop. Okay?" The young man nodded again. The middle-aged man continued. "We are staying in a hotel in Barcelona itself, to give you some space," he said it as if he was doing the young man a favour, but Pete thought he had all the sincerity of a Nigerian prince trying to offload his inheritance. The man continued: "so we are at the Hotel Rec near the Arc de Triomf, but you shouldn't need us unless there's an absolute emergency."

"An absolute emergency!" Exclaimed the woman, really emphasising the emergency part. The whole thing sounded a bit fishy, in Pete's opinion.

"So, Steve, son," The man carried on. "Which hotel are you staying at?"

There was quite a pause before the young man finally spoke. "The Olympiad!"

"Well done, lad. Which stop is it?" Before the young man got a chance to answer, the woman interrupted. "Come on, Mike; he knows what he's supposed to be doing. Now let's go, I want to have a few more cocktails before we board. Okay, Steve, we'll be on the plane too love, but in case we don't see you, have a nice time and stay out of trouble, okay?"

Pete heard the young man repeat his instructions, finishing off with "Bye mum, bye dad. Love you." Pete was still staring out of the window, but he had managed to observe the exchange, after a fashion, in the reflection. He was pretty amazed to see the pair of them just turn on their heels and leave. There were no displays of affection, no handshake, no hug, not even a peck on the cheek. He could hear the click-clacking of the woman's heels receding as the pair headed back to the main precinct in the departure area. "Well, that wasn't odd at all," he thought. Without looking at the young man, Pete went and sat down again. Picking his phone up, he began doing whatever it is that most people do when they sit in airports looking at their phones. Before long, the call to board his flight came over the PA system, and by this time, the waiting area at the gate had become quite busy. Pete got up to join the throng as they queued impatiently to get on the plane. Looking down the queue, Pete couldn't see the young man anymore and assumed he was in the line somewhere. He glanced around at the other passengers, and then down at the door that led to the plane. As he looked that way, he caught a quick glimpse of a red and white striped shirted figure in a blue hat get escorted through it. Pete just assumed that the young man's folks had paid for priority boarding or something, and didn't give it another thought. The queue slowly began to move forward and, before long, Pete was on the gangway heading into the plane. He handed his ticket to the female flight attendant. She looked at this ticket, then at him. "Mr Kelly, is it?"

"Yes, Mr Kelly," Pete replied hesitantly. "Call me Pete though, no one calls me Mr Kelly, well no one except my parole officer." Pete gave a little laugh. The look on the attendant's face let him know he'd maybe misjudged his audience. "Sorry, that was just a joke, I'm not, I'm not really on parole." Pete could feel his face get hot as he started to blush. "is there something wrong?" His voice went higher at the end of his question, like a guilty child who wasn't quite sure what he was guilty of.

The attendant smiled. "Oh no, Pete, it's just, we wondered if you'd mind changing seats is all. Someone has requested a seat change because they don't want to sit," a pause "near the door, you see."

"A seat change, you say?" Pete could see a woman he presumed was the other passenger stood just behind the attendant. She looked a little embarrassed and seemed to be doing her best to avoid actually looking in Pete's direction.

"Yes, instead of the middle seat in row 'F,' you'd be sitting in an aisle seat near the door. There's no seat in front of you so plenty of leg room." That last bit was said with a big smile and a 'two thumbs up' gesture. "You'd be doing me a huge favour." The attendant gave another big smile.

Pete smiled back "You had me at 'plenty of leg room'" he said jokingly, although inside he really had already decided to agree when the attendant had mentioned the extra space.

"Awesome. Thank you so much, Pete. You'll be sitting just here." She motioned to the seat literally behind Pete. There were only two seats. His seat in the aisle and a seat near the window. In front of them, once everyone had boarded, he anticipated it would be a spacious paradise. Result. The female passenger was led down the plane to middle seat hell while he quickly stowed his bag and sat down. Turning to greet his fellow paradise citizen, he was surprised to see that familiar red and white shirt and blue hat. A bespectacled face with a beaming smile greeted his gaze. "Hi, Steve!"

"Hi" Pete responded. "No, my name's Pete, not Steve, Pete!" He recalled the conversation he'd witnessed earlier. "You, your name's Steve, I think." He added.

"Hi Steve!" Came the reply. The young man held his hand out for Pete to shake, which he duly did.

Meet Steve. Twenty-four years old, eternally happy and always smiling, slightly overweight, loves drawing cars, doing word searches, cracking corny jokes, has a passion for quoting his favourite TV Shows and films, and - essential to mention although he doesn't let it define who he is - born with an extra chromosome!

Wikipedia has the following, handily brief, description of Down Syndrome:

Down syndrome (DS or DNS), also known as trisomy 21, is a genetic disorder caused by the presence of all or part of a third copy of chromosome 21. It is typically associated with physical growth delays, mild to moderate intellectual disability, and characteristic facial features.

In case it wasn't clear before, it's also worth noting that although they had brought him on holiday, Steve's parents had pretty much abandoned him. Sticking him in a cheap shitty hotel at a resort that was over fifty kilometres away. Although on the same flight, they had just dumped him in the airport with just his passport, his travel ticket and twenty euros that he was under strict instructions only to spend in an emergency. "It's an all-inclusive hotel, after all," his mum had said, several times. He also had his backpack that had his meds (Steve had a few minor health problems that required regular medication) one spare pair of pants and socks, his sketchbook, pencils, and three new word search books. The biggest kicker in all this was that they had paid for their flights and four-star hotel with Steve's disability allowances.

Steve reached over and gently pinched Pete's cheek. "No, I'm Steve, and you're Pete, silly." He burst out laughing, and his whole face lit up. Pete couldn't help but smile at Steve's mirth.

"Okay big feller," said Pete. "Pleased to meet you." Inside, Pete considered that the lady he'd swapped with had other reasons than the door for wanting to move. "Her loss!" He thought. Twenty minutes into the flight, however, Pete wasn't so sure she had made the wrong choice. Yes, the extra room was nice, and it also didn't hurt that the attendant who made this paradise possible kept bringing him complimentary snacks and drinks. The downside, if you'll pardon the pun, was that Pete was treated to a running commentary on the flight, the world outside the window, all imparted as if he was talking to an imaginary version of himself. Quite often, Steve would end his sentences with "that's a Jim Bowen joke." This was his favourite saying, in fact, Steve particularly liked to use this one after he'd said something he found funny adding a little laugh that made his whole face light up.

For those of you who are unfamiliar with his work, Jim Bowen was a famous seventies comedian who's crowning glory was shooting to cult figure status as the host of a cheesy Eighties game show called Bullseye. The basic premise involved general knowledge and darts skills. The prizes were shit, and the main prize that was rarely won was usually a speedboat or caravan. Britain in the Eighties was a roaring place! I'll let you delve into 'Bully's' delights on your own time. I have a story to tell.

So, Pete was all ready to open the Airplane door and see if he could make the news as 'Man Survives Fall From Plane Sans Parachute' when Steve suddenly looked at his watch, reached down between his legs, pulled a word search book out of his backpack and began looking for words in total silence. "Oh," thought Pete, "Okay." Pete retrieved his iPod from his pocket and unravelled his headphones. Attaching the phones to his hears, he reclined his seat and settled down for a snooze.

Popular UK talk show host, Graham Norton, inexplicably dressed as Batman, was just about to give Pete a 'Bat Enema' when he awoke with a start. Pulling his earphones from his ears, he stretched before returning his seat to the upright position. As Pete took a moment to pull himself together, he glanced at Steve, who looked like he literally hadn't moved. His word search book was still in one hand, held up in front of his face while he used the pen in his other hand to trace over all the letters looking for the hidden words. Every now and again, he would grab the book with his pen hand and use his free hand to push his glasses back up the bridge of his nose with his index finger. Leaning over slightly, Pete discerned the hidden words were all clothing related. He began to point words out to Steve. Steve, in return, ringed the words and crossed them off the list, not speaking a word or even looking across at Pete. Pete was fascinated by how meticulous Steve was with it. Every time he ringed a word, it was perfect. Lovely straight lines along the top and bottom and perfectly rounded at the ends. When he crossed out a word from the list, the line started and finished exactly at the beginning and end and appeared to be perfectly straight. "That's quite a talent you have there, mate." Pete offered. Steve just smiled and gave him a quick glance before continuing.

Eventually, it became time to land, and the two men packed their backpacks and stowed them overhead as instructed while they waited for the descent. Steve was avidly looking out of the window, and Pete thought about how he was going to get to his hotel. There would be taxies, he supposed, but for over fifty kilometres he reckoned it would cost a small fortune. When he consulted his maps app, he saw that it looked like Calella was on the main coastal train line and getting a taxi to the station and then a train might be the cheaper option. There was, of course, a third option! Pete remembered that he heard Steve's parents tell him that he was staying at what sounded like the same hotel as him. As the plane began to descend, Pete leaned into Steve and nudged him "Hey, Steve mate."

Steve nudged him back, greeting him with "Hi Steve!"

Pete laughed. "Listen, mate: what hotel are you staying at?"

Steve began to recite what his father had told him a few hours earlier. "Hotel Olympiad, Calella! Fifty Kilometres away! Last coach stop. Don't bother us at the Hotel Rec unless it's an emergency!"

Pete feigned a look of surprise. "No! The Olympiad? That's amazing! I'm staying there too. What are the odds, eh?"

Steve laughed and pointed at Pete. "Never tell me the odds!" He laughed again. Pete laughed too.

"Yeah, nice," Pete missed the reference but humoured him, still grinning, he cut to the chase. "Listen, how are you getting to the hotel? Was it, did you say there's a coach? Because if there's a coach I might try and get a ticket for it, see. Do you have the details?"

As he'd already checked the travel coupon, Steve recited the info contained therein; "Coach 34, Car park C, Row 6!" He smiled that million dollar smile again.

"Great stuff! Thanks, Steve. I really appreciate it." By now, the plane was all but done with the landing and was taxiing to the terminal. Steve kept looking out of the window, chatting away to himself "What's he like? He's all right, Steve. Does he like word searches, Steve? Yes, Steve, but he's not very good at them." He laughed before adding: "Yeah, I'll keep him right, Steve. I look after my friends. Yeah."

Bemused and a little confused, Pete stood up as the plane had finally come to a stop and the seatbelt sign had gone out. Reaching up into the overhead locker, he retrieved his bag first, then Steve's. "Here you go, big fella." Pete handed Steve his bag. "Right, you'll probably want to go and get your case or whatever. Car park C, Row 6, Coach 34, right?" Steve nodded, giving that colossal smile again. "Great stuff, thanks. Listen, mate, I might see you on the coach or, even back at the hotel. If not, you have a great holiday, okay?" He had no intention of spending any more time with his new 'friend' than he had to, but nevertheless, Pete smiled at him and held out his hand for a handshake. Steve, having other ideas, smiled and stood up to give Pete a hug. Pete was taken aback. "Okay then, I'll see you in a bit maybe." Steve released him, and he quickly turned and headed off down the gangway that was now open for disembarkation. Before he turned the corner to enter the terminal, he glanced back up into the corridor and into the plane. The attendant who had greeted him at the door earlier was helping Steve get his backpack on. She then put her arm through his and began walking him towards Pete. Pete also noticed Steve's parents - he recognised them from Newcastle Airport - he was pretty shocked to see them walk right past Steve and his chaperone without any kind of acknowledgement. He felt a little guilty at this point. He'd fully intended to head over to the coach try his luck at getting on and then try and hide from Steve, not just on the coach but for the duration of his stay. However, the sight of Steve's folks just completely ignoring him, coupled with that big warm bear hug, melted his heart. Other passengers were filing past him as he stood there, looking down at the terminal and then back up into the plane. He shook his head, and said: "Shit" under his breath. He turned around and walked back up the corridor to Steve. Steve was pleased to see him again so soon and gave him a big smile. "Actually mate, let's go get your case together." Turning to the attendant, he said: "don't worry, love. I've got this. We are at the same hotel so I'll look after him from here."

The attendant smiled and looked at Steve. "Are you okay with that, Steve?" she asked. "Do you feel comfortable going with this man?"

Steve smiled, nodded, and gave her a big hug too. "Thank you." He said through his smile."Bye for now!" Then, as he turned to Pete. "Come on, Steve, Let's go catch a bus!" With that, he headed into the airport. Pete waved at the attendant and gave her the thumbs up before heading off at pace after the surprisingly swift Steve. They breezed through passport control and Pete quickly discovered that Steve didn't have any other luggage apart from the bag he was carrying. It was an average sized backpack, but Pete could tell it was absolutely rammed to the gills. They left the arrivals terminal, and Pete looked for an information desk to find out where precisely they needed to be for the coaches. As soon as they left the air-conditioned sanctity of the airport, they were hit by a wave of pretty fierce heat. Pete was pretty amazed at the difference and actually walked back inside and back out again, marvelling at the contrast. This was not really that odd as he had only been abroad twice in his life. Once was a college trip to Amsterdam where they'd travelled by ferry, the second time - and the first time he flew - was his 'honeymoon'. He didn't really have fond memories of that trip, though. He had been married to Gemma at least six months before they managed to get it together to go abroad. It was memorable for being his first trip on a plane and for the fact it was also when he first swam, not just in the sea, but ever. He'd never learnt as a child as his mum never really bothered with anything that cost money. He'd always bunked off school during sports so, again, he'd missed the opportunity to learn.

Anyway, he and Gemma went to Limassol, in Cyprus. It was a perfect honeymoon destination or would've been had his wife not insisted on bringing her best friend, Belinda, with them. Pete wasn't happy, but he submitted to Gemma's will, as he always did. In retrospect, it did have its upside. Pete had managed to stand on sea urchins with both feet within the first 6 hours of being in a foreign country. Gemma would not go near his feet as she had a bit of a foot phobia. Belinda had stepped up and meticulously extracted every last Sea Urchin Spine from his foot with tremendous care and patience.

When the boys finally made their way outside to the coach park, Steve kept chatting away to himself about nothing in particular while Pete kept his eye out for the coach he hoped would take both of them to the Olympiad. Once he knew he'd found the right coach, Pete stopped and turned to Steve. "Right, mate." He said, "I don't have a ticket right now, so I'm going to try and bribe the driver. Hopefully, there are a few empty seats left." Steve just looked at Pete, who wondered if he actually understood him. "If not, I'll probably have to get a train or something, but I'm sure I'll see you at the hotel at some point." Pete looked at Steve again as he started to fish in his pocket for his wallet, so he could have some cash ready in case he had to do the old 'special handshake'.

The old 'special handshake,' as Pete liked to call it, was basically a case of palming a variable amount of cash (usually notes) and passing it surreptitiously to an intended recipient during the process of — our survey says — shaking hands! Pete had seen it on more than one TV show and had worked hard over the years to perfect it. In his mind, it made him look smooth and sophisticated!

Rifling through his wallet for some notes, he was about to ask Steve how much he thought would be okay when Steve reached over and took hold of his hand. "Trust me, Steve!" He said, smiling. "I've got this!" With a quick wink, he began to lead Pete over to the coach, still holding his hand like a small child would. The driver was stood smoking outside the coach door. The luggage compartment was open, and it appeared he was just waiting for more passengers to come out, hand him their travel coupons so he could cross them off the list, and get them onboard. This was his last run of the day, and the late afternoon sun had made him hot and bothered. He longed to be back in the air-conditioned comfort of the coach and, he was sure, his not too distant future held a cerveza or four. Steve, still clutching Pete by the hand, strolled right up to the man with tremendous confidence. "Excuse me, mister. Is this the coach for Calella?" Pete kept silent, but his face told a story of amazement and wonder as he watched Steve work.

The driver was looking at his list. "Si! Name please?"

"Here's the thing, Mister, my name is Steve Oldfield, and this man is Pete…"

"Kelly!" Pete interjected." Peter Kelly!"

Steve winked at Pete. "Y' see, Steve, I've managed to lose our travel coupon. I'm supposed to be going to the Olympiad Hotel in Calella with my carer here." Steve motioned to Pete despite the driver not even looking up as he took another drag of his cigarette.

"Name is Bartolo," he said, pointing at his name badge, "not Steve!" He didn't even make eye contact. "No coupon, no travel, señor!" He was managing to look anywhere but at them.

"Here's a man who hates his job." Thought Pete. He tried to let go of Steve's hand and get his wallet. "Even the special handshake might not be enough!" Steve tightened his grip on Pete's hand and, to Pete's complete amazement and utter horror, he began to wail like a banshee! He wasn't just crying, he was going full Christian Bale and channelling all the pain of the human race from the last two millennia.

"Nooooooo!" He managed between wails. "What are we going to dooooooooo?"

"Holy shit!" thought Pete. "Outstanding work!"

The wailing had come on so loudly and so suddenly that it had almost knocked the driver off his feet as if it was some sort of sonic blast. He looked at the source and, obviously, the first thing he noticed was Steve's condition. "Señor! Señor! It's okay! Okay! Please! You calm down. Is alright!" Steve continued, he began to slap his chest too, for added effect. The driver, just wanting to shut this down without having to call Fathers Merrin and Karras, frantically scoured his list. "Oh, look at that señor," he remarked as he held up his thumb and forefinger, "two for Oldfield. No problem, please to be on board." He motioned to the door.

Steve immediately stopped wailing. He smiled, patted the driver's arm and, heading for the door, he said, "Thanks, mister!" Pete quickly followed, mumbling his thanks as he passed the driver.

They went straight to the back of the bus. Steve sat down while Pete just stood in front of him in a state of shock. "What the hell was that?" screeched Pete quietly. "I mean, that was just, wow!" They both burst out laughing, and Pete took a seat next to Steve. About ten minutes after they had boarded, the coach was on its way. Only about ten other people had joined them, and most of them got off at stops along the way. Steve's parents had been the first to alight, pretty much as soon as the coach had started its journey. Steve, meanwhile, had retrieved his pen and word search book from his backpack and was concentrating intently again. Pete just looked out of the window and watched the sights go by. He was looking forward to getting the hotel, especially since he'd booked for all inclusive, something he'd never done before. As he had no frame of reference outside of a few sitcoms he'd seen set abroad, in his mind, he had a picture of delicious food and exotic drink on tap every hour of the night and day, with room service, and poolside service and silver service and ALL the service! The coach finally pulled up outside the hotel at around seven pm local time and Pete, Steve, and the one other passenger still left on the coach quickly exited it. The third passenger went to get his luggage, but as Pete and Steve were carrying everything with them, they headed into the hotel. The images Pete had reviewed when booking the hotel made it look like a sumptuous palace. He remembered being very impressed at how it looked for a three-star hotel: Spacious reception, modern decor throughout, loads of cool facilities, great looking rooms, and it was only a stone's throw from the beach.

As he entered, he couldn't help but utter "bloody internet!" The building itself looked very similar to the one in the photos, just a little more… weathered! Pete guessed it had been built in the seventies and that the pictures he had seen were maybe taken in the late 90s, which was when he estimated it was last decorated. By 'decorated' he meant that it looked like it had been done by the handyman from some run down old folk's home. The woodwork was thick with paint that looked like it had been applied with a spoon, and the walls were covered in what looked like painted over wallpaper. The fittings were old and dirty, and the floor was discoloured. They'd entered the building up a set of steps that were dead centre in the middle of the building. Either side of these steps were two swimming pools, children's swimming pools, he assumed, mainly because there were kids everywhere and the deepest end of the pools didn't look too deep. Outside the front door, about ten people were stood about. Some were smoking, some were vaping, some were wearing socks with sandals. Pete did not like where this was going. Once inside, things didn't really improve either. Bratty kids ran around screaming, chasing each other and throwing stuff about, their parents presumably in the bar or, who knows where. Steve went straight over to the reception desk to check in, as he'd no doubt been instructed to do by his caring and sharing parents.

Pete had to pee, so he scanned around and saw the universal signs for toilets. Walking through the lobby, he was amazed at how genuinely grubby the place was. The paintwork beyond reception was also thick and clumsy, and there was dust on most surfaces and grime in all the corners. The toilets weren't too bad, though. Surprisingly, they didn't stink of piss, which Pete attributed to the rather large, wall mounted, industrial air freshener. He did his business, washed his hands, then headed to check in. Steve was nowhere to be seen. Pete felt some relief at this. Although he was grateful to Steve for getting him on the coach, and if he saw him about he'd 'buy' him a drink, he really wasn't planning on spending the whole week with him.

As he emerged from the restroom, the reception was relatively quiet. It seemed the other arrivals had already checked in and the only other people were guests making their way between bar and elevator, with the occasional deviation out the front door for a smoke. At the desk, a man Pete estimated to be around the same age as he was stood waiting to welcome the last of the new arrivals. At first glance, Pete thought the man looked incongruously smart compared to the hotel itself, but as he got closer, he could see the man's uniform had seen better days. Checking the name badge, Pete greeted the clerk: "Hello, Alejandro. I would like to check in, please."

The gentleman looked at him, "Okay, mate, no problem. Got your details?" Pete wasn't sure what surprised him more; the sudden chirpiness or the Yorkshire accent behind it. Handing his passport over, he looked around the hotel reception again as the clerk checked his passport and hit a few keys on the computer keyboard in front of him.

"Have you got your booking reference there?" 'Alejandro' asked, looking up at Pete. Pete pulled his phone out of his pocket and opened his email. Having found the email regarding his booking, he passed it over to the clerk. His face must have given some clue as to his confusion over the name badge, and the desk clerk laughed. "The name badge?" Pete nodded. "Yeah, I lost mine, so I nicked this from the staff room." Pete just smiled and nodded. He was suddenly tired and just wanted to get to his room at this point. Alejandro passed him his key card and explained how the hotel worked. "This is not just your room key, it's also your passport to happiness in the hotel. You'll need it for the bars and restaurant and to access the hotel after midnight. Yours is blue to denote fully inclusive, but I have to let you know that the restaurant closes at seven pm. There are snacks available in the bar, but they are not included in your package."

"So I can get some food in the bar if I get hungry tonight?" Pete asked.

"That is correct, sir. The restaurant opens at seven am sharp, for breakfast, breakfast finishes at ten, lunch is from twelve to two thirty, and evening meals are four thirty through to seven. Now, you are in room 323 - a balcony room as all our rooms are. To get to your room, you basically get in the elevator. Third floor, turn left." He motioned to the elevator behind Pete. Thanking Alejandro, Pete headed off to find his room, thinking about his next move. On the one hand, he wanted to rest, on the other, he fancied a drink. The best course of action, Pete decided, was to get to his room, shower, change, then head out to explore, starting in the bar. The room was easy to find with Alejandro's instructions, once inside, he was again amazed at the universe of difference from the photos he'd seen and the actual reality.

"Jesus Christ!" He exclaimed. It was like some seedy little Bed and Breakfast. In fact, it was so grim, he wondered if he'd bump into Reginald Christie in the hallway. Still, he'd not come all this way to sit in his room and watch telly — which, incidentally, was a good thing seeing as the TV was covered by a huge yellow sticker that bore the words "Peligro: no usar" along with a picture that was either a man being electrocuted or Thor warning up to kick some ass! Sighing heavily, he sat down on the bed, half expecting it to feel like an ironing board, feeling pleasantly surprised when it was surprisingly quite soft and inviting. So inviting, that Pete laid back, placing his hands behind his head and settling down into its sweet embrace. He laid there, staring up at the, oddly, wallpapered ceiling, and his mind began to wander to the events of the last few weeks.

The next thing he knew, he was waking up with the sun streaming through the still open curtains. Yawning, he checked his watch. "Only just gone eight! At least I can get some breakfast" he thought. He went into the bathroom and started running the shower. It was a pretty standard hotel bathroom, if a little dated. In the corner, next to the hand basin, was a single louvred door. It was about the size of a kitchen cupboard door, and it stood out like a dog in a cat's sanctuary. Unable to help himself, as his curiosity welled up inside him, he tugged at the door. It was a bit stiff at first but, after a little persuasion, it opened to reveal a chasm that seemed to run from roof to basement. It was only a few feet wide and was mainly taken up with what Pete assumed were water pipes and conduits. Beyond the pipe, he also noticed the inside of a door similar to the one he was peering through. The light beyond suggested that it too was in a bathroom of an adjacent room. He quietly closed the door and checked the shower for temperature. "Good enough," he thought and commenced with his ablutions. The shower was glorious. He'd not had one in 48 hours and, to be honest, he was happy just to stand and let the warmth wash over him. He eventually emerged, clean and quite refreshed, quickly drying himself off and getting dressed before heading down to breakfast.

The breakfast room was just off the reception area, and Pete was happy to find it did, in fact, look like a room from at least this century. The food itself was the usual European breakfast affair; a selection of cereals, meats, fruits, cheeses, yoghurts, bread, and pastries along with typical English breakfast items such as beans, sausage, bacon, etc. Starting with a coffee, Pete opted for an English style breakfast along with a few rounds of toast and honey. After he'd squeezed the last slice of toast onto his plate, he grabbed his coffee and looked around the room, thinking he might see Steve. When Pete could see no sign of him, he grabbed a seat at one of the smaller tables nearest the buffet bar and tucked in. The food wasn't bad, if a little lukewarm, and after the second round of toast and coffee, Pete decided he needed the toilet. Having the common British phobia of defecating in public restrooms, he headed back up to the sanctity of his room and his own bathroom. As the elevator came to rest and the doors opened, he found himself almost running to his as the extra coffee he'd had seemed to be having an adverse effect on his bowels.

Ten minutes later, having just narrowly escaped faecal disaster, he was sitting on his bed looking at maps of Calella on his phone. It didn't seem to be that big a place, and he decided he would have a little look about then locate the train station and head over to Barcelona to have a wander around there. The 'Low Battery' alert popped up on his phone, so he plugged it in to charge and, while he waited for it to charge, he set about unpacking the few things he'd brought with him, placing them into the dilapidated wardrobe before putting his valuables in the safe. With all this complete, he went out onto the balcony to sit in the sun until his phone had a decent charge. The website for the hotel had shown great views over the hotel pool and, as the hotel was on a hill, out over Calella. Strangely enough, and not entirely unexpected, Pete's balcony view was nothing like that. He had a view of part of the hotel - including the bins, a tiny and apparently derelict building site, a small farm and some hills where a few affluent residences were nestled. "Great!" He said out loud. "Just great!"

The balcony itself was reasonably spacious with a table and two chairs. Each balcony was separated by a large smoked, frosted glass partition. Pete pulled one of the chairs around and sat down, placing his feet up on the balcony railings. He sat there in silence for a little while, relaxing in the reflected rays of the sunshine. Although the bins were three floors below and some distance away from where Pete sat, he'd managed to convince himself he kept catching a faint whiff of their stench. Alone with his thoughts again, his mind began to wander, and his eyes began to droop, so relaxed was he. Sleep slowly overcame him, and he was drifting into a pleasant dream when suddenly…

"Hi, Steve!"

Chapter Three: Bad Medicine!

As his eyes burst open, Pete was greeted with the sight of what he thought was Steve's possibly disembodied head floating in the sky. Such was his fright that he kicked his feet off of the balcony, which then caused him to topple backwards in his chair. The chair hit the deck and his head, in turn, hit the large bottom pane of the window behind him, cracking it a little at the base. "Ow, shit!" he exclaimed, immediately reaching up for his head with one hand while trying to raise himself with the other. After a brief but amusing struggle, he just lay back down, holding the back of his head. He looked up again to see Steve's head poking around the glass partition, this time he took a little more time to process the information from his eyes and the unmistakable silhouette of Steve's body behind the glass gave Pete some cause for relief. "Steve! What the hell, man?" Steve just looked at Pete with that massive smile on his face. Pete straightened his chair up and sat back down, rubbing the back of his head where it had collided with the window. "You nearly killed me, man! How come you have the room next door?"

"How have we got the room next to Pete, Steve? Ah! I'm not sure, Steve." Steve responded, shrugging as he spoke. They both looked towards Pete's door as they heard a pinging sound. It was Pete's phone, signifying he'd had a text.

"Hang on, I'll be right back, big guy." He said, shooting Steve a quick, backwards glance as he nipped inside to check his phone. The good news was it was fully charged, the even 'gooder' news was that the text was from Gemma. The expletive-laden message basically told him that, for whatever reason, it had taken her until now to actually get into her own bed and she'd discovered the little 'treat' he'd left for her. "Mr Corleone thanks you for your update." He sniggered, wondering if it would be solid like a dry Weetabix by now. Emerging back onto the balcony from inside the room, he started to speak to Steve, "Hey, big guy, you'll just never guess what I did yesterday." Beginning to recount the tale of his unplanned slumber, bending down to pick up his chair. As he straightened up, he realised Steve wasn't there. "Steve?" Pete went to the edge of the balcony and peered around the partition. On the table was a word search book, which looked like a sketchbook, pens and pencils. There was no sign of Steve, though. He tried to see into the room, the sunlight made it hard to peer into the unlit gloom inside, but after straining his eyes for twenty-seconds or so, Pete made out Steve's shape in the darkness. He was just sat there on the edge of his bed, staring at the wall, or maybe the TV. Perhaps his TV was working! He shook his head. "That would just be just grand!" He said out loud. "He gets a decent TV, and I'm left looking at the walls in my quiet time." Sighing, he put all the furniture straight on his balcony. He gave Steve another quick glance then, rather than attract his attention, Pete chose to take this as his cue to make his escape. His phone was charged, the sun was shining. Time to see the sights! He'd gotten as far as down to the lobby when his conscience got the better of him. All he could think about as he waited for the elevator, and indeed as he descended in the elevator and then crossed the reception area, was Steve just sitting there all on his own. "Okay," he said to himself as he was about to leave the hotel. "Shit!" He turned around and got back in the elevator and headed up to his floor. Rather than knocking on Steve's door, he headed back into his room. Inside, he walked out onto the balcony to see if Steve was still about. A peek around the partition revealed Steve had apparently not moved. "Steve!" he called out. The balcony door was closed and, as the windows were surprisingly quite well soundproofed, Steve didn't hear him. Calling louder, he tried again. Still no response. "Right then, plan B!" he murmured. Plan B basically involved just knocking on Steve's door, like he should have done in the first place!. It took a minute or so before Steve finally answered the door, opening it only partially and peering around it as if there were some invisible chain in place. "Hi, Steve!" It was Pete who made the greeting this time. Steve opened the door wider and stood there, looking at Pete. He pushed his glasses up his nose.

"Hi, Steve!" He smiled as he replied back.

Pete cut right to it "Look, mate, I'm going to go out and explore a bit. Y'know, get the lay of the land and that, I just wondered if you'd like to come? You seem to be at a loose end, and I figured safety in numbers, and all that!" He smiled at Steve, who smiled back the biggest smile he could muster to mirror his excitement. This wasn't the first time Steve had been dumped in a hotel on his own. In fact, it was more common than not.

On the one hand, Steve was grateful that his parents took him abroad. Especially as they kept telling him how lucky he was to get all these holidays with his 'condition.' It was always the same procedure, though. They would stay in a separate, and usually, upscale hotel, while Steve was left to languish in a cheaper hotel on his own, out of sight and presumably out of mind. Steve had never let his Down Syndrome get in his way, though, and had, in the past, tried to be sociable and mix with the other people in the hotels he'd stayed in. Sometimes people were helpful and friendly, sometimes they weren't. Once, he'd met another boy with Downs, and they had struck up a bit of a friendship. Sadly, the boy turned out to be "a bit of a prick" and so Steve spent most of that holiday avoiding him. The other trips abroad he'd had, usually ended up with him just staying in his room doing his word searches or drawing cars. Steve didn't so much draw cars as trace them. He was very meticulous, and he had his own 'process' He had a large hardback book of cars that listed every model ever made from the Model 'T' Ford, right up until the latest models as of 2016 when the book was last printed. It was quite a weighty tome, and each page had about eight or so images with a small write-up on each one. He would select a page and carefully attach a sheet of tracing paper over it using paper clips. He used paper clips because he knew that pins or tape usually resulted in damage. Then he would trace all the cars on that page. Once he was finished, he would very carefully cut around each one, and he would place them in a large bankers box in his wardrobe. On a Saturday afternoon, when Steve was at home, he would sit on his bed and watch football while pulling out random cars and colouring them in, using some of the hundreds of felt tips he had in a bedside drawer. It was a simple past time, but it gave him tremendous pleasure. On holiday, he would keep up his weekday routine of drawing cars in his room because he usually had nothing else to do. He was a lonely soul, venturing out only to get some food or a drink. His parents had been bringing him abroad like this, twice a year since he was seventeen years old. He was twenty-four now, and this was the first time in those seven years that anyone, other than the aforementioned "prick," had bothered to ask him to do something with them. Pete had already shown him more kindness than anyone else had in a long time, and when he asked him to go out for a walk he was so happy at that point, he could have popped with excitement right there. Pushing his glasses up his nose again, his face beamed as he nodded at Pete and said; "Would you like to go for a walk out with Pete, Steve? See the sights? Yes, please, Steve. Yes, please!" He reached out and gently patted Pete's cheek.

Pete still hadn't got used to this little routine of Steve's. He pulled his face back from Steve's hand and gave him a pat on the arm, saying: "Cool, get your stuff together, and I'll wait out here for you." It was only a matter of minutes before Steve came out of the room, hat on head and backpack over his shoulder, all ready for an adventure.

As they exited the elevator in the lobby, Steve grabbed Pete in a big bear hug. Pete could see people staring, and he smiled awkwardly as he eased himself out of it. "Alright big guy, settle down. People think I just proposed to your or something." Steve laughed and asked if that was a Jim Bowen joke. "I don't think so. Come on, Dora, let's go!"

"Dora?" Steve looked around.

"Dora The Explorer?" Pete began to explain. Seeing the lack of recognition on Steve's face, he told him "never mind." And off they went.

Calella! Situated on the Spanish coast, it was once a thriving holiday destination, full of life and activity. These days, it was a bit down on its luck. Although it still made a reasonable trade in tourism, the sun had long since set on its heyday. The Olympiad was one of the few big hotels still open. Indeed, Pete had noticed, on their way down to the main town, a large hotel — much more significant and more beautiful looking than theirs — that appeared to be derelict. Given that it was mid-August, it should have been a hive of activity, but alas, it just looked closed and sad, very sad. The saving grace for Calella was that it was also a large town, fortunate enough to be situated on the main train line into Barcelona. As it was only an hour away, many people commuted to work in the big city while living in the, still quite picturesque, seaside town. The moderate tourism influx that the town did experience was an added bonus to a, relatively busy, local economy.

As they walked in the morning heat, they were both quite taken with one of Calella's more unusual features: a broad and open storm drain that seemed to run right through the town and down to the beach. It was lower than street level and divided the main street right down to the sea, bisected every two or three hundred yards or so by a 'bridge' that was really a road that ran off elsewhere. Okay, so maybe the drain in itself wasn't impressive, but the massive amount of amazing graffiti that adorned it was. Both Pete and Steve were fascinated as they walked alongside it, looking down at all the cool murals. Every so often, you could see remnants of past paintings poking through the new ones. Eventually, they came to the intersection of the main road that ran perpendicular to it. The drain disappeared underneath it and, as they discovered, didn't reappear until just before it reached the beach. Once they had crossed the intersection, there was the usual mix of bars and restaurants and cheap souvenir shops one found in towns like this the world over. In actual fact, it reminded Pete of Redcar, a small seaside town near where he lived, only Calella was classier and had better restaurants. Over to the right side of the main drag, once you got behind the shops and bars, the commercial area gave way to more suburban sprawl, and after realising there was not much else to see the pair turned round to explore the other side. This side was much better: there was a maze of side streets that contained a mixture of regular shops and restaurants. It was almost like being back home, thought Pete, such was the mundanity of it all. Steve seemed to be enjoying himself, though. He didn't say much but had a smile on his face most of the time, his favourite part seemed to be when they found a shop that had rude things in the window and laughing hard when they saw chocolate penises in a sweet shop. He laughed so hard that Pete couldn't help but laugh too. Every time a tourist or local passed by and gave them disapproving looks, they laughed harder. Both of them were quite breathless and a little sweaty when the mirth finally subsided. "Awww man, I haven't laughed like that in a while," said Pete.

Steve smiled. "They were funny, Steve! Aye Steve" He replied. "You should buy one for your mum." He continued, giving a little laugh, then he started a short conversation with himself "You can't do that Steve, dad won't be happy. No, he won't be happy. Be funny, though. Aye!" He started laughing again. The exchange reminded Pete of Gollum in Lord Of The Rings but less sinister, and Steve was definitely better looking.

"Come on, mate." Pete interrupted, looking at his watch, "Let's go grab some lunch, it's getting on, you know."

"Ooh, it's getting on," said Steve, mimicking Pete, "let's go get some lunch." And then he started laughing again.

They wandered around a bit more first, seeing what else of interest they could find. Eventually, the pair of them discovered the train station and, checking his watch, Pete decided he'd just hang around in Calella for the day and keep Steve company, but he told Steve to wait outside on a bench while he popped into the station and had a look at the train times. The Barcelona train seemed to run every hour and a quarter past the hour, from what he could see on the timetable. The first train was at a quarter past seven in the morning, the last was at a quarter of an hour past eleven in the evening. He assumed the last train back would be around that time too, although he could always check that once he arrived in Barcelona. Outside the station, Steve was still where he'd left him chatting away happily to himself. "Right, big fella! Hungry?" Steve nodded, smiling, as always. "Come on then," Pete beckoned, "let's go grab some food." Because they were already out and about, Pete decided he'd see what the town had to offer in terms of food, rather than go back for the free 'all inclusive' restaurant at the hotel. The choice of restaurants in the town was pretty varied, but Steve didn't want to eat at any of them. As a last resort, they ended up back on the main drag, in a McDonald's. "When in Rome, eh?" Pete had joked as he bought them both lunch.

Steve just looked at him and said; "We're in Spain!" Then he laughed.

He was about to say something more, but Pete beat him to it. "Let me guess, that's a Jim Bowen joke." Steve joined in at that last bit then reached over and rubbed Pete's arm, Smiling and chuckling, then they both tucked into their meals. Pete had kindly sprung for the food as a payback treat for getting him on the coach. Steve was grateful for the meal and even more grateful when he saw Pete had also bought ice creams for them both. A little while later, after finishing their meals, they were both messing about blowing straw wrappers at each other when Steve suddenly stopped. He was gazing past Pete with a wide-eyed look on his face. Pete, just about to blow another straw wrapper at him, noticed Steve was looking past him, and he turned to see what had caught his eye. Now, if this was a film, this is the bit where the camera would cut to a long shot then some tight shots of what the boys were looking at. There would be a soft filter on the lens, some artistic lighting, and some anthemic rock track playing on the soundtrack, maybe 'Bad Medicine' by Bon Jovi (if you can't bring that to mind - use your own choice of song) This is kind of how it was for Pete, and he assumed Steve was having the same experience. Into the restaurant, two girls had walked in. One was about the same height as Pete, curly brown shoulder length hair, and a figure to die for. Meet Melody, Mel for short. Pete was mesmerised as she giggled her way up to the counter. In a fantastic stroke of luck, or maybe good writing, Melody had a companion; Joanna. Joanna, who also had a thick head of curly brown hair, was about the same height and build as Steve, estimated Pete. Pete also noticed that Joanna also had Down Syndrome.

"She's beautiful!" Exclaimed Steve.

Steve couldn't stop staring at Joanna. Pete, similarly transfixed with Melody, broke the spell. "Hello, ladies!" He offered, smiling cheekily.

"Aye, Hello ladies" also offered Steve.

The two girls turned to look at the two boys. "Can we help you, boys?" enquired Melody. She smiled at both of them.

Pete looked at Steve. Steve, having no experience in these sort of situations, just nodded and smiled at Pete. "Well, girls," replied Pete, turning back to face them. "We just wondered if you'd like to join us?" His voice rising a little too high at the end.

He could hear Steve start to ask himself questions behind him "Ah, do you think they want to join us, Steve? I don't know Steve. Petes sorting it out. She's pretty, Steve."

Joanna turned to Melody and whispered something in her ear, they both laughed. "Okay, boys, we'll come and join you, I'll have a 'Big Mac' meal, large with a diet coke," pointing to Joanna "She'll have the same but with a Sprite, please."

"Oh!" Replied Pete. "Okay, you want us to buy it?"

"Is there a problem?" It was Joanna who spoke this time.

Pete looked at Steve, who just smiled and pushed his glasses up his nose. "No, no problem! If you ladies would care to take a seat, I'll go and sort it." As he headed off to the counter to order the food, the two girls sat down.

Joanna pinched his seat and sat opposite Steve, Melody sat next to her. "Hello, handsome!" He heard Joanna say to Steve as he walked away. When he returned with the food, Joanna was talking away while poor Steve just sat staring with that massive smile on his face, occasionally the finger would come up and push his glasses back up his nose.

"Here you go." Pete set the tray down, and the girls took their own meals off it. They both said their thanks to Pete and Steve and began to tuck in.
"Mmm" Melody muttered, swallowing hard. "Sorry, I'm Melody, but most folks call me Mel."

Steve suddenly found his voice singing a few lines from a Neil diamond song - Melody Road.

Pete looked at him. "Random!" He said.

Mel smiled at them both and gestured to Joanna, who was busy murdering her burger. "And this lovely lady is Joanna, most folks call her Jo." Before Pete could stop him, Steve began singing a few lines from, as it turned out, a Cliff Richard song of the same name. Pete laughed, nervously.

Steve laughed then followed up with "That's a Jim Bowen joke, Steve!"

Joanna laughed in between bites of her burger. "You're funny, I like a man with a sense of humour! Especially a handsome one!" Pete could see Steve was blushing. Mel threw her head back and laughed. It was a sound like Pete had never heard before, magical, like some enchanted music. She noticed Pete staring and asked if he was okay? Pete snapped out of it, literally giving his head a shake before he laughed, and he introduced himself and then Steve.

"Pleased to meet you both," smiled Mel. "How long have you worked with Steve?" She asked him, nodding at Steve.

"Excuse me?" Pete replied, hoping it would appear as if he hadn't heard the question while he tried to process it. He had no idea what she was on about.

"How long?" Mel motioned at the pair of them. Then a look of horror crossed her face. "Oh shit, is he your brother or something? I'm sorry." She laughed again, and Pete could swear it made his heart tickle. "I always just assume people are support workers, like me."

The penny dropped, and Pete realised she thought that he was maybe a support worker. In a hot minute, he weighed up his options; "Tell her the truth that I just met Steve yesterday and am hanging around with him because that won't sound a little creepy at all. Or I can pretend to be a support worker, which will look less creepy and it will give me some common ground on which we can build a splendid future together." "Aaaaah, sorry!" Pete said, smiling. He shook his head and looked over at Steve then back at Mel. Option B it is then. "Oh, we've not long been working together, have we mate?"

Steve looked at the both of them in a moment that seemed to last forever. "Come on, Steve." Pete was screaming internally "Please don't let me down here." He'd only just met Mel, but there was something about her, something special that he just couldn't put his finger on. He'd never been one for subscribing to the whole 'love at first sight' thing, but he couldn't deny there was some sort of spark. Steve was currently having a 'deer in the headlights' moment. He had never had much to do with girls other than his mum or people in shops. There was a sudden shyness to his demeanour. After an awkwardly long pause, during which Pete was sure he made some sublime telepathic connection, he looked at Pete and then at Mel and said; "Yeah. Just new," and smiled.

"Oh! Thank Christ!" thought Pete, trying not to look too relieved. Quickly turned the tables: "What about you? How long have you and Joanna, is it? How long have you two been working together?"

Mel took a drink of her coke before answering."Over two years now, I think. This is our third holiday together. She lives in supported living, back home. Her parents are always popping in, but they want her to live as independent a life as she can. They figure they won't always be around to look after her, and besides that, they wanted to treat her as normally as possible, and a lot of girls her age are living away from home, so." She took another drink. "She's actually a dream client. She is quite independent, and she's hilarious. She has me in stitches. She's obsessed with finding a boyfriend, though. Driving me nuts!" She looked over at Jo, who had taken a breather from talking to Steve and was taking a sip of her drink while listening to Mel. Mel gave her a wink, and she winked back, finally releasing her grip on the straw and letting out a big satisfied sigh. Mel smiled at her and Pete could see the genuine affection she held for her ward. As she continued eating her meal, Pete couldn't help but stare at her. He'd immediately noticed the Deadpool t-shirt she was wearing as she and Jo were walking up to them. As she took a bite out of her burger, he noticed the small 'Face-hugger' tattoo on the inside of her wrist. "As if she likes Marvel and Alien!" He thought to himself, before breaking the silence "Yeah, it's a bit different with Steve. His parents want him at home, for various reasons," he said out loud while thinking; "like taking advantage of his benefits, for one, I bet!" "They're very, er, busy though." He continued, diplomatically, Pete was now making this up as he went along. "They're not always around, so I go in and help him with stuff, bring him on holiday and that." He continued, nodding his head sagely.

"Do you, now?" said Mel, smiling a little. Pete wasn't sure what she meant, but she was smiling, so he figured it wasn't a wrong kind of question. Besides, he could look at that smile all day.

"Oh, yeah! All the usual stuff, like" he stammered.

"Interesting! And what does your wife think of you getting free holidays like this?" Mel asked.

"Excuse me?" Pete was on the run again.

Mel looked at his left hand and then back up at him. He subconsciously grasped the ring between thumb and forefinger of his other hand. "Oh, right, the ring! Yeah, that's a long story, partly the reason why I'm here." Mel looked perplexed. Before she could ask what he meant, Pete continued. "I took this," he searched for the right word "assignment. I took this assignment at the last minute. Someone else was supposed to come, but they dropped out, and I needed a bit of time away."

Mel took a sip of her drink. "Things not good at home, then?"

Pete laughed. "you could say that. Actually, things are pretty fu…grim at home. In fact, it's pretty safe to say there is no home, anymore." He took a sip of his own drink and just stared at the table.

"Oh, dear! Sounds bad" exclaimed Mel, "I'm sorry. I am a nosy cow sometimes. I didn't mean to pry."

Smiling, Pete waved his hand dismissively. "Don't worry about it, honestly. It's been a rollercoaster couple of weeks, but I'm moving forward, surprisingly quickly. Working with Steve has been a blessing." They both looked over at Steve and Jo, Jo was busy chatting away while Steve just looked at her, smiling. Occasionally he'd laugh and push his glasses up his nose. Pete turned back to Mel. "Are you staying locally?"

Mel, after another sip of her drink, replied; "Yeah, we're in the Olympiad, the old hotel back up the hill there."

"No way," said Pete, "that's our gaffe too. We only just arrived late yesterday, so we're having a bit of a wander to get the lay of the land."

"We've been here a week already," said Mel. "We're on a two-week break. Jo normally goes away twice for a week at a time, but she couldn't go earlier in the year as she wasn't well, so she decided to get away for two weeks now, instead."

Just then, Jo interrupted their chat "Come on Mel, stop making eyes at dreamboat over there and let's get on the beach. I want to swim." She laughed.

Pete blushed as Mel gave Jo a playful shove. "Behave yourself, missus." She said, laughing.

Jo laughed again then, looking at Pete, she said; "don't worry, sweetheart, I like a little extra something in my men."

"Joanna." Mel said, in an almost cautionary tone.

Pete just looked confused, a small nervous smile crossing his face. "Extra something?"

"Yeah," she laughed "like an extra chromosome." She winked at him and giggled. Pete did not know what to do at this point. Should he laugh? Should he stay silent? He really did not know the social etiquette for this sort of situation.

Mel saved him. "Joanna Smith! You'll be getting us both in trouble." She said, in a faux school matron tone, then she too laughed. Meanwhile, poor Steve just kept looking at everyone. When Mel started laughing, he also began to laugh, but it was the laugh of someone who wasn't sure why he was laughing, he just knew someone had said something funny.

Turning back to face Pete as she stood up, Mel asked if the boys wanted to join them. "Well, we'd love to, but we haven't got any gear."

"Gear?" It was Jo who asked the question. "What gear?"

"You know, towels and shorts and that." Came Pete's reply. Mel looked perplexed again.

"Did you bring a towel, Steve? No, I didn't, Steve!" Was Steve's response.

"You both came on holiday to Spain, but you haven't brought any beach gear?" She feigned an exaggerated look of confusion.

Pete looked at Steve, Steve smiled back. Calm Pete took over. "well, funny story, the bloody airline only went and lost our luggage!"

Mel and Jo both looked shocked as, in unison, they both said; "No way!"

"Yes, way!" Steve joined the fray. "Lost our luggage." Then he laughed.

"Yeah," Pete continued, "they lost our luggage. Well, it's not lost as such, it's just not here. They know where it is, and they are trying to get it back to us." Of course, Pete was lying. He couldn't say that he'd come away, as a support worker for Steve, with just a backpack that contained two t-shirts, three pairs of pants, no spare socks, or any other clothes for that matter, an iPad, an iPod and his wash bag. Worse still, how could he explain his 'charge' also had only a backpack with him, the contents of which were mostly a mystery, save for a word search book, a sketchbook, and an assortment of pens and pencils.

"Where is it?" Jo asked.

"Would you believe," began Pete, wracking his brains to think of somewhere far enough away for it to take a while to get their lost luggage back.

Steve, having spent last night looking for South American countries on his word search grid, saved the day; "Pargay!"

Pete shot him a bemused look "Pargay?" He laughed, realising what Steve meant to say. "Yeah, Paraguay! It's gone to Paraguay. They're trying to get it back to us as quickly as possible." On a roll, he went on; "Tell you what, you go and get yourselves settled on the beach, Me and Steve will have a look into the shops and get some stuff," he shot Steve another quick look and nodded at him, Steve nodded back, "and then we'll come and join you."

"Yes," said Steve, "join you, we will" in his best Yoda voice.

"If that's okay with you, of course?" Pete added, hopefully.

"Oooh, I don't know. What do you think, Jo?" Asked Mel, smiling.

Jo put her hand on her chin and cocked her head, looking up at the ceiling. "Oh okay then, if you have to!" Then she laughed. Like Steve's smile, Pete found he couldn't help but be warmed by it. It was a musical laugh, and much like Steve's big smile, it was full to the brim with genuine mirth and joy. Outside the restaurant, the group made arrangements about where to meet later and said their good-byes.

As Mel and Jo headed off down towards the beach, Pete and Steve headed towards the shops. "What are we doing, Steve?" Steve asked.

"We need some trunks or shorts or something mate and towels." Pete looked up at the sky. "Some sunblock might be a good idea too. Do you have any of those things back at the hotel? Shorts or a towel, sunblock?"

"There's a towel in the bathroom." He said.

"That's a no then!" Sighed Pete. "Okay, well, we'll just go find a shop that sells this sort of stuff and get sorted before we go back and find the girls."

"Ah," said Steve, "we'll go and find the girls, Steve!" he said to himself, "Aye Steve, go find the girls. Do you like Jo?" he replied. "Yes, Steve, she's beautiful!" Pete said nothing, he just listened as they walked side by side. "We have to go and buy some shorts and a towel." Steve continued. "Aye, what with, Steve, brass buttons?" Steve started laughing and finished off with his customary Jim Bowen jocular classification. Pete stopped and turned to face him.

"Brass buttons?" He asked, not quite sure what Steve meant.

"Yeah, brass buttons!" Steve replied.

"Don't you have any money?" Pete asked.

Steve just looked at Pete and shook his head. "I have twenty euros for emergencies only that my dad gave me." Then, as if mimicking his dad; "Don't spend it unless it's absolutely necessary!" He said, jabbing his finger at Pete.

Pete took a step back in disbelief. "So, let me get this straight," he said, "your mum and dad bring you on holiday." Steve nodded. "They put you up in a hotel, not their hotel, a different one. In this case, one that is fifty kilometres away." Steve nodded again. "Not only that, but they don't even give you any spending money?" Steve nodded then pushed his glasses back up his nose. "Are you kidding me, there?"

Steve looked at the floor. "I'm sorry, Pete." He said, then, to himself: "What're you sorry for, Steve? Pete's angry at me, Steve! Because you're useless? Yes, Steve!" He put his hands in his pockets.

"What? Wait, no, no, no, whoa!" Pete realised how he must have come across. "No, Steve!" He placed his hands on Steve's shoulders and tried to look into his eyes. "Hey big fella! I'm not mad at you. I'm mad at your folks. I think it's shit how they treat you."

Steve looked up at Pete. "You're not angry with me?" Pushing his glasses up his nose again.

"No, mate, I promise. I can't be mad at you, you're too cool, buddy." Pete gave him a wink. Steve smiled that big smile again. Pete knew he wasn't short of funds himself, he figured this was a small price to play if he managed to spend some time with Mel as a result. "Come on, big guy. Let's go get some stuff!"

"Yeah!" Steve shouted, actually raising his fist in the air.

A short while later the pair were heading back towards the main drag. They had both managed to find a large department store that, conveniently, pretty much had everything they needed. Pete just picked out a pair of khaki cargo shorts. They would do for the beach, and he figured it wouldn't matter too much if they got wet. Steve followed suit, for no other reason than Pete got them, and Pete was his new, and only, best friend. For his seating and drying needs, Pete selected a plain red beach towel. Steve, although tempted to get the red towel, couldn't resist the lure of a huge Star Wars beach towel. Pete looked at it. It was more of a blanket than a towel. Also, Star Wars! As they headed to pay, Pete surreptitiously swapped his red towel out for a Star Wars towel too.

They went straight back to the hotel first. Pete wanted to get changed and pick up his backpack to keep his towel and the sunblock in. He had also grabbed a small four-pack of beer, to share with Mel. Coming out of his room, he found Steve waiting for him, clutching his towel, dressed in his new shorts and a new pair of flip flops, (that also matched Pete's) and looking very proud of himself. "Hi, Steve!" He greeted Pete.

"Nice shorts, big guy!" Pete responded, causing Steve's smile to get even wider. "Come on, let's go and impress some girls." Steve patted his shoulder, and off they went.

It wasn't long before they were passing the McDonald's they'd eaten at earlier. Straight on past there they came to where the storm drain re-emerged from under the town. Just past that, it was spanned by a bridge that carried the rail line, and another bridge for pedestrians. The only way to get to the beach, without having to walk about five hundred meters out of the way to use a rail crossing, was to head down a ramp to the storm drain. From there you could use the little footpath that went under both the rail bridge and the footbridge and out onto the beach by way of a broad path that ran the entire length of the beach, right up to the train station. The beach itself looked quite nice but, as their feet made contact with the sand, they both realised that looks can be deceiving. Pete bent down and grabbed some sand in his fingers. "Jesus!" He exclaimed. "This is like building sand. I think I finally figured out where sand-paper comes from!"

Steve, who had also bent down to examine the sand, laughed. "Aye, sand-paper!" He laughed again then his eyes shot wide, and he pointed down the beach. Pete followed his direction and saw the girls.

"Nice one," he patted Steve's shoulder, "come on, Jim Bowen!" Pete set off with Steve bringing up the rear and pushing his glasses up his nose and smiling. Jo had already spotted them and began waving. "Hello boys!" she shouted as Mel turned to see where they were.

The beach itself was relatively flat, but when you got to the water's edge, it dropped down a few feet in a quite steep incline. As rough as it was, the sand was a lovely golden colour that contrasted sharply with the deep azure of the mediterranean sea. The beach, overall, was quite quiet. A few couples were laid out on the sun nearby. In the distance, an elderly man in a Panama hat was strolling down the beach with his dog. A few seagulls padded about on the beach while more swooped and soared out to sea, their cries crisp and urgent in the afternoon breeze. The boys reached the girls just as Mel was applying sun cream to Jo's arms and face. Quick as a flash, Pete retrieved his own sun cream from his backpack and motioned to Steve to stretch his arms out.

Taking his cues from Mel, he applied sun cream to Steve's arms, legs, and the back of his neck. Steve brushed his hand away as Pete tried to put some on his face. "Oooh no," he said, Pete smiled and pulled his hand away, applying the cream to his own arms and legs.

He was about to stow the cream in his bag when Steve grabbed it and put some in his hand. "Neck!" He said and began to apply it to Pete's neck before Pete had a chance to protest. Everyone laughed at this while Pete pulled his towel out of his backpack. Steve hadn't seen Pete's towel when he bought it, and his face lit up when he saw their towels matched. Once Steve was sorted, Pete placed his towel on the beach next to Mel and sat down on it. Reaching into his backpack, he retrieved two of the beers, offering on to Mel.

"Thanks" she said, taking it from him and checking the alcohol content before twisting the cap off. "I'm not really supposed to drink while I'm on duty, but it's only three percent and one won't hurt. Thanks!" She held out the bottle and Pete lightly tapped it with his own.

"Cheers!" He offered. They both took a swig and Pete noticed Mel had a small 'Death Star' tattooed on her other wrist. "I like your tattoo."

"Sorry?" Mel responded before she realised what he was referring to. "Oh, my Death Star!" She laughed. "Just wearing my allegiance to the Empire on my sleeve, like you do! Don't tell me you're a fan of those Rebel scum?" They both laughed and she pointed out her 'Face-hugger' tattoo on the other wrist.

"Yeah, I clocked it back when you were eating. Nice!" Pete smiled. "You like that sort of stuff?"

"Oh god, yes!" Mel replied. "I love it all. Always have, right from being a little girl. My mum despairs at it, thinks it makes me look like a tomboy." She took another swig. "But my dad actively encourages it. He's pretty much the reason I'm into it all. Right from an early age, he let me stay up and watch old science fiction and horror films with him. He bought me my first comics too! What about you?"

Pete hadn't really heard the question, he was too busy swooning at these revelations. He realised she was looking at him expectantly and he repeated the last words he'd heard her say: "What about me?"

"Yeah," she responded, smiling, "what are you into?"

"Oh!" Pete took a swig. "Pretty much the same sort of stuff. I have quite a collection of films and comics and stuff. Toys too!"

"No way!" Mel responded. "I have loads of stuff like that! What's the chances?" They both laughed and the afternoon descended into a game of geeky top trumps as they both listed off their prized pop culture possessions. Jo and Steve, meanwhile, kept chasing each other in and out of the sea while Pete and Mel sat and observed from the safety of the beach towels, sipping on the beers Pete had brought.

The conversation eventually lulled and Mel changed the subject. "Steve seems like a dream job." She said. "He's got a really kind way about him. Do you do any other support work, or is it just Steve?"

The question caught Pete off-guard. Think, fast! "Yeah, I do a few others too. Steve's the main one, though!"

"Are they all like Steve? We have a core client base, but they all have different issues; autism, physical disabilities, some developmental issues. Jo is the one I work with the most though. We get on so well that her mum has asked that I work with her as much as possible. When I first started working with her, she'd not long since moved into the supported living accommodation. She was a bit overwhelmed by it all and would act out with the staff and the other housemates. It was such a massive change for her, but she soon settled into it. She's a little more independent than the others now. She's not as badly affected as some DS sufferers."

"DS?" Pete looked lost.

Mel gave him that sideways glance again. "Down Syndrome?" She said.

Pete rolled his eyes. "Idiot!" He thought to himself. "Oh yeah," he said. "Sorry, I'm not firing on all cylinders today. DS, of course." He said, out loud.

"Yeah," Mel continued, "she still has short term memory issues and stuff like that but her mental age and reading skills, vocab, things like that, she's above average for her condition."

Pete smiled. "Yeah, she's definitely not shy." He agreed. "What about you? What sort of things do you like to do, when you're not doing this?" He asked, trying to change the subject before he got asked any more uncomfortable questions. Mel laughed, much to Pete's bewilderment. "What?" He asked.

"The old 'getting to know you' open questions routine. Smooth!" She laughed again. Pete looked a bit startled, and Mel gave him a playful shove. "I'm just messing with you" she laughed again then her face suddenly went deadly serious. "Seriously though, this isn't that sort of holiday. You're married, as far as I know, and I'm just not interested. I know I'm killing the ambience right now, but I'm just setting my stall out for you, so there's no misunderstanding further down the line. Okay?" She held his gaze for what seemed like forever until he murmured a meek "okay." She burst into laughter again. "Your face!"

"That laugh!" Thought Pete. It was like a butterfly fluttering its wings in his chest. He wasn't usually given to waxing lyrical like this but that laugh, and the way her smile seemed to blot the rest of the world out. In that split second, time stood still for Pete as he regarded the smooth beauty of her skin, The mystical allure of her deep, electric blue eyes, and the luscious and full natural redness of her lips. He quickly snapped out of it. "Stop it, fella!" He said, inside. He knew this was probably just his mind looking for solace to calm the raging storm of emotions deep within him, caused by that, that…

What was it his grandmother had called Gemma? Oh yeah, "That filthy bloody hooer!" He figured this was just a rebound thing.

Steve came over and picked his towel up. He began rolling it up with a purpose. "What's to do, big guy?" Pete asked him.

Steve continued to roll his towel up as he looked at his watch and said; "It's half three."

"Okaaaay!" Said Pete. Jo was heading back from the water and Mel was watching the exchange.

"Meds and word search!" Steve explained. Mel looked concerned.

"Oh yeah, meds!" Said Pete. "Silly me, come on then, let's get you back."

Mel still looked concerned. "How long have you been working with Steve? I only ask because, y' know, forgetting med time is pretty bad!" Steve had already started walking off towards the bridge.

"Shit!" Thought, Pete. "Well, back at home, they have Alexa reminding him all the time. I downloaded the app, and it was supposed to go off to remind me. I guess I screwed it up. Good job Steve has an alarm on his watch." Mel didn't look convinced. She started to say something, but Pete was on the move. "Look, I better get after him. I don't want him getting lost. Might see you back at the hotel. Maybe in the bar for a drink later?" He was shouting the last part as he started running to catch up with Steve, who had covered quite a distance despite being a little overweight and having shorter legs. Pete caught up with him just as he was leaving the beach to go under the bridges, back up to street level. "Hey, big fella, what's the hurry?"

Steve was sweating a bit in the heat. "I have to get back for four o'clock to take my meds and do my word search."

"Can't you give the word search a miss today?" Pete asked, panting.

"Nope!" came the reply.

"Oh! Okay then." Pete was a bit taken aback by Steve's sharp tone. He walked on in silence a bit then said: "What meds do you take?"

"Just stuff for epilepsy." Steve replied.

"Epilepsy?" Steve nodded in response. "Do you get seizures often?"

"Nope, Steve, not had one for years." Steve pushed his glasses up his nose.

"Maybe it'd be a good idea to keep your meds in your backpack while we're here. Especially if we're going to be out and about with the girls? You could bring your word search out too, maybe. How's that for an idea?" Steve put his hand on his chin thoughtfully as he walked then he turned to Pete and stuck his thumb in the air. They remained silent for the rest of the walk back to the hotel, and once they were back, Steve went straight up to his room. Pete decided to go to the bar.

Situated just off the main lobby, the bar was quite a sizeable room. There was a stage at the far end, a view out to the front of the hotel along the left side of the room and the bar itself ran almost the length of the right side. At the end of the bar were two sets of double doors that led out to the pool area at the rear. The section of the bar near the doors had hatches that opened out so pool patrons could get beverages without having to keep coming in. The bar was quite busy. Pete looked around and marvelled at the amount of cheap nylon shorts he could see. He reckoned that every other t-shirt was either a George Cross or a Union flag. With the rest being football tops, and that was just the women. "Christ!" He thought, "This must be what it's like in the Jeremy Kyle Green Room of a morning!" He went to the bar and was surprised to see 'Alejandro' serving. 'Alejandro' was now wearing a badge that read 'Dave.'

Dave saw Pete and smiled. "Now then Irish, what can I get for you?"

"I'll just have a pint of Lager, please mate," Pete replied, adding "and get one for yourself, is that possible? I mean, do you need money for that or, how does it work?"

Dave laughed. "I just need your key card," he said, "don't worry about getting me one, we have a, er, *special policy* on staff drinks!" He gave Pete a wink and pulled Pete's pint, setting it down on the bar in front of him. "So, sir, where's your friend?"

"Hey, call me, Pete, please. My friend?" Pete responded, taking a sip of lager.

"Okay, Pete. Yeah, your friend! The guy you went out with this morning? Special looking fellow, if you catch my drift."

"Oooh!" The penny dropped. "You must mean Steve. He's not really, we're not really friends. I literally met him yesterday. He just seems to have latched on to me."

Dave grabbed himself a quick shot of vodka and leant on the bar in front of Pete. "That's a nice thing you did then, taking him under your wing."

"Yeah well, it wasn't completely philanthropic."

"How so?" Asked Dave, grabbing another quick shot.

"Well, see, there's this girl, and she does that sort of thing for a living, I figured"

Dave jumped in, "You figured you'd pretend to be in the same line of business to 'get closer' to her?"

Pete raised his glass. "Bingo! I mean, it makes me sound a bit sleazy, but yeah." Dave emptied his glass, and glancing at Pete's wedding ring, shook his head. "What?" Asked Pete.

"Well," Dave began "I see that wedding band, and I'm conflicted. I'm usually a good judge of character, and you just don't strike me as the cheating type, yet here you are. What's that about? I mean, I don't judge. I've seen some shit in this line of work - a lot of it right here in this lovely hotel" Pete chuckled. "But you really don't strike me as 'that guy'"

"Well," countered Pete, draining his glass, "fill me up, and allow me to tell you a little tale of love, infidelity, and the need for speed!"

Dave looked at Pete for a moment. He pulled two pints and called up the bar. "Hey, Alejandro!" As a handsome looking Spaniard turned around, Pete was bemused to see the real Alejandro finally make an appearance. "I'm taking a break, okay?" A nod from Alejandro and the two of them went and sat at a table in the window. Pete began to regale Dave with the sordid tale of Gemma's infidelity.

Thirty minutes later, and two pints deep, Pete had gotten to the faecal finale of his last home visit, they were both howling. Dave was banging on the table with his palm, tears rolling down his cheeks. "Oh, no!" Dave said trough the tears of laughter. "That is without a doubt," he said, wiping his eyes "the best infidelity stroke revenge story I've heard in a long time."

"You really had to be there." Pete said, draining his pint.

"I bet." Said Dave. Pete suddenly jumped and reached into his pocket.

"Lucky for you, I have some footage." Beamed Pete as he started the video off and handed the phone to Dave.

A minute later, Dave handed the phone back to Pete as he wiped more tears of laughter from his eyes. "Oh, man, that is outstanding! I must admit, I was a bit sceptical. The whole Top Gun thing just sounded a bit far fetched to me, but that was brilliant. What did Mel think?" He asked, before whistling loudly and motioning over to Alejandro for two more pints.

"Oh no, I haven't even told her what went on, let alone shared the video with her. I just told her things weren't good. The thing is, I know I just met her, but she's really nice. When I first saw her, I definitely wanted to Goose her Maverick!" They both laughed. "But the truth is, mate, I just feel this connection. I can't explain it. I know this sounds incredibly stupid and corny, but there's something about her that… I don't know, man. She's got this smile and this way about her, and that laugh!" He rolled his eyes "I've only heard it a few times, but already I want to do whatever it takes to hear that laugh every day for the rest of my life. She loves all the stuff I love, too. Gemma made me box all my stuff up and store it in the attic, Mel has loads of stuff like mine too. Shit, Dave. I know I should come clean about all of it, Steve, Gemma, everything but I don't want to tell her because I don't want her thinking I'm just looking for rebound sex or that I'm just, you know, vulnerable and all that. Or worse, a real creep!" Alejandro brought the drinks over. Dave took a big gulp of his and looked thoughtful.

"I see your dilemma. This is a tricky situation. I suggest you keep your new friend close and see how it plays out. Worst-case scenario, you get nowhere, but you make your mate, Steve's holiday the best he's ever had, by the sounds of it. Best case is that you manage to win the heart of the fair maiden. Either way, it's a win on the wheel of Karma!"

Pete finished his drink. "Yeah, I guess. Maybe I am on the rebound, though. I mean, I've only known her for like, six hours now and here I am contemplating spending the rest of my life with her"

"Yeah, life is never simple, Pete. As for the rebound thing, I reckon the fact that you're aware that it's a possibility rules it out. I mean, I'm no expert, but when you're on the rebound, you usually don't care about being on the rebound or don't realise. It's like when they say mad people don't know they're mad, or that thing when stupid people don't realise how stupid they are. There's no harm in getting to know her. You never know, by this time next week you might be sick of the sight of her."

Pete nodded in agreement. "Yeah, I guess you're right. Anyway, I'll be getting myself upstairs to see what's going on. Thanks for listening." Standing up, he offered his hand to Dave, who stood up, shook Pete's hand and picked up the empty glasses.

"No worries. Listen, I'm always around here somewhere. If you need anything, come find me." He gave Pete a wink and went back to work. Pete headed out of the bar and over to the elevator. "Time for a kip!" He thought to himself.

Up in his room, Pete showered then, wrapped in a towel, went out to sit on the balcony. He surveyed the view and cursed his luck at getting such a shitty room. It was apparent to Pete, squinting through the partition, that Steve was not out on his balcony. Straining his ears, he could hear the faint murmurings of Steve chatting away to himself in his room, and he got up and peeked around the side of the partition. Sure enough, there sat Steve at the little table in the room, pencil in hand, concentrating intently on his word search book. Sitting back down, Pete wondered if Steve would have ever ventured out of his room without his intervention. He also considered what a pair of poor excuses for humans Steve's parents were. Yes, it was great they'd brought him on holiday but to dump a vulnerable adult fifty kilometres away with next to no cash and to not even let him bring a case with him. "Bastards!" He thought. He went back inside and got dressed, before rummaging through his backpack for the last of the beers he bought earlier. Returning to his balcony perch, he cracked the beer open, sat back and surveyed the mountains in the distance. It was a little after seven, and the sun was beginning its journey down towards the end of the day.

Bird song was the only noise he could hear as he sipped his beer and soaked up the atmosphere. If he strained his ears, he could faintly make out the sound of kids playing somewhere, maybe the pool. Below him, one of the staff was emptying something into the oversized wheelie bins. High above him, he could see a plane, its vapour trail cleaving a thin white paper-cut through the deepening azure of the early evening sky. He wondered what Mel and Jo were up to at that moment, then his thoughts turned to Mel and the effect she'd had on him in such a short space of time. Being a practical sort of bloke, he told himself that this is definitely a rebound thing. "I mean, she's incredibly hot, and I would definitely like to get to know her better. But I don't think she's 'The One.' I mean, I've only known her for like, seven or eight hours or so." He was talking out loud and hadn't realised that Steve had emerged onto his balcony and was listening, silently. Pete finished off his beer, just as his phone gave a familiar 'ting' from inside the room to let him know he had a text message. Placing his empty bottle in the waste bin just inside the door, he went to retrieve his phone. It was Terry:

"What the hell did you say to Hashimoto? For god's sake, Pete! He's sent a letter saying that due to what he perceives as an act of moral bankruptcy on my part, he feels the need to review our business relationship as he does not feel he can trust us in business due to such a blatant lack of integrity! Wants to see me next week to discuss it! He's not returning my calls

or anything. MORAL BANKRUPTCY? WHAT THE HELL! Is this your doing, you vindictive little prick?!! It's one thing to bugger my relationship with Clair, but this is my bread and butter too! There are some lines you just don't cross 'mate!'"

Pete shook his head in disbelief at the last part. "Utter prick!" He said out loud. This was terrible news, though. As much as he wanted to see Terry suffer, this would affect the livelyhood of all the other staff too. He hadn't considered this when he broke the news of his departure to Mr Hashimoto, although he had no control over how the man reacted to the news. "Still, not much I can do right now. I'll speak to Mr H next week and see what I can do to change his mind." He began typing:

"At least he only feels the need to review your contracts. He could have been feeling the need…" He hit 'send' the followed it up with: "For speed!" 'Send.' "You twat!" He inserted the emoji of the hand with its middle finger raised and hit send on that too. Then he blocked Terry's number. That prick had already ruined his life, he didn't want him ruining his holiday. Rumblings from his tummy reminded him it had been quite a while since he'd eaten and checking his watch revealed it was past seven o'clock. "Shit!" He'd missed the restaurant again. There was always the bar, but he decided against that. Mainly because there were too many 'England' shirts knocking about, and he didn't want his accent getting him into any altercations, the second reason being that he'd caught a glimpse of what passed for snacks in the bar - carrot batons between two slices of buttered bread, shrink-wrapped on a plastic tray with some rather limp looking crisps. It was the kind of horror show your granny's dog would turn its nose up at. In the face of those tantalising facts, he decided he'd head back down to the town and maybe get shawarma or a pizza.   If he was lucky, he thought he might even run into Mel… *if* he was lucky. But given his luck lately, he probably had more chance of getting squashed by a whale falling from the sky. Using the stairs, he was halfway down to the lobby when a thought entered his head: Steve! If he was to pursue his ruse that he was Steve's carer, then he couldn't leave him behind. If Mel and Jo had eaten in the restaurant, they more than likely would have noticed that he and Steve hadn't been in. If they bump into him heading off to get food Mel might want to know where Steve is and why he hadn't eaten in the restaurant. Even if they hadn't missed them, Mel might find it odd that Steve wasn't with Pete when Pete was supposed to be looking after him, or maybe he was just overthinking everything. "Ah, shit," he sighed, before turning round to head back up the stairs. It took Steve a few minutes to open the door after Pete knocked.

Steve peered around his partially opened door with some suspicion. "Hi, Steve!" he said to Pete.

"What about ya, big fella?" Pete responded. "Listen, I'm hungry, and the restaurant is shut here, so I'm thinking of heading down to town for some food. Would you like to come?"

Steve shook his head, saying a prolonged "No."

"Oh!" Said Pete, a bit surprised. "Have you already eaten?"

Steve gave the same response.

"Okay," said Pete. "Aren't you hungry? Surely you must be hungry if you haven't eaten since earlier." Steve just looked at him for a moment or two, then he nodded, smiling slightly as he did so. "Right, come on then, let's go get something to eat!"

Steve just looked at Pete again, before answering. "You haven't got any money, Steve! No, Steve only for emergencies!"

The proverbial penny dropped. "Ah, sure, no need to worry about that." Pete said, smiling and waving his hand in a dismissive motion, "I'll sort you out. Come on, grab your gear and let's go." Steve stared at him again for a moment then he gave Pete that big broad smile, and nodded his head before opening his door wide while he went to put his shoes on. Pete looked into the room. Not a thing was out of place. Steve must have finished his word searching for the day and packed everything back into his backpack. The only thing that stood out was a picture frame on the little built-in stand next to his bed. While Steve pulled his shoes on, Pete wandered over and picked it up. The picture in the frame was of what Pete presumed was a younger Steve with his mum and dad. The sight of the photo made Pete both sad and angry. He felt sorry for Steve as he clearly felt something for his parents, hence the need for the picture. Steve was quite sweet in his own way, and the fact that they seemingly treated him so poorly made Pete angry, furious, in fact. Yeah, Steve moved slowly, he didn't talk much (except to himself), and he was certainly not someone Pete would have chosen to hang around with under any other circumstances, but he was sweet, friendly and polite, and don't forget that smile!

They headed out of the hotel and down towards the town, walking on the opposite side of the road this time, to look at the graffiti on the other side of the storm drain. As dusk was beginning to creep in and chase the last of the sunlight out, the light wasn't that great, but they could still make out all the cool murals, Pete's favourite was one with the giant insects, the details were insane, given that they appeared to have been spray painted like the other murals. Steve liked the one with the Super Mario characters he saw. They found a little shawarma place that did pizzas and parmesans too. Pete had chicken shawarma. "What will you have?" he asked Steve.

Steve spent a few more minutes looking at the menu before answering: "Pizza, please."

"Pizza? A good choice!" Steve smiled. "What will you have on your Pizza, then?"

"Just Cheese, if you please," Steve replied, laughing when he saw that it rhymed.

"So, one Margarita Pizza for you, and one Chicken Shawarma for me!"

"No, I just want cheese on mine," Steve said, looking serious. Pete started to explain that that's what a Margarita pizza was when he saw the gleam in Steve's eyes. Realising he'd been caught out in one of Steve's jokes, Pete smiled and started to nod his head. Steve gave a massive roar of laughter and reached out, playfully putting his hand on Pete's forearm and giving it a friendly rub. People had looked up from their meals and conversations to see what the fuss was and this made Pete feel a little embarrassed, and he picked up the menu again, burying his head in it as if he was still deciding on what to have. Eventually, a waitress came and took their order. Pete ordered drinks for the pair of them as well as the food. Just soft drinks, he'd already had a couple of pints earlier, and he was feeling quite dry. Besides, despite his intake over the last few weeks, he was not really a big drinker and afternoon drinking often gave him a headache later in the evening. He could actually feel one brewing now, prompting him to try and rehydrate a bit.

They sat at a table out in the front of the restaurant and ate their food in relative silence, enjoying the night air and, in Pete's case, keeping an eye out for Mel. "What do you think of Mel and Jo?" Pete asked Steve.

Steve shrugged his shoulders. "I like Mel, she seems really kind, Steve." He said.

"Yeah, she does, I guess. I get where you're coming from. What about Jo?" Pete asked, raising his hand to try and catch the waitress's eye.

Steve smiled, not his usual smile, but a shy smile. He blushed. "She's all right." He said, to the floor.

Pete smiled. "Just 'all right,' or a bit of all right?" He asked, giving Steve a wink.

Steve laughed. "A bit of all right, Steve. Aye, Steve!" He laughed again. The waitress arrived at the table and asked if everything was okay. They both agreed it was perfect, and Pete asked for the bill. As they walked back up the road, Pete pressed Steve about Jo again.

"So, you like her, then?" He asked. Steve went unusually quiet, nodding quietly, Pete smiled. They walked on in silence.

Half an hour later, after a slow meander back up the road, the boys arrived back at the hotel and looked around for the girls. They checked the front pools, the rear pool, and the bar, all to no avail. "Never-mind, Steve." Steve lamented, "Maybe tomorrow. Yes, Steve, maybe tomorrow!" Pete was disappointed they had come up empty in their search. He did consider asking his new friend Dave to look up her room number, but Dave was also nowhere to be seen and, besides, he knew that was a cheeky request. Defeated, they had a drink in the bar. Having shaken off his headache, Pete threw caution to the wind and had a pint, while Steve had a half pint. Pete was reluctant to buy it for him at first, but Steve reassured him it was ok and reminded him he was old enough to drink what he wanted. Pete conceded this and got the round in with his key card. They didn't talk much as they stood at the bar, Steve just kept sipping on his half and making the same pantomime sigh after each sip that Jo had made earlier. As much as Pete would be the first to admit that Steve would not be his first choice of wingman in any situation, he couldn't deny that he had a charm and a wit all his own. In fact, as much as he really hadn't fancied the idea of spending time with him, he had had fun. As Steve took his last sip, Pete downed what was left of his drink.

"Come on then, big fella!" He patted Steve's shoulder, "Let's get back to our rooms. Tomorrow is another day." Five minutes later, they were both stood outside Steve's door. "Right mate," Pete said, "I'll see you in the morning." A thought passed through his head as he was about to turn and got to his door. Aside from the food he'd bought him, he wasn't sure Steve had eaten anything. "How about we say… nine o'clock? That way we can get some free breakfast downstairs."

Steve smiled. "Nine o'clock!" He said, putting an emphasis on the 'ock' part of the last bit. Pete started to turn to head back to his room when Steve grabbed him in one of his bear hugs.

"Thanks Steve!" He said into Pete's shoulder. Smiling, Pete reciprocated, patting his back to signal a release. "See you in the morning."

Chapter Four: Parrots, Parks, and a Perfect Dream!

09.48am

On a Thursday!

Pete found himself awake early and was showered and dressed well before he had to meet Steve. He plugged his phone in to charge and because he still had an hour to kill before he met Steve, he decided to wash his underwear in the sink. He'd literally just thrown a few things into his bag when he decided to take this trip, and, upon arrival, Pete realised that enough underwear for the week was something he had neglected to cross off the 'list of stuff I really must take!'

An hour later, he was heading down to breakfast with Steve in tow. The pair perused the wide selection of cereals, bread, pastries, hot food such as eggs and bacon, and cold stuff such as sliced meats and cheeses and fruits, that were on offer. Pete devoured a massive plate of bacon, eggs and toast. He'd had one of these breakfasts a few times before and he loved the crispy, streaky bacon that the Europeans seemed to favour over traditional back bacon that the English preferred. Steve, meanwhile, had eaten quite a healthy breakfast in comparison —some cereal and some fruit and yoghurt washed down with orange juice... a lot of orange juice! They were just about to head out of the restaurant when Steve suddenly sat upright and pointed past Pete. Pete turned in his chair to see the girls walking in. "Awesome" he thought, and he waved frantically until he caught Mel's eye. Mel spotted him and, with her hand, motioned over to the buffet tables and then her watch. Pete checked his watch and saw it was getting on for ten o'clock and that meant the girls would have to hurry to avoid missing out. Around the room, Pete could see that the restaurant staff were already starting to clear some of the breakfast things away. Waving his acknowledgement to Mel he stood up to get another cup of tea. "Are you wanting another drink there, Steve?" Steve held his glass up and smiled winking at the same time. "Orange juice?" Pete enquired. Steve gave him a 'thumb up' and nodded, the big smile on his face still. The girls sat down soon after Pete returned with drinks and both of them seemed to have chosen healthy options of cereal and fruit with a side of coffee for Mel, and juice for Jo. Pete returned with the drinks and they all made small talk while the girls tucked in. Well, all but Steve, who just sat and observed proceedings wearing that heart-warming smile. Once or twice, Jo would address Steve directly, but he would just go red and laugh.

Twenty minutes later, after the food was all finished, and plans for the day were all finalised, they all went back to their respective rooms to get quickly ready for the rest of the day. Fifteen minutes later, Pete and Steve were coming out of the elevator and waving to Mel and Jo who had beat them down to reception. During their breakfast discussion, they'd all decided that they'd head over to Barcelona and do some exploring and sightseeing. Mel and Jo had already spent some time over there, so they put themselves in charge of 'the tour.' The sun was shining as the four of them set off towards the town.

Even though it was only ten in the morning, it was already quite warm, and they'd not gone more than three hundred yards when Mel stopped to put sun cream on her and Jo. Pete followed suit, with himself and Steve, and they all resumed their trek, Jo was at the front with Steve. Pete could see that Jo was chattering away, and Steve just seemed to be nodding and smiling. He hoped the lad was holding up under pressure. As they walked, Pete and Mel began chatting again. Pete was surprised at the complete lack of awkwardness between them.

"What's the first film you remember watching as a child?" He asked her.

Mel thought for a moment before answering: "I think it was Forbidden Planet. I remember watching so many old sci-fi films with my dad, but this one stands out the most. What about you?"

Pete didn't hesitate and answered straight away. "Metropolis!"

"Really?" responded Mel. "I haven't actually seen that one, would you believe?"

Pete smiled. "It's a bit of a forgotten gem, really. I still vividly remember being unable to read the story cards as they flashed up on screen, but I somehow managed to grasp what was going on just by watching it. I loved how it looked and I loved the robot, Maria."

Mel nodded. "It's a silent film, then?"

"Oh yeah, silent and black and white." Pete responded. "I remember when Queen did that video for Radio GaGa using footage from it and how it made me feel so nostalgic. I used to have this limited edition bust of the Maria robot, it was worth a fortune but I had to sell it to buy…" He trailed off. He'd sold it to buy an engagement ring for Gemma, he took quite a bath on it too, not even getting back a half of what it was worth. He didn't want to start talking about his soon to be ex-wife in front of Mel though.

"To buy what?" she asked.

"Oh, I sold it to raise cash to buy a car." He quickly replied. "It was my first car, actually. A shitty old Toyota Corolla!" Pete smiled as he thought back. "Only had it a year before it had to be scrapped."

Mel laughed. "I bet that was a bit of a kicker."

"You're not kidding." Pete responded, his head swimming from the intoxicating sound of her laughter.

The station wasn't far away when Pete suggested they get some drinks. They were passing a small shop and it seemed prudent. "It's really warm now, and it'll only get hotter. Better to get one now while we are passing a shop." Mel agreed, pointing out it was an hour on the train with no trolley service or buffet car. Pete stopped at the shop and called ahead to Jo and Steve. The pair turned and slowly made their way back, and then the four of them went into the shop. While Jo and Mel picked their drinks, Pete grabbed a bottle of water and asked Steve what he wanted. Steve didn't move, he just looked at Pete. Pete realised why. "Don't worry, it's my treat." He offered.

"Ah!" Said Steve. Smiling, he looked at his options and settled on a two-litre bottle of orange juice.

"More orange Juice?" Pete queried. "That's quite a lot of juice, mate. You must've had a pint at breakfast as well." He pointed out.

"It's okay," responded Steve. "I like orange Juice, and it's good for you too! Yes, Steve, keep you fit and healthy!"

"Okay, mate…If you're sure." Pete sighed and took it off him to go and pay. They were soon back on their way again, and it wasn't too long before they arrived at the train station. Realising he was going to have to pay for Steve's ticket as well, Pete sighed as he queued at the ticket window. Mel was an old hand at this by now and she had told him to get a ticket to the Arc De Triomf station, so he asked for two return tickets and braced himself for the damage.

"Twenty euros please, Señor." The clerk replied.

Pete was confused. "Er, per favor, I need two tickets." He held up his thumb and forefinger like he'd seen local people do.

The clerk looked at him, then his screen, "Si, señor. two return tickets are twenty euros!"

"Crikey!" Exclaimed Pete. Based on the last time he'd bought a train ticket back home, Pete had been expecting to pay a small fortune for two return tickets to go all the way into Barcelona yet the price of these seemed incredibly low. Nevertheless, he handed over the money and took the tickets and they all exited out onto the platform hastily looking for some shade. Luckily they didn't have to wait too long before their train arrived, though. Pete was amazed at the whole experience: the ticket price, the punctuality of the train, how spotlessly clean the train was. In fact, the train was so clean that it gleamed the gleam of a practically new train.

The route was mainly along the coast until they reached the city, and all four of them took it in turns to point out cool things as the landscape whizzed by. Jo won the game when she spotted a stretch of beach that was obviously for nudists. Pete was taking a swig of water when she gleefully exclaimed "Look, willies!" This caused him to do a spit take over the seat-back in front of him. Mel and Steve and Jo laughed, partly at Jo's discovery and partly at Pete's misfortune. He looked around the rest of the carriage, no one was really bothered about his sudden oral evacuation. He could see one or two people smiling, though, possibly at Jo's exclamation. The rest of the journey was relatively uneventful and they continued to point, and "ooh" and "ah" at everything of interest. Jo kept talking to Steve and Steve kept taking nervous swigs of juice every time Jo spoke to him, his smile never far away. The train finally reached the Arc De Triomf station about an hour or so after they'd set off and after alighting from the train they headed up the steps out of the station to street level. Mel and Jo had spent a lot of time in Barcelona already, so they had volunteered to be the tour guides for the day. The first stop was the Arc De Triomf itself, which was, handily and not unsurprisingly, around the corner from the station entrance.

The Arc itself was ok, Pete thought. There seemed to have been some sort of event going on previously as there were a lot of barriers piled up near the monument, and a stage was being dismantled nearby. At Mel's direction, the group walked down the long avenue that led from the monument to a big map of Barcelona that was embedded in the floor at the end. In the meantime, Steve had pulled out a little Lumix compact digital camera from his backpack and was busy taking pictures of just about everything they passed. After crossing over the road, they walked into the Parc De La Ciutadella where Pete was relatively unimpressed at first. To him, it looked like any other park back home, with people sat on the grass chatting, reading, or just relaxing in the sun. Young kids were running around as a street-performer was filling the air with huge bubbles from some sort of homemade bubble wand. The street performer would dip it in a huge bucket and wave it frantically, releasing hundreds of decent sized bubbles into the hot noon air. Every so often, he would carefully wave the wand in one direction and release a massive, worm-like bubble that seemed to weave its way through the minefield of smaller bubbles. Some would pop as it passed close to them, some would attach themselves to the 'worm' before being fully absorbed by it. Pete was mesmerised by this. He'd seen bubbles before, of course, but not like this.

What really blew Pete's mind, though, was the parrots! He'd not been able to process what he saw at first. They'd sat down on the grass for a bit while Jo chased bubbles and Steve took some photos of her with his camera, when Pete saw something suddenly fly past his head. "Whoa!" He screamed. Mel laughed when she saw what had happened. Pete saw something green land on the grass about ten feet away and thought someone had thrown something at him at first. He looked around but saw no obvious culprit. Pete turned back to the UFO and, as he stared at it, he realised there were more, a lot more, and they were moving. Looking up at the palm trees and the other trees around him, he realised there were more green things up there too. "Holy shit! Parrots!" He shouted, in a moment very reminiscent of Jo's 'Willies' revelation. Mel was laughing hard by now. Having visited the park previously, both she and Jo knew of the parrot's existence. There were Nanday Parrots, Rose Ringed Parakeets, and Monk Parrots. All were very similar in appearance, and all were utterly enchanting to Pete, who had only ever seen a parrot when he had volunteered at a local animal sanctuary with work. He was thrilled, and he whipped out his phone to film them. He called out to Steve. "Steve! Steve! Look!" Pointing when Steve looked over, he shouted again. "Parrots, man! Parrots!" He laughed in disbelief as Steve smiled and clapped. Turning to Mel, Pete asked; "Shouldn't they be, like, in cages or something? I mean, do they just roam free or what?" Mel explained, to Pete's amazement, that they did indeed just roam free. Once Pete had managed to overcome his astonishment, and when Steve and Jo had had enough of the bubbles, they moved on.

The Park itself was quite the treasure trove. There was a boating lake, and more than a few statues dotted around the place, but the 'pieza de resistencia' was the 'Cascada' fountain.

Built in the late 1800s, the 'Cascada' fountain is a two-tier fountain that is truly wonderful to behold. What a lot of visitors don't realise is that the water tank and hydraulics were designed by the famous Antoni Gaudi while he was still a student and way before he became famous for his weird architecture and that crazy basilica!

After Steve had photographed the heck out of the Cascada, they all agreed it was lunch time, and after a little wander around, they found a nice little bistro and took a table outside. Pete was glad he had sequestered all of the cash from the joint account when he realised he'd be picking up Steve's tab again. "What do you want, mate?" he asked Steve, anticipating the usual cat and mouse game, he also added, "My treat!"

"Your treat?" Mel asked before turning to Jo and telling her "Don't you be getting any ideas, young lady," and smiling. Seeing the way Pete was looking at her, she asked him "Do you often pay for Steve?" Pete's face adopted a more confused look as he struggled to work out what she meant. "You DO know that in our line of work, clients are supposed to pay for everything on these trips, right? Or was Steve's wallet in your lost luggage?" She chuckled.

Pete, realising what she meant, responded "Yes! The lost luggage bit. Left his wallet in his suitcase. I have to keep all my receipts."

"Okaaaay." said Mel, not sounding entirely convinced. Before she got a chance to question him more, the server arrived to take their order. They all ordered their food and drinks, nobody batting an eyelid when Steve ordered yet more orange juice. Over lunch, Mel and Jo debated on where to take the boys next.

Steve kept saying: "Camp Nou" to no one in particular, which was good because no one was really paying attention. They settled collectively - almost - on the Sagrada Familia. "Camp Nou" repeated Steve, dejectedly.

"Okay I'll bite," said Pete, "what the hell is 'Camp New?'" Steve Just smiled. Mel and Jo looked at each other and then at Steve before finally looking at Pete with a look of feigned disgust on their faces. A pair of teens at a nearby table also looked at Pete with looks of disbelief and disgust, although he suspected the latter was not feigned.

"It's not 'new' it's 'nou'... But that's kind of the same thing as it means 'new camp' or something." Said Mel. This did little to clarify anything for Pete.

"Is it like a theme park or something?" he asked.

"Or something!" Replied Mel, grinning. "Camp Nou is only the football stadium for Barcelona FC! Good god! Do you not know anything?" Mel laughed, as did Jo and Steve. The two teens across the way shook their heads and smiled at each other as they continued tucking into whatever was on their plates.

"Football?" Pete looked like someone had farted right in his face. "You want to go take a tour of a football ground?"

Steve, happily munching on pasta, smiled with a mouth full and nodded. Swallowing hard, he said, "Yes, Camp Nou!"

Pete shook his head, "I dunno, big fella. I mean, what's to see?" Then, mimicking a tour-guide with a plummy British accent, he began narrating fictional tour; "Yes, on the left here one can see the seats where fans will sit. To the front, one can see a large expanse of grass, This is the playing area or 'pitch' as the players like to call it. Now, if you'd care to follow me, ladies and gentlemen, we will visit the changing rooms, and you can see the team toilets where Ronaldo has left a poop so big, the handyman has had to go and fetch the sacred team 'Poop Knife' in order to get it to flush away!" Mel and Jo howled with laughter, more at his accent than anything else. Steve smiled, then shook his head. "What?" Pete asked.

"Ronaldo doesn't play for Barcelona."

"Well, I don't know. Are you sure? It's a Spanish sounding name." Pete countered.

"He plays for Juventus. It would be Messi's poop, not Ronaldo's" then he added "aye, Messi's poop, Steve!" and laughed before turning and calling to no one: "Fetch the poop knife!" Then he laughed some more.

Jo laughed and gleefully added "Messy poop!" This caused Steve to laugh a bit louder.

Pete, slightly embarrassed at his lack of knowledge, assumed a look of indignant disdain, "I can't believe we're arguing over the owner of a fictional arse biscuit!" He said, sending Jo into a further fit of laughter, an infection that quickly spread to Mel, then Steve and, eventually, even Pete succumbed. After the laughter had subsided, they finished their meals and drinks. Mel and Pete sorted the bill out for the four of them, and they set off again. It had been decided they would now visit the vast, Gaudi designed, Sagrada Familia.

The Sagrada Familia, for those who don't know, is a huge and epically quirky Basilica in the heart, though not the centre, of Barcelona. Envisioned initially by a bookseller, Josep Maria Bocabella, work began in 1882 under the architect Francisco de Paula del Villar, who resigned the following year and was replaced by Barcelona's favourite son - Antoni Gaudi. Gaudi oversaw construction until his death in 1926 and was once asked why construction was taking so long, to which he apparently replied that his client was "not in a hurry!" Work is still continuing today, some 137 years later (at the time of writing).

The gang arrived at the Basilica just before two o'clock, and by the time they'd queued for tickets they found they were eligible to buy the cheap tickets, which were still the best part of twenty euros. Pete was obviously relieved at this as it cost him double. The place itself was stunning, and they stayed in there for a good few hours. Pete, not usually one for taking photographs, found himself getting his phone out more than once to capture some of the awesomeness. Several times during their tour around the Basilica, Steve asked if they could visit Camp Nou next. Several times he was met with a "We'll see, mate," or a "Maybe tomorrow, eh?" This made Steve sad. He loved football, not as much as drawing cars or doing word searches, but he loved football. He didn't love it enough to be able to tell you who his favourite player was in his favourite team (Liverpool!), but he loved football. Steve loved watching it. He loved to look at sports pages and nod his head sagely as if he was deep in thought about whatever football news was on the page in front of him, even though he didn't really read the paper. He just loved football. When he found out he was coming to Barcelona, he found out which football grounds were there by researching at the local library, which consisted mainly of him asking library assistants and random library patrons about it. From his 'research,' he'd found out about Camp Nou and Barca FC and some of their players. One kind patron had even put him on the internet at the library and showed him the website for the ground, explaining that there were tours of the ground available. This was great news to Steve, as it meant that he was going to be in a place where he could, if he wanted to, go on a tour of a football ground. He'd only been on one tour before, in his home town. The local team had a stadium built by a local entrepreneur, but the team had long since been relegated out of any proper league, and the stadium was now occupied by the local rugby team. But you could still get tours for eight pounds a time, twelve with a pie and a pint! Steve knew he'd never actually get to Camp Nou at that point. He knew his parents wouldn't have time to take him, and he knew he wasn't brave or smart enough to find it on his own, especially when he wasn't even staying in Barcelona. That was before he met Pete, though. Pete was his new best friend!

Steve didn't have any friends back home. His parents saw him as dependant enough as to need state benefits in order to make his life easier, but independent enough for them to spend the money mainly on themselves. Steve hadn't had the benefit of a support worker or anything like that. His parents didn't take him to any special clubs or any social gatherings of people that shared his 'condition' as his mum referred to it. The usual excuse was that they were just too busy, or that they thought, he was happy enough with his own company. The only things they did for him, or rather allowed him to do, was to let him pick five items just for himself on the weekly shop. You'd be forgiven for thinking that this was just food items and that his word search and art supplies were separate to that concession. You'd also be sadly mistaken. Steve's life was quite a lonely one. He spent most of his time in his tiny box room of a bedroom, watching his old DVDs or looking out of the window when he wasn't doing his word search or drawing cars. Having no company, Steve often talked to himself to pass the time, a habit that had spilled out of his bedroom and into his everyday life. On the plus side, his parents had at least furnished him with a bus pass so he was able to take himself into town every now and again, where he'd wander about, looking in shops or just watch people going about their daily business.

Every two weeks, and always on a Saturday, Steve would go to the library with his library books in his backpack. He'd generally just check out the same few books on a rotation basis. Books on cars and books on football. The football books he'd just flip through and try and memorise who played for which team. The car books he'd use to draw from, using his special method of attaching tracing paper to the book, ever so carefully, with paperclips. Sometimes he would try and draw cars in his sketchbook. They were quite good too. Some looked like the cars he had traced, some looked like a project from Top Gear.

Aside from word searches, this was his main pastime, and he had tens of sketchbooks with plain black and white pencil drawings of cars in them. His collection of sketchbooks was, in fact, nearly as extensive as his collection of tracings. Eventually, it got to the point where he was running out of space, and his dad had taken some out of his room and "put them in the attic". Steve had asked his dad a few times if he could get them out to look at, but his dad always found an excuse as to why that wasn't going to happen. Maybe one day, he'd get them down for him.

Now, though, things had changed a bit for Steve, and this was because he'd met Pete! Pete was great. Pete didn't shout at him, Pete didn't leave him out of stuff, and Pete talked to him like a person. Pete had bought him things too. No one had ever just bought him things like that, not without asking for the money later. He took a big swig of the orange Juice Pete had bought him, finishing it off and marking its demise with a massive pantomime sigh. Steve liked Pete, and he felt sure Pete would take him to Camp Nou. Maybe not today, but soon, and before they went home. Carefully, he put the empty bottle into his backpack as littering was a bad thing. Then he went up to Pete and hugged him for no other reason than just because he was Pete, and Pete was his friend.

Pete was working on Mel with his charm and patter when Steve hugged him. They'd been swapping stories about their teenage years and laughing as they tried to outdo each other with tales of drunken silliness and early sexual calamities. Jo saw Steve giving Pete a hug, and she went to give Steve a hug when he'd broken off from Pete. Steve backed away a little from her, though. Undeterred, she went in again, "Come on, Robert Downey Jr! Don't be shy!" She smiled at him as she said it and he let her hug him, his discomfort plainly visible. Pete didn't get it at first. He knew Steve liked her and it was obvious she liked him. Then Pete considered that this might be like being in the playground and getting a hug from your first crush, and maybe a little overwhelming for Steve. Pete couldn't speculate out loud that Steve was maybe really shy though, as that might give the game away to Mel that he was, to all intents and purposes, with Steve under false pretences and had no real clue as to what made him tick. Steve, meanwhile, continued to stand still and let Jo hug him, but he didn't reciprocate. In truth, though, despite looking terrified, he was thrilled to bits that she was hugging him.

They finally exited the Basilica, after Jo bought a souvenir shirt from the gift shop. Pete bought one too, it was for Steve, though and it prompted another massive hug from him when Pete had given it to him. Steve carried it proudly in a plastic bag, and they slowly headed back to the park near the Arc De Triomf where they spent the rest of the afternoon relaxing and messing around in the sun. Jo kept trying to engage with Steve, but Steve was on his word search mission again. Arriving back to the park a little after four, and as soon as they had found somewhere to sit, Steve had rummaged in his backpack for his meds, before beginning his wordy quest. Today's grid was, coincidentally, words associated with holidays.

As the four of them lay or sat about on the grass, the afternoon sun not so much caressed their skin as assaulted it and, although they were in a foreign country, Pete marvelled at how familiar the sounds were. Closing his eyes and listening, he could hear kids playing and laughing, the general chatter of people catching up with each other or having fun, and the occasional squawking of one of the resident parrots. He felt incredibly happy at that moment and wished he could lay there forever. Mel, who had been quietly creating a daisy chain as she lay on the grass, broke the spell. "He seems quite the loner at times." She said, motioning to Steve. She and Pete were both laid side by side on their stomachs, with just enough space between them to demarcate their friendship, as opposed to being closer, like a couple.

"Who, Steve?" Pete said, sitting up and spinning around on his backside so he could look at her face. Mel nodded. "You mean the way he's tuned it all out while he does his word search?"

"Yeah."

"I guess he's not so much a loner as he's very set in his ways." Mel thought for a moment before asking if Steve was on the spectrum. Pete had no clue what this meant, so he erred on the side of caution. "No, no," said Pete, also letting out a small, nervous laugh. "he just doesn't like to break his routine much." He added. Mel just looked at him and murmured a soft "Okay." Attempting to change the subject, Pete pointed out that Jo seemed quite enamoured with Steve. "I mean, she seems to enjoy his company and that." Mel turned her head to look at him, bringing her hand up to shield her eyes from the sun. Nervous again, Pete just kept speaking. "She really seems to like him, you know? I was wondering, what's the protocol for that sort of thing?"

Mel laughed."Protocol? What the hell?"

"Well, you know," said Pete, "are they allowed to date? Is she allowed to have a boyfriend?"

"Allowed?" She laughed again. "How long did you say you've been doing support work?" Before Pete had a chance to answer, they were distracted by Jo's excited squeals.

"Look, look" she shouted, pointing excitedly at Steve. Steve had been laid on his tummy for most of the time in the park. While Jo was sat a short distance away trying to make daisy chains, he was laid there, resting his chin on the one hand and using the other to move his pen over the book looking for words. He'd managed to stay so still, for so long, that one of the Rose Ringed Parakeets had come and perched on his back. Jo clasped her hands together as if trying to contain her excitement right there between them. Steve, of course, was utterly oblivious to his new status as an Avian park bench! Everyone gasped as another Parakeet came and joined its green feathered friend.

Pete rose to a half crouch very slowly, so as not to startle the bird. With his phone in his hand, he carefully moved around so he was looking at Steve at an angle where he could see Steve's face *and* the bird and he took a few photos without Steve noticing. He was about to put his phone away when a third bird landed on Pete's back. Pete, meanwhile, was oblivious and intently focussed on his word search. Pete took a few more photos before attempting to gently catch Steve's attention. Steve looked up just as a fourth bird came and landed on his back but he still seemed oblivious to the feathery shenanigans occurring behind him. Pete smiled at Steve and showed him that he wanted to take a photo. Steve gave his best smile, and Pete took a few shots, then he put the phone away, giving Steve the thumbs up. Steve, still totally unaware of the birds perched on his back, just went back to his word search. Jo, who had also got her phone out and was busy filming the whole thing, exclaimed, "He's just like a Disney Princess!" This cracked Mel and Pete up. Steve looked up to see what was funny, startling the birds in the process. He just smiled as the birds fluttered off. Jo let out a cry of dismay and put her phone back in her bag.

"Come here, lovely." Mel beckoned to Jo as she sat herself up. Jo duly came over, and Pete watched as Mel gently placed the newly completed daisy Chain on her head like a fairy crown. "There you go." Mel smiled when Jo clapped her hands and gave her a hug, she then thanked Mel before pulling her phone out of her little bag to use the front camera as a mirror. Pete continued to watch Mel as she, in turn, sat and watched Jo. Once again, he was struck by her beauty. The afternoon sun seemed to make her skin shine with some sort of heavenly radiance.

Having spent the last six years or so with Gemma, he could tell when a girl was wearing no makeup, a load of makeup and a load of makeup that looked like no makeup. Gemma was pretty much always made up, and heavily so. "My mum says a lady never lets her man see her without makeup on!" She'd proudly tell him, especially when she was drunk, bizarrely. In fact, he remembered how she used to boast that she hadn't washed her face properly since she was eighteen, relying solely on the occasional use of make-up removal wipes. He'd once earned a slap when he suggested her face might be coated with several layers of paint, not unlike an old door in an old house. Mel, in complete contrast, didn't seem bothered with superficial beauty. He could tell she wasn't wearing any makeup, not even any lipstick. Gemma always had to be dressed up too, there was no way they would have come to a park and (*cue sharp and horrified intake of breath*) sit on the grass! Yet here was Mel, making a pair of tatty Chuck Taylors, well-worn jeans and a Goonies t-shirt look like catwalk material while sat making daisy chains on (*cue look of abject horror*) grass! He checked himself, this was the first time in over twenty-four hours that he'd thought of his ex-wife. It also occurred to him that he wasn't full of melancholy, just regret. He was, in truth, quite surprised to find he wasn't so much regretting the split as regretting it not happening earlier in his life. All things happen for a reason though, he told himself. If he'd split from Gemma at a different time in his life, he would not be sat here in Barcelona, occupying the same airspace as Mel.

He was brought out of his daydream by Mel placing her latest daisy creation on his head, her touch sending an electric shock through him, snapping him back to reality. "There you go, hotshot!" She said, her face inches from his.

"Jesus," he thought, "even her breath smells amazing." He looked up then brought his gaze down and their eyes locked, and they both seemed frozen in time for the longest minute. It was Jo who broke the spell, clapping when she saw what Mel had done. "You look like a Disney Princess too!" Jo laughed, Mel laughed, Steve looked up from his word-search and laughed. Pete thought that he might not ever take his new crown off of his head!

"I could get used to being a Disney Princess!" He said, jokingly. Jo laughed again, and Mel smiled at him.

"You might need to lose that scruffy facial hair." She said, chuckling. Pete feigned a look of hurt indignation and she gave him a playful shove. "Oh knock it off, you know I'm only joking." She smiled again and Pete gave her a playful wink, making her blush inexplicably.

"Actually, I was just thinking the same about you." He responded, with a poker face. She laughed and pushed him backwards. As he went, he grabbed her hand and pulled in an effort to steady himself. Because of the way she was sat, though, this action caused her to topple forward, right on top of him. For a brief moment, their eyes met and they both seemed to hold the pose, and their breath, as they stared again into each other's eyes. The sudden laughter of a passing child snapped them out of it and they both scrabbled to move and regain their composure.

"We should think about hading back soon." Said Mel, still blushing. Pete nodded his agreement and looked over to Steve, who had finished his words for the day and was putting his book back into his backpack. Jo, who had waited patiently for him to finish, went over to tell him what had happened with the birds. Pete could hear sounds of laughter and disbelief and then he saw Jo quickly retrieve her phone to show Steve the proof.

Steve laughed and looked quite pleased with himself. "Jim Bowen did that once!" Pete heard him say before they both laughed, and he was really pleased that Steve had finally opened up a bit. After a short discussion abut what to do next, they all headed back to the bistro they'd been to earlier, to have some more food before heading back to Calella. They knew they'd miss the hotel restaurant and the journey would take an hour from whenever they could get the next train, so it seemed like the best thing to do. Everybody ate Pizza and Steve had not one, not two, but *three* glasses of orange Juice. Steve liked orange Juice, possibly more than football and word-searches. Actually, Pete had never seen anyone so addicted to orange Juice like Steve was, and he wondered if maybe he didn't get to drink a lot of it at home. He did! OJ was one of his 'five items.' Actually, sometimes it was two of his 'five items.'

Later, on the train ride back to Calella, Steve and Jo were keeping each other company. Jo sat on one chair at the window, and Steve sat near the window on the seat in front. Well, he was not so much sat there as kneeling up and looking at things as they whizzed by. Jo especially was avidly scanning the lay of the land, looking for more willies! Pete, meanwhile, had sat next to Mel a few seats back from "the kids" as he kept calling them. "Hey!" He said to Mel. "Does Jo have like a set bedtime or anything?" Mel looked at him strangely again. "What I meant was," he continued, "would you fancy meeting downstairs for a drink, just you and me? A bit later on maybe?" He looked hopefully at Mel.

Mel looked back at him intently, as if studying him. "What was that?" She asked, half smiling.

"What do you mean? I was just asking."

Mel cut him off, "I know what you were just asking. I just want to know *why* you're asking? Did I... was I not clear yesterday?" Pete just looked at her, puzzled. She sighed. "Okay, once more down the Death Star Trench. You see, Pete, it's like this; I'm just wondering what your intentions are here. I mean, I still can't help but notice that you have a wedding band on. I also know you've told me that there's a bit of an issue there, but I only have *your* word to take for it. Now, don't get me wrong, we've had a lovely day today, and you really do seem like a nice guy. But!" Pete raised his eyebrows in anticipation of what 'but' meant. Mel continued; "Despite the nice day we've had today, I hardly know you, and as nice as it was, today - one day - hardly qualifies as a shining character reference. Do you catch my drift?" Pete nodded. "For all, I know you could be Ted Bundy's bastard love child, on the run and on holiday and looking to franchise for his father and expand into new territories! Not just that, but that wedding band, I dunno! I mean, what kind of a girl do you take me for?"

Pete's face seemed to expand in astonishment. "Wow!" he exclaimed, but before he could continue, Mel cut him off again.

"This is what it is; If you're looking to meet up and have a few drinks as *'new friends'* then that's fine. I'm thrilled with that idea." Pete smiled, but before he could speak,

Mel continued; "However, if you see me as some leg spreading, air-headed holiday bang girl, you maybe should jog on because, like I said, I hardly know you, you appear to be married, and, most importantly - I'm just *not* that kind of girl!" She sat back and just looked at him with a stony face.

"Okay then... I guess that's me told!" Pete said. "Look, Mel, I really don't think you're that kind of girl. I just wanted to meet you for a drink and maybe get to see what kind of girl you actually are." Her eyebrows raised this time. "No, I don't mean like that. I just meant I'd like to get to know you a bit better. I won't lie, I do like you, but I'm not into that whole 'holiday hook' up thing either." He was partly telling the truth... mainly because he'd never been on holiday as a single man before, well, not as an adult at least. Holding up his hand with his ring band, he went on. "As for this, there's quite a funny story that goes with it. How about you meet me for that drink? I will tell you exactly how far down the toilet my life has gone in the last few weeks?" Mel regarded him for what seemed like an age. He held her gaze for as long as he could before it became uncomfortable.

Eventually, with feigned comic reluctance, Mel let out an "Okay."

"Excuse me?"

"Okay," she said. "I'll meet you for a drink in the bar. It has to be in the bar though, as I can't leave Jo alone in the hotel. I have to be nearby, and I'm sure the same applies to you with Steve." Pete nodded. "Pete, I'm upfront with you here, though. This is just a drink, nothing more."

Pete nodded and held out his hand for a handshake. "Deal." Mel shook his hand, laughing. They had stopped laughing and resumed looking out the window when Jo squealed and clapped excitedly. Mel and Pete both looked at each other and said: "Willies!" before bursting into laughter again.

They arrived back at Calella Train station and began the trek back to The Olympiad. Jo was looking in all the shop windows as they wound their way through the narrow streets, Mel and Pete meandered along behind her a little, pointing stuff out to each other. No one really noticed that a rather pale looking Steve was lagging behind a bit. Eventually, Pete noticed Steve wasn't in his field of vision. He looked around and saw him about fifty yards back. "Come on, mate! Catch up." He shouted. Steve kept ambling along with a strange gait, he looked right at Pete and shook his head. "Odd," said Pete to Mel. "Hang on, I'd best go see what's up." Soon he was in front of a rather unwell looking Steve. "Hey, big fella, what's the crack?" he asked.

"I need the toilet, Steve." He said, somewhat sheepishly.

"That's okay mate, we're not that far from the hotel, can you make it back?" Pete asked.

Steve looked at him, not only was he really pale but Pete noticed he was also sweating a bit. "Can you wait Steve?" He asked himself. "No, Steve. Really need to go now!" He replied to himself. Pete patted his shoulder and looked around to see if there was anything nearby. He spotted a shawarma shop.

"No worries, mate, Let's have a look in there." Pete waved to Mel and indicated for her and Jo to go on as he manoeuvred Steve over to the shop. A bell rang as he opened the door and Pete could see one guy behind the counter, apparently chopping veg. Pete assumed he was prepping food for the evening's trade. There was another guy who sat this side of the counter, he was flicking through his phone and sipping what looked like an espresso, but Pete assumed this was maybe a Turkish style coffee as it appeared to be Turkish takeaway shop with a few seats and tables inside. He saw the sign for the toilets and directed Steve to them as the guy chopping veg looked up and just stared at Pete. Feeling awkward, Pete tried to break the ice; "Hi there," he greeted the stony face, "have you got any chips on the go?" He added, reckoning it wasn't so much of a piss take if he bought something.

Stony Face looked at him and, in a thick Spanish accent asked, "You want fries, señor?"

"Yes, yes, fries… please." Pete smiled and reached into his pocket for some cash. Steve was still nowhere to be seen when Stony Face passed the tray of fries over to Pete and took his money off him. Pete motioned to the guy to keep the change. Stony Face said something in Turkish to Mr Coffee who looked at Pete before they both laughed. Just as he was tucking into the fries, Steve appeared. He didn't look too happy. "Everything ok, big man?" He asked as he moved closer to him.

"I didn't make it!" Steve said, in a not very quiet voice.

"Excuse me, now?" Pete asked.

"I didn't make it!" Steve repeated, a little quieter as Pete was now in front of him. Steve looked down. Pete looked down.

The realisation of the situation hit Pete about the same time as the smell did. "Shit!"

Steve looked at him. "Yes, shit!"

"Okay, right, so when you say you didn't make it," Steve nodded and Pete paused, wondering how to proceed, "did you, er, did you get any of it in the toilet?" Steve shook his head. "Is it all…" Pete nodded down to Steve's trousers "Y'know?" Steve shook his head again. Pete looked back at Stony Face and Mr Coffee. The former was concentrating on not slicing his finger as he chopped what might have been onions, The latter had looked up from his phone and was watching Pete and Steve now. Pete hoped the man couldn't hear their conversation over the 'chop, chop, chop' of Stony face's labour. "So, if it's not in your pants… and it's not in the toilet…"

Steve looked at Pete and with a deadpan face simply said; "Floor," Pete stared back "and maybe walls too, Steve."

"Shit," said Pete, "okay! Okay. Okay, be cool. Come on." He grabbed Steve's arm "Let's go." Turning back, he waved and shouted "Gracias!" They then bundled out of the door before the two men had a chance to respond. Outside, the girls had kept going as per instructed and were now nowhere to be seen. As he didn't have to worry about catching them up, Pete steered Steve right and then right again, and they headed down a side street towards the railway line. They emerged near the crossing and Pete motioned they go over there to head along the boulevard back to the footbridge. Pete kept looking back to make sure they weren't being followed. In his head, he could see the headlines 'Brit holidaymakers stabbed in faecal fallout!' This spurred him on a bit faster. Steve was struggling, though. It was hot and incredibly humid, and as he was a little overweight, he was struggling to keep up with Pete. Not only that but things *down below* weren't good, and Steve was starting to suffer from some bad chafing as a result of his mishap. In fact, he was walking like he was riding an invisible horse. Pete saw this but just assumed that he was just uncomfortable. He slowed down though, confident that they were now out of danger and not about to bump into Stony Face, who was now no longer called Stony Face. Now he was 'Señor Stabby'…

"My name is Señor Stabby. You shit all over my stall. Prepare to die!"

As they sauntered on, Pete became aware that people they passed were staring at Steve, one or two were pointing at him too. He surreptitiously had a look at Steve to see what was attracting the attention and, in some cases, looks of disgust and laughter. He shook his head when he realised just how obvious it was that Steve had soiled himself. Steve's shorts were white, once, but now, particularly around the back, they looked like someone had spilt some self-tanning lotion on them, and down the back of Steve's legs. "Bloody hell!" He muttered. "Hold up, mate." He gently grabbed Steve's arm and guided him to one of the many benches that lined the boulevard. "Sit there a minute, man. Have a rest, eh?" He thought for a moment. He could see the bridge ahead, and as moderately busy as the beach boulevard was, he knew the main drag would be at least twice as active, and he didn't want to have Steve run that gauntlet as he felt sure there would be some cocky bastard that wouldn't hesitate to cause a scene. Even if he could call one, there's no way a Taxi would let them in with Steve covered in shit. There was only one thing for it, he began unbuttoning his shirt. The shirt itself was new, being one of the new tops he'd purchased on his little impromptu shopping trip with Steve the day before. As much as he liked it, and as much as he lamented the fact it had cost him thirty-five euros, he couldn't let Steve go through it all with people pointing at him. Slipping it off, he motioned for Steve to stand up. Positioning the shirt around Steve, so the bulk of it covered the back, he tied the sleeves up in the front and patted him on the shoulder. "There we go, champ. Let's get back then." Steve smiled and nodded, and off they went.

It took them a while to get back, mainly because Steve was walking ever so slowly. Pete still hadn't realised that Steve was sore and Steve still hadn't volunteered that information. By the time they reached the hotel, he was really struggling and starting to sob a little. Pete finally noticed "Hey, what's up, champ?" He asked, putting his hand on Steve's shoulder.

In between sobs, Steve asked himself "What's the matter, are you really sore, Steve? Yes, Steve, really sore!" He quickly answered.

"Ooooh!" Pete responded as he realised what the issue was. "Right, let's get you upstairs then we'll see what we can do about it." They slowly and carefully navigated their way through the lobby. Dave was back on the desk, and Pete gave him a quick wave before he and Steve entered the elevator. They weren't the only passengers and, as the doors closed, Pete became acutely aware of something he'd only slightly experienced until now: the smell! Pete could tell by the look on the other lift passenger's faces that they noticed it too. "Wow" he suddenly exclaimed, causing the middle-aged woman nearest him to jump a little. "It's a hot one today, isn't it." He smiled at the other passengers. "Smells like the hotel is having problems with the drains again." He was doing his best to deflect attention away from what was only a glance away from being obvious.

"That's not drains, is it Steve!" Steve piped up. "No Steve, it's not"

Pete let out a laugh that was a bit too loud and obviously forced. The woman jumped again, the two other passengers just looked at each other as if speaking using telepathy or some secret blinky code.

Steve continued; "It's not the drains, it's me, Steve." He said. "Ah, it's you is it? Yes, Steve, I've shit all over meself!" Pete just grimaced and rubbed his forehead while the other passengers slowly moved to the opposite corner to Steve. As the lift came to rest and the doors opened, the other passengers were forced to circumnavigate around Steve and Pete as he was stood next to the door. The woman unashamedly pinched her nose as she passed by. Pete just gave her an incredulous look as Steve just smiled and let out a little laugh. The lift doors closed and the lift resumed its journey, and the pair were soon outside Steve's door. Pete was helping him get his key in it when Mel appeared with a big smile on her face. "Hello boys!" she chirped, her smile slowly dissipating as she began to catch a whiff of what was actually a familiar smell, given her line of work. Surveying the scene with fresh eyes, she quickly deduced what had transpired. "Oh dear," she remarked, "was this why you stopped, earlier?"

"Kind of," Pete replied, "it kind of happened when we stopped." Mel raised her eyebrows. "Let's just say we need to avoid going past a particular take-away if we go into the town again." Mel just nodded, knowingly, a smile crossed her face. They got Steve inside his room, and Pete turned to leave. Mel looked at him. "Oh, he's going to have a shower I think," he offered. Mel still stared at him, a quizzical look on her face.

"You're not going to leave him like this, surely?" she asked, although it sounded more like a statement than a question.

"Well, he's going to get a shower, and I need to get ready for our date, our drink!" He corrected himself.

Mel shook her head "You can't leave him like this." Seeing Pete's reluctance to get involved in any kind of cleanup, she told him to go and start the shower off while she turned her attention to Steve. "Come on, Steve, let's get these things off you." Reaching into the back pocket of her jeans, she pulled out a pair of blue latex gloves. Personal care was not something Mel had to do a lot of with Jo, but she'd had plenty of experience in that area and she'd learnt the hard way to always have a supply of gloves with her, in case of any emergencies. Mel began to help Steve take his clothes off, carefully pulling the t-shirt off over his head so as not to touch him with the dirty parts and she soon had him stripped down to his underpants. "Right, Steve. You take those off in there and put them in the bathroom bin, okay?" Steve nodded and headed into the bathroom "And get a shower while you're in there!" She shouted after him.

"Yes, Steve!" Came the reply.

After a brief glance around the room, she grabbed the waste bin from under the table and removed the plastic bag from inside it. Carefully, she placed the soiled shorts, t-shirt, and Pete's shirt into the bag before removing the gloves and dropping them in the bag too. She tied up the bag and dropped it outside the room door. As Steve entered the bathroom, Pete emerged from it just in time to see Mel disposing of the clothes. "Oh, shit!" he cried. Mel asked what was wrong and Pete reminding her that their luggage was missing, adding that he didn't expect that the hotel had a laundry service.

Mel laughed. "They don't even seem to be able to wash their staff uniforms that well," she said, "so I think that's a dead end. I take it there's still been no word on the luggage then?" Pete shook his head and sat on the edge of the bed. Looking at his watch, he asked Mel what time the shops usually shut mid-week. "It varies," she replied, "some of the shops on the main drag stay open until around ten, the other shops in the side streets seem to close when they feel there's no more money to be made."

"It's only eight o'clock." Stated Pete. "If we get a crack on we could get something for Steve then get back for that drink." He looked at Mel, hopefully. "That is if you don't mind?"

"Mind? Don't be daft," Mel scoffed, "I'll go and quickly change, and we can set off. Do you need to keep an eye on Steve in the shower?"

"Why?" Pete asked, quickly remembering he was supposed to be his carer. "He'll be fine. Really, Mel! He's fine, really. Showers all the time on his own at home." Outside, Pete was displaying casual confidence while inside he was silently praying that Steve didn't slip and crack his head on anything. Mel gave him that funny look she wore so well then disappeared out of the door. Pete sat on the bed, "What a day" he thought to himself. Pete began daydreaming about possible outcomes for the evening. He liked Mel, *really* liked her, but he figured it wasn't going to be one of those nights, given her express reluctance to even entertain the notion of anything happening between them. To be honest, Pete wasn't really sure what to do either. In fact, he was in quite a quandary. It had been several years since he had to try and woo a woman, especially one that didn't want to be wooed. Still, stranger things had happened. At best, he reckoned, he'd get to know Mel a bit better and show her that he was quite a decent bloke. Aside from the need to prove he wasn't some sleazy creep who preyed on vulnerable people, top of his list was explaining what had happened in his marriage and trying to convince her he wasn't on the rebound. Actually no, scratch that. That was not the best case scenario. The best case scenario was locking lips after Mel realises he is her soul mate and that she needs to spend the rest of her life with him... stranger things have happened, he thought. Before long, he heard the shower shut off, and after five minutes of what sounded like a towel getting a massive workout, Steve emerged from the bathroom. His glasses were steamed up, and his hair was tousled where he'd attempted to rub it dry with the towel that was now wrapped around his waist. He smiled and gave his customary "Hi Steve."

Pete asked him how his chafing was feeling. "Sore" he said, as he half walked, half waddled across to the bed. He looked around for his clothes. "Where are your clothes, Steve? I don't know, Steve... Maybe they've been stolen! Aye, that's maybe it, stolen" He put emphasis on 'stolen' and laughed. Pete explained what had actually happened to his clothes and outlined the plan.

"Will you be okay? I mean, we won't be too long. We'll come straight back and get you sorted. I want to be able to wine and dine Mel without any further distractions. Give her the ol' Kelly Charm" he explained, winking as he gave Steve's arm a playful tap. Pete had said this more to boost his own confidence than to impress Steve, who remained suitably unimpressed and just kept smiling, looking at him through slightly steamed up lenses. Pete headed for the door "Right, big fella! I'll see you soon. Why don't you go and try sitting out on the balcony? Keep your towel on, mind, but try and… y' know… air your business, if you get me." He winked again and was gone.

As soon as he was back in his room, the first thing Pete did was take off the daisy chain crown, that he was still wearing. He looked about for something to put it in. After a fruitless search in his bag and the bedroom, he checked the bathroom. Here he found a small plastic pouch that currently contained a shower cap. Tossing the shower cap aside, he carefully placed the daisy chain into the pouch and put it in his backpack. Pretty soon, after the worlds quickest shower and change, he was popping his shoes on just as there was a knock on his door. "Room service, señor!" Came an odd sounding female voice from outside. Pete twigged it was Mel but played along. Quickly opening Google Translate on his phone, he typed 'one moment I am just shaving my testicles'.

From outside, the voice piped up again; "Señor?"

"Un momento, me estoy afeitando los testículos!" Pete replied, in the worst Spanish accent ever, but he didn't for one minute think that Mel might have a decent enough grasp of Spanish to understand what he'd said anyway. There was a pause followed by silence and then more silence. A full minute went by, and there was no answer. Pete panicked. What if Mel had ordered some sort of room service or what if the lady had the wrong room. He quickly opened the door. "I'm really sorry, I thought." The sight of Mel, with her hand over her mouth, clearly struggling to not burst out laughing like a lunatic, stopped him in his tracks. "Ah, well done. You got me. Very good." He closed the door then gave her a faux round of applause. "Of course, you realise that this means war?"
Mel looped her arm with his, "Oh, come now, Mr Kelly. Don't be like that." And off they went.

Walking at a steady pace, they were soon down at the main drag. Mel wanted to search for a clothes shop first, so Pete took them to the store where he and Steve had first purchased their swim gear which, as fortune had it, was still open. After some discussion around sizes and some more funny looks from Mel, they managed to get a few shirts and pairs of shorts for Steve. Pete also grabbed some pants for him, as well. He'd found some adult sized Star Wars briefs that he felt sure Steve would love. As they walked, they both took turns again to point out the funny stuff they saw. A game had developed where they tried to spot "Shit tattoos." A point for each shit tattoo spotted and a bonus five points every time a Cross of St George or a bulldog wearing one was spotted.

Mel was ahead by twenty points by the time they were on their way back. "Oh, wait!" she exclaimed, as she spotted a Farmacia. This intrigued Pete. Maybe she needed something for Jo, or perhaps she needed something for later in the evening!

He smiled at this thought, then gave his head a shake. "Not going to happen, hotshot" he told himself. Once inside, he was dismayed to find she just wanted to get some cream for Steve's chafing. His dismay soon turned to adoration again though, when he saw her conversing in quite fluent Spanish with what he assumed was the pharmacist. "Is there seriously *nothing* this girl can't do?" he thought to himself. Mel turned around, a paper bag in hand, to see Pete staring dreamily at her. As if to reinforce her earlier assertion that this was just a friendly evening get-together, she cocked her head at him and to break the spell, she asked Pete how long his flies had been open. Pete snapped back to reality, desperately scrabbling at his trousers, quickly realising he was wearing fly less shorts. He laughed. "Well done," he smiled. "I'll be having to get you back for that as well, though."

"Whatever you say" Mel replied as she brushed past him and opened the Farmacia door. An image of Steve, still sat in his room with just his towel flashed through Pete's mind so he suggested they'd best go straight back to the hotel and sort him out before they went for any kind of drink. Mel agreed. They left the Farmacia and walked on in silence at first. It was Mel who broke the silence, "Y'know, I've had a really great couple of days, Pete Kelly." Pete gave her a sideways glance and smiled. "Don't be thinking I'm getting all mushy on you, mind" she laughed. "I just… These holidays are usually just Jo and me. There's not usually any other sort of company. I'm sure you've seen how people can be when they're around people like Jo and Steve. Unless they have any experience with disability or down syndrome, they're either super patronising or super rude, in my experience."

"Yeah," agreed Pete, remembering the way he ended up sitting next to Steve on the plane "super rude!"

"Meeting you and Steve has been fantastic. Spending time with someone else who is in the same line of work and who has a friend for Jo, it's been great." She quickly added that it was great for Jo, too.

Pete smiled again. "Yeah, she and Steve really hit it off. I mean, I think he really likes her, I mean really likes her! The problem is he's just super shy."

It was Mel's turn to smile. "Yeah, Jo likes him. She didn't stop talking about him when we got back. I'm going to make sure I get some details off you both so I can keep them in touch." Pete nodded his agreement. "And then there's you," she continued.

"Me? What about me?" Pete asked, smiling hopefully

"Down boy" she laughed. "I mean, you're not bad, for an Irish man!" They both laughed as Pete pretended to be wounded to the core, holding his hands over his breast as if trying to heal a broken heart. "I mean it though," she continued again, "there's something about you, Pete Kelly, that I can't help but like." Pete was smiling again, nervously, unsure how to respond. "I'll be honest, I'm not one for falling in love or even crushing on a guy at the drop of a hat, but despite what I keep saying, I think It would be really nice if we kept in touch maybe… who knows." She smiled and looked down as they walked. Pete smiled, too, and they walked on in silence. After a few yards, he surreptitiously tried to hold Mel's hand. She wordlessly gave his hand a slap, and they walked on. They'd walked maybe another three or four yards before she quietly reached out and took hold of his hand. They walked on in happy silence.

Before long, they were knocking on Steve's door. As they waited for a response, they heard a chair scrape and the soft padding of bare feet approaching. Inside, a familiar voice could be heard "Might be room service, Steve! Haven't ordered anything, Steve! Ah!" The door opened, and they were both bathed in that big beaming smile. "Ah, it's the lovebirds, Steve," he said then he laughed, heartily.

Mel laughed too, while Pete just stammered before saying: "Okay then, let's get you sorted." Mel turned to leave, and he nervously asked: "Wait, aren't you coming in?"

Mel shook her head. "I'll give you boys some privacy, you'll probably need to apply the cream we got him, and he wouldn't want me watching, would you Steve?" Steve just laughed. "Anyway, I'll just pop along and make sure Jo is ok. See you in about ten minutes?" Pete gave the thumbs up and off she went. As she sauntered down the corridor to the lift, Pete and Steve went into Steve's room. As Pete closed the door, the full impact of what Mel had just said hit him. "Apply the cream?" he said out loud. "What the hell?"

Imagine!

Imagine posing as a carer for someone just to try and seduce a girl.

Imagine posing as a carer to seduce a girl who is also a carer.

Imagine posing as a carer to seduce a girl and, to all intents and purposes, having your bluff called, albeit unknowingly.

Pete considered that he would do pretty much anything to help someone, but... well, he wouldn't do that. Pete wouldn't even apply the cream to his dad's arse, let alone a relative stranger's arse. "What if it's on his ball bag?" He thought. "Oh, sweet jumping Jesus!" Pete said this out loud. He stood there, his back to the door, clutching an oversized carrier bag and staring at Steve. Steve stood there, about eight feet away from him, staring back, smiling, as usual. "Right then, I guess we'd best get you... done!" Pete reached into the bag and started to pull out some of the things he'd bought for Steve. "I'd better at least get to kiss her tonight," he said as he placed the different items on the bed, "you're costing me a small fortune so far, too." This was indeed true. With their first shopping trip, meals out, drinks, train fares, this bag full of stuff, Pete had spent about two, maybe even three hundred euros. He shook his head. Steve just smiled, then walked over and gave Pete a hug. Pete reluctantly hugged Steve back, patting his clammy back. "Hey! Jim Bowen! Make sure that towel doesn't drop!" Steve laughed. On the bed were a five pack of Star Wars boxers, two pairs of shorts, two t-shirts and some socks. Pete reached back into the bag and pulled out the last item: the cream to soothe Steve's chafing. "Shit!" He said out loud again. "Steve, mate, is there any chance, any chance at all that you can apply this stuff yourself?" Steve was about to answer when there was a knock at the door. "That'll be Mel, I expect," Pete said and went to let her in. Mel was surprised to see Steve still stood in his towel.

"What have you boys been doing? I thought you'd be all done by now!" She exclaimed. Before either could say anything, she continued; "Steve, Jo wants to know if you'd like to come down for a drink in the bar too? Sort of a double date, but not a date because this is just friends having a drink." Pete stood behind Mel and waved his hands in front of him, trying to get Steve to decline. Steve looked past Mel at Pete and cocked his head like a quizzical puppy. Mel turned to see what was happening, and Pete quickly began fanning himself with his hands.

"Ooof! Is it me or has it gotten really hot in here?"

"Why don't you go stand over by the balcony door, you big chimp!" Mel gave him that look again and turned back to Steve, watching Pete as he moved past Steve to get cooler. Mel continued; "Have you put some of that cream on, Steve?" She asked. Steve, still smiling, shook his head. She turned her attention to Pete, "Have you not done that yet? I'd have thought that would have been the first thing you'd have done!"

Pete squirmed, "Well, the thing is, I'm not… it's not something I've done before." At least he was honest.

Rolling her eyes, Mel shook her head and grabbed the cream off of the bed and motioned towards the bathroom. "Steve, would you like me to put this on for you?"

"It's not just the, er, backdoor y' know!" Pete piped up. Mel asked what he meant. "Well, it's his, er, his coin purse too." Mel just looked at him, lost. Pete gestured to his own crotch and continued with "His coin purse? His bean bag?" Mel now understood what he meant, but she continued to play dumb, seeing how far he would go before he actually said the right name. Pete continued; "His chicken skin duffel bag? His berry basket?" Still a blank look. "Jesus H. Christ, woman! His ball bag, sorry, his *scrotum*!" Mel frowned, comically. Pete realised he'd raised his voice, and he repeated it again, in a softer tone "His scrotum might also need some attention." Mel smirked, and Pete realised she'd been winding him up. He smiled and nodded, wagging his finger at no one in particular. "Every bloody time!"

Mel chuckled, and she turned to speak to Steve. "Are you okay with me helping you put this cream on, Steve?" she asked.

"Yes, Steve," he responded, nodding and smiling.

Mel gave a thumbs up and continued "If I put the cream on round the back for you, can you put it on your nether regions." She pointed to his crotch as she said it.

Steve turned his head to the side as if talking to some unseen companion. "Can you put the cream on *down there*, Steve?" He pointed to his crotch as if showing 'other Steve' then he continued, "Aye, Steve! Mel is going to put it on the other sore bits, we'll do all them bits." He smiled again, and gave Mel the thumbs up.

Mel smiled too. She reached into her back pocket and pulled out another pair of disposable, blue latex gloves. Pete was mesmerised. "Always carry a pair in this line of work." Mel responded to his look of awe. "Don't you?" she asked. Pete just shook his head. "Right!" she said, turning to Steve. "Why don't you and me pop into the bathroom and we can get you sorted." She motioned to the clothes on the bed. "Grab some pants and a shirt, so you can get dressed afterwards."

"Ah, good idea, Steve, let's get dressed as well!" Mel and Pete smiled at each other and Mel gave Pete a wink before disappearing into the bathroom with Steve. Pete went and sat on the chair out on the balcony, to wait until it was all over. Twilight had melted away and the night was getting darker.

Pete checked the time; 21.30. "Bugger," he thought, "time is getting on." He sat back on the chair and put his feet up on the balcony railings and waited. It actually wasn't long before Mel emerged from the bathroom, snapping the gloves off, rolling them up and tossing them into the bin in one practised movement. Steve followed close behind, smiling, as always.

"All done!" Mel chirped. She turned back to face Steve. "Are you sure you don't want me to go grab Jo, so you can come with us? She'd like that."

Pete watched Steve. Normally he always smiled. When you ask him a question — smile. If you tell him something — smile. Look at him — smile. He drops an ice cream — believe it or not, smile! When Mel mentioned him 'double dating' with Jo, he noticed Steve didn't smile, at all. This was odd. Pete knew Steve liked Jo, and he was sure that Steve understood what Mel was asking him, but it just didn't raise a smile. He actually noticed Steve take a step back from Mel when she asked him.

Steve just shook his head saying, "Oh no, Steve."

"Are you sure?" Mel persisted. Looking uncomfortable, Steve confirmed this with a nod. Sensing his discomfort, Mel dropped it, adding "Okay, never mind, lovely. Jo will be disappointed, but I'm sure there'll be another time before we go home." Steve had already moved away and was rifling through his backpack. He pulled out a packet of crisps that they'd bought earlier in the day.

"Ah, crisps, Steve!" In his bare feet, he padded out onto the balcony and sat down on the chair.

Mel looked at Pete. "Shall we go get that drink then?"

There was a subtle inflection in her voice that told him something was off. Pete could sense it, but what? "Everything okay?" he asked.

"Yeah, course. Why wouldn't it be?" Mel responded, smiling slightly. "Come on, let's get down to the bar." Pete wasn't convinced that all was okay, but he followed behind her as she headed to the elevator. On the way, he slowly reached out to try and hold her hand, she pulled back as soon as she felt his fingers touch hers and they entered the elevator in silence. Pete pressed the big green G button, and the doors slid shut.

Chapter Five: "Can you turn those crickets down?"

As the elevator doors opened, and Pete and Mel emerged into the reception area. The evening had gone so well so far, and despite the little blip upstairs, Pete was feeling confident. He wasn't expecting any miracles, but knowing Mel was warming to him made him optimistic, the earlier bit of hand-holding more so. Pete knew it was all very fast, and he could hear his mother's voice in his head, reinforcing this notion. "You've just got rid of that snooty, slack-fannied bitch." She wasn't exactly a massive fan of Gemma, as you can maybe tell! "She's only been out of your life a few weeks, and you're already lining up the next flighty, soul stealing, drama junkie! You'll be giving your head a shake, or I'll be giving it a shake for you!"

Pete chuckled to himself as they made their way through to the bar. He knew all too well the pitfalls of impulsive decisions, the last big one he made ended up with him marrying a girl that seemingly was easier to spread than margarine, but he couldn't help himself. He had always been one to follow his heart, for better or worse, and this was no exception. Down in the bar, Pete asked Mel what she wanted to drink and went and ordered.

A familiar face greeted Pete at the bar. "Hey, man!" he greeted Pete, holding out his hand. Bemused, Pete shook it and gave his order. "Coming right up." Dave brought the drinks, two pints of lager. Pete handed his room key over for Dave to swipe. "I take it that these are for you and your crush?" Pete laughed and gave him a brief rundown of the last couple of hours. "Sounds promising. It's none of my beeswax, but I'd play it cool, if I were you though, and tell her the truth about everything. Start with a clean slate, y' know?"

Pete nodded. "Yeah, I've already decided to come clean about Steve AND tell her about Gemma too, and what happened. I mean, what's the worse that can happen? I think you're right, a clean slate is best." Dave nodded sagely and gave him a wink. Pete nodded, picked up the drinks and went to find Mel. It didn't take long to find her, she was stood at the other end of the bar, a cheesy pop act had set up shop. With a woman old enough to be your mother's older sister on the keyboards and an old guy who looked like Benny Hill and Thor's bastard offspring singing and playing guitar, they just fired up and were currently murdering Abba's 'Dancing Queen,' at an unforgiving volume, much to everyone's apparent delight.

Motioning to the rear door, Pete suggested they go sit outside by the pool. Mel gave a thumbs up, and they headed out. Outside, the sun had long since gone to bed, and the moon shone brightly in the balmy night air. At first, no one spoke. Mel was unusually quiet again, and this struck Pete as odd. They sat there for a while, both just staring out into the night. Pete looked around and saw they were the only people out at the pool. He broke the silence. "A beautiful night like this and everyone is sat in there, in that shithole, listening to that, that, Peter Stringfellow lookalike murder Abba!" Mel looked back at the bar and then up at him before smiling. Emboldened by this apparent change in the wind, Pete continued. "I wonder why that is? Don't you wonder?"

Mel shrugged, "Hadn't given it much thought, to be fair." She looked around, her face looked distant, as she didn't really want to be there.

"You see, I reckon that it's this: the average brits on holiday are just lazy bastards. Even when faced with sitting out on a lovely night like this, simply because it's self-service at the bar. The hotel has closed the hatches and so they don't like the idea of having to walk too far to get their own drinks, and they have to have their drinks, I mean, why else do they come on holiday? It can't be for the sights around here, lovely as it is, it's hardly a cosmopolitan centre of culture, is it now." Mel laughed. Pete continued. "I reckon, if they had table service out here, I guarantee it would be heaving. So now we've got," he paused before affecting a lousy cockney accent, "no table service? Bugger me, I'm not walking all that way back to the bar, come on Karen, let's just bleeding well sit right here, right next to the bar!" Mel laughed again, heartily. Pete joined in.

At this point, Pete expected the conversation to flow a bit. Instead, the laughter petered out again and gave way to silence. That is to say, there was a lack of communication, as it certainly wasn't silent. They were sat far enough away from the closed bar door for it to muffle the sound of Queen's 'Crazy Little Thing Called Love' being brutally slaughtered. Louder than that, though, was the sound of the crickets. To Pete, who didn't have much experience (practically none) of travelling, particularly in hot countries, the sound of crickets, the sound of crickets *this loud*, was completely new to him. It was something he had probably only heard in the background of films and tv shows. As he sat, he looked around trying to find the source of this, quite alien, and very annoying sound. Obviously, crickets are small and really, not so easily seen, especially at night. A cursory glance about revealed no definite source and Pete deduced the sound was coming from the speakers mounted at various points around the pool area. "I think they must be faulty!" He said, looking at Mel.

"Excuse me?" Mel looked puzzled.

"The speakers!" He replied, motioning around the pool to the various mounted cabinets. "That weird chirping noise seems to be coming from them." Mel laughed. Pete laughed too. "Maybe it's some sort of rodent deterrent."

Mel gently bit her top lip, as if stifling a smirk. "Oh," she exclaimed, "you're serious."

"What do you mean, 'serious?' Can you not hear that chirping?"

"Well, yes, I can but," she was about to explain the source of the noise but instead, seeing the look on Pete's face, she played along, "I can hear it, but I thought it was just the mosquito repellers."

Pete nodded sagely. "Yeah, *Mosquito repellers*! That's what I thought it was too. I saw something about it on the Discovery channel, a few weeks back, I'm sure."

Mel, suppressing the urge to laugh, vigorously jiggled an index finger in her left ear. "I tell you what, it's driving me insane too, why don't you be a love and go and ask at the bar if they can turn it down, or off?"

Sensing a 'hero moment,' Pete quickly responded; "Yes, right, I'll go and do that, I need another drink anyway. How about you? Drink?"

"Please."

"Same again?"

"Why not! I'm technically off duty right now." Mel watched as Pete got up and picked up their glasses. She followed him with her eyes as he circumnavigated the pool. There was a brief burst of an out of key 'Wig Wham Bam' as he opened the door to the bar area. Thankfully he closed it quickly, thereby muffling the musical holocaust. Five minutes later, the door opened again, allowing some mangled and bloody lines of 'Sunday Girl' to escape as Pete appeared, carrying two pints. He had to place them down on a table before he could close the door. This prolonged the cacophonous agony. With the door closed and screams quelled, Pete picked up the pints and made his way back over. Mel watched as he approached, placed the drinks on the table, and sat down. "There you go," he said.

"Thanks. I'll fetch the next one."

"Yeah, no worries."

"So?" She asked, desperate to hear what had occurred.

"So what?" Pete feigned ignorance.

"What did they say?" Mel asked, almost gleefully.

"What about?" Pete was entirely straight-faced at this point. Mel wasn't sure if he had maybe been joking after all.

"The 'mosquito repellers'! What did they say? They seem to have got louder. You did ask them to turn them down, didn't you?"

"Oh, that… yeah, I mentioned it." Still deadpan. Pete *had* mentioned it. First, he said it to Alejandro who really had no idea what Pete was on about. Alejandro then called Dave over.

Dave listened straight-faced as Pete explained the situation. Then he laughed. Then Pete's face made him stop laughing. "Oh shit, you're serious!" Was his response, followed by more vigorous laughter. "It's bloody crickets, mate! Crickets!" A bit more laughter followed. "Mosquito repellers!" Followed by more laughter. "Oh, Pete! I have to say, if these drinks weren't already free, I'd shout this round for you. The funniest bloody thing I've heard in ages."

"What did they say?" Mel was desperate to hear now.

"Oh, they said they can't turn it down, something to do with local bylaws or something like that." He took a sip of lager.

Mel bit her lip and paused a moment, trying to stifle laughter. "Local bylaws, is it?"

"Mm-hmm."

"They told you that? Local bylaws?"

"Yeah, local bylaws… and the fact that crickets don't have a volume button!" Mel burst into a fit of laughter. "You absolute bastard!" Mel was laughing so hard tears were rolling down her cheeks, now. "You knew! You bloody well knew!" Pete tried to admonish her but she was struggling to breathe, she was laughing so hard. Pete began to laugh, too, as he recounted the whole tale. By the time he got to Alejandro having to go and get Dave, they were both struggling to breathe, such was the intensity of their laughter. Eventually, they settled down, the previous awkward atmosphere seemed to have warmed a little. Mel and Pete were soon four beers and two whiskeys deep and getting on like the proverbial burning house. First, they swapped funny stories about their childhood. They'd shared funny stories about quite a lot, really, and they'd laughed lots. At one point, Mel had pushed Pete about his work in care. Pete felt he'd managed to keep his subterfuge going as he fudged a few answers and changed the subject, He knew it was stupid though. He knew she would have to know at some point unless he could manage to walk into a care job when he got back home. It was getting late, and so, at her insistence, Mel went to get them one more pint before they called it a night.

Pete moved his chair a little closer to Mel's while she was gone. "This is going to be it!" He told himself. "No time like the present. If I don't tell her now, I'll never find another good time. Besides, she's had a few drinks, and we are getting along like old mates. She'll probably laugh some more when I tell her. Yeah, it's definitely time to spill to beans, cut the crap, pay the bill, and clean the slate." He took some deep breaths and quickly thought about what he was going to say. He was piecing his 'mea culpa' together when he heard the door open, releasing the death rattle of Robbie William's 'Let Me Entertain You'. This was probably the most merciless murder to date, thought Pete as he looked up to see Mel approaching, pints in hand.

"It's looking like an episode of Shameless or something in there." Mel commented. Pete laughed. She took a sip of her lager, set the glass down and sat back in her chair, looking up at the night sky. "So tell me," she began, "what exactly happened to your marriage?"

Pete took a drink and set his pint down too. "Ah! The million dollar question!" Pete sat forward, looking at the ground. "Basically, in a nutshell, it just didn't work out."

"Why's that then?" Mel pushed.

"Let's just say she had… an addiction to speed." Pete laughed.

"An addiction to speed? A drug habit, then?" Mel looked surprised, "And you left her for that?"

"Well, it's a little more complicated than that but, yes! Yes, I did." Inside he was waging a loud and fruitless war with himself. "STOP DODGING, YOU WEAPON!" he screamed internally. The truth was that he just didn't want to start going into great detail with Mel. He was happy to tell all the gory details to a complete stranger like Dave, but when it came to Mel, he really liked her, and he was quite unsure as to how she might feel about him being cuckolded like that. He hadn't even thought about how to explain hanging around with a lad with down syndrome for no legitimate reason, he just kept thinking about 'Topgungate.' He was worried it might reflect poorly on him and, moving quickly to change the subject, he asked; "what about you? No man, or woman on the horizon?"

Mel took another drink. "Nope," she exclaimed as she sat back in her chair. "I was in a relationship for three years, but that ended last Christmas."

"I'm sorry to hear that." Pete offered. "What did he do?" He asked, adding quickly "or she"

Mel laughed "He! It was a He! He didn't have a drug habit." She said, alluding to Pete's half-arsed tale of, in her opinion, questionable woe. "No, he was addicted to injections, though. He was actually quite fond of meat injections." Pete looked puzzled.

"Turns out he was gay but didn't really realise until well into our relationship."

"Oh!" Pete said, solemnly "the old 'Freddie Mercury Equivalence!'"

Mel looked at him sideways before asking: "The what?"

"Freddie Mercury Equivalence." Pete repeated. "He was in love with a woman, Mary… Mary…" Pete rubbed his forehead to kickstart his memory. "Austin! Mary Austin! Anyway, they were engaged and everything, and she didn't have a clue about his love for men." Mel just looked at him, speechless. Pete continued digging: "I mean, he came clean and all, and they remained friends right up until his death from AIDS complications, Then she inherited the bulk of his fortune. I have no idea why I thought that was relevant, really. I'm talking too much, I'll stop now. How did you find out?"

"Well," said Mel, shaking her head and raised her eyebrows, "we went to a Christmas party. We both worked for the same care firm, and they had organised a party for all the clients. It was lovely. They hired a local function room, had food, a disco and even a Santa." Pete took a drink and leaned forward in his chair, intrigued. "He disappeared just after Santa had finished dishing out all the gifts. I went looking for him and found him."

"And?"

"It wasn't Santa's sleigh he was riding if you catch my drift."

Pete paused a moment, then the penny dropped. "Oooooh. Shit!" It occurred to him that his tale of Top Gun and infidelity wasn't perhaps quite as bad as he'd first thought. "This is it," he thought, "time to spill the beans!" A moment later, he opened his mouth to pour his heart out when Mel cut him off.

"If you're about to make a 'Santa's sack' joke, don't!" Pete bottled it, and he took a drink instead. They sat a moment in silence before they both looked at each other and burst out laughing again. As the laughter subsided, Mel held her glass up, as if checking the volume of what was left, then she leaned forward in her chair, "I like you, Pete." Pete sensed this was his moment, and he leaned forward also.

"I like you, too." He responded, smiling. "Look," he started, but Mel cut him off again.

"No, I really like you, Pete." She stared right into his eyes. Something was off, thought Pete. He couldn't put his finger on it. "You're funny, you're kind, you come across as really honest, you work in care just like me. You don't live that far away from me back home. If I was that kind of girl, this might have been your lucky night."

"Well, let's not be hasty," Pete stammered, "i mean, I'm not suggesting... y' know... but I really like you too, and..."

Mel smiled. "Is there anything I need to know?" In a split second, Pete decided his moment was lost, and as he felt he was on the verge of greatness, he decided that for now at least, discretion was the better part of valour, although he was feeling like a massive coward right now!

"Tell you? No, what would I want to tell you? Other than, of course, that I really like you. I mean, I'm not gay, or anything like that, if that's what you mean?"

Mel leaned closer to him. "That's good to know." She moved in as if to kiss him. Pete drunkenly convinced himself he'd made the right decision in keeping quiet, and then he leaned in too, closing his eyes, only to open them quickly as lager suddenly ran down his face.

"What the hell?" He opened his eyes, wiping the lager out of them, just in time to see Mel place her glass on the table.

"Good to know, but these are not the droids I was looking for." Mel stood up to leave.

"I don't understand! I thought we were having a moment?" Pete was pushing his dripping hair back.

"Oh, we were having a moment." Mel seemed incredibly angry. Pete was utterly at a loss. "We could have had a moment, in fact, despite my misgivings I had intended to have more than a moment with you tonight, you know, what with the 'Kelly Charm' and all that!"

"Wait, what?" Pete's brain began to spin into overtime. "Kelly charm?"

"Oh, I'm sorry, was I not supposed to know about the good old 'Kelly Charm?' Silly old Mel!" Pete cocked his head and pursed his lips as if he was about to say something.

Mel pointed at him and shook her head, adding "Don't!"

Bravely, he spoke anyway "Look, Mel… I literally have no idea what you're on about. One minute we were getting on fine, the next I'm in a war zone, and I'm taking fire without any cover whatsoever." This wasn't strictly true, for inside, Pete was going over all the things he could have said, the truth about everything, for example!

Mel sat down again and took a few deep breaths. Pete just sat and looked at her, unsure of what to do. He decided silence was his best course of action right now. Mel picked his drink up and took a swig. "I have given you several opportunities over the last few days, and finally tonight. You could have come clean at any time."

"Come clean?" she couldn't know, well she could, but how? Most likely, he'd just been so bad at portraying a care worker that she sussed him, he figured.

Mel continued: "Pete, right from the first day I met you, I was conflicted about you. I have only known you a few days, literally! But in those few days, I... you have really gotten under my skin, and I really like you." Mel gestured with her hands to emphasise that last part. "You make me laugh, you're not entirely unattractive, and you seem like a kind person." A nervous smile crossed Pete's face. Mel saw it and wiped it off quickly, though. "You've lied like a fucking flatfish, though!"

"What? How so?" Pete could hear the words coming out of his mouth. It felt like he was in one of those dreams where you're supposed to do something specific but say everything else other than the things you should be saying. Inside his head, Pete's raging sense of stupidity was stood over the corpse of 'Calm Pete' and was yelling:

"TELL HER.

THE TRUTH.

YOU TOTAL BLOODY MORON!"

Outside, Pete's nervous smile had faded away, and his whole face now hosted a look of confusion and despair. He wasn't drunk. No, wait, yes he was. He wasn't that drunk though. Actually, yes he was that drunk, and his brain was misfiring on all cylinders right now. He just sat there, meek and quiet, while Mel raged on.

"Sod off, Pete. I know you're not playing dumb now." Her sarcasm was tangible. "You only met Steve last Tuesday. You've literally only known him a few days, and the only reason you have been hanging around with him is to try and get in my knickers!"

"Whoa, that's not true!"

"Pete!"

"Well, that's not completely true." Pete prepared to bare his soul and come clean about how he felt and why he had posed as a carer for these last few days. Mel wasn't about to let him get a word in, though.

"The stupidest thing is, you didn't need to pretend. I like you... I liked you. Now, I can't trust you. I mean, you tell me your wife is out of the picture now."

"Oh, she is you've..."

Mel cut him off, "Shut up! Shut the hell up! I really don't care what bullshit tale of misfortune you have, because I really can't believe anything you say. I know you might feel I'm overreacting, but you have lied to me." She took another drink of Pete's lager.

Pete sat and thought for a few moments in the lull. The realisation of what must have happened washed across his face like a breaking wave. "Steve!" He said out loud. "For god's sake!" He looked over at her. "When?"

"Excuse me?"

"When did you find out? I'm guessing it was Steve who told you, I just wondered when."

"To be honest, I had my doubts that first afternoon on the beach. You were cagey about everything. You were dismissive about your wife, and then you were very vague about working with Steve. There have been loads more times since then that have triggered my spidey-sense!" The reference wasn't lost on Pete none of the references she'd made were, in fact. Despite the gravity of the situation, it still made his heart flutter a little. She sighed and paused. "You know, if you had actually been telling the truth, I might have taken some details from Steve and raised my concerns with the authorities, or social services, or someone when I got back to the UK. You seemed like you just didn't have a clue what to do with Steve and in this line of work that can be dangerous. But, yeah, Steve bubbled you tonight. In fairness, he didn't want to drop you in it and kept avoiding the question. I managed to get him to admit he had only met you on Tuesday and that he didn't normally have a carer. I mean, I'm not really sure why you were hanging around with a vulnerable adult in the first place but, anyway," Pete was about to try and explain but, again, Mel didn't give him a chance, "Steve told me your plan for tonight and assured me that the 'Kelly Charm' had nothing to do with Jim Bowen." Pete laughed at this, then pulled his face straight when he saw Mel was not amused. "You lied, though. You lied and you obviously thought I was an easy mark."

"Well, you did just say that we could've shared 'a moment' just now." Pete countered, right before his glass came whizzing past his head so fast he barely managed to dodge out of the way. The glass landed in the pool with a strange, audible 'plop'. As he straightened up, he saw that Mel was already at the hotel door. In a blast of…was that Agadoo? In a blast of pushing pineapples and shaking trees, she was gone.

Pete sat back in the chair and ran his fingers through his wet hair. He looked back at the door, murmuring, to no one in particular: "Well, that went well!" He was about to go on back up to his own room when he looked at the pool. "Shit, the glass!" He took his shirt, shoes and jeans off and climbed down into the pool near where he thought the glass has entered. Mel had thrown the glass in at the deep end, but it was still going to be dangerous if he left it in. Someone could step on it and get a nasty gash. The pool, out of the light of day and with no heating on, was unbearably cold. His breath was stolen from him with each descending step, and he had to wait a good five minutes while his body acclimatised. Struggling to keep his breath and trying to keep his head above water, he began to sweep his foot back and forth along the bottom of the pool to locate the glass. This was not so much an ingenious way of looking for the glass as a cowardly way of avoiding having to dive down to look for it. The water was just ridiculously cold. As time moved on, he was losing hope of finding it using his feet. He was just about to brace himself for the dive when his foot nudged something. Eureka! He manoeuvred the glass further up the shallow end until he could reach down and retrieve it, relieved it hadn't smashed. He got out and contemplated what he should do next. No towel, no dry pants. The night was warm and as he fully emerged from the pool, the warm night air was a welcome contrast to the icy pool water, and so he sat back down for a little while to try and dry off. "Ah, shit!" He said out loud. "shit, shit. SHIT!" Sitting back, he looked up at the stars. A movement caught his eye, and in the gloom, he could just make out a couple on a second-floor balcony. He looked around and realised there were at least five other occupied balconies. "Of course there are!" He said softly, wondering how much of the show the onlookers had witnessed. "Sod it!" He pulled his jeans on over his wet boxers and then his shirt, turning it outside in first. After putting on his shoes, he hastily made his exit from the pool area and headed back up to his room, stopping by the bar to get another pint and two, make it three, double whiskies. Tipping the spirits all into one glass, he headed on his way. Up in his room, he quickly got changed into drier clothes. Picking up his wet boxers and damp jeans, along with his pint and his whisky, he headed out onto the balcony, where he draped the jeans over the back of one of the chairs, and the boxers on the arm. He pulled the other chair around and flopped into it. Taking a sip of beer and then a sip of whiskey, he sat back and pinched the bridge of his nose. The night was quite calm. Warm and calm. The sound of the crickets had subsided somewhat, and an almost silence reigned. Pete kept taking alternate sips of his drinks. He did this for a little while before opting to finish the whole of the lager in one go. He let out a huge belch and set his glass down on the floor of the balcony, sipping at his whiskey again. With no food since lunchtime and the drinks he'd had with Mel, the whiskey soon made him feel warm and fuzzy inside. By the time he'd finished the glass he was no longer just 'quite drunk.' He was well on the way to being 'quite battered.' Pete wasn't 'falling down, slurring speech' drunk, just kind of 'not thinking things through and quickly overreacting' drunk.

As he continued to analyse the evening's events, he grew more and more annoyed that Steve had dropped him in it like that. But Pete did not once consider the fact that Mel will just have questioned him and Steve had no reason to lie to her, and it would have been unfair to even expect him to. This thought, that he had been 'betrayed' started off as a small seed but, as the whiskey slowly fertilised it, it grew into a giant, bitter behemoth. Fuelled by grain alcohol and a misguided sense of injustice, Pete got more and more angry until he could stand it no more. He stood up and walked over to the partition, trying to look around it to see if he could see Steve. The curtains were closed, and the room looked dark. "Screw it!" He went inside, through his own room, and out into the hall where he began to bang on Steve's door. "Steve! Steve! It's Pete! I want to talk to you, mate!" He put his ear to the door but couldn't hear any movement inside. "Steve!" He banged on the door again "STEVE! Open the door, you little prick!" There was still no sign of life inside. Undeterred, assuming Steve was maybe hiding, he began shouting through the door. "You had one job mate. One! Job! I've bought your food, I've bought you clothes and a towel, a Star Wars towel! And don't forget those bloody Star Wars underpants! I've actually spent a small fortune on you. Besides that, I've included you in stuff every day, and all I asked was that you let me pretend to be your carer in front of Mel. All you had to do was keep pretending. You know I really like her, and now, because of you opening your big stupid mouth, it's all screwed, blued, and tattooed! You have royally shafted me. Well, that's it, mate! I didn't even want to spend any of my holidays with someone like you, anyway. So that is it! The bank of Pete is CLOSED, and you can find your own fun from now on! I'll tell you what as well, if I see your folks on the ride home, I'll be giving them a sodding bill. STEVE? STEVE!" He banged again for good measure.

Steve wasn't in his room. Mel had checked in on him after her little spat with Pete and persuaded him to come to play some cards in her room with her and Jo. He'd been really reluctant, not because he wasn't sociable, but because he really liked Jo. Steve had never had any friends that were girls, well, he'd never really had any friends, and he was nervous and found he just couldn't find anything to say. Mel wasn't taking no for an answer though, and she'd persuaded him with the promise of crisps and coke, as she'd bought some for Jo earlier. Steve was peckish and was never one to pass up free food - who doesn't want free crisps? So, he'd gone along with Mel. They'd all been getting on really well and having fun, but when Jo had moved her chair really close to his and leant her head on his shoulder, Steve had suddenly decided it was time to go. He'd scurried off pretty quickly, with Mel following up behind to make sure he got back to his room. This was just about when Pete decided to confront him. He'd got back to his room just as Pete began his tirade, standing undetected, about ten feet away. Mel had seen he had got back safe and was about to turn and head back when she heard Pete's tirade too. She had moved about ten feet behind Steve.

Pete finished his floor show and turned to go back into his room. There stood Steve. Steve's ordinarily smiling face looked sad, incredibly sad almost close to tears, in fact. Steve pushed past Pete and went into his room, closing the door slowly. Pete shrugged and turned to go into his own room. Then he saw Mel, their eyes meeting for a few seconds. Mel broke the silence. "You are such a class act, Pete Kelly!" She turned to go back to her room. "I'm so glad I found out who you really are before I…" She didn't finish the sentence. She just shook her head and carried on walking. Pete felt sure he saw her wiping her face as if wiping tears away. Pete swore softly under his breath and went back into his room. He closed the door and clumsily staggered over to his bed, collapsing down on it. Within a few minutes, he was snoring away in a deep, drunken sleep.

The next morning — Friday morning, in fact — sunlight streamed through a small crack in the floor to ceiling curtains in Pete's room, striking him squarely in the eyes. He was still asleep at this point, but the bright, warm death ray was practically piercing his eyelids, and he soon began to rise from the depths of his slumber. His eyes blinked open, and the light immediately hit him like a good hard slap, causing him to quickly roll over to avoid any further pain. Reaching out for his phone, he checked the time and groaned, tossing the phone back onto the bedside table. As he lay there, his sleepiness started to subside, and his hangover began to rise. Feeling nauseous and gripped by quite a fierce headache, he tried to lie there as still as possible. Then it hit him.

We've all been there: when you suddenly remember a key event from the previous night, and the cold icy fingers or realisation and regret take a tight hold of your heart. Then you get hit by that accompanying rush of adrenalin that jolts you right out of your hungover daze, smashing you back to a harsh reality that you'd rather pretend never happened.

"Shit!" He pulled the covers over his head as his brain, in some act of retribution for the punishment it was now receiving, replayed through all of the events of the previous the night in full, unstoppable, and highly cringe-worthy detail. Actually, he thought, it's not that bad. At this point, he had only recalled the complete verbal arse kicking he'd had from Mel down by the pool.

You know how the next bit goes, we've all been there too: The Brain, ever thoughtful, lulls you into a sense of false security. "Here you go, here's the bad stuff! How do you feel now? Oh really? Not so bad, you say? Well, buckle up, buttercup!" Then it slams you with the coup de grace, rendering you paralysed with fear and humiliation.

Pete's brain let him rest a moment, pondering on what he could do about his spat with Mel, then it started to feed him little micro clues. The walk from the pool... The bar... Whiskey... "Whiskey?" Pete didn't like where this was heading. "Three... Only three whiskies, that's a relief... Oh, wait... Doubles? Doubles! Oh shit!" Pete realised why his head was so bad. He'd hardly eaten anything after lunch, and he and Mel had drunk at least four or five pints by the pool. Well, four and a half, in Mel's case. He ended up wearing that other half. "But wait, there's more!" Interjected his brain. He sat bolt upright as his mind played an uncannily detailed replay of his visit next door, and the aftermath. "Bugger me!" Pete was horrified. He'd actually stood there and shouted abuse at that sweet young man who, if he was honest with himself, was completely innocent in all this, and as for Mel's reaction he knew any chance of pulling any of this back was pretty much screwed right there, right then. "Shit, shit, shit!" Pete shouted, laying back down. He reached out for his phone to recheck the time: 09.36. There wasn't much point to actually getting out of bed, Pete reasoned, pulling the covers up over his head again.

Five minutes later, he jumped up, immediately regretting it as his head throbbed like it was about to burst and his stomach felt like he'd swallowed battery acid. He wasn't a bad person, although all the evidence from last night did suggest otherwise. He wasn't a bad person, and he needed to show Mel and Steve, and probably Jo, that he wasn't a bad person. Time to go and eat some humble pie! Pete quickly did the whole' shit, shave, and shower' routine and threw some clothes on, taking particular care to clean his teeth as his mouth tasted like he'd been chewing on a zombie's forearm. If he hurried, Pete reckoned he might just make breakfast, and in his head, Mel, Steve, and Jo were all sat at a table in the breakfast room. They were all sticking pins into Pete shaped voodoo dolls and eating bacon and eggs - except Steve, who was obviously having cereal and fruit and loads of OJ. He pressed the button for the lift but, being impatient and desperate to get his 'mea culpa' going, he opted for the stairs and raced down them, arriving at the breakfast room with five minutes to spare before the morning deadline. Dave was on the door, and he just waved Pete through instead of making him sign in like the other guests. After a quick exchange with Pete, he turned and pointed over to the far corner. Pete nodded and headed over to meet his fate. In the far corner, he found Mel and Jo sat, just chatting with no sign of Steve. Jo looked up and gave Pete a smile and a cheery "Hello, handsome!" Mel, who was looking at her phone, did not make any effort to acknowledge his presence.

"Mel?" Pete tried to get her attention.

Mel did not respond at first. Then she sighed and said; "Jo, can you smell something?"

"Only bagels, bacon, and your bum," said Jo, laughing.

"Mel, come on, please let me just try and explain." Pete pleaded

Mel cut him off. "Come on, Jo, let's go. There's a shitty smell in the air around here." They both got up and started to head off, Jo giving a little wave. Pete tried to engage Mel again and met with the same response or lack of one. Defeated, he headed to get some food in an optimistic attempt to quash his hangover. As he sat down, Dave came and joined him.

"How's it going? I'm no expert, but I would say that Mel seems a little bit…" he searched for the right word. "Hostile?"

"No, shit!" Pete then recounted the whole sorry tale. When he'd finished, Dave burst out laughing, much to his annoyance. "Come on, man. This is serious. What do I do?"

"I'm sorry, Pete," Dave said, still chuckling, "that's quite a spectacular tale of catastrophe! I wondered why your little buddy was down here so early."

"Who, Steve?" Pete perked up.

"Yeah, he was down here first thing for breakfast. He looked a bit off his game too, he normally smiles from ear to ear but this morning he looked like someone had shit in his Coco Pops. Poor fella!"

"Well, that helps!" Said Pete, shaking his head. "Shit! I feel terrible. He was really just an innocent bystander and technically, I was using him to get to Mel. He didn't deserve me tearing into him like that."

Shaking his head, Dave asked; "what will you do about Mel?"

"You're joking, aren't you?" Pete found himself laughing this time, at the sheer absurdity of Dave's question. "I have well and truly shit my pants there. I can't even get her to look at me, let alone speak to me."

Dave sighed and shook his head again. "Sorry man, I told you, though, I said: 'come clean'. I wish I could offer some sage advice on how to fix it, but I think this is in the lap of the gods now. Shit!" He stood up quickly and started to clear Pete's table.

"What's up?" Enquired Pete.

"The hotel manager is in, that sweaty looking fella over there." He motioned over to the doors with his head.

"Manager? Really?" Pete was surprised by this. "I honestly thought you ran the place."

Dave smiled. "Technically, I do. Manuel is the owner's son and he just lets me get on with it. He's a lazy bastard, see, and so he just buggers off and does god knows what all day. His dad knows he's a shiftless little bastard and he knows I can handle it. Every now and again though, Manuel likes to pop in and show his face. Pretend like he's the boss and he knows what he's doing." Pete just shook his head. "Hey, this'll cheer you up." Pete looked up at him, expectantly. "He's only called Manuel, AND he only comes from Barcelona!" Dave laughed. Pete just looked at him still, completely clueless. "Fawlty Towers?" Pete was again drawing a blank. Dave looked at him in disbelief before continuing: "You absolute savage. Keep me posted and shout up if you need any help with anything!" He gave Pete a wink, and he was off.

By now it was almost 11.00 am. Pete went into the bar to get a drink, a soft drink as he desperately needed to rehydrate. After grabbing a coke from the bar he headed poolside, hoping to nab some shuteye on a sun-bed, but when he saw that Mel and Jo were outside, he thought better of it and went inside to sit in the bar instead. The pain in his head had subsided a little, but Pete felt he might benefit from some pain relief, so he grabbed his coke and headed back up to his room where Pete felt sure that he had a box of paracetamol. Before long, he was laid on his bed again, waiting for the pain relief to kick in. As he lay there staring at the ceiling, he recapped his life so far in the last four weeks and wondered just how much worse, if at all, it could get. Eventually, his thoughts turned to Steve. Getting up off the bed, he went out onto the balcony to see if Steve was out there. He could see no sign of him on the balcony itself. "Fuck it," he said out loud and went out of his room and knocked on Steve's door. There was no answer. "Steve?" he called out as he knocked again. Still no response. He went back into his own room, back onto his balcony, and tried to peer into the gloom of the next room, to no avail. What he did notice, though, was that Steve's balcony door wasn't shut. After a brief internal debate about how stupid it would be, he climbed over his balcony railing and, holding onto the railings for dear life, shimmied across to Steve's balcony and climbed back over the railing. Steve definitely wasn't there. All that was there in the room, was a pile of badly folded clothes on the bed, and the now half empty tube of cream he'd bought for Steve the night before. Closer inspection of the clothes revealed they were all the clothes Pete had bought for him, the Star wars pants and Towel were there too. On top of the pile was a torn out word search page with the words 'for Pete' on it. "Ah shit, Steve!"

Chapter Six: Just Like Tiger Woods!

Pete was in panic mode. Steve was missing, and it looked like, to all intents and purposes, he'd run away. On top of that, it was pretty much all Pete's fault. Pete went back down to the bar to see if he could see Steve, but there was no sign of him. Steve wasn't in the bar, the front pools or the big pool out back. Pete double checked the restaurant in case he'd gone for lunch. Nothing."Bollocks!" He'd already spotted Mel and Jo by the pool and, in desperation, headed over to them. As he approached, he could see that Jo was pleased to see him, as always. Mel, who was not so pleased, sighed in disgust as she turned the page of the book she was reading. "Mel, Jo, I'm really sorry to bother you again, but have either of you seen Steve?"

"I saw him last night," said Jo, smiling. Pete smiled back as best he could. He was really hoping that the girls had seen Steve.

"Thanks, Jo. That's great, but I was wondering if you'd maybe seen him today at all?"

Jo frowned as she thought for a moment, "No, not today" she replied.

"Shit!" Jo giggled at the naughty word. "Mel? Have you seen him?" She continued to ignore him, turning another page. "Mel, please!" the panic evident in his voice, "I know you hate me, I don't blame you, I've behaved like an absolute cock slap" Jo giggled again, some pool patrons looked on and scowled. "But I can't find Steve anywhere. Dave saw him in the breakfast room really early, which is not like him, and I've just tried his room, and there's no answer, I'm a bit worried that he's taken off."

Mel turned another page and, without looking up, said; "Jo, tell Pete that Steve is a big boy and apparently doesn't actually need a carer and I'm sure that, whatever he's doing, he's perfectly safe."

Jo smiled at Pete and shrugged. Pete uttered a silent "Shit's sake" and spoke to her, all the while looking at Mel, who continued to ignore him. "Jo, please would you tell Mel that I'm really concerned as I actually climbed into Steve's room earlier, and he's cleared out everything but the stuff I've bought him, and I know he only has twenty euros on him and, well let's face it, he's hardly... y' know... smart!" Realising how that sounded he quickly added "street smart, he's hardly street smart" as he rubbed the back of his neck.

Mel shook her head. "Jo, please tell Pete that, again, I'm sure that Steve is okay. He must be capable of getting around and looking after himself or his parents wouldn't allow him on holiday on his own." Jo smiled and shrugged again.

Pete sighed. "Shit's sake! Okay, Okay. Have it your way." He turned to Jo, "Jo, Please, if you see him, tell him I'm looking for him and ask him to wait here for me."

Jo smiled and nodded "Roger Roger!" she exclaimed.

Pete turned on his heels and went back inside. Dave was at the reception, so he went over and asked him if he'd seen Steve again since this morning. Dave hadn't, but he asked Pete to wait and picked up the phone, pressed a button and waited. "Hola Alejandro! ¿Has visto al tipo que estaba colgando con mi amigo? Ya sabes, el tipo con las... ah... necesidades especiales?" a pause "Si, si, gracias." He put the phone down and looked at Pete. "Alejandro says he saw him about an hour ago. He had his backpack on, and he was headed out the front door."

"About an hour ago?" Dave nodded. Pete headed for the door, turning back as he went. "Thanks man, I owe you!" Dave waved and sat down behind reception, fanning himself with some old check-in forms. Outside Pete began to head for the town, continually scanning the street for Steve's familiar gait, his red shirt and blue hat. He stopped dead as he had a sudden flash of inspiration. "Wait a minute!" Quickly, he pulled his phone out and opened the browser. Steve had left those clothes with a note. He wasn't coming back, or at least that's what it looked like. If he wasn't coming back then it was a pretty safe bet that he was going to find his parents, he must be! Pete tried to recall the name of the hotel. Steve's dad had told him they were staying at in Barcelona. It was on the tip of his tongue, but he just couldn't recall it. "Arc De Triomf!" He remembered something helpful: Steve's dad had said it was near Arc De Triomf. He typed 'hotels near Arc De Triomf, Barcelona' into his phone hoping the results would jog his memory. "Hotel Rec! YES!" he shouted, scaring a passing elderly lady half to death. "Sorry, sorry!" He said to the lady as he took off running to the station.

Of course, he didn't get that far. It was midday almost, and very hot, and he was more hungover than a builders belly on a belt. He reduced his 'run' to a relatively brisk walk, arriving at the station just in time to get on the next train to Barcelona. When he was getting on the train, he checked the platform just in case Steve was still about, no sign of him. It was, mid-morning and the train itself was not very busy, and seats were in high supply. As the journey was about an hour long, he sat back and closed his eyes. The events of the previous evening played through his mind again. In all honesty, he didn't know what was worse: the way he'd blasted Steve or the way he'd completely mishandled the whole thing with Mel. He could have maybe avoided all of it if he'd just spoken up a bit earlier, like when he first met her maybe. He remembered his phone and the video footage of Gemma, kicking himself for not showing it to Mel. After all, that alone would surely have got him at least a sympathy hug maybe. After further consideration, he decided he felt equally bad on both counts, but that perhaps the business with Steve had the edge. He pushed it all out of his mind. He's learnt pretty quickly that dwelling on stuff bought nothing but grief and solved nothing. Better to focus on the here and now and see what can be salvaged than going back over what could have been done differently. When he set off on Tuesday, he certainly didn't envisage spending most of his break with someone like Steve, but Pete couldn't deny that the whole drama with Mel notwithstanding, he'd had some fun. In fact, if truth be told, he was actually missing not having Steve in tow, right now. "Deal with Steve first," he thought. Make sure he's okay, at least, and hopefully persuade Steve to forgive him for his outburst. With that done, he could see what, if anything, could be salvaged with Mel. Not that he was too optimistic on that front.

Over an hour later, after one change, Pete was standing on the platform at Arc De Triomf. The station was underground, so he headed for the exit and out onto the street. After checking the address of the hotel in the phone's map app, he set off in search of it. Using the map app and looking around the streets, it didn't take long for him to find it. In fact, he'd spotted it quite quickly as he could see 'Rec' written in big turquoise letters at street level on a large building ahead. "Bingo," he said out loud, smiling at a couple of passers-by who looked across at him. Walking towards the big letters, he kept scanning the street for Steve. As he got closer to the hotel entrance, a flash of red in the trees opposite the hotel caught his eye. There, sat on a bench doing what he felt sure was a word search, Pete could see Steve. "Thank Christ!" he exclaimed, letting out a massive sigh of relief.

Steve had been sat there for about an hour. He knew where his parents were staying, and he'd managed to get a train, including the change over, all the way to Arc De Triomf. After wandering around for a while, he'd found a policeman and asked him where the Rec was. The CNP officer had walked him there as it was not far from where they were. Steve had politely thanked the officer, and after failing to find the courage to actually go into the hotel, he had been sat there, patiently, in the late morning sun, with one proverbial eye on his word search book and the other on the hotel entrance. He knew this was his parent's hotel, but he didn't know what room they were in, or even if they would be in the hotel right now, so he figured his best course of action was to sit outside and just wait. Sooner or later they would either come out or go in, and he'd be able to catch them and tell them he wanted his ticket so he could go home. Obviously, the plan had a simple, yet a quite significant flaw, but as bright as he was, Steve didn't understand that planes weren't like buses and he couldn't just use his ticket on the next flight to England. Pete had spotted him at the exact same moment his father had spotted him. "Steve! Steve! What are you doing? Eh? Why are you here?" Pete saw the man he had observed back in Newcastle Airport, talking to Steve. He was dressed like a crossover episode of Magnum PI and Miami Vice. Despite the fact they were in the middle of a big, busy city, his voice carried all the way up to Pete. Pete began walking towards them. "Bloody hell, son. You can't be doing this. We've told you this before, me and your mum need a bit of 'our time'. We explained this to you. Now come, son. I know you're a bit light, but you're not that stupid. So tell me, what's going on? What's the crack?"

Meet Marion Oldfield — 'Mike' to his friends. Actually, it was Mike to everyone except when he had to formally identify himself. His mum was a huge John Wayne fan and already had a son whom she'd named 'John' when 'Mike' came along. She did toy with the name 'Rooster' for a while, but in the end, she opted for Marion. This wouldn't have been a problem so much if he'd grown up in the Thirties or Forties, or even the Fifties and Sixties, but as a child of the Sixties who grew up in the Seventies and Eighties, in the mean, mean streets of... Milton Keynes, it was a curse. His parents had slowly migrated further North over time, mainly for economic reasons, and at some point, some bright spark of a friend decided it was funnier to call him Mike rather than the endless cycle of shit 'Marion' jokes, and it had somehow stuck. If Pete had known this little bit of history, he might have had a little bit of sympathy for the man... might. Anyway, then followed the usual stuff: Met Diane, fell in love, got married — at twenty-one — settled down to married life. Now, Mari...Mike never wanted children. Diane did, but it was something they never talked about. Mike always insisted she takes 'The Pill,' which she did, very dutifully, for seven years. Then she stopped. She would flush them down the toilet every morning rather than take them. It didn't take long for her to fall pregnant either. Mike was livid, he accused her of doing it deliberately, which she obviously had done, but she always maintained her innocence. Then he had demanded she "get rid of the bleeding thing," this again resulted in a lot of arguments, but again, Diane got her own way. Eventually, along came Steve. When he was born, and finally diagnosed with Trisomy 21, it was Diane's turn to try to get rid of 'it' and Mike's turn to dig his heels in. Mike steadfastly refused to allow her to put him up for adoption. Now, before you develop any kind of soft spot, I should point out that this was not down to any paternal empathy or any other sentimental reason. No! Mike wouldn't let her put Steve up for adoption simply because, simply put, he's a twat. He spent a lot of time reminding Diane how he wanted to get rid of Steve when she was pregnant, and how she'd refused. Well, now she was going to have to live with that decision. This made for some very frosty days, and nights, then weeks, then months, then a few frosty years.

Now, don't jump to conclusions. Neither of them were model parents, but they never mistreated Steve, well, not in a 'News At Ten' kind of way. He was looked after in as much as he was always clean and tidy, he was always fed and watered and always had clothes and shoes and essential stuff, he just didn't get a lot of love and affection. Eventually, things in the Oldfield household thawed, and an *entente cordial* was achieved. In fact, they sort of became a happy family, especially when the money from Steve's different benefits came rolling in. Although the money was for Steve to live a normal life as best he could, Mike told him it was "what we get paid to look after you, see?" Steve didn't know any better, and he trusted his folks not to lie to him.

One of the benefits of living at home with such caring parents was that they took him on holiday with them, every time they went away. What Steve didn't know, was that they were too scared to get someone in to look after him while they were away, and because they neither of them had any family that they bothered with, they had no other option. They'd kept Steve away from any kind of Down's support network and support teams, in case they were rumbled, and their free money dried up. It was Diane who'd first suggested taking him away with them but putting him in a different hotel. They'd tried it first when he was eighteen and, despite a few minor hiccups around Steve getting completely lost in Limassol,

Cyprus, it had gone pretty well overall and that is how, six years later, they were in Spain enjoying the same holiday but in different locales. They hadn't always dumped him miles away. That first holiday in Cyprus, they'd put him in a little hotel called the Arsenio which wasn't that far from the apartments they'd booked in Amathus Beach. They soon discovered though, that the closer Steve was, the more likely he was to just turn up and hang about, which they quickly grew tired of.

Steve was lucky really, despite having Trisomy 21, he was quite capable and able to be quite independent. After Cyprus, there were no more major incidents or mishaps, and so Mike and Diane soon settled into a routine when it came to these trips. Mike was the one who came up with picking all-inclusive hotels on the cheaper end of the scale. He reasoned that this way, Steve wouldn't need any money at all. He was bright enough to know when the restaurants were open and when to eat. They knew they couldn't leave him on his own at home as their neighbours were too nosey and they were simply too tight to spring for any third party care and, besides, they didn't want to risk anyone rumbling them and calling social services. They didn't want to lose their cash cow. As far as anyone knew, they were model parents. They always took their boy on holiday with them. Nobody knew the real story.

Back outside the REC, Mr Eighties Throwback hadn't given Steve any chance to speak, though he bravely kept trying to interrupt. "What is it? Go on, spit it out. What's going on?"

" Do you want to go home, Steve? Yes, I do Steve." Steve managed to get a word in.

"Stop that, talk to me not yourself, what have I told you? Now what? You want to go home? You can't go home! Bloody hell, son! You think you can just jump on the next plane back to England? Get a bloody grip, will you! Now, you get yourself back to Calella and let's have no more of this nonsense." He reached into his pocket and pulled out his wallet. After a brief fumble, he produced a twenty euro note and thrust it into Steve's hand. He then paused a minute as if thinking about something, he reached into his wallet again and pulled out another ten euros. "That twenty is for emergencies - again! The tenner... well, let's call it an advance on your pocket money, eh? Treat yourself to ice cream or a souvenir or something. But hey! You'll be paying this back, you've already had twenty, I'm not a bloody bank." He put his wallet back in his pocket and pulled out a handkerchief, mopping his forehead and brow. "Right, I'm off to the shop for some stuff for your mum. You'd best not be here when I get back." Steve stood up and grabbed Mike in one of his hugs before Mike had a chance to stop him. Pete saw he looked uncomfortable with it and he was looking around as if making sure no one could see and he quickly broke it off. "Now go on, be off with you, and behave yourself!" With that, he was off on his own way.

Steve had not spoken or smiled much at all. He just kept nodding and pushing his glasses up his nose. During the exchange, Pete had managed to get himself behind Steve so he could observe the pair of them a bit better. He was pretty angry at what he'd seen. A soon as Steve's dad headed off around the corner, Pete's first thought was to follow him and have a chat with the man. He figured that was not the answer, though, and the last thing he needed was to get arrested in a foreign country. Besides, Pete was a lot of things, but he'd be the first to admit that he wasn't really a violent man and Steve's dad was a good foot taller than him, so he might not have come off well in a fight. Instead of confronting Sonny Crockett, he went up to the bench where Steve was still seated. As Pete approached, he could tell by the movement of his shoulders that Steve was sobbing a little. Without a word, he just sat down next to him. At first, neither spoke. Pete looked across at Steve and he felt his heart break for the poor lad. Carefully, he slowly shimmied his bum until he was sat next to the still sobbing Steve and put his arm around his shoulders.

After a little while, Pete broke the silence: "Your dad." Steve wiped his eyes and pushed his glasses up his nose, turning his head to look at Pete. "He's a bit of a weapon, isn't he." He turned to face Steve who was now managing half a smile. "There it is, a little smile." Pete gave Steve a playful squeeze then removed his arm from his shoulders, and the pair drifted back into silence. Again, Pete broke it: "Steve, mate, I am so, so sorry about last night. I was drunk. Actually, I was shit-faced, and I was angry, I wasn't angry at you though, I was angry at myself. I made a huge mess, and I just took it all out on you instead of being grown up about it." Steve just looked at him and smiled a bit more. "I should not have lied to Mel, and I really shouldn't have asked you to help me lie to Mel, and I REALLY shouldn't have gotten angry with you when you blew the lid of my stupid ruse. I didn't mean anything I said last night. I think you're great guy, I really do, and I have had some great fun these last few days hanging out with you." He stood up in front of Steve. "What

I'm trying to say is, can we, I mean, it would be really great if we could be friends again?" He held out his hand for Steve.

Steve put his hand to his chin as if contemplating what Pete had said and looked up at the sky. "Hmmm, Steve, can we be friends with Pete? I dunno Steve, what would Jim Bowen say? I think I think he'd say let's take a look at what you could have won, Steve!" He looked at Pete, his face a picture of seriousness. Pete looked back at Steve, raising his eyebrows. Steve looked at Pete then leapt up, brushing Pete's hand aside, to give him a hug. A big hug. " I love Pete, Steve. Me too, Steve! Me too!"

Tired and still hungover, Pete was caught off guard emotionally, he felt tears well up as he hugged Steve back. He wiped his eyes before releasing Steve fully. "Are you hungry?" Steve nodded. "Come on, let's go get something to eat then." They stood up and started heading towards the train station, and as they walked, Pete glanced back over his shoulder and saw Steve's father going back into the hotel carrying a plastic bag. The way the guy had spoken to Steve, the way they both treat him. This wasn't over, Pete thought, not by a long shot.

Before they got the train back to Calella, they grabbed some food. They'd passed quite a few takeaways and restaurants on their way back to the station, all vetoed by Steve, when they came across a street vendor, right outside the central station, selling chips or 'patatas fritas,' as the locals called them. They weren't cheap at three euros a tray full, but it was quite a mountain of fried potatoes, and there was a wide choice of dips. Steve just had good old Heinz ketchup while Pete opted for Garlic Mayo. Grabbing some napkins, they headed into the station to wait for the next train back to Calella. On the platform, they sat on a bench, and Steve sat and tucked into his chips straight away, while Pete checked the train times. "Cool," he exclaimed as he too began to tuck into his chips, "the next train is in ten minutes" They both demolished their food pretty quickly, and Pete's hangover was now a distant memory. Steve's smile was back and in full effect too. As Pete watched Steve daintily select each fry and gracefully dip it into his ketchup before stuffing it into his mouth, he couldn't help but smile too. Pete smiled. "Mate," he said, "I really am sorry about, you know, last night."

Steve nodded, still munching. "No, really, I look back on everything, and I really have been acting like a proper dick. I'm thrilled we managed to make up. Truly!" He held out his fist for a fist bump.

Steve, seeing the fist, dropped a chip back into the tray and wiped his hand on his top before bumping it with his own, looking up at Pete, smiling. "Aye Steve, Pete's a good lad," Steve reached up and put his hand on the side of Pete's face. "Good lad!" He smiled again then went back to his chips.

Pete had just finished his and tossed his rubbish into the trash when he heard 'Calella' mentioned in a tannoy announcement. Checking his watch, he stood up and nudged Steve. "Come on, big fella. Time to go."

An hour later they were once again exiting the Calella train station. Rather than heading through the town and risking running into Señor Stabby, they walked a little way beside the track and used the crossing to get over to the beach side, where they then headed down to the water's edge to take the more scenic route. Pete was surprised by the lack of people on the beach. He'd noticed it a few days ago too. The beach seemed to mainly be used by locals walking their dogs than by any of the tourist clientele. As they walked, Pete wondered if the coarse sand had anything to do with it as it was so rough that he was convinced if he checked Wikipedia for Calella, it would state that the town's economy relied entirely on its global export of building sand. He laughed to himself, Steve laughed too, despite not knowing why Pete was laughing. The laughter subsided and they walked in silence for a while before Pete tried to talk to Steve about his parents. "Tell me, big man, is your dad always..." He chose his words carefully. Steve looked up at him, pushing his glasses up his nose. "Is he always so strict?"

"He's always a bit stern" Replied Steve. "Aye Steve, someone should tell him to calm down."

Pete laughed, before continuing. "Your folks, do they get any money for you?" Steve looked blank. "Do you get money from anywhere, like benefits and stuff?"

"Ahh!" Steve nodded, realising what Pete meant. "My dad handles all that. Then he gives me my pocket money every week."

"Pocket money? Cool!" Pete nodded his approval.

"Yeah, I get twenty pounds every other week, Steve," he said proudly, "but I have to pay my dad petrol money when he takes me to the shops. That's five pounds a week, isn't it, Steve? Aye, Steve! A fiver! Yes, because adults pay their way, Steve!" He pushed his glasses up his nose.

"Wait!" Pete stopped and put his hand on Steve's shoulder. "Hang on a minute, mate. Let me get this straight in my head, here. You're telling me that your dad gives you twenty quid a week, and that's your 'pocket money'?"

"Aye," Steve nodded, smiling.

"But, to spend it you have to go to the shops, and your dad takes you?" Pete was absent-mindedly waggling his finger around as if illustrating some invisible point.

"Yep!" Steve responded, still smiling.

Pete continued: "And then because he's taken you to the shops, he charges you a fiver for petrol, and that?"

"Yep!" Steve pushed his glasses up his nose as they resumed walking.

"Un-bloody-believable!" Exclaimed Pete. "I mean, what a cheeky twat! Do you not think it's cheeky?"

"Noooo. Cars don't run on fresh air and friendship." Came Steve's reply. Pete suspected it was something his dad probably said to him to justify taking the money. Greedy little bastard!

They carried on walking along the beach in silence. Pete was pretty angry, not at Steve, obviously, but at his parents. They were obviously just keeping Steve around for the income, and he wasn't even getting the real benefit from it. What could he do, though? Up ahead, the footbridge was getting closer, and that meant they were also close to the town. "What shall we do, Steve?"

"What do you mean?" Steve asked, pushing his glasses up his nose again.

"Well," Pete looked at his phone, "it's only about half three. We can go back to the hotel if you'd like, or we can go and explore a bit."

Steve looked puzzled. "Explore, Steve?"

"Yes, I mean, we've had a good look around this bit" he motioned to his right and the old town, "but we've not had a look around that bit" he pointed beyond the footbridge.

"Aye," said Steve. "Shall we explore? Yes, Steve, that's a good idea, let's go explore" He pushed his glasses up his nose and smiled.

"Great stuff" Pete patted his back. "Let's go, then!" They headed off the beach towards the outlet and made their way up, under the bridges, and up to ground level where they branched off to the left. It didn't take them long to realise there was nothing there. Well, there were plenty of buildings, but they were mainly residential homes or hotels. They did find a big hospital with what appeared to be a large, Olympic sized open-air swimming pool to the rear, but there wasn't much else. Hotels and houses, and that was it. It was pretty quiet too. Not much in the way of traffic or people. Feeling the heat and a little exhausted, Pete sat on a kerb outside the hospital to rest for a moment, Steve joined him. Looking on his phone, Pete deduced that the road they were on would lead them right back to the main street, so he nudged Steve, and up they stood and off they went, mainly walking in silence with the odd spurt of conversation as they took turns to point things out to each other. This was the most chatty Pete had seen Steve and the most times he'd talked to him directly. "So!" he said as they trudged along, "Jo?"

"So, Jo!" Steve said, almost mimicking Pete, then he laughed.

"Don't get me wrong, I mean I'm no expert with women, and lord knows the events of yesterday proved that." Steve laughed. Pete continued, ignoring Steves laugh. "But it seems to me that Jo really likes you." Steve just laughed again. "Don't you like her?" Steve fell silent, and they walked on. "Tell me to mind my own business, Steve." Pete paused for a moment, not sure how to say what he wanted to say. "Look, mate, what I'm clumsily trying to say is, I haven't had much experience of people with." He nodded at Steve, still unsure of how to put it.

"Downs?" Steve offered.

"Yeah, Downs!" Pete responded. "I mean, have you ever had a girlfriend?" He thought for a moment. "Or a boyfriend? Is that it? Is that why you don't like her?" Steve put his head down, and they continued walking.

They'd only gone a few paces when Steve piped up. "I like Jo, Steve. She's kind and pretty and funny. Yes, Steve, I like her too." He'd dropped back to talking to himself instead of to Pete.

"Okay. That's great! She's great. So here's an idea, mate: why don't you ask her on a date?" He looked at Steve, who was just shaking his head as he walked. "Hear me out, big fella! We've only got a few days left here. I mean, I know I've shit the bed with Mel, but there's no reason why you can't get to know Jo a bit better." It occurred to Pete he was out of his depth right now. He had no idea what happened in this sort of situation, but he did know that everyone gets lonely. He had no idea what Steve's idea of having a girlfriend was, but what the hell! Everyone deserves a chance at love! Right? As they walked on, Pete asked "Why don't you ask her out, just down to the hotel bar when we get back? You could both have a drink and a dance." Steve started shaking his head again, only slightly, but the message was clear. Pete couldn't understand what the problem was. It's not like he hadn't already spoken to her or spend time with her, so it couldn't be shyness. Even though the sun was shining, Pete felt like a dark, sad cloud had slowly descended on them both, following them as they walked. Neither of them spoke for about ten minutes, as they just kept strolling along slowly. Every so often, Steve would push his glasses up his nose. Pete didn't know what else to do or say. He didn't want to push the whole dating thing as it was obviously a sore point, but he didn't want to just carry on and ignore Steve's sudden sadness. Out of the blue, Steve spoke.

"My dad says I'm not allowed," he said, solemnly

"Sorry, what?" Pete wasn't sure what he'd heard.

"My dad," Steve started again, "he says I shouldn't have a girlfriend because I'm 'a downie and downies aren't supposed to have girlfriends. He said we are too stupid and the last thing the world needs is a load of downies doin' it and having more idiot downie kids!"

"He actually called you a downie?" Pete asked, trying to contain his anger. Steve nodded, and Pete realised he was maybe focussing on the wrong part of that statement. "He said you're not allowed to have a girlfriend because you're… because you have downs?" Steve nodded again. "Wow!" Pete was dumbfounded. "Then he said all that about having kids, and that?" Steve nodded again. "Bugger me!" He said as he moved closer to Steve and put his arm around his shoulder, wishing he had given Steve's dad a piece of his mind earlier now. In fact, this latest revelation from Steve made him very determined to make sure that Steve's dad got a few choice words off of him next time he saw him. For now, he needed to put his anger aside and see what he could do to bolster Steve's confidence. He moved in front of Steve, causing him to stop and stand there, looking down at his feet. Pete began to talk: "Look, mate, I'm sorry to say this out loud, but someone has to tell you that your dad is a huge twat! I'm sorry, but it's true." Steve just kept looking down. Pete put his hands on Steve's shoulders "Look at me!" he said. Steve slowly raised his head and made eye contact with Pete, then he gave his glasses a quick push. "Mate, you aren't stupid. I mean, obviously, you're not likely to win The Chase anytime soon, unless there's a load of questions on Jim Bowen jokes." Steve's mouth gave a little twitch, the beginnings of a smile. "But you're not stupid at all. All those word searches you do, you need brains for them. Seriously! You're funny and kind too, just like Jo. Your dad hasn't got a Scooby or a Doo about you. I mean the *real* you!" Pete moved his face closer to Steve's and lowered his voice. "Look, mate, everyone, EVERYBODY deserves a chance at happiness; you, me, Jim Bowen!"

"Jim Bowen, he's, he's, he's dead," said Steve. He was smiling as he said it, which made Pete do a second take.

"Okay! That's my mistake, but you know what I mean. Why don't you ask her out for a drink, tonight?" Steve, still smiling, shook his head. Pete sighed. "Okay Steve, okay. Look, there's plenty of time to change your mind. Have a think about it, I mean, what is the worst that can happen?" He held out his fist, and Steve dutifully bumped it while simultaneously pushing his glasses up his nose with his other hand, and they resumed their journey. Steve stayed silent, but at least he was smiling now, and as they approached a corner in the road, they came across what looked like a bowling alley. Steve went for a closer look. "Do you like bowling?" Asked Pete. Steve nodded.

"I like crazy golf more though, Steve!" He said as he pointed to a large sign that showed people playing crazy golf. Pete looked at the sign and read out what it said in very bad Spanish "Golf loco: doce hoyos de diversión, hmmm." A quick check on his phone, and he repeated it in English "Crazy Golf: Twelve holes of fun! I knew a girl like that once." Steve gave him a blank look "never mind. You fancy a game?"

"Aye, Let's play golf, Steve!"

"Okay, then!" They went inside, and after a bit of back and forth with the desk clerk, they were heading through a door, each carrying a golf club and a ball. Blue for Pete and red for Steve. The got to the first hole, and Pete pulled a coin from his pocket. "Heads or tails?"

"Heads" Steve smiled.

"Heads!" Pete tossed the coin up in the air and let it land on the ground. "Aaaand heads it is. You can go first then." Steve gave a little air grab, and they moved to the first hole. The crazy golf course was quite busy. In fact, this was the most people he'd seen in one place doing something since he arrived. This meant they had to wait before they could tee off on the first hole. While they waited for their turn, Steve asked him loads of questions about how to play. In fact, he asked so many questions he prompted Pete to ask him if he'd actually ever played before. Steve nodded. "Are you sure? I mean, you're asking me an awful lot of questions for someone who, not long ago, told me he likes golf… I'm just saying." Steve smiled and pushed his glasses up his nose. He put his hand on his chin and grimaced before turning to Pete.

"So, the one who takes the most hits of the ball wins?" Pete, unsure if he was being wound up at this point, just laughed. Steve laughed too. "Is that not right?" If Steve was winding him up, Pete reckoned he had the best poker face he'd ever seen. With a sideways look Pete confirmed this was correct.

Still unsure if he was being wound up, Pete had an idea. "Tell you what, big fella, how about a wager?" Steve smiled but looked blankly at him. "A wager?" Still nothing. "A bet? How about a bet?" Pete saw the penny drop and Steve nodded his approval. "Great stuff! Okay, If I win, you have to ask Jo out for a date, and if you win… what do you want?"

Steve put his hand on his chin and looked skyward. Pete wasn't sure if he was doing this for comic effect or not. "If I win, we go see Camp Nou tomorrow." Pete stood and thought about it for a moment. He knew he was no Tiger Woods, but he reckoned it wouldn't be that hard to beat Steve, all things considered.

His assumption that Steve would be mediocre at any sporting activity simply because of his condition was his first mistake of the day. "Okay, if I win, you ask Jo out. If you win, I take you to Camp Nou!"

"Tomorrow!" Steve added.

"Tomorrow!" Pete agreed. He held out his hand to shake on it, and Steve grabbed it, laughing. That wager was his second and most costly mistake. The first hole was more or less a straight line to the hole, and so Pete just put it down to beginners luck when Steve hit it straight in on his first shot. As the ball dropped into the hole, Steve half lunged and did another comical air grab. "Okay, big fella, don't be getting cocky there, now!" He marked the scorecard for Steve then passed the card and pencil to over to him so he could take his shot. After one long shot and three putts, he finally sank the ball.

"Not a good start, Steve!" Said Steve, pinching Pete's cheek. Throughout the next ten holes, Steve taught Pete a valuable lesson in humility. He sank the ball on average, in two shots. The eleventh hole was a bit tricky as it went around a very snakey 'S' bend and then through a little tunnel. Although Steve had taken a lot of time planning his trajectory, he hadn't factored in the slight rise near the tunnel, and so his first shot fell short, much to Pete's elation.

"Yes, yes! Haha, in your face!" he shouted as he danced round Steve, wildly pointing at him. Several people looked up from their game to see this crazy Irish guy taking the piss out of a poor down syndrome lad for missing a shot. Pete could feel the judgement and, in his peripheral vision, he could see people shaking heads. He patted Steve's back. "Just joking, big fella, take your shot now, go on." He pointed down the course to the tunnel, It took Steve five shots to sink the ball on this hole, Pete had gotten to nine before he finally sank it. Again, they had to stand and wait for the players at the next hole to take their shots. Pete looked at the scorecard and winced, looking up from the tragedy just as Steve was taking his shot. The hole was on a small hump and at the end of one of three possible tunnels. There was no way Steve would get this in, surely? In fact, Pete was hoping he might be able to pull it back here if Steve took enough shots. The next thing he knew, Steve was hoisting the club aloft in both his hands and sinking to his knees. "You've got to be kidding me!" Of course, the number of shots it took Pete to sink the ball ran into double digits. When he missed the hole for the third time, he shouted "SHIT!" very loudly. When he missed it for the fifth time, he threw the club at the ground in a fit of pique. When he finally managed to sink the ball, he let out another loud exclamation: "Thank Christ!" Steve gave him a round of applause, and Pete just shook his head. People were still giving him sideways glances, and he could still feel their judgement. Pete was gutted he'd lost, not because he now had to take Steve to Camp Nous, although he didn't yet realise just how expensive that was going to be. No, he was gutted because he wanted to get Steve and Jo on a little date together. He had it all planned out in his head. "Ah well" he thought. As they walked back to hand their clubs in, he asked: "Steve, tell me... have you played this game before?" Steve smiled and nodded. "If this were a film, this would be the part where I find out you are like, the super talented progeny of Shooter McGavin or something." Steve grinned at this. " You've proper had my pants down there, haven't you?"

Steve laughed and started doing a clumsy dance singing "Camp Nou, Camp Nou, I'm coming for you" before laughing heartily.

"Fair play, a deal is a deal, so it's Camp Nou tomorrow." Steve clapped his hands, then gave Pete a big hug. Pete looked around, then broke the hug. "Okay, okay. Knock it off. People will think we're on a date!" Steve laughed again and started singing 'get me to the church on time'. They both started laughing as they left the leisure centre.

On the way back to the hotel, they made what was becoming a regular stop at McDonald's to get something to eat. Pete paid, of course, and while they sat and ate they talked about the game and how Steve was some sort of golf savant. There was a lot of mutual laughter, and for the first time since his marriage break up, despite the shit show of the previous day, Pete realised he was actually happy. It wasn't some little peak before a deep trough, he was genuinely in a happy place. He realised he hadn't really thought about Gemma for a few days and, despite the absolute horror show of the previous night, he was genuinely happy. Okay, that's maybe a stretch. He wasn't precisely delirious with happiness, but he wasn't unhappy. Yes, he regretted everything that had gone on with Mel, but he wasn't devastated. Now, you might think that this is a sign that he wasn't really that much into her — au contraire! He was mad about her. Still, he was angry at himself for messing it up, but he wasn't convinced it was all over before it had even begun and he would cross that bridge after he'd sufficiently mended the bridge with Steve. As for Gemma: Gemma who? Two weeks ago, he felt like his heart had been ripped out, but now, two weeks later, it was all like a distant memory of a bad dream. Right there, in the hot Spanish summer sun, he could honestly say he was over her. Even if, heavens forbid, he didn't manage an eleventh-hour reprieve with Mel, he was okay with how his life was going. "In fact," he thought, "this is going to be the bookend to the last ten years of my life. When I get back, it's going to be a brand new chapter. No! A brand new story!"

Feeling more positive than he had in weeks, he looked across at Steve, and he couldn't help but feel some sort of bond between them. Unbeknownst to Pete, Steve felt attached to Pete too. Despite the bit where Pete had shouted at him the previous night, this had been, by far, without doubt, the best holiday he'd ever had. Ever! Pete broke the silence and the spell. "So, about Jo!" Steve looked up, munching on a chicken McNugget."Is that it? Are you still not going to ask her out now? Even though I lost the bet?"

Steve finished chewing and took a sip of his drink. "A bet is a bet, Steve!" giving Pete a wink.

"Yeah, I know that. I just thought, maybe… you know, you could still maybe ask her on a date… even if it is just for a few cokes in the bar."

"Noooo!" Steve popped another nugget in his mouth.

"But you do like her, though?" Pete asked.

"Yes, Steve," he replied between chews.

"But you don't want to see if she likes you too?" Pete kept pushing.

"My dad said it's wrong." He had a look of sadness on his face that nearly broke Pete's heart. He didn't want to see his new friend so sad, but he knew he couldn't push it any further.

"Okay. That is a shame. I truly think Jo really likes you and I think every golf legend should have a beautiful girl to share his life!" Pete ducked as Steve tossed a crumpled napkin at him and they both laughed.

After they left the restaurant, they had a walk back down to the beach as Steve said he fancied a paddle in the sea. Pete had nothing else to do, so he agreed to accompany him. They made their way down to the water's edge and kicked off their shoes, as they weren't planning on going swimming or anything, Just a paddle. Pete emptied his pockets and put his stuff in one of his shoes, for safety. Steve watched Pete do this and did the same, using his shoe exactly like Pete had, despite having his backpack there. The sand down by the water was just as coarse as everywhere else, even under the water, it felt rough.

Back home, Pete and Gemma had often gone for walks on the beach as they only lived about thirty minutes from the coast. When they first got married, they'd had a dog. Gemma's family dog, in fact, that she couldn't bear to be apart from, or so she always said. It was a daft old Labrador that was old even when Pete met him. Deefer was his name, and he liked the beach, particularly when he found big puddles to roll in. He'd deteriorated quite quickly in their second year of marriage and had to be put to sleep. Pete remembered those walks fondly, though. In particular, he remembered all the *treasure* he would find on the beach. Odd looking pebbles, bits of shells, even sea glass. He looked around on the beach they were on as Steve noisily made his way into the water, but he was both surprised and dismayed to see absolutely nothing. No shells, no rocks, definitely no sea glass. Just that horribly coarse sand. He gave up looking pretty quickly and paddled in after Steve. The water was quite cold on his skin at first, but after a while, his feet acclimatised, and it actually felt quite warm. After an hour of messing about and trying to splash each other, they decided it was time to head back to the hotel. "We really should think about getting an early night as we have a big day ahead of us tomorrow." Pete said. Steve nodded, and Pete continued: "I mean, we need a good early start if we are going to go camping…"

Steve, who had just pulled his sandals back on, stood up and pinched Pete's cheek playfully. "Ah, Camp Nous, not camping! Silly!" Steve said, as he gave Pete another pinch and a wink. Pete laughed as they set off back for the hotel, talking about what Camp Nou might actually look like when they got there, and before long they were back at the hotel and stood outside their respective doors.

Pete opened his door with his key as Steve did the same, they both turned to face each other and Pete spoke: "Right, buddy. I'll give you a knock early doors in the morning, say about eight?" Steve nodded and repeated the time. "Good, good! Right, get some sleep, and hey!" Steve looked up at him "Thanks for all the fun today. I'm glad we're mates again."

Steve gave him a big smile and then a big hug before entering his room, singing "get me to Camp Nou on time," followed by hearty laughter as he closed his door. Pete laughed too, as he entered his own room. Kicking his shoes off and laying down on the bed, his thoughts quickly turning to Steve and how the poor lad was maybe missing out in his reluctance to ask Jo out, he clearly liked her.

"Sod it!" Pete jumped up and put his shoes back on before heading out of his room for the elevator. Down in the lobby, he was relieved to see Dave on the front desk. "Dave!"

Dave, who was sat down, reading an old copy of an English newspaper, looked up and smiled. "Pete! What's the crack?"

"Dave, I need a favour."

"Sure, man, fire away!"

"I need to know what room Mel is in."

Dave winced "Ooof! I can't help you there, mate. You know how it is. It's more than my job is worth to be divulging the personal details of other guests." He had scooted over to the desk as he talked and he began typing on the old, 'Windows 98' looking desktop situated there.

Pete looked on in dismay. "Really?"

"Oh, absolutely! It's a pretty serious thing." He winked at Pete. "I mean, If I were to tell you that a guest you were trying to contact was in room 389, I'd be fired for sure!"

"Shit!" Said Pete before he realised what Dave had just said. "Yes, yes! That would be a shame. I certainly wouldn't want you to be fired on my account, I'm sorry to have even asked you, and I will bid you, goodnight sir!" He held out his hand, and Dave shook it, winking again as he did so.

Pete ran back to the lift as Dave sat back in his chair and opened another old newspaper, raising his feet up to rest on the reception desk. "I am a generous God!" he said out loud to no one in particular.

Pete took the lift up to the third floor and was soon in front of room 389. He raised his right hand to knock, then pulled it away, clasping it in his left hand. He took a few deep breaths. "Sod it! No guts, no glory!" He knocked and from within the room he heard Jo's familiar squeal of excitement followed by a brief flurry of footsteps before the door opened. Jo poked her head around the door, holding it open only a little way.

"Pete!" She exclaimed excitedly. Before Pete had a chance to ask for Mel, Jo was already calling her. "Mel, It's Pete. Come see." She turned back to Pete. "We're getting ready to go down to the disco. Do you like discos?"

Pete was caught off guard. "Well, I, yes, I guess."

Jo clapped her hands. "Cool! You should bring Steve down, and we can all have a dance. You and Mel can come and get down with Downs!" She laughed hard but was startled by Mel who suddenly appeared behind her.

"Go get ready, Jo," she said, sternly.

"Oh! I was talking to Pete, though!"

Mel smiled and gave her a playful tap on the end of her nose with her index finger, "Go on, silly, or we'll miss the disco!" Jo sighed and disappeared from the doorway. Pete took a deep breath and was about to speak when Mel just shut the door.

"Bloody hell!" he murmured. He knocked again. From inside the room, he heard Mel tell Jo to ignore it and what sounded like sounds of dismay from Jo. He knocked again.

This time the door opened in a quick angry motion. It stayed open just long enough for Mel to spit a quiet but firm "Get lost" at him, then it was closed again. Pete considered knocking again but thought better of it.

"Right, well… I'll be off then. Good talk!" He went back to his room and laid out on the bed again, thinking about what he could do next. A plan formed, and he again got up and headed out, this time he was heading back down to reception. The sight of Dave, still reclining with his feet up on reception, made him breathe a small sigh of relief. Just as he approached the desk, some new guests arrived, and Dave sprang into action, checking them in. There were only three couples, but Pete still ended up having to wait for about thirty minutes, not wanting to interrupt him or talk about his plan in front of the other guests.

Finally, Dave waved off the last couple to their room. "Hey, back again so soon?" he greeted Pete with a smile.

"Dave, I know I hardly know you and in the scheme of things you have no reason to do this, but I really need your help!"

Dave leaned across the desk, looked left, then right and then said, "Diiiiiiiamond Dave, at your service! Tell me more, mi amigo! How can I assist a fine upstanding gentleman like yourself?"

Chapter Seven: Nou Thing!

0800

Saturday

When Pete knocked on Steve's door, he opened it like he was stood waiting on the other side, which of course, he was. Steve could hardly contain his excitement, in fact. He was smiling from ear to ear as they went down to the breakfast room, and Pete had to keep reminding Steve to eat because he was so excited that he just kept singing his Camp Nou song and spouting random facts about the place. Before they'd even set off, Pete knew it was completed in 1957, had a seating capacity of nearly one hundred thousand but had hit a record capacity of one hundred and twenty-thousand back in the mid-eighties and had undergone several renovations over the last thirty years. Pete had anticipated it being busy as it was a Saturday, so he had pre-booked tickets online. Wanting to give Steve a trip to remember, Pete bought the 'Tour Plus' tickets that also boasted a VR experience and he felt sure this would be a winner with Steve. The poor boy was almost popping with excitement now, and they hadn't even left.

The journey over was pretty mundane. They got drinks for the trip (no OJ for Steve), and took the usual walk through the town. With great ease, they got on the train to Barcelona, sitting back to admire the scenery. In a welcome break from the usual train monotony, some buskers boarded the train at Sant Pol De Mar, and a pretty Spanish girl sang some Spanish folk song. The girl had musical accompaniment from a backing track pumping through what appeared to be a battery operated karaoke machine on wheels, while a similarly pretty companion went up and down the carriage holding out a tin for donations. Pete gave them all his change, knowing it would be no good to him in a few days. The girls, having exhausted all revenue streams in Pete's carriage, moved on to the next carriage. They must have stayed on the train past the next stop as Pete saw them later, stood on the platform at Arenas De Mar.

When they finally reached Barcelona, Pete was also well prepared. He had programmed the route into the map app on his phone, and he knew it was only a couple of kilometres away from the main station. They stopped for a quick coffee at a little cafe in the train station. After a couple of refreshing coffees and more macaroons than Pete cared to admit to eating, they were ready to set off on their grand adventure. Barcelona itself had a wonderful atmosphere, thought Pete. People seemed really friendly, and he was amazed at how clean it was. Much like Calella, and the trains, Barcelona was spotless. There was no littler, no dog poop, not even any discarded cigarette butts. Pete knew streets back home, where all three of these things could be found in abundance. He was also amazed at the number of flags everywhere. They were hanging from lampposts, they were hanging in shop windows, they were hanging from just about every upper floor window and balcony on every street. Walking at a steady pace so as not to get too tired in the balmy heat, it took them about an hour to reach their destination. They were chatting away about nothing in particular when they turned a corner, and it came into view, at which point Steve let out a triumphant roar and did a double air grab. Pete smiled and put one arm around his shoulders, giving him a little squeeze. They made their way right up to the stadium and joined the queue to get in. As Pete had already bought his tickets, they were able to join the priority queue, which was moving down pretty quickly.

Once through the gates, they had a long walk along a covered walkway to get into the ground itself. Again, there were two queues. One was for people who wanted a photo, the other was to bypass this and get straight into the grounds and start the tour properly. Steve had already joined the non-photo queue. He stood in line for a few minutes before turning to ask Pete something. When he turned and saw Pete was stood in the photo queue, waving for him to come to join him, his face lit up, and Pete thought his head was going to pop, such was the look of excitement on his face. Their turn in the booth came round, and he and Pete had to stand in front of a green screen and pretend they were celebrating a goal or kicking a ball. Three shots were taken, and Pete was handed a ticket that he could redeem later in the gift shop. He waved it at Steve and gave him a wink before putting it safely in his wallet.

Pretty soon they left the walkway, and they were free to wander around the outer grounds before entering the actual ground and starting the tour properly. There wasn't much to see outside the ground except a couple of statues and a large seating area near a food and drinks outlet shaped, bizarrely, like an alpine cabin. The boys decided to have a rest after all the walking, so they sat down in the bar area and ordered a quick drink before they went in and started the main event. Half an hour later, after a brief toilet stop, they were finally entering the stadium for real.

Once inside, Pete handed over his phone, so the desk clerk could verify his E-tickets. After that was done, they were then both given a wristband that singled them out as Tour Plus visitors, and they were given special VR headsets before being directed to a holding area. After about ten minutes, when enough people had arrived for their group to start the tour, a guide appeared and explained how the tour would work. They would go through a specific route and see everything from the boardroom to the changing rooms to the trophy room to the pitch itself, and everything in between. There would be many photo opportunities and photos were encouraged throughout the tour, and they were advised that they would be directed when to use the VR headsets.

For Pete, who had no prior interest or knowledge of football, this was all quite an eye-opener, he certainly hadn't anticipated this level of detail. Once they started, he actually found some of the tour really interesting. They first went right up to the top of the stadium to see the press boxes. Tiny little individual cubicles where pundits could observe and narrate the games below from a proverbial 'eagle's perch'. Then, they saw the press briefing room where many a press conference had been held. This wasn't some old hall where chairs where laid out when needed, this was a bespoke facility with fitted seats, a beautiful podium and desk complete with what appeared to be built-in mics and some sort of wall mounted media centre. After that, they saw the trophy room and, even to Pete, that was mind-blowing. The trophy room was as opulent as it was dramatic. It was arranged in such a fashion to serve as a curated history of the club, with photos, trophies and artefacts dating back to the club's inception in 1899. The whole place was lit in a very understated and atmospheric way, and Pete wondered whether this was for effect or if it was for more practical purposes, such as preserving the integrity of some of the items. There were interactive displays, there were big cardboard standees of players for photo ops and, of course, there were the VR segments. These were really well done and enhanced the tour greatly. A large chunk of the VR stuff was more 'augmented reality' than virtual reality, giving greater life and depth to some parts of the tour - like seeing a press conference live in the press room, or seeing snippets of archive footage for each trophy. They even had the players cavorting round in the changing room with just towels on. He wasn't so bothered about it, but he did hear some of the women — and men — gasp when Suarez and Boateng climbed down into the jacuzzi. One thing that did strike Pete as odd was the inclusion of a well known branded refrigerator display right in the middle of the changing room. "Go figure!" he thought out loud. Steve meanwhile was like the proverbial kid in a candy store. He was like Charlie touring Wonka's chocolate factory, like... you get the picture, I'm sure. He had pulled his little Lumix compact out of his backpack and had been going nuts! Pete stood back and let him get on with it, occasionally taking the camera from him to get pictures of Steve with various things along the way. Pete was pretty impressed with the camera, not that he had a clue about them. Pete asked Steve where he'd got it from, pretty certain his dad hadn't got it for him.

"It was a Christmas present from my uncle a few years ago. He made me promise to hide it from dad, so he didn't take it off me." Steve answered. He had taken it out pretty much as soon as they started the tour and he had not stopped taking pictures since. Every now and then he'd thrust it into Pete's hand, and Pete would take a photo of Steve with whatever he was posing next to. Of all the parts of the tour, though, the coolest part was probably getting pitch side. They got to walk out of the player's tunnel and sit in the team's dugout. The area they were in was enclosed, and the guide called the tour plus visitors over to one end.

"Okay so, because you have selected the Tour Plus option, you get an extra benefit. I would advise that you make sure you put your headsets on while," he reached behind him and opened one of the enclosure fences that turned out to be a gate, "you have a wander out on the pitch!" The rest of the visitors clapped. Pete turned to get Steve's reaction, only to find he was the first one out of the gate and already on the pitch. Before Pete could join him, he was off and running around like a loon, pretending he was scoring goals and pulling his shirt up over his head in celebration. Pete still had the camera from when Steve had insisted Pete get a shot of him sitting in Messi's pitch-side chair. He quickly took a couple of shots of Steve as he played make-believe on the pitch before calling out to him and motioning to put his headset on. Steve stopped and obliged, his antics on the pitch changed gear as he began to relive great goals scored in the stadium. Steve was in his element.

As with all good things, the time came for the tour to end and they headed to the endpoint to hand in their headsets and check out the gift shop. As they entered, they were asked for their photo ticket and directed to a booth to redeem it. When they got there, Steve looked sad. "What's up, big man?" Pete asked.

"It's thirty euros for the photos."

"And?"

"I only have ten. I have another twenty, but it's for"

"Yeah, yeah, it's for emergencies," interrupted Pete. "I know, I know. Listen, look at me!" Steve raised his eyes to meet Pete's. "Have you had a good time?" Steve nodded. "Good! Now tell me, on a scale of one to ten then, how good has this been?"

Steve did that whole comedy hand on chin thing again. "A ten, maybe a hundred and ten!" He grinned.

"Right answer! There you go, you've won our top prize: a free photo and a tour program! Let's give him a round of applause, ladies and Gentlemen." Pete made his best attempt at a Jim Bowen impersonation. He wasn't old enough to have watched the show when it first aired, but he had watched quite a few episodes on the Challenge channel. Looking over at the clerk, Pete smiled and nodded, the clerk reached back on the shelf behind him after checking the number on the ticket and grabbed one of the hardback tour books and placed it in a unique FC Barcelona carrier bag. Steve hugged Pete so hard and fast he nearly fell over. "Whoa there, Nelly!" Pete laughed.

Outside, They took a few last minute photos and then they set off back to the train station. It didn't seem to take long, mainly because Steve was walking on air for most of the journey down. In fact, Steve was so happy it was coming off him in waves, like some happy microwaves. Pete couldn't help but smile every time he looked at him. They stopped for a drink along the way, mainly to rest as he didn't want Steve overheating. He also wanted to make sure they took as many toilet breaks as needed... just in case. As they walked, Steve didn't shut up about the stadium, holding his bag aloft and making crowd noises, even when they were on the train heading back to Calella. Pete checked his watch and was surprised to find was only half past two. They'd be back in plenty of time for phase two of 'Operation: Steve's Best Day'. Steve was carefully flicking through the pages of his souvenir program, chatting away to himself. Pete lay back in his seat and closed his eyes. "Wake me when we get back," he said to Steve, before dozing off.

Back in Calella, after leaving the station, Pete and Steve took the less scenic route back. There was a method to Pete's madness though, he wanted to get Steve a nice shirt to wear, so they went through the town instead of down by the beach. Firstly, they got something to eat in a cute little bistro facing the beach or at least facing the beach over the railway tracks. Both of them had a Spanish Omelette followed by some ice cream before they headed on their way. Using the subterfuge of wanting a new shirt for himself, Pete dragged Steve into a few clothes shops where they perused shirts and other tops. When Pete finally found a shirt he thought suited Steve (and one that he liked for himself, too) he got Steve to try one on along with him to check the size. Eventually, he found the perfect shirt. Plain and white with a grandad collar. Keeping his plan secret meant Pete had to buy two shirts, but he figured if his plan were successful, it would be worth it. Outside the shop, Pete checked the time. It was five — only a couple of hours before showtime! "Come on, Steve. Let's get back. We can get changed then see what's to do in the hotel."

Steve grinned "Aye, hit the town like a couple of swells, Steve!" He laughed. They got to the hotel just as a bus was picking up guests to take them to the airport and so the foyer was quite busy. Pete saw Dave was on the desk again and gave him a wave. Dave waved and gave him a thumbs up. That was the signal that everything was good to go. Pete pointed to his wrist as if to confirm the time and Dave responded by holding up eight fingers. Eight pm thought Pete. Good, good!

Outside their rooms, Pete turned to Steve, "Right mate. I've an idea." Steve smiled and asked what it was. "Well, let's go back to the room, and we can grab a shower." Steve gave him a puzzled look. "Not together, you goon!" Steve laughed. "We can get a shower and make ourselves look nice then we can come down and see what the crack is. We haven't really spent any time in the hotel bar. They had a band on the other night, so maybe they'll have some entertainment on tonight as well. We can maybe come down and have a bit of a dance and that. How does that sound?"

Steve pushed his glasses up his nose and said, "That sounds like a plan, Steve."

"Great stuff," said Pete. "I'll see you at about a quarter to eight, okay?" Steve nodded then gave Pete another hug then they both bid each other adieu and headed inside their respective rooms.

At seven forty-five sharp, Pete opened his door to find Steve stood there, already waiting for him. He had put his new shirt on and had left his hat in his room, opting for a side parting. From the waist up, Steve looked like a different person almost, from the waist down, he was still wearing his usual shorts and sandals. Pete gave him the once over and was a bit surprised at first as he'd not seen Steve without his hat on, that he could recall.

"Wow!" he exclaimed. "Excuse me, sir…I'm looking for Steve, have you seen him?"

Steve laughed "it's me you goon," they both laughed, and Steve hugged Pete again.

"Right" Pete urged, looking at the time, "let's get a crack on!" They headed to the lift and Steve pressed the button for the lobby. Pete had already made some arrangements with Dave, giving him rough timings for everything, and so far, things were running right on schedule. They got down to the lobby, and Dave came straight over. "Are we set?" asked Pete.

"You betcha!" came the reply. "I got flowers too, like you asked."

"Damn! I completely forgot about the flowers. Shit! How much do I owe you?"

Dave laughed, "Don't be daft, man. I'm always happy to help loves young dream. Besides, they cost me nothing, let's just say the hotel had a surplus this week." He gave Pete a wink.

"You are an absolute star. I really do owe you, mate." Said Pete as he reached out and touched Dave's elbow. "What about… you know who?"

Dave leaned in and whispered, "She's already out there. I had to tell them they'd won a competition for a free VIP experience. They are just having drinks right now."

Pete smiled, "You are worth your weight in gold, my friend." He turned to Steve. "Right, let's go." Pete paused as a thought crossed his mind. Mel! He needed to get her out of the picture. He turned to Dave again: "When we head out, can you get Mel in with a fake call or something?"

Dave nodded "Yeah, no problem. Look, the only place I could do it was out back under your rooms."

Pete looked concerned "Where? I mean, I know where you mean, I just don't understand where you would do it."

Dave laughed again "Unless you've been out there, you wouldn't know it, but directly below you there's a small grassy patio…Kind of a patio, more like a small paddock

175

or tiny, fenced lawn. It used to be a kid's playground. Kids would go out and play while mum and dad got pissed in the bar. Then Maddie McCann went missing, and parents wouldn't let their kids play on their own anymore, and they didn't want to be all that way away from the bar, and so it never got used. Then two years ago someone pinched all the equipment, and so Manuel just had it grassed over. It's surprisingly nice and peaceful down there, trust me." He gave Pete another wink."Right! Are we ready?"

"Yes, just give me a minute." Pete turned to Steve, who had been watching the exchange between the two men. He pushed his glasses up his nose. "Right buddy, I have another surprise for you. Now, I know you won the bet, and so you didn't have to ask Jo out." Steve nodded. "Well, I kind of took the pressure off and asked her for you." Steve looked a bit worried. "No, no, no! Don't panic." Pete put his hands on Steve's shoulders and leaned in close "In a moment, I'm going to take you outside to sit and have a special romantic dinner with her. All you have to do is go out and be your charming, loveable, happy self. If you need me, I'll be right here inside, and I won't go anywhere, I promise. Just do one thing for me: if you like her, tell her before the evening is through. Can you do that for me?"

Steve looked down at the floor. "I'm not supposed to have girlfriends, my dad said!"

"Look, mate. No offence, but your dad is a huge twat, and he has no business telling you that. We are all allowed to be happy: you, me, Jo" Steve pointed to Dave. "Yes, Dave too, all of us are. Now, I don't know much, but I know the girls are going home next week and you might not see Jo again unless you tell her how much you like her. Maybe you're meant to be together, maybe not, but there's only one way to find out, and if you don't go out there and tell her, you'll regret it. Maybe not today, maybe not tomorrow, but you will regret it someday. So, what do you say?"

Steve looked at Dave, who nodded at him, then he looked back at Steve, before looking back down at the floor. He looked down for a few more moments before raising his head slowly. He looked at Pete and pushed his glasses up his nose. "What do I say, Steve? I say, I, I, I say let's do it!" It was Pete's turn to air grab.

"Right, Come on." He motioned for Steve to follow him and he gave Dave the signal to go ahead. Dave passed him a small but perfect bouquet of flowers and headed outside. "I won't be a minute."

While Dave got ready to begin his mission, Pete gave Steve a final once over. "Right, let's have a look at you." He looked him up and down and gave him the thumbs up. "You can do this, big fella! Time to light the fires and kick the tyres." Steve gave him a smile and nodded, Pete signalled to Dave, Dave turned and waved to Alejandro, letting him know he was going to be indisposed for the next few hours. Alejandro gave him a nod. Dave gave a quick wink to Pete before he headed out to the 'Executive Patio' as he was now calling it. Pete put his hand on Steve's shoulder while Dave went and told Mel about her nonexistent phone call. They stood there for what seemed like an age, Steve just waiting for Pete to tell him what was happening and Pete waiting for Dave to come back in with Mel. He was just about to peek through the little glass porthole in the door when the door burst open with Mel in full flow.

"I just don't understand why anyone would be calling me at the hotel is all! There's no need to be snippy." As Mel continued to berate Dave, Dave just looked at Pete, not really sure what he was supposed to do next. Pete dived in.

"Mel!"

She span around, venom in her eyes."What the hell, Pete? Please don't tell me you sent this idiot outside to do your work for you?"

Pete put his mouth close to Steve's ear. "Right, big fella, you're up! Off you go, and remember, just be yourself." Then he motioned for Steve to go outside and join Jo. He turned back to Mel. "Mel, I"

"Seriously, Pete, what in the hell is going on?" She cut him off. "Not content with being a complete twat, are you now trying to kidnap my, my" she struggled for the word, what was Jo, exactly?

"Ward?" offered Dave.

"Yes, thanks. My *ward,*" she nodded at Dave. Pete gave him a little shove and motioned outside.

"Oh! Right, yeah!" Dave went out to offer drinks and present them with their choice of fine dining for the evening. Mel watched him head out the door, the confusion visible on her face.

"Mel, please, I can explain everything. Just calm down a mo." Pete had put his hands together as if praying to some unknown deity for mercy. "Please! I can explain all of it if you just give me ten minutes." Mel turned her full attention to Pete. She folded her arms and took a deep breath, in and out, through her nose. After a pause, she went over to the door and cupped her hands up to her eyes on the glass so she could see outside better. Happy that all was well out there, she turned back to Pete who said: "please" one more time.

"Ten minutes?" Pete nodded. "Okay, this better be good."

Outside, Dave had taken the drinks orders from his special guests. He'd worked all afternoon to make the seldom-used play area look presentable. This had entailed a lot of litter picking, a lot of scrubbing of patio tables (and chairs) and finally, a lot of messing around with the strings of lights. The lights were possibly the worst part of all this as Dave reckoned they hadn't been used since the Conquistadors had set sail. He'd managed to pull it all together nicely though. He'd even managed to hook up the old mounted speakers to the hotel PA and was currently channelling Imagine Dragons through it as, apparently, they were Jo's current favourites. He looked around and marvelled at what he'd achieved at such short notice. Earlier that day, he'd caught up with Mel and Jo as they headed into town. Under Pete's direction, he had told them they'd won a special hotel draw, and the prize was a candlelit dinner for two on the 'executive patio'. Mel, although sceptical, had agreed that they would be there at the specified time.

Jo had wanted to get dressed up and so was looking quite swish when Steve walked out to surprise her. She had squealed with delight when she saw him. "This is just like in a movie!" she exclaimed.

Steve grinned and nodded before walking round to where she was sitting and handing her the flowers that Pete had given him. "These are for you," he said as he handed them to her. She immediately squealed again, jumped up and gave Steve a massive hug.

"No one has ever given me flowers before" She grinned. "Oh!" her smile turned to a frown, "I haven't got you anything though."

"That's okay, isn't it, Steve? Aye, Steve! A gentleman doesn't give to receive!" Steve said, then he laughed. "That's a Jim Bowen joke," he told Jo. They both sat down, and Dave appeared, ready to take their drinks order. They both ordered diet cokes, and he dutifully scribbled it in his pad.

"If I can also turn your attention to our specials menu, sir... Madam." He held up a chalkboard with a couple of options written on. He wasn't sure what either of them liked, and Pete hadn't thought that far ahead, so he'd put down a couple of staples that he knew were pre-prepped in the kitchen and hoped for the best. Steve and Jo both opted for chicken nuggets, chips, and beans. Dave let out an almost inaudible "Thank you" as he grabbed the board under his arm and headed out for their drinks. He opened the door and headed inside just as he heard Jo squeal again and start chatting ten to the dozen.

Inside, things weren't going quite as well. Pete had persuaded Mel to listen to him, and they'd sat at a table right near the door - Dave had thought of everything. There was even a jug with iced water on the table and a couple of glasses. Pete offered to pour one for Mel, she just gave him a death stare. "Okay, well I'm having one," and he poured himself a glass, taking a big gulp of water before he started his 'mea culpa.' "First of all," he pointed over his shoulder at the doors to the patio, "that is just my attempt at pulling some karma back and spreading a little happiness in the world, rightly or wrongly," he could see Mel gearing up for another round of shouting. "Look, before you kick off, hear me out." She stayed silent, and Pete continued. "Steve has a shit life, I think. Yeah, I know, I've only known him since last Tuesday, but I've seen and heard a lot. For instance, did you know his parents are actually here?" Mel's face softened a bit as confusion washed over it again.

"Here in the hotel?"

Pete laughed "Here in the hotel? Good one! No, they're nowhere in the hotel. In fact, they're not even in Calella!"

"I don't understand!" Said Mel.

"His mam and dad are actually staying in a hotel not far from the Arc De Triomf!" He saw her looking more confused. "You know. The Arc De Triomf!" He pointed in the direction he thought the monument might be. "Over in Barcelona," he added, just in case he wasn't clear.

"I know where it is, Pete!" She snapped. "I just don't get it. Why would they book a hotel all that way away from Steve?"

"Well, I can shed some light on that for you. You see, basically, from what I can gather they have this huge problem," Pete offered.

"Which is?"

"Well, they don't like having Steve around on account of they are both a pair of massive bastards!"

Mel looked more perplexed as Pete went on. "I don't get it though, they could at least have had him in the same hotel."

"Aye, well you'd have thought that wouldn't you, but like I said." She looked at him "Massive." Then he paused for effect before adding: "Bastards!" He nodded knowingly as he said that last part and he was surprised when she actually, albeit briefly, laughed at this.

Her mirth turned back to anger, though. "How do I know this is true? How do you know it's true?" She asked.

"When we were flying out, before I actually met Steve, I was minding my own business in the departure lounge at the airport, when I heard this fella talking to some guy. That guy turned out to be Steve and, as I now know for sure, the guy who was talking to him was, *is* his dad. I heard him tell Steve where he needed to get off the bus." Mel poured her self a drink of water, taking a sip as Pete continued: "I heard him tell Steve where he and the missus —Steve's mum — are staying." Mel took another sip. He could see she was weighing up what he was telling her and he would swear it looked like her face was softening a little. "Yesterday, after you," Mel looked right into his eyes, "when I…when *we* fell out, Steve disappeared. You remember I was looking for him everywhere? Well, it turns out I knew exactly where to find him - Hotel Rec! Right where his dad said he was staying. I headed out there to try and catch up and apologise, and I actually heard him, his dad, talking to Steve." It was Pete's turn to take a drink. He drained his glass and reached for the jug, pouring himself another one. "I mean, he was speaking to Steve like he's a bloody idiot. Seriously! I mean I know he's…"

Mel cocked her head. "He's what, exactly?"

Pete could sense that she was like a coiled cobra, ready to strike. "He's…well, he's special, obviously. Y'know, what with the extra chromosome and everything, but that boy is no idiot. He's kind, and he's sweet, and he's funnier than he realises." Mel still didn't look convinced. "Look, he makes me laugh, and I mean I laugh *with* him, not at him. He's got some magic powers too." Mel laughed at this. "I swear he gets you in one of those bear hugs of his and he melts your heart, you know? You find yourself wanting more, like he's dishing out some sort of *huggy heroin* or something!" Mel laughed again this time it was a real deep and genuine laugh. It was that laugh she had that worked a kind of magic of its own. It made her face light up and warmed the hearts of those who were worthy enough to hear it.

"That hug is some really serious shit, mind," she agreed. They both laughed this time.

Pete continued: "Seriously, though," he didn't want to kill the mood, but he knew he had to make this count. "He was left here with no friends, and all he has with him is his backpack with his word searches and some sketchbooks and twenty euros, which he's only allowed to use in emergencies."

"So how has he been able to eat and get drinks off-site? What about his clothes and everything else?" Mel looked shocked.

"How do you think he's been able to do all that?"

Mel paused thoughtfully for a moment, "You, it was you!" She said, her tone belied her incredulity. "It was you who paid for it all?"

Pete raised his eyebrows and smiled a tightlipped smile, nodding his confirmation. "You can scoff all you want but what was I supposed to do? Look, I know I screwed up, but I'm not a bad person, I just made some stupid decisions is all. I'd have made sure Steve was okay, even if we'd not met you guys. I was already out with him the first day we met." Mel looked down at her feet for a few minutes before reaching out for the water jug again. "Hang on!" Pete stopped her. "Let me go and get some proper drinks, and I'll fill you in on everything else." Mel stood up and went to the door to make sure everything was okay outside. After peering out through the glass, she came and sat down again.

"Okay, I'll have a lager." Pete grinned and rushed off to the bar, feeling pleased with himself. He'd managed to at least avoid getting slapped, and he'd now had more than the ten minutes Mel had agreed to. "Fortune favours the brave!" He said this out loud, to no one in particular.

At the same time as Pete was heading to the bar, Dave was coming out of a side door with food for love's young dream. As he approached the table, he could see they were both laughing. Jo looked up and saw Dave approaching with their food, and she squealed again, clapping excitedly. "Sir, Madam!" Dave gave them both a stately nod and placed their plates down for them. He reached behind him with both hands and pulled out two fresh bottles of diet cola. Dave placed one on the table while he reached for the bottle opener, suspended on his belt on a retractable line. He opened first one, then the other and poured them out slowly and with the air of a Maitre D from the poshest hotel. Once the glasses were both topped up, he turned to face Steve. "Can I get you anything else, sir?"

Steve smiled and looked at Jo, who mouthed "ketchup," to him.

"We'd like some ketchup, my good man!" Steve said before giving a hearty laugh.

Dave smiled and nodded. "As you wish, sir!" He turned on his heels and went to quickly procure some ketchup muttering silently "Alfred Pennyworth can kiss my arse!" as he went.

Steve, meanwhile, had found his groove and was coming out with a string of jokes bad enough to make your dad cringe, but Jo loved them. "What's E.T. short for?"

"I don't know" she replied.

"Because he's only got little legs!" Followed by squeals of laughter.

"Why was the calendar worried?"

"I don't know," came the reply.

"Because its days were numbered!" Followed by more laughter from Jo.

"What do you call a fly without wings?"

"I don't know!"

"A walk!" Even more laughter. Every time he hit her with the punch line, she laughed, and laughed hard! Even Dave found it hard not to laugh as Jo's laughter was infectious.

Back inside, Pete set two pints of lager down on the table and resumed his tale of woe, love, and down syndrome. "Steve told me that back home, his dad handles all his money. He doesn't work apparently, and his mam's a part-time cleaner somewhere, yet here they are, staying at a not too cheap hotel in the heart of Barcelona while sticking junior in a shitty dive, fifty kilometres away!" Mel shook her head. "I mean, I'm just putting two and two together, you know? But I can't help but get five. See, he also told me he gets twenty quid a fortnight for pocket money."

"At least it's something," Mel suggested, taking a sip of her lager.

"Well, yeah, you're right. However!" Pete mirrored her and took a sip too. "His dad has to take him into the town if he wants to spend it and his dad then charges him a fiver for bloody petrol!" His voice rose at the end of the sentence as his anger showed itself. Mel shook her head in disbelief.

"No way?"

"Oh, yes, way! I found this out yesterday when I caught up with him outside their hotel. He'd spent his twenty euros getting there, and so his dad had to give him another twenty 'for emergencies'. Credit where it's due though, he did give him an additional tenner. At first, I thought it was a guilty conscience, but then he told him it would all come out of his pocket money when he got back home. Poor bugger. He wanted to see his mum and dad because he was upset after the other night…" Mel shot him another quizzical look as if she was sarcastically wondering what could have upset Steve. Pete picked up on this straight away, holding his hands up as he continued "…and rightly so. His dad, though, basically just told him to bugger off back here. He couldn't get rid of him quick enough."

"Unbelievable!" said Mel.

"I know, right! Anyway, on the way back, I asked him about Jo. It's not hard to see she's sweet on him and I reckoned he was sweet on her too. I couldn't figure out why he kept seemingly dodging the issue though… so I asked him what he thought about her." He paused to take a drink and Mel followed suit. Pete continued: "Anyway, he told me he really likes her." Mel smiled "I asked him if he wanted to ask her on a date, and he just said: 'no' then went all silent."

"Why do you think?" Mel asked, taking another drink.

"Well, We walked on and eventually he tells me that his dad has told him, and I quote: downies aren't allowed to have girlfriends and that! I mean, I'm paraphrasing here, but that right there, it broke my heart, it really did. He's a lovely lad, and I know he likes Jo, and it couldn't be more obvious that Jo likes him." Mel smiled again. "The only reason he hasn't really shown any interest is that his dad, well," he sighed "his dad's a bastard…but I think I already covered that bit?" Mel, still chuckling, nodded her agreement. "So, anyway, I hatched a plan, see. I spoke to Dave — Dave's my new best friend, by the way. I don't know if you've had much to do with him during your stay, but he's really a top guy, and I owe him such a lot — anyway I spoke to Dave yesterday, and he helped me put all this together. Actually, to be fair, I just told him my idea, and he single-handedly took it upon himself to create this wonderland out there. I took Steve out to Camp Nou earlier, while he set all this up."

"Steve got to see Camp Nou?" Mel remembered Steve was desperate to go visit the other day.

"Yes, he did. Funny story: we had a bet over a game of crazy golf, and he played me like a cheap fiddle! I lost and, as per our bet, I had no choice really — a bet is a bet, after all. So, yeah, I managed to overcome my complete and utter hatred for football, and I took him over there and did the full top tier tour. I have to admit that, as tours go, it wasn't bad. Don't get me wrong, I'm not about to start watching Match Of The Day anytime soon, but it was quite interesting. The big fella was absolutely buzzing, I mean he was literally buzzing with excitement." Pete shook his hands vigorously as if to illustrate this. "He walked on air the whole way home, so it was totally worth it." He took another drink of his lager.

Mel gave Pete a little round of applause, "Well done, Mr Kelly! You might get your angel wings, yet!" They both laughed.

Pete continued: "Anyway, it was me that got Dave to come and tell you about the prize draw."

"I knew something was fishy," she laughed.

"I planned to get you both down here. Give you the old 'fake phone call' - which always seems to work so well in old spy films - and then sneak Steve out to work his magic with Jo." Pete got up and went and opened the door slightly, so he could see how it was going. "It seems to be going really well." Mel came over to join him at the door. Out on the patio, Jo and Steve had finished eating and were now slow dancing to Celine Dion - the only romantic CD Dave could find. As the theme song from that film about the big ship oozed out of the speakers, Steve and Jo swayed to the music, punctuating the night air every so often with their own rendition of the chorus, followed by Jo's trademark squeals and Steve's inimitable laugh. Mel stared at Pete, and a smile graced her face, causing Pete's heart to physically ache, he couldn't help but notice there was sadness in her eyes, though. She went back inside and sat down. Pete joined her, and they both sat there in silence for a few minutes, each taking a synchronised sip of their own pints. Pete broke the silence. "Look, Mel, I'm sorry," She just looked at him, the sadness seemed to spill out of her eyes and fill her face. "Really, I am SO, so sorry. I should never have lied to you about Steve and me. I just wanted to spend some time with you, and I figured having some common ground was a good start, and besides, I thought you might think I was a bit creepy, you know? Just a grown-up dude hanging around with a vulnerable adult he'd literally just met on the plane... nothing shady there!"

Mel ignored the last bit. "Common ground? The care thing?" Pete nodded, "You absolute muppet. I do this sort of work for a living. I mean it really does totally consume my time." She shook her head and took a sip of lager. "To be honest, Pete, the last thing I would do is date someone who does the same line of work as me. Jesus Christ! Can you imagine what scintillating bedtime chats we'd have?" She made a poor attempt at imitating Pete's accent. "Oh! Hello darling! How many piss bags did you empty today? Really? My, my, that's a jolly good show!" Accents were definitely not Mel's strong point and, after a passable start, the accent quickly descended into what may or may not have been Apu from the Simpsons. Pete laughed nervously, not sure how to respond as Mel continued. "Hell no, Pete! I love my job, but I want to be able to totally separate myself from it outside of work."

"Really?" He asked. Mel gave Pete a wide-eyed nod of the head. "Shit! I really did screw up didn't I?"

"Yep!" Mel nodded again. "I'll tell you a secret, though." He cocked his head and raised his eyebrows as he took another drink. "I was seriously starting to wonder if I could break my 'no carers' rule for you." Pete smiled and shook his head. "In fact" she continued "I was about ready to break a few rules for you on the first day." She blushed and avoided his eyes. "I really like you. Despite my spider-sense telling me something wasn't quite right, I felt comfortable with you. You make me laugh and, despite your whole subterfuge, I can tell you're a really kind person deep down. If you hadn't been married, you'd have been in with a real shot!" She gave him a smile, still avoiding eye contact, then she took a drink herself.

"Shit!" Pete said out loud. "I'm such a total idiot," not hiding the frustration in his voice.

"You'll not hear me arguing, sunshine," she laughed.

They were silent for a few minutes. Pete took a drink and then let out a sigh. "I can explain the wedding ring," he said, "I mean, I really wasn't lying about that."

"Maybe you were, maybe you weren't." She replied. "The problem I have, is that I don't know if I can believe you now. Do you see my dilemma, Pete Kelly?"

Pete Kelly did indeed see her dilemma, it was time to come clean about everything. He had no reason not to bare his soul now. "Okay, look! Cards on the table time."

Mel stared at him a moment as if weighing him up. "Go on then, I'll bite. Let's hear it."

Pete chuckled, "Okay, well, strap yourself in. See, I'm really not lying about my marriage. The only reason I was cagey is that …well…it's all bit embarrassing, really… and very… raw." He stared at her, waiting to see what she said.

Curiosity filled her eyes, and she smiled at him. "Okay, Pete." Mel said, still smiling "embarrass yourself…Show me what you got!"

"Where to begin?" Pete settled back and regaled Mel with the full, and sordid details of his soon to be ex-wife's transgression. He didn't embellish it, he didn't have to.

As he talked, Mel would punctuate his storytelling with "No way!" and "Holy shit!" And, of course, laughter. Lots of laughter!

"So, you can maybe understand why I was a bit cagey. I mean, It's bad enough she did the flirty dirty, but the way I found out…" he went silent.

Mel clapped, causing Pete to give her a puzzled look. "Bravo!" She said.

"What?" Pete was flummoxed. "You don't believe me?"

Mel laughed. "Oh, come on, Pete, you don't seriously expect me to believe that, do you?" She laughed again but stopped when Pete didn't. His face was deadly serious, "Well done, though." She continued "You had me right up until the whole 'need for speed' bullshit." She laughed again and stood up. "Right, it's been nice knowing you, I'm going to get Jo and go back to our room. You can…" she paused. "I'm going to be polite because you have been so nice to Jo and Steve, but you can go get lost. 'Need for speed.'" She turned and headed to the door, stopping to peer out of the little portholes first, to see what Jo and Steve were up to. Pete dug in his pocket and pulled out his phone. He quickly opened his camera roll, queued up the relevant video. He checked the volume was on full, and he hit play.

Almost immediately, Gemma's voice rang out saying the very words Mel had just scoffed at. Mel span round to see what the source of the sound was. Pete stopped the video and walked over to her. He started it again and handed her the phone before returning to his seat. Mel's chin nearly hit the floor as she saw the horror show on the screen. The clip was only short, and when it stopped, she looked over at Pete, who was doing his best to look everywhere but at her. She walked quietly back to her seat and sat down, still speechless. Shaking her head, she looked at the phone, then up at Pete, then up at the ceiling as she rolled her eyes, then back to Pete. Without saying a word, she put the phone on the table and slowly slid it across until it was in front of him. As she looked at his face, Mel could see the hurt in his eyes. "Pete, I," he picked up the phone and put it back in his pocket before he looked at her.

"It's pretty screwed up isn't it!" It wasn't a question.

"I'm so sorry I…" Pete didn't know Mel that well, but if he did, he'd know this was one of the rare times that she was genuinely at a loss for words. Yes, he'd seen her be silent, that was different though, that was a deliberate silence. This? This was a whole other ball game. She really did not know what to say.

Pete relieved her of the burden of trying to find words. "Funnily enough, it's not the fact that it's over that bothers me, if I'm honest, we'd already drifted apart. It's just, it's the way it happened. Of all the people, it had to be my useless, narcissistic, idiot boss! I lost my whole life that day. I lost my job, house, wife, everything. That's mainly why I ended up here. I was living in a Premier Inn, and I just got sick of the sight of the same four walls and drinking myself stupid. I decided this was a bookend trip. I'll come away, close out that whole part of my life, go back and start afresh. A brand new chapter, so to speak. Now more than ever, I realise that what happened," he motioned to his phone, "was a blessing in disguise. I have to say though, I didn't think, for one minute, that I'd create a whole new chapter in one week alone." He finished his drink off. "Well, not so much a chapter as a novella… a tragicomedy at that!"

Mel could tell that, even though he was making light of it, he really was hurting inside. With a sigh, she reached out and took hold of his hand. "Look, I'm not saying I forgive the whole 'let's lie to Mel' thing, but I kind of understand it. Especially about the whole Top Gun thing!"

Pete looked confused, a look he wore all too well lately. "Sooo… what you're saying is?"

"I'm saying that hostilities are ceased." Pete gave a little sigh of relief. "But I'm still salty at you."

"Okay, I'll take that… I can definitely work with that," he responded eagerly.

"I think it's a good thing we didn't hook up though," Mel continued.

"How so?"

"Well," she said, "I think you are maybe still in quite a bad place emotionally, if you're telling me the truth."

Pete shook his head and laughed "What? You've seen the video evidence, and you still don't fully believe me, is that it?"

Mel laughed. "No, I believe you." She let go of his hand, "Seriously though if I WAS about to have a relationship with you — which I really am NOT — but if I were, I'd be anxious that I was just a rebound thing."

Pete finished his drink off and thought about what she said. "You're maybe right, but," it was 'go for broke' time, "I really do like you. I know it's corny, but you have really got under my skin, with your magic laugh and weaponised smile." Mel laughed, unsure how to respond "I know I've just been through a bit of a thing, and I get the whole rebound concern, but I know deep down it's not a rebound thing. I know I messed up and I really can't tell you how incredibly sorry I am. I wasn't just trying to."

Mel interrupted him with "give me that Kelly Charm?"

"Shit, yes, I know how that must've sounded. I didn't mean anything by it, I was just grandstanding for Steve… if anything, it was me trying to conquer my nerves. I wasn't out to get a one night stand on holiday. In fact, the night I said that to Steve, I was planning on telling you all about Gemma and my pending divorce… you know… coming clean and that. But you sort of preempted it all."

Mel stood up and ruffled Pete's hair. Pete stood up to meet her eyes as she reached out with her hand and touched his face. "Ah, Pete," she lamented. "I really wish you'd been honest right from the start. What you've done for Steve and Jo out there, that's amazing. Truly amazing, and I'm going to get some details off of Steve so I can make sure he and Jo keep in touch. But, I'm sorry, this is it for you and me though."

Pete reached up and held her hand to his face. "It? I'm sorry, It's just, I'm a bit cloudy on the whole 'this is it' thing… can I get some clarity?"

Mel smiled, staring deep into his big brown eyes "I mean it's the end of the line."

Pete stared back.

"The end of the road, the fat lady has sung. The…"

"Okay, okay, I get it. But it doesn't have to be, does it?" He didn't attempt to hide the desperation in his voice.

"You did a great thing here tonight, and I really do like you, but I cannot trust you and heaven knows I've had enough bullshit this past year to last a whole lifetime." She let go of his face and looked at her watch. "I really must get Jo. We still have to pack."

"Pack?" Pete felt dizzy.

"Yes, pack…We go home tomorrow. I thought you knew?"

"Tomorrow? Since when?" He shook his head "No, you go home on Tuesday, with us, on the red-eye." Pete's voice cracked a little as if he would break down in tears any moment.

"Tuesday? No! Where did you get that idea from? We came here two weeks ago on a Sunday. I thought we told you." She hadn't. In fact, the subject of homeward flights had never actually come up in conversation. Pete had just assumed they were going home the same time as he and Steve were. "You do seem like a great guy, Pete. I'm sorry this has to end like this."

"Before it's even started?" He smiled a sad smile.

She nodded. "I hope you find happiness. Maybe we'll bump into each other again, someday." She leaned in and held his face in her hand again, tenderly kissing his cheek. Her hand lingered on his cheek before slowly sliding off as she moved past Pete and went out onto the patio. He heard her call out. "Okay, Frankie and Johnny. Time to…" her voice trailed off as the door closed. Pete sat back down just as Mel and Jo burst through the door.

"Pete!" Jo squealed. "I've had the BEST time, ever. Thank you!" She bent over and gave him a huge hug as she planted a kiss on his cheek.

"Hey, he's making moves on your girl, Steve." Pete heard Steve's voice from somewhere behind Jo and they all laughed, all except Pete who managed a faint smile. He looked up at Mel who gave him a wink. Jo and Steve shared one last hug and pecked each other on the cheek, and then Mel and Jo turned and headed off to the lobby. Steve sat down in Mel's seat. He was beaming from ear to ear at first. Then, as the realisation that Jo was going home tomorrow set in, his smile slowly faded. He and Pete just sat there in silence, brothers in arms, both bathed in love's sweet sorrow. The camera draws back away from them down the corridor.

"Shit, Steve! Aye, Steve, shit!"

Chapter Eight: "Well, that was unexpected!"

09.30

On a Sunday

Pete awoke from a short but deep sleep that seemed a relatively small reward for spending a long night peppered with extended periods of staring at the ceiling and feeling sorry for himself. He rolled out of bed and into the bathroom to relieve his bladder. As he washed his hands, he stared at his face in the mirror, his hair was all over the place, his eyes puffy and his face covered in sleep scars. "Jesus! You look like shite," he admonished his crumpled looking reflection. Reaching into the shower cubicle, he turned the tap on with one hand while he turned the sink tap in front of him on again, before scrabbling for his toothbrush and toothpaste. Half an hour later, he emerged from the bathroom, still feeling like shit, but at least now he didn't look like he was about to join the cast of The Walking Dead.

The previous night had been bittersweet, and he headed out onto the balcony to sit for a while and see if thinking about it in daylight was going to make him feel any better than the many hours he'd lost to it during the night. It didn't, everything was still shit, but on the plus side, he'd managed to salvage his friendship with Steve. Additionally, with a little help from his other new friend, Pete had managed to give Steve a night to remember and, who knows, maybe kickstarted something special for him. Also on the plus side, he'd managed to build a bridge with Mel. Granted it was more of a pontoon bridge than any sort of solid suspension bridge…or maybe it was more of a 'felled tree spanning a swollen river' than any sort of decent bridge, but it was a start. On the flip side, though, there was everything else. By everything else, he meant the fact that he found out Mel had liked him from the beginning and he didn't need to have played Captain Caregiver to Steve. And here he was: sat on his balcony, the lost love of his life heading home later that day, and him sitting in his boxer shorts, all showered, shaved, and shit out of luck.

"Knackers!" He shouted out loud at the absurdity of it all. Somewhere above him, someone mimicked his call, and he heard "knackers" ring out. It then struck him that, after being outside and talking out loud, he would typically have been treated to the now familiar greeting of his fine friend. Getting out of his chair, he peered around the balcony partition, hoping to see a familiar face. Surprisingly, the balcony was empty, and he tried to peer into the gloom. He could see signs that Steve hadn't run away again, but he was perturbed that there was no sign of life. He got dressed quickly and, grabbing his phone, wallet and room key, he headed next door to give him a knock. There came no answer. He tried again, this time putting his ear to the door. Nothing! He knew he'd totally missed breakfast at this point, but he figured he'd pop down and have a look to see if he could see his missing friend. Friend! He realised that he did indeed consider Steve a friend and this made him smile. Pete arrived at the elevator at just about the same time as housekeeping.

The maid was pushing the laundry/cleaning cart ahead of her, but Pete couldn't help but notice that she was really trying to keep it at arm's length, her face was twisted in a strange look of anger and disgust. Then the smell hit him. "Oh! Oh! Shit!" He shouted as he tried to bury his nose in the crook of his arm to mask the smell.

The maid, upon seeing and hearing Pete's distress, launched into a tirade in Spanish; "putos animales sucios. Cagan la cama, la mierda el baño, cagan por todas partes. bastardos repugnantes!" She looked him in the eye and, gesticulating like an old Italian Housewife, repeated the last bit in English: "FILTHY BASTARDS!" The elevator arrived, and the maid began to push the cart into it.

"I'll, er, I'll take the stairs," he said, followed by "el stairoes" as he pointed to the door to the stairs. The elevator doors closed and he raced to get away from the god awful smell. "I pity anybody getting in that lift over the next hour or two," he thought.

The breakfast room yielded no results. Just as Pete had expected, it was closed off and empty of guests. Against his better judgement, he decided to head up to Mel and Jo's room to see if they were in. Just as he was heading back to the stairs, he caught sight of Dave who, as usual, was sat behind the reception desk sipping an iced coffee and reading old newspapers. "Morning, mate," he greeted Dave, who glanced up and smiled.

"Morning, Irish," he grinned as he rose from his chair and extended his hand. "How's it going?" he asked as they shook.

"Well, you know, could be better." Pete half laughed as he said this. "Listen, I didn't get a chance to thank you for last night. Mate, you pulled an absolute blinder. I really don't know how to repay the favour." Dave held up his hand and playfully dismissed him.

"Don't be daft," he smiled. "I had a blast, and I got to spread some happiness, and I'm always up for spreading some happiness. I'm guessing the happy couple are now just that - a happy couple?"

"Well, that's the thing, Dave. I have no idea. I can't find Steve again this morning. I haven't checked in with Mel and Jo yet, but I'm hoping he's with them."

Dave nodded sagely, "Gotcha. Listen, don't panic. I saw the three of them heading out earlier, that's why I assumed cupid's arrow hit its mark. Your man looked proper happy, all smiles and whatnot!" He raised his eyebrows three times in a row and grinned.

"Yeah, that's what he looks like all the time," Pete responded, smiling. "Happy!"

"Ah, but what if I told you him and Princess Jo were holding hands?" Dave replied, still grinning.

"Really?" Pete asked, excitedly. Dave nodded, and Pete did an air grab. They were interrupted by the maid that Pete had seen outside the elevator. She just seemed to appear and start shouting at Dave in Spanish. Dave and the maid exchanged Spanish and hand gestures for a good five minutes — at one point she took her apron off and threw it on the floor, spitting on it — before the shouting finally stopped.

Frowning, Dave went into the till and pulled out a ten euro note, handing it over to her saying: "Tómate una hora de descanso, ve a tomar algo, mi regalo." The maid took the ten euros and held it in front of her, raising an eyebrow. The pair now seemed locked in some mystical staring contest. Dave acquiesced first. "For god's sake," he exclaimed, reaching into the cash drawer again and retrieving another ten euros.

"Gracias," said the maid, blowing him a kiss before turning to retrieve her apron. "adiós por ahora," and she was gone.

Pete had just stood and watched the whole thing go down with a mixture of wonder and amusement. "What the hell was that all about?" he asked.

"Shit," came the reply.

"Shit as in 'just stuff,' or shit as in… shit?"

"Shit as in Shit," said Dave. "It seems a couple of new arrivals decided to try and buy some MDMA in a local bar last night. Silly bastards got royally shafted when some crafty local charged them thirty notes for what wasn't MDMA but what was, apparently, powerful laxatives. Their room - 237 - was an absolute massacre. Not so much 'The Shining' as 'The

Shittening,' less 'Icecapades' more 'shitscapades!' We had to move them to a completely different room because it smells like a tramp's taint in there. Mind, I should have made the daft little bastards stay there, teach them a lesson." They both laughed. Pete asked what the hotel will do about the mess, and Dave explained they'd clean it up and bill them. "I've already been up and confiscated their passports. What a pair! A skinny ginger lad and a scruffy little fat lad who looks like he's never had a bath in a month of Sundays. They pissed and moaned about it and tried to get all macho. I just held back my laughter said: 'okay, I'll just get the local constabulary on the phone then, boys' and they couldn't get their passports out quick enough. They're only here a week, thankfully, but I'm guessing there will be more shenanigans before their week is out." They both laughed again.

"I don't suppose they said where they were going, did they?" Pete asked.

"Who, Ginger and The Fat-man? No," Dave replied with an air of incredulity, he stared at Pete, straight-faced. Pete gave him a stare back, and he burst out laughing. "I'm sorry, mate. I can't help myself. No, they didn't. I didn't speak to them, to be honest. I just saw the tail end of them as they headed out. Sorry, man."

Pete sighed and looked around. "Never mind, I'll go and see if I can see them about anywhere." They exchanged a quick handshake and Pete was off.

Pete headed straight down into the town to start his search for the others. The first thing he did, though, was grab a bite to eat. The lure of McDonald's couldn't compete with the freshly prepared food from the bistro he'd been to with Steve the other day. He found a table outside and waited for the waitress to come and take his order, scanning the street while he waited. The waitress didn't take long to arrive at his table to take his order, and after a quick perusal of the menu, Pete ordered a potato omelette and a coffee. While he waited for his food, he took his phone out to catch up on social media and see what was happening in the rest of the world. His phone showed that Pete had a missed call and a voicemail from Mr Hashimoto. "Strange," he thought, wondering how he missed it. Checking the time of the call, he figured it was during the exchange between Dave and the Hotel Maid. He gave a little chuckle before checking the voicemail:

"Kelly San, I apologise for this intrusion. I realise that you are still in Spain and I imagine that you will be returning to England this coming week - Tuesday, perhaps? I Know that I advised you to take some time and contact me when you are ready, but I would greatly appreciate you calling me on your return, as a matter of great urgency. Things here have… shall we say… taken an unexpected turn. I look forward to speaking with you soon."

At this point, Pete was half tempted to call Mr Hashimoto back. "No," he thought, "mister H said when you get back, and that's when I'll call." He knew Mr Hashimoto well, and he knew that he would not be offended if Pete did not call straight away, only if he called long after his return or if he didn't call at all. The temptation to unblock Terry and call to see what was going on was quite strong. He almost gave in, but then he remembered everything. "Shit!" Everything came flooding back in stunning, hi-definition detail. As a wave of emotions washed over him, he began thinking about his 'reset week' and how badly it had gone, and how deep in the toilet his life would still be when he got back. As the waitress set his food down in front of him, he looked up and thanked her through teary eyes. She asked if he was okay and he just smiled and told her it was his allergies. Grabbing a napkin, he wiped his eyes then blew his nose before thanking her again. She smiled and wandered off, leaving Pete alone with his tears and his omelette. After finishing his food off, Pete settled the bill and set off to look for his friends in earnest. He searched all through the town, he scoured the beach, he stopped for ice cream, he explored the beach some more, all to no avail. In a last-ditch attempt to find them, he tried the bowling alley and crazy golf course. Again he came up empty. "Bugger" he lamented. I just can't seem to catch a break, he thought. He checked the time and was surprised to see that it was nearly four o'clock. It occurred to him that he'd better head back to the Olympiad lest he miss Mel and Jo altogether.

He arrived back at the hotel just after four thirty. Alejandro was on the desk, and Pete gave him a quick wave. He didn't bother checking the bar, or anywhere else, instead he headed straight up to see if Steve was back in his room, listening intently as he strained to hear movement from inside the room after he knocked. The scrape of a chair on the tiled floor and the soft padding of bare feet on the tiled floor from the other side of the door made him sigh with relief. The door opened, and there, smiling and executing his signature glasses push, was Steve. "Mate!" Pete exclaimed. "So glad to see you. I've been out looking for you and the girls all afternoon. What have you been up to? Do you know where the girls are or what time they leave?" Steve just stood there smiling, waiting for Pete to finish, then he paused a moment before answering.

"We've been on the beach, then to lunch, then we went to play golf at that place," he said, smiling still. He leant forward and gave Pete a wink "I won," followed by a big grin.

Knowing Steve's skill on the crazy golf, he grinned back. "You're a monkey," he said as he reached out and gave Steve a playful poke in the tummy. Steve laughed. "But where are they?" Steve brought his watch up to his face to check the time.

"It's five o'clock" he noted, "they'll be heading down for the coach soon. I said I'd meet them at a quarter past."

"Thank Christ." Pete sighed, visibly relieved. "I really thought I was going to miss them. What time are they actually leaving, do you know?"

Steve raised his right hand to his chin in a comical display of thoughtfulness "Five Thirty!" he said, after a momentary pause for dramatic effect. He grinned.

"Five thirty! You're sure?" Pete was surprised it was so soon.

Steve nodded. "Yup!"

"Well, that's that then, I guess!" Steve just stood and watched as Pete lamented his situation. "I wouldn't care, but I looked everywhere, trying to find you. I thought maybe…" Steve was hanging on his every last word. "Ah shit! I guess this just really wasn't meant to be." He ran his fingers through his unruly mop of hair, then he turned to Steve. "Do you think it will be okay if I came down with you. To see them off?"

"Yeah, Steve, you can come." Sensing his friend's sadness, Steve grabbed him and gave him a hug.

"Okay, cool," said Pete, hugging him back. "I'll just nip for a quick visit to the bog. I'll meet you out here, and we can both go down together… okay?" Steve nodded.

Ten minutes later, Pete emerged from his room to be greeted by Steve who was already stood waiting for him. They walked along to the elevator when Pete remembered something. He told Steve to carry on down and he rushed back around to his room. Once inside, he scrabbled in his bag for the small plastic pouch that contained the daisy chain Mel had made for him earlier that week. Placing it in his pocket, he rushed down and met Steve in reception where they both stood about like a pair of nervous schoolboys. All around them, people were dragging their luggage around. Some were handing their keys in. Some were quickly swigging down their last drinks from the bar before handing their keys in. Pete looked outside and just over the front hedge he made out the top of what was probably the coach as it hove into view.

The coach itself had come almost directly from the airport and was dropping off new arrivals before making the return journey with the outbound holidaymakers. A steady stream of people began to enter the reception area, forming an orderly queue at the desk, as the departing holidaymakers started to file out in a surprisingly orderly fashion. "Typically British" Pete said, under his breath. He jumped when a familiar voice squealed behind him.

"There's my handsome boy," Jo Squealed again. Pete and Steve spun round to greet her. Jo, grinning like a Cheshire cat, held her hand up in front of Pete and said: "Hold up Pete, you're handsome and all but," she placed her hands either side of Steve's face "he's downright perfect!"

Pete laughed. "where does she get these lines from?" He thought. The sweet sound of Mel's laughter came from behind him. He turned round to see her smiling at Jo and Steve and struggling with their luggage. "Here, let me help you with that." He reached out to take one of the bags, which Mel gratefully passed over to him.

"Thanks," she said as she rebalanced everything. She nodded over to Jo and Steve. "You did a great thing there, Pete Kelly. If you do nothing else of note in your life, you should be proud of this."

"Nah," he smiled, "I just gave cupid a chance to work his magic." He looked over at Steve as he was giving Jo a massive bear hug. "They did the rest." As he looked back at Mel, he asked: "What will happen when you get home? How will you keep in touch with Steve?"

"I've taken his number and his address. I'll be able to chase him up once we've got home and got settled."

Pete nodded. "Just a word of warning" Mel looked at him. "You might get a bit of resistance from his folks. His dad is" he chose his words "a bit of a twat, y' know? Did I mention that part?"

Mel laughed, "Oh, I know, and yes you did mention something, but don't worry. I'm quite tenacious." They both looked up at the same time, and their eyes locked for what seemed like an age before they both looked away. "Come on, Jo. We best get on that bus." Jo gave a 'thumbs up' without breaking off from her hug. Turning back to Pete, "Well then, it's been… an experience." Pete nodded and smiled. She smiled back at him, and Pete felt his heart break at the sight of it.

"Yeah, you, er, you take care of yourself," he managed, unsure of what else to say. He began to move closer, planning to give Mel a hug and a kiss on the cheek, but Mel quickly turned and began heading out to the coach.

"Come on, Jo." She called back behind her. Jo gave Steve one last squeeze, and they shared a kiss. It wasn't a passionate kiss, Pete noted, it was more like the kind of closed mouth kiss you gave your playground sweetheart back in infant school. It still made him feel warm inside, though. Jo broke off from the hug and began following Mel, when she got to the door, she turned and looked back at Steve, giving him a little wave and blowing him a kiss. Steve pretended to catch the kiss and put it in his pocket, then he reciprocated. Pete went over to him and asked him if he was okay. Steve smiled, pushed his glasses up his nose and nodded, but Pete could see his eyes were wet and misty. A tear began to make its way down Steve's left cheek and, putting his arm around him, Pete suggested they head out and wave goodbye. Steve smiled, nodding his agreement before he patted Pete on the back, and they made their way to the front of the hotel. As they were descending the hotel steps, the coach driver was just finishing loading the luggage into the special compartment. Jo and Mel were sat at the back of the bus, and Pete knew this because Jo was patting the window with the palm of her hand to attract their attention, then waving madly. Steve dried his eyes and gave a wave back.

Pete could make out Mel sitting next to Jo, and he could see that she was looking at her phone or something. She looked up and stared right at him, but before he could wave at her, she looked down again. Pete was gutted. He'd felt bad after he found Gemma and Terry, but somehow this felt worse. "What the hell is wrong with me?" He hadn't even known Mel a week, and here he was, feeling like it was the end of the world because she was going home. She was going out of his life, and his heart literally ached at the thought it all, and the idea of that, the stark reality that he would probably never see her again made him feel so dreadfully sad. He'd been sad when it all ended with Gem, but his sadness came more from all the deceit and the upheaval of his life, than the actual loss of Gemma. But this? This was a whole other ball game. It was like he had known Mel all his life, and she had suddenly died, and he was never going to see her again. He couldn't bear it. He wouldn't be able to bear it!

The coach began to set off, and as Pete stood there watching it go. Jo was now waving like a lunatic out of the rear window. As he watched, Steve grabbed the cap off his head and began waving it like he was Jenny Agutter waving at the Flying Scotsman or something. Meanwhile, Pete's panic began to spill out of his head into his reality, and he turned to Steve, who was leaking from his eyes again. "Steve! What if she's the one? What if I… what if I let her go and I never see her again, and the rest of my life is shit as a consequence? What if I spend the rest of my life trying to find Mel, or someone like her?" Steve just looked and smiled before giving Pete a hug.

"Use the force, Luke!" Steve whispered into Pete's ear as he hugged him, quoting his favourite part of his favourite film. Pete grabbed Steve by the shoulders and looked him dead in the eyes.

"You're right!" he kissed Steve on the forehead. "You're totally right, I have to tell her" he set off running "I HAVE TO TELL HER!" he called back. Steve looked on as Pete ran off. He scratched his head and smiled that massive smile of his. Then, placing the cap back on his head, Steve set off at a leisurely pace to follow Pete.

He'd gone a few steps when he suddenly stopped and uttered: "Use the force, Steve! Aye, Steve!" He chuckled before following it up with "The force will be with you, always." In what was probably one of the best Alec Guinness impersonations that no one had ever witnessed. Chuckling loudly to himself, he carried on walking.

Meanwhile, the coach had driven to the end of the street and turned a corner. Pete knew it would then double back behind the derelict hotel opposite the Olympiad, passing by the bottom of the street it had driven up, before joining the main street down towards town.

It would then head through town and follow the coastal road on to Barcelona and the airport. Pete ran down to the end of the street to intercept it, getting there just as it was approaching the junction. Waving wildly, he ran out in front of it to make the driver stop. Luckily for him, the driver, and everyone on board, the coach had enough room to slow to a graceful stop. This threw Pete a bit. He was expecting some sort of movie style reprieve where the vehicle stops inches from the hero, who's stood there with his arms up and his eyes closed, waiting for the imminent impact. Regaining his composure, as much as he could, given the situation, he ran round to the door at which point he began pleading through the glass to the driver for him to open it. The driver looked at Pete. Pete looked at the driver. He brought his hands up to his chest, clasping them together, making a pleading motion. The driver looked at his watch and, shaking his head, reached for the door mechanism.

The door swung open, and Pete thanked the driver, profusely. "five minutes, loco bastardo!" Pete nodded and headed straight to the back of the coach.

As he moved up the aisle, he was greeted by a sea of faces. Some looked confused, some looked angry, some were already asleep and blissfully oblivious to the drama that was unfolding before them. "Sorry, sorry!" Pete repeated his mantra of apology as he made his way closer to Mel. Jo was already clapping her hands by the time he reached them, and Pete gave her a little wink and a smile.

From the front of the bus, the driver yelled at him to "Hurry up, mierda cabeza!" Pete looked at Mel, who was just sat, staring at him. Her face was expressionless but her eyes, her eyes were clearly saying: "What the hell!"

"Mel!" He began, pausing for a moment to gather the words in head before continuing. "Look, I know I screwed up, believe me. I mean, I know if there were an Olympic category for total bloody idiots, I'd be a solid gold medal winner. A reigning champion, without a doubt!" Mel smiled. This gave Pete a morale boost as he continued. "I know I hurt you by lying, but it wasn't done out of malice. It was done out of… I dunno… fear, I guess. My ma always says that the road to hell is paved with good intentions and I reckon I could probably get a taxi straight along that road after this. But I'm sorry, and hard truth of it is, I just don't want to lose you. I get that you don't want to be… *romantically* involved with me, and I really don't blame you. But, honestly, I'd settle for just friendship."

He sighed and ran his fingers through his hair. "I'll be totally honest, Mel, I've spent the best part of the last eight years or so, with a girl I thought I loved, and when it ended I felt that my life was over."

Mel looked stared at him, then past him, then back at him again. "Is this revelation supposed to win me over?" she asked.

Pete glanced around behind him and saw a sea of expectant faces. Every person on the bus was now wide awake and transfixed. He turned back to Mel. "Shit… look I thought my life was over, but the very next day, I didn't miss her. I don't miss her. In fact, would you like to know what goes through my head when I do think of her?" Mel shook her head. "When I think of Gemma, I do't miss her. I miss my life and the routine I had. But when I think of her now, I just wonder how many other guys she banged during our time together. Seriously! I reckon she's had more meat go through her than a high street butcher shop!" Behind him, he heard somebody laugh, causing him to give a backwards glance before continuing. "I look back, and I know that we should never have been together. She hated everything I liked, and liked everything I hated, and here are you making Spiderman and Star Wars references while you're tearing me a new arsehole the other night. I gotta tell you, Mel, with all my heart, the thought of you driving off into the sunset, never to be seen again… well, it fills me with absolute bloody terror. It terrifies me. I feel like my chest is being crushed and I can't breath. I nearly had a bloody panic attack just now, at the thought of not seeing you again."

The driver, worried that he might get caught in traffic, was growing impatient. "Hurry the hell up, hijo de una puta irlandesa!"

Pete turned and gave him a wave as if to say okay. "Mel, I know I've only known you for a few days, and I know I'm acting completely irrational right now, but you have touched me." There was a gasp from behind him, causing another, exasperated, backward glance from Pete. "Bad choice of words… you have gotten under my skin. You and I, we've talked loads, and you love all the stuff I love, You laugh at the same stuff I laugh at. And that laugh. Man, that laugh. I swear on everything holy that your laugh could heal the sick!" He held his right hand up and put his left hand on his heart. "When you laugh, it's like getting bathed in puppies!" Jo squealed and clapped, stopping as Pete continued. "Your smile makes me want to be a better man and meeting you here has made me question every decision I've ever made in my entire life, right up until now. Until this moment, right here," he put both hands on his heart, " and I totally understand you not wanting to get involved romantically, but please, PLEASE, let's just stay in touch… see how it goes." He stopped and stared right at her, making his best 'puppy dog' eyes. Behind him, he could hear a few murmurs, and it sounded like someone was sniffing and sobbing. It quickly died down, though, and the bus fell silent. Everyone, including Pete, seemed to be holding their breath as they waited for Mel to speak. Mel put her phone down and sat up a little, holding his gaze. She then leant forward, shuffling forward in the seat until she was perched on edge. The silence was deafening, and Pete kept eye contact with her as she moved, looking hopefully into her eyes. Mel smiled, and she slowly reached her hand up to touch his face and Pete leant forward to meet her hand, closing his eyes as the soft skin of her fingers caressed his cheek.

"Pete… Oh, Pete," she said softly, lightly caressing his cheek with her fingers still. Pete was actually feeling a bit dizzy, although he wasn't sure if it was his posture or the sheer energy of Mel's touch. This is like some kind of fairytale, he thought. It's like a scene from a film. He and Mel were like some up and coming Hollywood stars when they appear in the usual bubblegum shite that rakes in cash and leads to them becoming 'Big Stars'. Romantic music was now playing in his head as he, the hero of the story, was about to fulfil the third act destiny hinted at in the first act.

The music in his head built to a crescendo, he looked into her eyes and managed to squeeze out an answer: "Y, yes?"

"Get the fuck off the bus, mate!"

If this were a film, the building crescendo of music would be replaced with the sound of a stylus being dragged across the soundtrack record. "I'm sorry, what?" Mel stood up and looked him square in the eye, pulling her hand away as she rose.

"I'll speak slowly because all the other passengers are probably now wondering if you're drunk, or on drugs or something." She pointed towards the door at the front of the coach. "Get! The fuck! Off! The bus!" She sat back down and looked at Jo, who was as stunned and silent as the everyone else on the bus, then she looked out the window, clearly unhappy with the whole situation. Pete stood up straight and turned to go, totally stunned. He turned back to face her, thought better of it, and began to make his way down the aisle.

He went a few steps and turned back round. Mel saw him retrieve something from his pocket before he walked back towards her. He took hold of her hand and placed the plastic pouch into, curling her fingers over it, before turning again to leave the bus. Everyone was watching his walk of shame, lowering their eyes though, as Pete passed them one by one. Halfway towards the front of the coach, he did turn back.

Mel looked at him and pointed to the door as she mouthed "Fuck off," at him. Dejected, and with all eyes on him, he continued with his exit of shame, thanking the driver as he alighted from the coach. The driver just shook his head and closed the doors as Pete finally stood on the roadside. The engine started up, and the bus set off again. Pete watched it go by and then watched the back of it as it rumbled along the narrow street. Jo was looking out the window again, but she looked sad as she gave Pete a little wave. Pete waved back just as the coach turned the corner. Then, it was gone.

On the bus, Mel looked down and opened her hand to reveal the pouch. She held it up in front of her eyes and saw the daisy chain. Jo, having stopped waving at the boys, was sat looking at Mel, who turned her head to meet her gaze. Both girls began to cry, Jo reached out to Mel for solace and the girls hugged each other.

Meanwhile, back down the road, as the bus had driven past Pete, it revealed Steve who was sat on the opposite kerb. Pete walked over to him, taking a look after the coach again. Sighing, he sat himself down next to his friend, who looked pretty sad himself. "Well, that was unexpected," said Pete. Steve pushed his glasses up his nose then put his arm around Pete's shoulders, and for the second time in two days, the boys found themselves sat together in silence, sad and alone.

"Shit," said Pete softly.

"Aye, Steve… Shit!"

Chapter Nine: "You had me at 'fuck off!'"

On a Monday

Pete stretched his arms and legs out in a huge yawn and, having forgotten he'd been asleep on a chair on the balcony with his legs on the railings for the last few hours, he promptly pushed his chair backwards and ended up on his back with his legs in the air. "OW, SHIT!" he cried.

"I think Pete's awake, Steve." Steve's words came drifting across the partition from his balcony where, to be more like his best friend, he had also spent the last few hours. Although Steve had just sat and watched the world wake up instead of dozing off like Pete had. "Aye, Steve, I think he might need a doctor too!" He laughed.

"Bugger me." Pete whispered under his breath, the absurdity of ending up on the floor like this, just like on his first morning, was not lost on him. He continued to just lie there for a while, with his legs in the air, looking up at the calm morning sky. "What are we going to do today, big fella?" He called across to Steve, trying to sound positive. That's the one thing Pete was good at. The world could be coming down around his ears, like it was right now, and Pete just keeps on keeping on. Terry used to say he was the glue that kept the ship afloat when things went tits up at work. Pete knew Steve was probably feeling pretty shitty with Jo being gone, so he figured it was up to him to keep his spirits up. That would also serve to keep himself occupied too, in theory. Eventually, he began to feel uncomfortable, and he started the struggle to get upright. Once on his feet, he discussed with Steve what they were going to do for the day. Straight away, Steve said Golf. "Hang on there, man. I don't mind playing a few games, but I'm not making any bets with you this time, not after the way you had my pants down the other day." He heard Steve laughing on his side of the partition. "Right" he exclaimed as he finally got upright, "let's get dressed and see what delights the breakfast room has to offer." He heard Steve laughing and chatting to himself as he went into his own room to get ready. It didn't take long for him to get showered and dressed and soon he was knocking on Steve's door. Despite Pete's best efforts, the mood remained somewhat sombre as they made their way down to the breakfast room

Steve clearly wasn't his usual smiling self, and he remained relatively quiet as he ate his breakfast. In fact, they both were silent as they sat and picked at their respective plates and bowls. Pete even thought there seemed to be an air of sadness across the breakfast room overall, although he suspected this had more to do with the shit breakfast buffet than his utter failure in love and Steve's pining for Jo. They both continued to pick at their breakfasts in silence, broken only by Steve's occasional commentary on what he was eating He went from "Ah, toast!" to "Ah, rice crispies… snap, crackle, POP!" to "Ah, cakes!" Pete couldn't help but smile as he watched Steve make his way through the massive tray of food he'd collected from the buffet. He had lightly fondled some very runny scrambled eggs and some bacon that could be used to build a shelter if one found oneself stranded out in the wild.

Pete managed to eat a little bit of the egg, which was tastier than it looked. But he decided to avoid the bacon as he figured that, at best, it would maybe break a filling, at worst it was sharp enough to give him an anal fissure as it exited through the gift shop, assuming it didn't damage all his major organs first, as it worked its way towards his back door. Pete watched as Steve gulped down the last dregs of his daily glass of orange juice — one a day, as agreed after the OJ induced 'shit shenanigans' the other day. Pete pushed his plate away from him and followed suit with his coffee. He gave his mouth quick wipe with a napkin and motioned to Steve to do the same as he had some flakes on his face from one of the three Danish Pastries he'd demolished after his cereal, and then they were off. They headed up to their rooms first because Pete reckoned that, as they had no real commitments, there was no real hurry. Besides, he could feel a need building up that he'd prefer to take care of on familiar territory, rather than using a toilet out and about.

They met outside their rooms an hour later and headed for the elevator. As it descended, Steve was gleefully predicting the outcome of the impending golf game. "Who's going to win the golf, Steve? Will Pete win? Nah. He won't win, Steve." Then he would laugh, citing Jim Bowen as the source, as usual.

"Did they even have crazy golf when Bullseye was broadcast?" Pete asked. Steve just laughed again. The doors opened, and they were greeted by what looked like someone being wheeled on a gurney out of the front the door by two paramédicos, closely watched by about a dozen onlookers. Seeing Dave was on reception, Pete walked to over to find out what was going on, Steve followed close behind him. Dave saw him coming and gave him a smile and held his hand out. Pete liked that about Dave; he always shook hands and was always pleased to see him. He probably did it with everyone, but it made Pete feel special, like Dave valued his presence as a customer, as a friend even. They shook hands and exchanged pleasantries.

Dave held his hand out to Steve, who dutifully shook it. Steve smiled and said: "I've been expecting you, Mr Bond!"

Dave laughed. "That's quite a grip you have there." Shaking his hand as if brushing away some sort of pain while laughing. "I hope you're not too sad now your girlfriend has gone home."

Steve pushed his glasses up his nose, "No time for love, Dr Jones." Dave gave Steve a friendly pat on the shoulder as the three of them laughed. Dave turned to Pete and asked him what was up to.

"Well, we're just heading out to go play crazy golf. I'm trying to fill the void if you catch my drift." Pete nodded in Steve's direction. Dave looked back at Steve, who was looking at a brochure from a stand near the reception desk. He looked back at Pete and gave him a knowing look and a nod. "What was that all about?" he asked, motioning to the doors and the now disappeared paramédicos.

Dave let out a loud laugh that startled Pete, not least because he wasn't expecting such levity when a guest had just been wheeled out on a stretcher. "I'm sorry, mate." He put his hand on Pete's shoulder when he saw the look of concern cross his face. "You won't believe this." He laughed again. "I mean, I've been on the desk now for five years, and I have never seen or heard of anything like this."

"Come on then, Dave. Don't keep a man in suspense, eh?" Pete urged. Steve had also come closer to see what his two friends were laughing about.

"Well!" began Dave. "You remember the two shit-weasels from yesterday?" Pete nodded. "Of course you do, after Maria's lovely outburst at the desk, how could you not. Well, it turns out one of them was ginger."

Pete was confused. "I don't follow? How is that a medical emergency?"

"Well," said Dave, ordinarily it's not and issue. "This guy, however, dyed his hair!"

Pete still wasn't following what Dave was saying. "No, mate, I'm still not getting it."

Dave held a finger up in front of him like a teacher "Allow me to explain, then. You see, our Ginger friend wanted a tan. He knew, though, that being a redhead predisposed him to just go red in the sun's rays." Pete still looked confused. "So, he reasoned that the best way to avoid sunburn and to achieve a tan was, not to use sun block and shade like most of us, but to dye his hair." Dave smiled at the boys, expectantly. The boys still looked blank. Sighing, Dave then explained "He thought that by dyeing his hair, he would fool his body, and the sun, into thinking he wasn't ginger, thereby avoiding the usual effects of the sun and also achieving the much coveted 'holiday Tan'!" Dave took a step back and held his arms open. Pete looked at Steve then at Dave and then he burst out laughing. Steve burst out laughing too, not because he knew what Dave was saying, but because his best friend was laughing. "Again I say: never in my five years of running this hotel, have I witnessed anything as close to this spectacular display of horsecockery," said Dave. "He appears to have literally dyed ALL his body hair!" Dave motioned over his body with his hands. "On his head, under his arms, his arse, on his coin purse, even his toes! In his little brain, this fellow reasoned that if he wasn't ginger, he wouldn't be as at risk from the sun and its evil ways. His second day here, he spends all day out by the pool sipping on free cocktails and foregoing the usual formalities, like clothes and sunscreen."

Pete was practically speechless, managing to squeeze out a barely audible "Shit!"

"I know, right!" said Dave. "He literally laid out there, in the hot, Spanish summer sun, all bloody day! He might have had half a chance if he'd not been hammering Mojitos all day too. Mojitos! I ask you, who the hell still drinks those? It's not like he wasn't warned, either. Alejandro told me he tried to tell him that the sun was scorching and he should think about covering up. Maybe something was lost in translation there, but he just smiled and told him to fetch more Mojitos. A couple of other pool patrons also tried to warn him, only to be told he was okay because he wasn't ginger! I mean, what an absolute weapon. Actually, more like a weaponised idiot! Anyway, by the time he went to bed, he was totally hammered and pretty much anaesthetised against the pain. He woke up sometime in the night and couldn't move. He tried to wake his mate in the other bed, but he too was battered, and he was sleeping the sleep of someone who had drunk a lot but hadn't spent all day in the sun without taking the proper precautions. Eventually, his mate woke up and the rest, as they say, is history." Dave stopped talking and looked at Pete and Steve. They all looked at each other before bursting into laughter again.

Pete spoke. His face a picture of disbelief and, to some degree, pity. "So, he thought by dyeing his hair, he would somehow magically deceive his own skin into accepting the magnificent bounty of the sun, without coming to any harm? Holy shit. I mean, I had a mate once who called customer support at Rockstar games as he wanted to transfer his in-game bank balance from his Grand Theft Auto player profile into his own, real life, bank account, and I thought that was, by far, the dumbest bloody thing I'd ever heard. But this!" He burst out laughing again.

"He looked like the bastard offspring of Freddie Mercury and Clifford The Big Red Dog!" They all burst into laughter again. Alejandro had appeared behind the desk, and he called over to Dave in Spanish. "Ah shit, I have to go lads. There's a bit of bother in the kitchens. I'll catch you later, okay?" He shook hands with Pete and Steve again before heading off towards the kitchens. "Right Alejandro, you big beautiful Spanish bastard! Let's you and me go sort these mutineers out!"

The ambulance was just pulling away when Steve and Pete emerged into the, already roasting, morning sun. They watched it disappear around the corner at the end of the street and Pete looked up at the sun and then across at Steve. "Y'know, I think we should maybe nip upstairs and grab the sunblock, mate." Steve smiled and nodded.

Fifteen minutes later, the pair were heading down into the town. Steve wanted to take a closer look at the graffiti in the storm drain, and so they had headed up the hill a little way so they could start at the top of the drain, to begin with. After finding a way down, they set off. Steve was fascinated with the graffiti, and he had his camera out the whole way as they sauntered down towards the town. Pete didn't mind, he was happy that Steve was occupied and not moping. In fact, Steve appeared to be dealing with Jo's absence really well. Pete thought about this as they walked, and he put it down to the fact that Steve was pretty confident that he would see Jo again. Pete, on the other hand, well, he didn't want to think about that. He wasn't a big drinker, but he was really starting to understand why people turned to drink in their hour of despair. The pair walked for what seemed like ages, mainly due to Steve's fascination with the wall art and the inordinate amount of sand that was heaped in piles along the way.

Pete wasn't sure about the origins of this sand, but he assumed it drifted up from the beach. On closer inspection, though, he noticed this sand was much softer than the beach sand. This revelation was a little disturbing because, as his feet would attest, there was no soft sand anywhere on that beach. So how did that silky soft sand end up in the storm drain? Was it washed up from the sea? Or maybe it was washed down from the mountains? Why would there be soft sand up in the hills and mountains? When they finally reached the town, they had to go right down to the beach to where the footbridge was to get back up to street level. The main street was its usual busy self. Holidaymakers and residents alike made their way back and forth across the wide street. Some went into shops or restaurants, some disappeared down the main little side streets. Pete looked at Steve and asked if he was hungry. A nod and a push of glasses up a nose later, and they were heading to the McDonalds they'd become so fond of during their stay.

The boys didn't rush their meal, there was no need. It was the last day of their holiday, and, with the absence of the girls, they were just going to amuse themselves. After lingering over value meals and McFlurries, they finally bit the bullet and began heading to the Crazy Golf course. They'd only just crossed the road after leaving the restaurant when Steve asked to have a look in the souvenir shop looming up ahead. "Yeah, sure we can." Steve entered the shop and Pete lingered outside, looking at the t-shirts, marvelling at how they could get away with some of the *'funny'* slogans and images that adorned them. Pete liked a laugh and even recalled when, as a teen, he'd thought it hilarious to wear a shirt that bore the legendary slogan: 'FBI: Federal Boob Inspector,' but these shirts? These shirts were way over the line and so far past the knuckle that you might lose your wristwatch! "Who comes up with this shit?" he pondered out loud as he perused t-shirts bearing slogans such as: 'Keep Calm & Slap Her', 'Fuck Isis' (written in faux Arabic - very witty), 'McFur Burger - I'm LOVING it' (complete with a very dodgy illustration), 'Sit On Me Face, I'll Guess Your Wait' (sic), and, his personal favourite: 'Glaze Me Like A Donut, Daddy!' (also available in child sizes! Let that sink in a moment). "More to the point," he said aloud, "who wears them?" As he rooted around to see just how low the depths of poor taste descended to, Steve appeared carrying a small and rather cute looking teddy bear that was holding a little red fluffy heart.

He looked at Pete and asked, "Can I buy this?"

Pete looked at the bear and then at Steve. "Course you can, big fella." Steve smiled at Pete, but instead of going to pay, he just stood there, holding the bear up to Pete. Pete stared at the bear again, then back at Steve, then back at the bear. Then he realised what the problem was. Steve only had his twenty euros 'for emergencies only' and an extra tenner. "of course." Pete said, reaching for his wallet. He reached over and checked the price tag and handed Steve twenty Euros. "Nineteen Euros? Jesus Christ, for that little thing? Here you go, mate, that'll cover it. Now off you go, people are gonna think you're proposing to me stood there like that!" Steve laughed his inimitable laugh and trotted off to the cash desk. "Hey! Ask the man for a belt for your trousers seeing he's had 'em down so fast!" He shouted, disgruntled, before heading outside to wait.

Five minutes later, Steve came out clutching a carrier bag in one hand and some change in the other. He went to give Pete the change and receipt, but Pete told him to put it in his own pocket, which Steve dutifully did before grabbing Pete in a bear hug. "Thank you," Steve said. Pete wasn't sure if it was because he was tired or miserable, or both, because even though Steve had hugged him and thanked him for something nearly every day of the last week, this time it seemed to resonate deeper and he felt a lump build in his throat as his eyes began to fill up. Fighting to keep his composure and holding back the tears, he hugged Steve back. Not the kind of perfunctory hug back that guys always give each other, but a tight, heartfelt hug, before he patted Steve on the back and made to break away.

"Right, come on, you big happy bastard," he said to a smiling Steve as he wiped his eyes, "let's go sink some balls!" Steve laughed and pinched Pete's cheek, and off they went.

Later, around teatime, they were heading back. Of course, Pete had taken a battering at Steve's hands on the crazy golf course. He got so fed up of losing, after three games, that he challenged Steve to a game of ten pin bowling instead. Sports of any kind had always been anathema to Pete. He just wasn't coordinated enough to be able to play any sport convincingly, but he figured bowling against Pete, with his 'condition,' surely he'd stand a fair chance of winning at bowls? Obviously, as well as being shit at most sports, Pete also didn't learn by his mistakes. He seemed to have totally forgotten that he'd made a similar assumption a few days earlier concerning crazy golf, and he'd also seemingly forgotten the humiliating defeat that followed that mistake, including the miserable defeats he'd endured today... After having his pants taken down three times in a row, he became convinced Steve was some sort of ringer. "Are you some sort of Paralympian, or something?" He asked Steve. Steve, pushing his glasses up his nose smiled and told him he used to play in a local disabled bowling league, explaining how they'd all get in a little community minivan once a week and travel out of town to a nearby retail and leisure park, where they'd play other disabled bowling teams in a special league.

"I'm team captain," he said, proudly.

"Of course you are," said Pete, nodding his head. "Do you still play? In the league, I mean." Still smiling, Steve shook his head. Pete asked why.

"The community group that organised it got their funding cut and they started charging £5 every time we went, to cover the costs. My dad said I couldn't go after that." A look of sadness crossed his face.

"Really? I'm sorry to hear that. What about golf? Are you the secret love child of Jack Niklaus or something?" Steve just looked at him blankly. "How are you so good at golf?" Pete asked.

"My uncle Brian used to take me with him when he played proper golf, but not when he and dad played. Dad said he needed golf as his 'alone time' so I wasn't allowed to go with them." Steve smiled but Pete saw this made him sad.

"Your uncle *used* to take you? What happened there then?" Pete was curious.

"He died," said Steve, still smiling, but not as brightly. "Aye, Steve, hit by a car he was. Hit and run! A hit and run? Aye!" His smile faded. "He showed me how to hold the clubs, how to stand, and how to hit the ball. Aye, Steve, always keep your eye on the ball and always look at where you want it to go before you hit it. Follow through, Steve!"

"Shit, man, a hit and run? That is dreadful... and they never caught anyone?" Steve shook his head.

"No, I remember the day well, Steve, because my grandad had died the week before. My uncle-John and my dad fell out a bit because my grandad left all his money to John in his whatchacallit?"

"His will?" Pete offered.

"Yes, his will," said Steve.

"Did your dad and grandad not get on? Was there no other brothers or sisters?" Pete asked, wondering why the man would snub one of his sons.

Steve walked on for a bit, looking thoughtful, then he answered: "No, Just John Wayne and Marion Wayne. Aye Steve, the Wayne brothers, ridin' into town!" and he laughed.

"You're kidding me! Your dad's name is Marion?" Pete could hardly contain his glee.

Steve nodded. "My nan was a huge John Wayne fan. I don't, I don't know why my dad is called Marion, though. Do you know, Steve? No, Steve, I don't. I do know he hates it, though. Aye, that's why he calls himself Mike!"

"Brilliant!" Pete was lapping it up. "So why did your grandad leave everything to your uncle? There must be a reason for it."

Steve shrugged his shoulders. "I don't know, really. All I know is that when my nan died, my uncle moved in with my grandad and took care of him." He pushed his glasses up his nose. Pete thought for a bit on what Steve was telling him.

"Ah, I think I get it: Your uncle looked after your grandad for the rest of his life after his wife died. I'm guessing your dad didn't really do much or go visit much?" Steve shrugged his shoulders again. Pete continued: "And when he died, he obviously left everything to the son who had given up his time and life to look after him! Was it a lot?" Steve looked at him, puzzled. "Was it a lot of money he got left?"

"I dunno," Steve responded. I know Uncle John was talking about getting a brand new car before, before, before the accident. He pushed his glasses up his nose, and they walked on for a bit before Steve broke the silence. "It all worked out well, though, Steve. How's that, Steve? Well, my, my dad got a new car instead, Steve. Just in time too!" Pete had gotten used to Steve's conversations now. He looked across at him and asked him what he meant. "My dad needed a new car as he broke his old one, Steve" came the reply.

"Broke?"

"Mmm Hmm," Steve nodded, "he hit a dog, a big dog."

"Your dad hit a dog in his car?"

Pete was a bit confused now. "And it broke his car?" Steve nodded. "Broke it?" Another nod from Steve.

"All the front was damaged, Wasn't it Steve? Yes, and the window shield was all cracked too, Steve!" he added.

Pete pulled a face. "Jesus, what kind of dog was it, a bloody horse dog?" Steve laughed and repeated what Pete had said but left out the sweary bits.

"He wasn't happy, was he, Steve? Nooooo. He was proper angry, Steve. Aye, he was proper angry, Steve. That was bad for us. First, he hits a dog and breaks his car, then he gets a call from the police telling him about Uncle John."

"Sounds like a horrible day, mate." Steve didn't respond, he just pushed his glasses up his nose. The boys walked on in silence again, and as they walked, Pete began turning over the events of the last few days. He couldn't help but feel like an absolute idiot when he thought back to when he first me Mel and the stupid charade he put on. It made Pete cringe so hard inside that he felt physically sick, and he actually muttered "Make it stop," as they walked. More so when he thought of the brutal way she'd murdered his hopes on the bus yesterday. "That was stone cold," he said out loud, absent-mindedly. Steve kept looking over at him and smiling every time he spoke, not sure at all what Pete was on about. Pete's thoughts then turned to Dave. What a guy! He'd known him for a little less time than he'd known Steve, yet this guy had been an absolute lifesaver, a wingman extraordinaire, and he got stuff done. Despite his own failure with Mel, he owed him a great deal. The way he'd pulled everything together for Steve, at such short notice, was phenomenal. He turned to Steve "You know what mate?" Steve looked up again. "We need to get Dave a little present, to say thank you, especially for Saturday night." Steve cocked his head quizzically. "Mate, It was my idea to get you two together like that, but I couldn't have done it without Dave's help." Steve gave a thumbs up and smiled. "What shall we get him?" Pete asked.

Steve looked thoughtful for a moment before holding up his carrier bag and saying: "Teddy?"

Pete laughed."No, nutter, we want to thank him not ask him to the prom." They walked on a bit, both deep in thought. Steve brought another idea to the table.

"Whiskey!"

"Whiskey?"

"Whiskey! My dad likes whiskey. We could get him a bottle too, to say thank you for the holiday. Aye, Steve, good idea!"

Pete was taken aback by this. Steve's dad was, by anyone's standards, a bit of a twat, he thought, yet here was Steve, wanting to buy him a gift to say thank you for said twattyness! "Whiskey, you say?" He said to Steve. Steve nodded his agreement, executing his now signature glasses move. "So, you reckon we should get Dave AND your dad, a bottle of whiskey… as a thank-you present?" Another nod from Steve. Pete was flummoxed. His natural instinct when it came to Steve's dad, was to dress him like a chicken and toss him to the Lions at Longleat. Yet Steve, who had the biggest axe to grind, wanted to buy him a gift. "There is literally not a bad bone in this boy's body," he thought, "or maybe he just judges everyone by his own happy and kind standards." Either way, Pete was torn. He begrudged spending money on anything other than a 'World's Shittiest Parent' mug for that tosser, but if he bought, say, a small bottle of whiskey… A thought crossed his mind. Well, not so much a thought, as a plan. "Okay mate, you're right. I'm a bit low on cash though so we'll get Dave a big one, and you're old fella a little one. How about that?" Steve gave a thumbs up, and his smile returned to 'full beam'. "Great stuff." They soon found a small convenience store, and sure enough, they found a standard sized bottle of whiskey for Dave - Laphroaig, in a beautiful little presentation tube - and a small bottle of cheap shitty whiskey for Steve's dad. Pete had asked Steve to wait outside, using the pretence that he had a carrier bag with him and some shops don't like that.

Steve was happy to oblige. He did this for the simple fact that he actually did suspect Steve didn't have a bad bone in his body and, as such, would not be capable of any kind of subterfuge which, given that Pete was now the man with the plan, would not do. Pete figured by leaving Steve outside, he was also leaving him in the dark, thereby giving him plausible deniability. They bought the whiskey, some snacks and a bottle of soda each for him and Steve. After he bagged it all, he met Steve outside, and they carried on their journey back to the hotel. Pete had everything he needed, he'd do the prep work later when Steve had gone to bed, or at least into his own room. "Right, matey. We'll give this to Dave tomorrow before we leave, okay?" Steve agreed and asked about his dad's gift. "Well, unless we get a train to Barcelona, he won't get it until he gets on the coach. I've bought some wrapping paper so we can make it look nice for him, okay?" Steve smiled and, predictably, hugged him. He really wanted to share his plan with him, but he didn't think Steve would find it funny or nice, or whatever. Besides, what Steve didn't know, wouldn't get either of them into trouble!

Departure time came around all too quickly, and Pete and Steve were already ahead of the game, having sat in reception, waiting for thirty minutes when the coach arrived. As this was a late, or so-called 'red eye' flight, there wasn't the usual drop off and pick up routine that happened with daytime arrivals and departures. This meant that there was only a skeleton staff about in the hotel at that time. As a result of this, Pete and Steve had sought Dave out earlier in the day to say their farewells and, of course, to give him his gift. Dave seemed genuinely touched when they gave him the whiskey, Pete had thought. At Pete's insistence, Steve had handed it to Dave, thanking him for his help and adding that he wasn't a bad sort of a guy to say he lacked that extra chromosome. "You've been hanging around with that Jo too much." Dave responded, and they all laughed. Pete had thanked Dave, too and given him his phone number.

"If you're ever up Darlington way, and fancy a catch-up, or need a favour or even just a place to stay, or anything, anything at all, look me up." Dave thanked him, telling him he might regret making that offer. They both laughed and shook hands. He went to shake Steve's hand, but Steve was having none of it, going straight in for a hug. They all said their farewells and that was that.

Later that night, as the boys stood waiting, the coach rolled into view outside the gates of the hotel. At the same moment, Alejandro appeared out of nowhere clutching two brown paper picnic bags. "Señor, Kelly!" Pete turned around, slightly startled, and greeted him. Alejandro held the bags out to him. "For you and Señor Steve, from Señor Dave!" Pete thanked him with a ten euro tip and picked his bag up. Looking inside, he was pleasantly surprised to see that Dave had prepped them both a packed lunch. Nothing fancy, just a sandwich, some crisps, a snack bar and a drink. Steve already had the snack bar out, and he was happily munching away. He laughed as they both headed out for the coach with the few other guests who were also saying goodbye to Calella, and Spain, today. As they approached, they were surprised to find the coach already had passengers. Because they'd been the last to be dropped off on arrival, Pete had assumed they'd be the first to board on their homeward journey. He wondered when the pickups had started and if Steve's parents would be on the coach already or if they would be picked up on the last stop before the airport. That was, of course, if they were even getting picked up at all; they may have made their own way there.

After handing their backpacks off to the driver to stow in the luggage compartment, they boarded the coach. Pete had kept hold of the carrier bag he had placed the nicely wrapped whiskey in, just in case Steve's parents were on the coach. As they climbed up the steps into the vehicle, they found the coach was almost full. Pete quickly scanned the other passengers, looking for a glimpse of Steve's parents. Bingo! There they were, halfway up. As he and Steve were the last to get on they had to sit in the last 2 seats available, right at the very front. Turning to Steve, he gave him a nudge and said: "I'll grab these seats, mate." Motioning down the coach to where Steves folks were sat, he then prompted Steve: "you go and give the whiskey to your dad, eh?" Steve smiled, nodded and then set off while Pete took the seat in the aisle. He sat there partly because, by now, Pete knew Steve liked the window seat and partly because he wanted to eavesdrop on Steve and his father, as best he could above the throng of chatter.

Steve walked right up to his parents, smiling that big bright smile. His father looked up as he approached and sighed. "What is it now, my lad?" Mike barked, impatiently.

Steve smiled and nodded at his mum first, then his dad."Mum, Dad."

"Yes, what?" said his dad, getting more impatient with each passing moment. Pete had shifted around so he could watch. He tried to be inconspicuous as he observed events unfold. With his head blatantly sticking out into the aisle, he failed miserably. But it didn't matter much because Steve's dad was too busy being a twat to notice his beady, Irish eyes. As soon as the man opened his mouth, Pete felt his anger begin to rise. This sort of reaction was unusual for Pete as he was usually quite a placid, laid back kind of person. He certainly wasn't one to be easily riled. In fact, it was a trait that used to drive Gemma mad. She would often get bent out of shape over the small stuff, and he would just shrug it off. The truth of it was that she just loved the sound of her own voice and loved to complain, whereas he would only complain when it was absolutely necessary, and even then, he would remain polite and civil, unlike Gemma who was like Attila The Hunny when she had an issue.

Back up the aisle, Steve held out the carrier bag. "I've got you a present today… to say thank you for bringing me on holiday. I've had a fantastic time, and I've." His dad cut him off before he could finish, reaching out and snatching the bag off of him.

"What is it?" He reached in and pulled out the small, nicely wrapped bottle of cheap whiskey. "Where did you get this from? Eh?" Steve shrugged and smiled. "You'd better not have spent your emergency money." Steve assured him he hadn't and started to try and tell him again about the great friend he'd made. His new best friend; Pete. Before he could get a word out though, his dad was asking for the twenty euros back, as if he still suspected Steve had used it to buy the gift.

"Perish the thought." Pete said to himself, under his breath. He watched from a distance as Steve's dad snatched the money from Steve before ramming it in his shirt pocket and ripping the paper off the bottle. "Ooh, whiskey, a good one too. Very nice!" Pete winced at that last bit. "I bet he pretends to 'know' wine too," he thought. "Bloody imbecile." Up ahead, Steve's dad opened the bottle, too busy telling Steve to go back to his seat to notice the safety seal had already been broken. Pete watched as he took a massive swig and handed it to his wife, who followed suit.

This was working out better than expected. "That's it," Pete thought, "fill your boots, ya manky pair of shite-hawks!" Steve squeezed past him and sat down, smiling at the window seat. Next up, the driver took his place and closed the doors and then they were off, airport bound. They'd not long pulled away from the hotel before Pete nodded off. He dozed for most of the journey there, while Steve sat and looked out of the window, straining hard to see into the gloom beyond the lights along the motorway. Every so often they would pass through a town and Steve would smile and chatter away to himself as he pointed out things he'd spotted.

In what seemed like no time at all, they were at the airport and Pete, awakened by Steve nudging him as they pulled up, gave a big yawn and stretched. Rubbing his face and eyes as he woke himself up, he suggested they sit and wait for everyone else to get off before they moved. He was a bit groggy still, but mainly he wanted to get off after Steve's parents and see if they had finished the whiskey off. Of course, they had, why wouldn't they have? After all, it was a small enough bottle. Sure enough, once the coach had emptied, Pete nipped back a few seats and spotted the empty bottle on the floor. "Typical!" He thought. "Of course, the lazy bastard left it there for someone else to tidy up." The boys grabbed their bags and got off the coach, heading into the terminal.

Inside the terminal, they were soon checked in and sat in the departure lounge. Fortune favoured them, and there were shops and places to eat that were still open, despite the lateness of the hour. Pete and Steve went and sat in a burger outlet and got something to eat and drink. From where he was sat, Pete could see that Steve's folks had gone and sat at a table in a bar over the way. He kept watching, and waiting for signs that his plan was working. He watched them closely, very carefully, all the while, making small talk with Steve. The boys stayed at the same table for the whole duration of their wait for boarding to begin. When they call finally came, they gathered their backpacks and dutifully made their way to the gate. It seemed to take forever to board as they kept shuffling forward a few steps at a time.

The mood in the lounge was quite sombre as people seemed quite tired. In fact, nearly everyone was quiet, almost everyone. Of course, Mike and Diane were chatting away loudly, well, mainly Mike. He was loudly bragsplaining how good the hotel was to Diane. As he was up ahead, Pete could keep an eye on him, and he smiled when he saw Mike start to rub his tummy a little. Soon, the boys were stepping into the cabin and, in a stroke of luck, the attendant greeting passengers at the aeroplane door, was the very same attendant who had asked Pete to swap seats on the flight out. As soon as she saw them, she pulled them to one side. Checking their tickets, she asked them about their holiday and commented on how nice it was they'd become friends. She motioned for them to stand to one side. "wait here," she said, "I think we might be able to get you two seated in the same place again." She gave them a wink and a smile. Pete thanked her and Steve gave her his biggest and best smile. Pretty soon they were both seated in the same seats they had flown out in.

Pete loaded their bags up into the overhead storage after Steve had retrieved his word search from his own bag. While doing so, Pete made several casual glances in the direction of Steve's parents. They were halfway back, and Steve's mum was in the window seat while his father was in the middle seat. Pete was amused to see the aisle seat was occupied by someone wearing one of the very same 'Fuck Isis' shirts he'd seen the previous day. Steve's mum was wearing her sunglasses, which struck him as odd, she was also fanning herself with a copy of the In-Flight magazine. They both seemed okay though, and although he found it odd, he wasn't worried. He knew 'it' was coming, it was now just a question of when. The cabin crew began the safety display, and Pete turned his attention to that, grinning as he dutifully sat down and paid attention. Twenty minutes later they were airborne, and the attendants were starting their rounds with the trolleys. First, the duty-free cart began making its way along, closely followed by the drinks trolley. Pete didn't bother with the duty-free, but he got Steve and himself a diet coke each.

Standing up, Pete pretended to stretch his legs and arms a moment. Pete mainly wanted to see how things were up the aisle. Fine. Everything was fine. Damn. "Okay," he thought, "not to worry." He looked down at Steve, who was gearing up for his word search. "Let's just sit back and let nature take its course," he told himself. So he did. He sat back, well he laid back actually, and he nodded off again. He slept for pretty much the whole flight, and he dreamt. He dreamt of Mel and him making a life together, with a house, and puppies, and kids! Then he dreamt of cars and dogs and hitting and running and. He awoke with a start. "Oh my god... he killed him!" He took a swig of diet coke and turned to Steve. "Steve, big fella, did you say your dad broke his car on a dog the exact same day your uncle died?" Steve smiled and nodded. "You're sure?" Steve gave another nod. "What happened to the car?"

Steve thought a moment. "He didn't ride it after that, except to take it to be scrapped when he got the money through, Steve." Pete thought about this a moment. Hitting a dog wouldn't do that much damage, surely not enough to warrant scrapping the car. "I can go ask my dad to explain it better if you like?" Said Steve, starting to rise.

Pete pulled him gently back down. "Noooo. No, no, no. No need for that, big guy. I was just passing the time. It's not important. Sit yourself down. We'll be landing soon."

Sure enough, a few minutes later the Captain came over the tannoy announcing that Easyjet BC1138 from Barcelona was preparing its final preparations for landing and advising the cabin crew to get everything sorted, which they duly did. It was then that everything took an exciting turn. They were on their final approach and the 'fasten seatbelts' signs were all lit up, everyone was buckled up and waiting for the plane to begin its descent. From behind him, though, Pete heard a commotion, and he tried to turn round to see what was happening. It seemed that Steve's mum was out of her seat and trying to get past a quite anxious flight attendant. "Madam, I must insist you sit down please!"

Diane just ignored her and tried to push past her, standing on Mike's toes in the process. "Owww, shit! You stupid cow!" Mike had just woken up and was not really sure what was going on. All he knew was that his wife was arguing with a flight attendant, and his stomach hurt like hell. "What the hell are you doing?"

Meanwhile, as both women completely ignored Mike, the flight attendant was really getting annoyed. "Madam, I really must insist that you take your seat and buckle up!"

Diane wasn't having any of it though. "No, no, no love, I HAVE to go to the toilet. I have to go NOW!" She didn't look well at all. In fact, Pete could see the sweat running down her increasingly pallid forehead. She tried to move forward again. The poor guy sat in the aisle seat was caught up in all this, an unfortunate innocent bystander, and it was obvious he was growing more uncomfortable with each passing moment. Around the plane, a few people were watching the drama unfold, some were still reading books or scrolling through their phones, some were asleep.

The flight attendant was doing her best to block Diane's way and pointing back to her seat. "Madam, I must insist you return to your seat. The Captain has turned the 'fasten seatbelt' sign on, and you have to return to your seat right now!" Diane wasn't having any of it though.

"And I am telling you I NEED THE BLOODY TOI…" she stopped abruptly and a look of horror crossed her face. At the same time as she finished speaking, a sound not unlike a gallon of baked beans hitting the ground after being tipped out of a third-floor window, made everyone look up. Diane had just 'sharted'.

The dictionary defines a shart as follows: 'To expel faeces accidentally while breaking wind.'

In layman's terms, Diane shit herself!

Now, we've all done it at some point in our lives. You might lie to yourself "No, not me!" but, deep down, you know I'm right. I don't mean when you're giving birth, ladies, and your midwife is eyes to eye with you, and you accidentally give her a few freckles when you're pushing your beloved offspring out. You get a free pass for that one I'm talking about the 'everyday situational shart' we've all tried to forget. Like, you lift your cheek in the break room at work to quietly 'let fluffy off the leash' and BAM! You follow through! Maybe you're in the bath, relaxing with a good book and sipping on some wine. Time to make some bubbles… the water runs brown! Or that time you were commuting, and you hopped off the morning train, planning to squeeze out a crop duster when — horror of horrors — you pooped, and you have to go all the way back home to change. Maybe you've sleep-sharted? Not so bad if you're asleep in your bed, but if you doze off on a bus…

Whatever your story, I'm sure you've only done it a little bit. It feels like a massive load in your pants when, in reality, it's tantamount to just a few melted chocolate buttons back there. Am I right? Sure I am. However, unfortunately for Diane (and Mike), this was a spectacular manifestation of said phenomenon. Diane, although over fifty, was still quite shapely and she liked to dress quite trendily. On this occasion, she had opted for a beautiful Indian print sarong, with a rather minuscule thong underneath. The scarceness of any real or substantial barrier between her backdoor and the outside world meant that when the (shit) levee broke, it just sprayed through said garments, all up her seat, all up the side of the cabin and the window and, possibly the worst part, all over Mike.

"WHAT THE FUCKING HELL?" Mike, who now looked like some faecal Jackson Pollock, was torn between kicking off more or throwing up, such was the smell. It only took a few seconds for his body to make its mind up for him, and he vomited all over Diane, who was still stood in front of him. Then he too suffered from a shart, although his was absorbed by his pants, trousers, and chair. Up at the front of the plane, near the door, Pete had pulled some napkins out of his pocket. He tore bits off and balled them up, popping one in each nostril. Pete then made two more improvised 'bungs' and, nudging Steve, motioned for him to do the same. Steve didn't hesitate, he trusted Pete, and this was obviously necessary. Lucky for the pair of them, the smell didn't hit them straight away, and they got their protection in place just in the nick of time. Around the plane, other passengers were not so lucky, and Pete could hear people retching and coughing. Pete double checked the integrity of his nose filters and smiled. He was feeling pretty pleased with himself.

Rewind to the previous evening. Pete and Steve had turned in at around nine. Once Pete was ensconced in the privacy of his own room, he commenced work on 'Operation: Shit Wolves!' He picked the title because he thought it was like Seawolves, but with less sea and (hopefully) more shit. He liked Sea Wolves and considered that and Wild Geese to be Roger Moore's best work outside of Bond and The Saint. But I digress. He'd opened the whisky and, using a fast food drinks cup he'd acquired earlier, he began to prepare his magic potion. Tipping the whiskey into the cup, he reached into the carrier bag from earlier and pulled out a packet of? You guessed it: laxatives! After removing them from the foil packaging, he then began to painstakingly empty all six of the plastic capsules into the whiskey. This took him about half an hour and, once done, he had to test it. Of course, he wasn't going to actually drink it. He just needed to make sure it looked ok and that, probably more importantly, it tasted okay. He took a small swig, swilled it around and spat it back in the cup. It tasted like, like, "Shit whiskey!" Success! That was until he reached for the bottle to begin the refill process, that's when disaster struck.

Pete watched in horror as his arm clipped the cup and the cup went flying in slow motion, off the table and onto the floor where it seemed to explode on impact, sending tainted whiskey in all directions. "Shit! Shit, and hairy balls!" he shouted. This put a massive spanner in the works. He'd lost the two main ingredients, the only two ingredients, of his master plan. He sat for a moment then he scooped the bottle and cap up off of the floor, grabbed his room key and headed down to reception. Luckily, Dave was on the desk and pleased to see him. They shook hands and Pete, desperate to get sorted, cut right to the chase: "Mate, I know I keep doing this, but I need a favour."

"A favour? I live for guests like you, there's always some shenanigans to relive the boredom. How can I help, mon frere?" Dave grinned and listened while Pete explained everything: Steve's folks, what a pair of bastards they were to Steve, and his plan for avenging his Jim Bowen loving friend. Dave rubbed his chin for a moment.

"I'm sure you don't need me to tell you just how bloody childish this is, right?" his deadpan delivery threw Pete.

"Well, I, yeah. But if you'd seen the way they treat Steve." Pete pleaded, trying to justify his plan.

Dave rubbed his chin some more, looking incredibly stern. Then he burst out laughing. "Nah, I'm only pulling your chain" They both laughed and Dave reached out to Pete. "Gimme the bottle, and wait here." He took the bottle off of Pete and disappeared into the bar. Four minutes later, Dave was returning with the filled bottle, a cocktail shaker, and a pair of pliers.

Pete ignored the other stuff and thanked him for filling the bottle. "I'm going to have to dash, I need to get back down to the Farmacia before it closes."

Dave held up his free hand. "Hold up, Buttercup!" he said. "Come with me," and he led Pete behind the reception desk into the back office! The back office was surprisingly well ordered and tidy, and Dave motioned to Pete to grab a seat as he reached up onto a large grey metal storage cupboard. He pulled down a large bankers box and set it on the desk in front of Pete.

"What's this?" asked Pete.

"This, my fine Irish friend, is our 'left behind' box!" Pete just looked at him, not sure what to say. Dave gave a comical sigh. "Okay, basically, loads of guests end up leaving stuff in the rooms. Generally, it's half empty boxes of biscuits, opened liquor, some porn maybe, even lube and, once, a massive pink dildo." Pete laughed. Dave continued. "Every now and again they leave medication though. All sorts of medication, from mundane asthma inhalers, to exotic pain meds, and everything in between and beyond, if you catch my drift." He whipped the top off the banker's box and waved his hand across it like a magician revealing the pay-off to his greatest illusion. "Et voila! I give you Farmacia Olympiad!" He stood there, grinning. "Right, let's find some laxatives!" They both began digging through the strips of tablets, the bottles and boxes. "Ooh, codeine!" Exclaimed Dave, his face lighting up as he pulled out a strip of tablets and slipped it into his back pocket. Digging right down to the bottom, Pete found something that looked promising. He pulled out several sachets and handed them to Dave as they appeared to be Spanish in origin. Dave inspected them and smiled. "Bingo! Let's get busy with the fizzy" he said, as he emptied the whiskey into the shaker.

Pete watched, intrigued. "What are the pliers for?"

"Ah," replied dave "false alarm! I got them in case we had to crush any tablets into dust." Pete nodded and agreed it was a good call. Ten minutes later, he was pouring the whiskey back into the bottle. Dave held it up to the light. "Perfect" he beamed, as he tipped the shaker up and let the remnants dribble into his mouth, spitting it back out immediately. "There's a bit of a tang to it, I think they're lemon flavoured." He pointed to the empty sachets. "It's ok, though. The whiskey is cheap and one step away from tasting like jet fuel, so it's hard to notice."

He passed the bottle to Pete, who took it and shook his hand. "Mate, you are simply the best! I can't thank you enough."

"No problem. Stay out of the blast zone, eh?" He grinned. This piece of advice turned out to be wise words, indeed!

Fast forward!

'Fuck Isis' guy had begun to liberally spray Drakkar Noir everywhere, one squirt at a time. This was obviously to try and mask the growing stench a shit and vomit which, in itself, was causing an emetic tidal wave. Diane, knowing she had no burning reason to be out of her seat anymore, flopped back down in surrender. She looked very green around the gills but had so far avoided vomiting herself. Mike also seemed to have managed to control his oral evacuations. He had not, however, been able to control his rectal evacuations, neither had Diane, for that matter. They both just wanted off the plane, so they dutifully sat tight and buckled up. The flight attendants, who had also managed not to toss their cookies yet, had notified the captain that the cabin was secure enough for him to proceed and the plane eventually started its descent. Despite the odd cough or dry heave, the aircraft descended in silence, there wasn't even a round of applause when the plane landed safely.

Once on the ground, as the plane taxied to the terminal, people could still be heard dry heaving. Some, like Mr 'Fuck ISIS,' had even broken out their duty-free perfume and were spraying it directly at their noses. Some passengers held the complimentary vomit bags on standby. Those that could stand without dripping puke or shit, did so and retrieved their luggage. As some of the few people to not have puked on or shit themselves, Pete and Steve managed to get off first. Walking down the gantry into the terminal, Pete could see several ambulances, and what looked like an extensive cleaning crew, gathering below on the tarmac. The boys got through Passport control quite quickly. Baggage claim was also easy as they were both carrying their luggage on their shoulders. As they traipsed wearily towards the doors that would take them into the main terminal and freedom, it occurred to Pete that he was still with Steve. This wasn't a bad thing as such, he'd gotten so used to him being around on holiday that he'd not given it a second thought as they'd gotten off the plane. Pete gave Steve a little nudge "Steve, what are you going to do?" Steve looked at him.

"With what?" he answered Pete's question with his own question.

"Well, we're home, mate. Your mum and dad, well, they're probably not going to be going home tonight. What will you do?"

Steve shrugged and thought for a moment. "How are you getting home?" He asked Pete.

Pete stopped and gave that question some thought. "That's a great question, actually." He'd also not given that any thought. "I'll have to get a train or maybe a taxi." He looked at his watch and saw it was now half past three in the morning. "Ah, I'll just hang about and get a metro over to Newcastle station then get the train home to Darlington in the morning."

"Darlington?" Steve's face lit up.

"Yes mate, why?"

"That's where I live, well, Cockerton, which is sort of Darlington. I could come home with you if you'd like?"

Pete laughed. "Sure, why not? We've come this far, we may as well make the final leg together. I'll get you back to Darlington and make sure you get home safe. You do have a key, right?" Steve smiled and reached into the neck of his t-shirt, pulling out a string necklace, at the end of which dangled a single Yale key. "Awesome!" Pete laughed. "Come on, let's get out of here." With that, they continued to head for the exit of the arrivals lounge. Pete was talking away to Steve as they passed through the automatic doors and not really paying attention to anything. Out of the corner of his eye, he saw Steve raise his gift shop carrier bag, the one that contained his little gift for Jo. Pete looked over to see that Steve was smiling as usual, but he seemed to not just be smiling for the sake of it, he was smiling and looking straight ahead. Before he could turn his head to see what he was looking at, he heard a familiar squeal. He whipped his head back round to see Jo jumping up and down and clapping her hands. "No way!" All at once, icy fingers of fear and warm spicy fingers of hope gripped his heart and gave it a squeeze in his chest as he realised that if Jo was there, it's more than likely that Melody would also be there. Adrenalin pumped through him, and he could hear his heart beating in his ears as he looked to the left of Jo. As he did so, he would swear he heard Bon Jovi's 'Bad Medicine' as if it was being sung A Capella by a heavenly choir as, bathed in a divine (spot) light beaming down from the sky (roof), there she stood, in all her 'Movie Of The Week, vaseline over the lens, soft focus' glory: Mel.

Time stopped for Pete. It was as if a secret pause button had been pressed and everyone stopped dead. Nobody moved, a perfect moment frozen in time, Even the planes and birds hung motionless in the sky. Jo, who was jumping up and down at the sight of Steve, was also caught like a statue in mid-air. "Wait a minute," he thought, "the last time I saw her, she told me to 'fuck off,' so her being here, now...none of this makes sense." He realised she was holding a sign, like when drivers pick someone up from the airport. The sign read 'Kelly.' He was suddenly brought out of his stupor when Steve nudged him. "Looks like we've both got a ride home, Pete," he said and gave Pete a wink. Before Pete could ask Steve why he was able to speak when everyone else had been frozen in time, Pete was suddenly 'back in the room' again. People started moving, planes and birds carried on their way, Jo landed safely and began clapping Pete walked over to Mel, keeping eye contact as he narrowed the thirty-foot gap between them. When he finally stood in front of her, he reached out and poked her arm to make sure she was real.

Mel gave him that funny look he now knew so well and exclaimed "Ooookaaayyyyy," before asking him: "are you all right there, Kelly?"

Her perfume made him dizzy, good dizzy, and she was smiling that smile, the smile he'd seen that first day. He just nodded and stared at her like a proverbial deer in the headlights. After a few moments with no words, Mel broke the spell. Holding up the sigh, she said: "Taxi for Kelly?" He dropped his bags as she grabbed him and kissed him, taking her in his arms. Time stopped again for Pete. Right there right then, a million romantic cliches passed through his head. Was this what love genuinely felt like? He'd never ever felt like this before, not even with Gemma. He couldn't say what love truly felt like, but the feelings he had as they held each other, the sheer euphoria of the feeling of her lips on his, right there he knew, he knew that, whatever happened, he had to spend the rest of his life in the company of this beautiful human being. When they eventually broke for air, Time started again for him. As they pulled away from each other's lips, they found Jo and Steve on either side of them, leaning in really close, both of them smiling like chimps in a banana stand.

"Woooooooo," went Jo.

"Woooooooo," went Steve.

Pete spoke: "Guys, come on, man. Give us a minute, will you?" He smiled and stared back at Mel. "So, last time I saw you, you told me to fuck off. You were pretty insistent on it, in fact." She smiled.

"Well, you see…" she paused.

"Go on," he urged, nodding playfully.

"Well, you see it turns out that the old 'Kelly Charm' is a real thing. In fact, I wouldn't be surprised if there are adverts on telly." Affecting a stern voice, she continued: "Have you ever been a victim of 'The Old Kelly Charm'?" She tried to continue, but Pete tickled her, causing her to break into laughter. "Stop, stop!" she blurted. She calmed down and continued, her grin subsided to a soft smile, and she stared into his eyes as she spoke. "I got back and I, I just couldn't stop thinking about you, Pete. Of course, it didn't help that this one," she motioned to Jo, "this one would not shut up about you and about how perfect you were for me and how I'd"

"Made a HUGE mistake!" Shouted Jo, laughing.

They all laughed, and Pete turned and gave Jo a hug. "So I have you to thank for all this, then?" Jo laughed some more, but it was Steve who spoke next.

"Someone had to help him out, Steve! Aye Steve, he couldn't pull a muscle, that Pete. Bless him!" Steve then let out a big roaring laugh at his own joke before he brought his hand up to Pete's face and gave his cheek a little rub. Pete waggled his finger at him and pretended to be angry then he gave him and Jo a double hug before turning back to Mel.

Pete smiled at her, but her face looked more serious. Taking his arm, she moved to one side, away from Steve and Jo. "Listen, Pete. I can't make any promises, and I really don't want to rush into anything," he nodded his agreement, and she continued: "but what say you and I see where this friendship takes us?" Pete brushed her hair off her face with his fingers. He stared into her eyes for what seemed like an age as if he was searching for something. Mel cocked her head quizzically.

He took a short breath in through his nose before he spoke."You had me at 'fuck off!" They both burst out laughing before kissing again.

Mel stopped and moved partially away from him so she could look in his eyes. "No more secrets!" she said, deadly serious. "That's not a request!"

Pete gave a partial nod before agreeing. "No more secrets!" They kissed again. Long and lingering. As they finally parted, Mel motioned across to the other two. "Come on," she said, "let's get out of here."

"Wait!" urged Mel, fishing in her pocket. She half turned away from Pete as she fumbled with something unseen before turning back around to place the now slightly dilapidated daisy chain on his head. "There we go," she smiled. "There's my princess!" They both laughed.

And so, Steve picked his bag up off the floor and looped his arm with Jo's. Pete also picked his bag up off the floor, then he took hold of Mel's hand. They stared into each other's eyes for a brief moment then all four of them headed to the door and out into the fresh, early morning air. The doors closed behind them, and they were gone.

Epilogue

The doors closed as the gang left the airport, but the story didn't end there. How could it? There were still one or two things that needed sorting. Mel had driven everyone home. She dropped Steve off first, and she and Pete sat in the car while Jo walked Steve to his front for and gave him a goodbye playground kiss. Pete was next, and as he had no fixed address, he had her drop him off at his mum's house. Mel got out of the car, and they shared a hug and another lingering kiss. "What are you going to do about Steve?" Mel asked him. He ran his fingers through his hair and sighed. He knew she was referring to the way his parents were taking advantage of him.

"Well, I'm not sure, to be honest, I think there's some more serious stuff to deal with there." Mel, concerned, asked him to explain. "It's nothing to do with Steve as such," he replied, "but I don't want to involve you in my crazy thoughts, so it's best if I just deal with it myself." Mel raised her eyebrows and folded her arms, this was enough to remind Pete of the oath he'd sworn just over an hour earlier. "You're right, you're right. No more secrets! This is just, it's pretty serious." And so he explained the tale that Steve had told him about his uncle, his dad, the will, and the car. "I mean, if it's true, then this whole thing is even worse than I thought because if it was a large inheritance and it went to his dad, after all, they're taking all Steve's money, and they don't even need to. They're greedier than a pair of Bombay Shite-hawks!" They could both see Jo in the car, and she had dozed off waiting for Mel.

"I'd best get her home," she said to Pete. "Bless her, she's been so excited all day. Look, do whatever you think is right, but if you need any help if you don't go the murder trial route, let me know. Now, get some sleep, and I'll speak to you tomorrow." They kissed again, briefly but with no less passion. With a wink and a quick hug, Mel was climbing into the car. Pete watched as they drove off and waited until they were out of sight before he began to sneak into the house. Pete knew he was going to head straight for the sofa and crash. He was totally exhausted. Elated, but exhausted.

Surprisingly, he was awake pretty early the next morning, he went through the clothes he had left there and grabbed a shower before getting dressed. His mum was up and preparing breakfast when he came downstairs. After his hearty, home cooked breakfast, the first thing he did, as requested, was call Mr Hashimoto. Mr Hashimoto was pleased to hear from him but about to go into a meeting and so he invited him to come to a meeting at his old workplace. Pete had been very reluctant, for obvious reasons, but Mr H had asked him to trust him and, as Pete had never had a reason not to, he agreed. Mr Hashimoto had always set high standards but had always been fair, acting with the utmost integrity at every step in his business dealings. Pete felt sure he wouldn't let him down.

The meeting had been set for three and Pete, as usual, arrived in good time. As he pulled through the main gates and into the car park, he was quite surprised to see scaffolding up at the front of the building. The scaffolding seemed to be being used by a couple of gentlemen who were… Cleaning? Were they cleaning the company sign? Pete couldn't tell. He parked up and headed into reception. Karen, the receptionist, was on the phone as he entered. Her face lit up when she saw him, and she motioned him to go on through and head on up. The main offices were situated on the first floor and to get there one had to go into the factory, along a small walkway and then up some stairs. As soon as he entered onto the walkway, the familiar smell of lubricant and hot metal hit his nostrils. The high whine of CNC milling machines and the distant booms of hydraulic presses were almost deafening. Pete reached the landing and took a breath before knocking on the door. "Come," boomed a familiar voice. Pete opened the door and was surprised to see Mr Hashimoto sat where he used to sit. "Hello, Hashimoto San," He said as he walked over to the desk. Mr H stood up and came round to meet him, and they shook hands, exchanging customary bows.

"Kelly San! Pete! It is good to see you." There was always a sincere warmth in Hashimoto's voice, and today was no exception.

"It's good to see you too, sir," Pete responded.

"Dai!"

"Excuse me?"

"Please, call me Dai!" Pete was now in strange territory. There had always been a quaint formality between the two of them. Even when Pete had visited 'Dai's' home as his guest, he had still maintained that formality. It was always 'Mr Hashimoto' or 'Hashimoto San.' In all the years he'd know him, he had never been invited to use is forename.

"It's good to see you too, Dai." Pete smiled nervously. There were two windows in the office. One looked out onto the car park, the other looked out onto the factory floor. Dai walked over to it, Pete followed. Below them, Telco was a hive of industry. Dai motioned with his hand. "This is a very well oiled machine," he said sagely. "Out of all my suppliers, Telco has always been the one I have had the least trouble with. I have always been confident in its performance, despite that imbecile being in charge." Pete assumed he meant Terry, who else? Pete had run the factory, but Terry was the main man. It was his company, after all. "I was incredibly saddened by the news you gave me, Pete." Pete nodded, solemnly, his gaze fixed on the window. "I was also very disappointed. You see, I believe strongly in honour and integrity. I conduct my personal life with honour and integrity, and I conduct my business with honour and integrity. In Japan, we have an old saying: 'honour is like a match, you can only use it once. You can abandon your own body, but never let go of your honour. Honour is like the eye, which cannot suffer the least impurity without damage. It is a precious stone, the price of which is lessened by a single flaw.'" He looked at Pete, and Pete nodded at him before they both continued staring out of the window. "Your news made me sad because it revealed Terry to be something I had long suspected: a man without honour. Pete, I do not do business with such men because, in my experience, this lack of honour ends up manifesting itself in treacherous ways." He turned to face Pete again, and Pete mirrored his move. "I have thought long and hard about what to do. I did not want to continue to do business with this man, but I was also aware that in ending my contracts with Mr Drake, I would also be potentially harming the livelihood of all these hard-working men and women we see below." He motioned to the window again. Pete remained silent, nodding and maintaining eye contact. "To punish them for something they had no part in, that would not be honourable." Pete nodded his head in agreement, still unsure where this was going. "I spent many hours, Pete, thinking about how I could resolve this matter." Pete nodded. "Many, many hours. In the end, I decided I must follow the examples set out in the Bushido code."

"Bushido code?" Pete asked, nodding again

"Yes, Kelly San! Honour and Loyalty are two of the eight virtues of the unwritten, yet very real, 'Code of the Samurai.' The eight virtues have long served to bring balance to the character of all who followed the code. I decided there was only one course of action. Only one way in which I could restore honour and balance." Hashimoto paused, staring hard at Pete. Pete grew more uncomfortable with each passing second until finally: "I had to take Drake San's head." Mr Hashimoto gave a curt nod, hardly moving his head before falling silent, staring hard at Pete again. Pete ran everything he'd just heard back through his mind. 'Bushido, honour, impurity, take his head'. Despite the muffled sounds of the factory that breached the mid-priced glazing and half-arsed soundproofing, you could hear the penny drop.

"Take his head?" Pete blurted out, incredulously. Hashimoto stood, inscrutable, unmoving. He stayed like that, watching Pete's face as Pete was still trying to process everything, for a good thirty-seconds before he burst out laughing. Pete, sensing he'd been had, let out a semi-silent "shit" before joining in the laughter.

"You got me there," said Pete, visibly relieved. "You got me good!"

This was a side of Mr H he'd not seen before. Hashimoto slapped him on the shoulder. "Come!" He motioned him to follow as he headed over to Terry's office. Pete figured Terry was in on the joke and that Mr H had some big reconciliation plan in mind. 'so much for honour' he thought. Hashimoto stopped outside the door and looked at Pete, his face serious again. "I did not take Drake-San's head." Pete lamented on this for a moment, then Hashimoto spoke again: "I took his company instead!" Pete laughed, thinking he was being pranked again, that laughter trailed off as he realised Hashimoto wasn't laughing this time.

"I don't follow." Pete was back in the land of confusion.

"I gave him an ultimatum. I could literally wrap his business up by the end of the day by pulling all my contracts, or he could sell the company to me."

"You are kidding me!" Pete exclaimed. "You bought the company?" he put two and two together, quickly.

Mr H nodded. "Mister Drake, was very reluctant, at first. He called my bluff by claiming that I would not be able to put a contingency in place quick enough. I pointed out that all the tooling technically belonged to me and so I would just transfer it to my own factory and begin temporary production there in the interim. He thought I was joking and so I invited him to test that theory because, as you well know, I do not make jokes!" He gave Pete a wink. "I gave him a fair price for the company, I am not a thief, I also threw in a small bonus incentive for him providing he signed my sales contract and vacated the premises by the end of the very next working day. He agreed once he saw the offer price. He signed there and then without even seeking legal counsel, which I did, of course, advise him to do. I now own this company. All those people out there now work for me. I have a problem though; I must keep this business separate from my own as it is a personal investment, not made through the company or with the permission of the board or shareholders. I am also a very busy man, Pete, and I do not have time to run two companies. That is, hopefully, where you come in." He stepped back from the office for and motioned to the name plaque. Pete looked in, stunned awe. 'Peter Kelly. M.D.' "The job is yours if you want it."

Pete felt his emotions bubbling over, and he quickly brought a hand up to wipe his moistening eyes. "I don't…I don't know what to say, sir."

"Yes, it would be a good start." Said Hashimoto, smiling.

"My god, yes, of course, yes… and thank you." He reached out and took hold of Hashimoto's hand and shook it firmly and vigorously. "I will not let you down."

Mr H looked him in the eye, smiled and said; "Of that, I have no doubt." He broke off the handshake and opened the door. "I can hold the fort for the rest of the week while you tie off all your loose ends. If you give Karen an address I can courier over your contract and a brief update on the business for you to review." Hashimoto smiled. "I anticipated your delight, and I have scheduled a meeting with all the department heads in attendance. It's scheduled to start in," he looked at his watch. "Five minutes!"

Five minutes later, Karen watched as Pete and Mr Hashimoto went into the conference room and closed the door. She heard muffled voices and then a huge cheer. She smiled and picked up the phone as it rang. "Good afternoon, Telco Engineering, a subsidiary of Hashimoto Enterprises! How can I help you?"

Pete's next action item was a place to live in. He couldn't crash at his parents, and he didn't fancy entertaining Mel at a Premier Inn, so he began searching online for houses to buy or rent in the area. In another bizarre twist, Karma worked its magic once again.

Following the fallout from her transgression, Gemma had found herself decidedly alone. The only person who was still speaking to her was her mother, and this was because she had managed to put a rather convincing spin on the whole situation, painting Pete as the bad guy. Gemma's biggest problem was she was hopeless with money. Okay, maybe it was her biggest problem AFTER the fact that Pamela Anderson and Kid Rock managed to stay together longer than her knees. Anyway, she quickly decided she couldn't live in that big house on her own, and she certainly couldn't afford the mortgage on her own, so she'd put it on the market and moved back in with her mum. Pete came across it that very evening as he searched for a house, and was surprised to see that it was on the market for the same price they'd bought it for. This suggested that Gemma wanted rid of it as soon as it was at all possible. He gave this some thought that night and the next day he got on the phone with his bank, securing a mortgage. Of course, it helped that Mr Hashimoto had thrown in an incredibly generous signing bonus with his new contract and that went a long way to help Pete get what he wanted, not just with the bank but with the house too. After the bank, he spoke to the estate agents offering them twenty-thousand above the asking price providing he could move in within a week. Although this was highly irregular, money talked, and Pete got his wish. He knew the house was worth more than he paid for it, so the extra twenty-thousand was worth it, he reckoned. Some people might have had a hard time moving back into a house that had such a negative association. Not Pete! He really wasn't bothered about stuff like that, and despite the way he'd left it, he had a soft spot for it and couldn't wait to move in, choosing not to tell Mel until he was in and settled. As soon as he got the keys, he immediately got on the phone and brought contractors in to completely remodel — after all, Pete could afford to now that he was a managing director! New kitchen, new decor all over, new furnishings, new hot tub, new everything! He even had his pop culture collection (a posh name for all his toys) all out on display, because he could now.

Within a week of coming home, Mike and Diane had made a full recovery from their episode. That fateful Wednesday morning, they'd been rushed to the hospital and quarantined as no one had seen anything like the shit fest they let loose on the plane. Within 24 hours it was ascertained they were free from any bacteria and had somehow managed to ingest some sort of Spanish Horse Laxative. At first, Mike had threatened to sue the airline but he soon back-heeled that idea when the airline threatened to counter sue for the complete cost of cleaning the plane and the reupholstering of eight seats. The pair of them returned home, exhausted and angry, on Thursday evening and found Steve sat at home, eating crisps and doing his word search.

Friday, there was a knock at the door around nine in the morning, and Mike, who was tucking into a light breakfast of scrambled eggs on toast, went to answer it. Imagine his surprise when he opened the door to a couple of detectives who wanted to question him in connection with the hit and run that resulted in his brother's death. The detectives were duly invited in, and Mike offered to make them a cup of tea. They declined the offer as they just wanted to get the questions over with. See, they'd apparently had some sort of anonymous tip-off about the, now year-old, case. The caller was quite specific about Mike's old car, and they just wanted to ask him a few questions and rule it out. They were pretty sure it was rubbish, but rules are rules.

All went well initially. Mike seemed fine and was laughing and joking with them, but the detectives couldn't help but notice the colour drain out of his face when they ask him about his car. His confident and jovial demeanour quickly evaporated, and he became a mumbling stuttering idiot. Crunch time came, literally, when he said he was just popping to the toilet and walked out the back door. The two detectives raced after him and emerged from the house just in time to see him trying to scale the fence at the end of the garden. Mike managed to get up onto the ten-foot-high wooden fence, but then slipped back down, landing badly on his arm. Obviously, the detectives had no choice but to arrest him on suspicion of causing death by dangerous driving and leaving the scene of an accident. They'd no sooner read him his rights when he pretty much confessed to everything which was ironic because he'd scrapped the only actual evidence that could have linked him to the hit and run. If he'd sat still and kept quiet, he'd have gotten away with it. Steve watched the whole thing from his bedroom window, happily eating a bowl of cereal, pausing every now and then to push his glasses up his nose. There, beside him on the windowsill stood a nice cold glass of orange juice.

Just over four weeks after he returned from that fateful trip to Spain, Pete was a happy man. Possibly the happiest man in the history of happy men! It was a Sunday, and he rolled onto his back and opened his eyes as he awoke from a delightful sleep, rubbing away the sleep as he let out a big yawn. The blinds at the window did little to hold back the bright sunshine, and he stared up at the ceiling, just resting and contemplating how to fill the day ahead. As he lay there, something stirred next to him under the duvet. Pete turned his head slightly to look in the direction of the rustling, just as a tanned and slender arm emerged from the depths and came to rest on his chest. Mel's voice broke the silence. "Morning, handsome!" She yawned at him, and he looked at her face, reaching out to move her bed hair out of her eyes.

"Morning yourself, gorgeous!" He leaned over to kiss her, she quickly dodged his lips, and his kiss landed on her cheek.

"Morning breath," she said, with a grin.

"Your breath is fine," he reassured her.

"Not my breath, yours, you dafty!" They both laughed as he began to tickle her. He was about to kiss her again when he heard the doorbell.

"Strange," he said out loud, looking at his watch. It was only ten, and it was Sunday. It could only be The Hawk, he thought. "Maybe there's been some shenanigans on the close, I'll go and investigate. Coffee?"

"Yes, please."

He kissed her forehead and grabbed his dressing gown off the floor. "Alexa put the kettle on," he said as he headed down the stairs. Alexa gave her customary acknowledgement, and by the time he reached the bottom of the stars, he could hear the steady hiss of the kettle as it began warming up. The doorbell rang again. "Okay, okay" he admonished as he unlocked and opened the door. "Hold your horses…" his voice trailed off. He was genuinely expecting to see The Hawk waiting for him when he opened the door. Instead, as he looked at the floor first, he went silent when he saw a wheelie suitcase with a Star Wars print on it.

"Hi, Steve!"

After a brief pause, Pete smiled and grabbed Steve in a hug. "Hi Steve, yourself!" He laughed, and they broke from the embrace. Over the way, he could see The Hawk, and he gave her a cheery wave. She gave him a smile, and a wave back then scribbled something down in her notebook before returning inside. He turned back to Steve, who was already barging past him with his suitcase. "Whoa, fella! What's the hurry?" he laughed.

Steve turned and looked at him and with a big smile on his face, told Pete: "My dad's going to prison."

"Prison, you say?" Pete tried to look concerned and surprised, although he was neither.

"Aye, prison. The police say they had a tip-off about dad's car." He smiled and pushed his glasses up his nose before telling Pete what he saw that day.

"The police got a tip-off? Fancy that!" Pete said, raising his eyebrows. "Your dad fell off a fence and broke his arm too? Eventually charged with murder? Well, I do declare!"

"Aye, and then my mum got instigated!" Steve continued.

"Instigated?"

"Yeah, instigated by the people, the people that give me my money."

The penny dropped. "Oh, you mean investigated!"

Steve pushed his glasses up his nose again. "Yes, Steve, investigated. That's what I said, Steve. Aye Steve, you did."

Pete smiled. "Of course you did, big fella. So what's happening there?"

Steve smiled. "She, she, she's in big trouble. Her and my dad are. He's in bigger trouble because he ran my Uncle John over, but she's in big trouble too as they reckon they've been stealing my money." He took a breath. "She might go to prison, Steve! Aye, Prison! Everyone's going to prison! That's why your here, Steve! Yeah, we better tell him!" Pete, still smiling, asked him what he meant. Steve smiled his biggest smile and just stared at Pete.

"Steve?"

Steve blinked a few times and took a step closer to Pete. "I, I, I've come to live with you, Steve!"

Pete was not really sure what to do at this point. He took stock in his head. He had the room, of that there was no doubt. Steve was technically an adult, although a vulnerable one. He'd need to speak to Mel about the long term legality of it all but, "What the hell!" he thought. He opened his arms wide, and Steve moved in for a hug. "Of course you are, buddy! Of course, you are."

THE END

(For Now!)